Tanith By Choice

Tanith By Choice

Tanith Lee

NewCon Press
England

Contents

If my sword is broken, my words, they will never be.
See you on the battlefield.

Remembering Tanith

Ian Whates

Tanith Lee is one of the finest writers to ever grace the field of speculative fiction.

I generally shy away from asserting such things with conviction, framing them with qualifiers such as 'in my opinion', because no such statement can ever be objective. Any review of a book, a film, an author's ability… all such things are coloured by our own personal filters and prejudices, which precludes them being wholly objective. At the end of the day, it's all a matter of opinion, no matter how well-informed we might consider that opinion to be.

In this particular instance, however, I'll make an exception: Tanith Lee is one of the finest writers to ever grace the field of speculative fiction.

I vividly recall John Kaiine telling me at the 2015 Eastercon that Tanith only had months to live. I cried; we both did, clinging to each other in the middle of the bar at a Heathrow hotel. Less than two brief months later, the news I'd been dreading arrived.

Tanith has left one hell of a legacy. The author of around 100 novels and several hundred short stories, she wrote two episodes of the iconic TV series *Blake's 7*, was the first woman to win the British Fantasy Award – which she followed with two World Fantasy Awards, shortlistings for all manner of accolades including Nebula and BSFA Awards – and in 2013 she received a 'Lifetime Achievement Award' from the organisers of World Fantasycon… Yet I still encounter people who say, "I've heard of Tanith Lee but I've never actually read anything by her."

My response to that is simple: "Do."

I first met Tanith when she was Guest of Honour at Eastercon, the British National Science Fiction Convention, in 2008. I had lunch with Ian Watson, Tanith, and her husband, John Kaiine. Shortly afterwards, John bought a copy of the anthology *Myth-Understandings*, which features all women authors. A week later, Tanith emailed to say she had read and loved the book and so wished she could have been in it. Could she please submit a story for my next anthology? *Could she…?* Tanith's "Under Fog (The Wreckers)" subsequently featured in the *Subterfuge* anthology, and was selected for Stephen Jones' *Year's Best Horror.*

Nor was this to be an isolated example of Tanith's modesty. In 2011 Tanith was present when I announced a new series of books, *Imaginings*. She congratulated me and said how much she would have loved to be a part of the series. I was dumbfounded: I could have published a whole *book* by Tanith Lee…? Her collection *Cold Grey Stones* duly appeared as volume one, selling out in six weeks. Then, in the summer of 2013, I received a phone call from John, saying that he and Tanith knew I was bound to be busy at World Fantasycon, but they were wondering if I could possibly find the time to conduct Tanith's interview for her Lifetime Achievement Award. I have never felt more honoured.

In addition to being a consummate writer, Tanith was one of the most supportive professionals I have ever encountered, eager to read the work of others and offer encouragement, support, and, where she felt the writing merited it, praise. Being told that you are a writer of rare talent by someone of Tanith's calibre goes an awful long way.

There is one other side to Tanith that should never be underestimated: her sheer sense of *fun*. Helen and I enjoyed a number of nights out and about in the pubs and bars of Hastings with Tanith and John. Tanith's capacity to laugh, to put on silly voices and indulge in pure daftness, her glee at hearing sea shanties sung in a back bar, her appreciation of a spontaneous joke, and her overriding zest for life, these are the qualities that even now remain freshest in my mind.

Tanith's greatest legacy is, of course, her writing. She has left such a wealth of stories spanning fantasy, horror, science fiction and beyond, that selecting a 'Best of' would be a challenge for anyone and is a task I would never dream of taking on; so instead I invited others to do it for me.

Tanith By Choice contains a selection of Tanith's finest stories, as picked by many of the people who knew her best. I hope it will delight established fans and new readers alike. Above all else, these are stories that deserve to be read and if there is any justice in the world they always will be. A few of the stories are accompanied by introductory notes from the author. I considered removing these for consistency's sake but refrained. Why would anyone want to delete words written by Tanith Lee?

Tanith passed away in May 2015, at the age of 67, finally succumbing to the cancer that had plagued her in later life.

I miss her. I suspect I always will.

Ian Whates
Cambridgeshire
July 2017

Red as Blood

The beautiful Witch Queen flung open the ivory case of the magic mirror. Of dark gold the mirror was, dark gold like the hair of the Witch Queen that poured down her back. Dark gold the mirror was, and ancient as the seven stunted black trees growing beyond the pale blue glass of the window.

"*Speculum, speculum,*" said the Witch Queen to the magic mirror. "*Dei gratia.*"

"*Volente Deo. Audio.* "

"Mirror," said the Witch Queen. "Whom do you see?"

"I see you, mistress," replied the mirror. "And all in the land. But one."

"Mirror, mirror, who is it you do not see?"

"I do not see Bianca."

The Witch Queen crossed herself. She shut the case of the mirror and, walking slowly to the window, looked out at the old trees through the panes of pale blue glass.

Fourteen years ago, another woman had stood at this window, but she was not like the Witch Queen. The woman had black hair that fell to her ankles; she had a crimson gown, the girdle worn high beneath her breasts, for she was far gone with child. And this woman had thrust open the glass casement on the winter garden, where the old trees crouched in the snow. Then, taking a sharp bone needle, she had thrust it into her finger and shaken three bright drops on the ground. "Let my daughter have," said the woman, "hair black as mine, black as the wood of these warped and arcane trees. Let her have skin like mine, white as this snow. And let her have my mouth, red as my blood." And the woman had smiled and licked at her finger. She had a crown on her head; it shone in the dusk like a star. She never came to the window before dusk: she did not like the day. She was the first Queen, and she did not possess a mirror.

The second Queen, the Witch Queen, knew all this. She knew how, in giving birth, the first Queen had died. Her coffin had been carried into the cathedral and masses had been said. There was an ugly rumour – that a splash of holy water had fallen on the corpse and the dead flesh had smoked. But the first Queen had been reckoned unlucky for the kingdom. There had

9

been a plague in the land since she came there, a wasting disease for which there was no cure.

Seven years went by. The King married the second Queen, as unlike the first as frankincense to myrrh.

"And this is my daughter," said the King to his second Queen. There stood a little girl child, nearly seven years of age. Her black hair hung to her ankles, her skin was white as snow. Her mouth was red as blood, and she smiled with it.

"Bianca," said the King, "you must love your new mother." Bianca smiled radiantly. Her teeth were bright as sharp bone needles.

"Come," said the Witch Queen, "come, Bianca. I will show you my magic mirror."

"Please, Mamma," said Bianca softly, "I do not like mirrors." "She is modest," said the King. "And delicate. She never goes out by day. The sun distresses her."

That night, the Witch Queen opened the case of her mirror.

"Mirror. Whom do you see?"

"I see you, mistress. And all in the land. But one."

"Mirror, mirror, who is it you do not see?"

"I do not see Bianca."

The second Queen gave Bianca a tiny crucifix of golden filigree. Bianca would not accept it. She ran to her father and whispered, "I am afraid. I do not like to think of Our Lord dying in agony on His cross. She means to frighten me. Tell her to take it away."

The second Queen grew wild white roses in her garden and invited Bianca to walk there after sundown. But Bianca shrank away. She whispered to her father, "The thorns will tear me. She means me to be hurt."

When Bianca was twelve years old, the Witch Queen said to the King, "Bianca should be confirmed so that she may take Communion with us."

"This may not be," said the King. "I will tell you, she has not been Christened, for the dying word of my first wife was against it. She begged me, for her religion was different from ours. The wishes of the dying must be respected."

"Should you not like to be blessed by the Church," said the Witch Queen to Bianca. "To kneel at the golden rail before the marble altar. To sing to God, to taste the ritual Bread and sip the ritual Wine."

"She means me to betray my true mother," said Bianca to the King. "When will she cease tormenting me?"

The day she was thirteen, Bianca rose from her bed, and there was a red stain there, like a red, red flower.

"Now you are a woman," said her nurse.

"Yes," said Bianca. And she went to her true mother's jewel box, and out of it she took her mother's crown and set it on her head.

When she walked under the old black trees in the dusk, the crown shone like a star.

The wasting sickness, which had left the land in peace for thirteen years, suddenly began again, and there was no cure.

The Witch Queen sat in a tall chair before a window of pale green and dark white glass, and in her hands she held a Bible bound in rosy silk.

"Majesty," said the huntsman, bowing very low.

He was a man, forty years old, strong and handsome, and wise in the hidden lore of the forests, the occult lore of the earth. He could kill too, for it was his trade, without faltering. The slender fragile deer he could kill, and the moon-winged birds, and the velvet hares with their sad, foreknowing eyes. He pitied them, but pitying, he killed them. Pity could not stop him. It was his trade.

"Look in the garden," said the Witch Queen.

The hunter looked through a dark white pane. The sun had sunk, and a maiden walked under a tree.

"The Princess Bianca," said the huntsman.

"What else?" asked the Witch Queen.

The huntsman crossed himself.

"By Our Lord, Madam, I will not say."

"But you know."

"Who does not?"

"The King does not."

"Nor he does."

"Are you a brave man?" asked the Witch Queen.

"In the summer, I have hunted and slain boar. I have slaughtered wolves in winter."

"But are you brave enough?"

"If you command it, Lady," said the huntsman, "I will try my best."

The Witch Queen opened the Bible at a certain place, and out of it she drew a flat silver crucifix, which had been resting against the words: *Thou shalt not be afraid for the terror by night. . . . Nor for the pestilence that walketh in darkness.*

The huntsman kissed the crucifix and put it about his neck beneath his shirt.

"Approach," said the Witch Queen, "and I will instruct you in what to

11

say."

Presently, the huntsman entered the garden, as the stars were burning up in the sky. He strode to where Bianca stood under a stunted dwarf tree, and he kneeled down.

"Princess," he said, "pardon me, but I must give you ill tidings."

"Give them then," said the girl, toying with the long stem of a wan, night-growing flower which she had plucked.

"Your stepmother, the accursed jealous witch, means to have you slain. There is no help for it but you must fly the palace this very night. If you permit, I will guide you to the forest. There are those who will care for you until it may be safe for you to return."

Bianca watched him, but gently, trustingly.

"I will go with you, then," she said.

They went by a secret way out of the garden, through a passage under the ground, through a tangled orchard, by a broken road between great overgrown hedges.

Night was a pulse of deep, flickering blue when they came to the forest. The branches of the forest overlapped and intertwined, like leading in a window, and the sky gleamed dimly through like panes of blue-colored glass.

"I am weary," sighed Bianca. "May I rest a moment?"

"By all means," said the huntsman. "In the clearing there, foxes come to play by night. Look in that direction, and you will see them."

"How clever you are," said Bianca. "And how handsome." She sat on the turf and gazed at the clearing.

The huntsman drew his knife silently and concealed it in the folds of his cloak. He stooped above the maiden.

"What are you whispering?" demanded the huntsman, laying his hand on her wood-black hair.

"Only a rhyme my mother taught me."

The huntsman seized her by the hair and swung her about so her white throat was before him, stretched ready for the knife. But he did not strike, for there in his hand he held the dark golden locks of the Witch Queen, and her face laughed up at him, and she flung her arms about him, laughing.

"Good man, sweet man, it was only a test of you. Am I not a witch? And do you not love me?"

The huntsman trembled, for he did love her, and she was pressed so close her heart seemed to beat within his own body.

"Put away the knife. Throw away the silly crucifix. We have no need of these things. The King is not one half the man you are."

And the huntsman obeyed her, throwing the knife and the crucifix far off among the roots of the trees. He gripped her to him and she buried her face in his neck, and the pain of her kiss was the last thing he felt in this world.

The sky was black now. The forest was blacker. No foxes played in the clearing. The moon rose and made white lace through the boughs, and through the backs of the huntsman's empty eyes. Bianca wiped her mouth on a dead flower.

"Seven asleep, seven awake," said Bianca. "Wood to wood. Blood to blood. Thee to me."

There came a sound like seven huge rendings, distant by the length of several trees, a broken road, an orchard, an underground passage. Then a sound like seven huge single footfalls. Nearer. And nearer.

Hop, hop, hop, hop. Hop, hop, hop.

In the orchard, seven black shudderings.

On the broken road, between the high hedges, seven black creepings.

Brush crackled, branches snapped.

Through the forest, into the clearing, pushed seven warped, mis-shapen, hunched-over, stunted things. Woody-black mossy fur, woody-black bald masks. Eyes like glittering cracks, mouths like moist caverns. Lichen beards. Fingers of twiggy gristle. Grinning. Kneeling. Faces pressed to the earth.

"Welcome," said Bianca.

The Witch Queen stood before a window of glass like diluted wine. She looked at the magic mirror.

"Mirror. Whom do you see?"

"I see you, mistress. I see a man in the forest. He went hunting, but not for deer. His eyes are open, but he is dead. I see all in the land. But one."

The Witch Queen pressed her palms to her ears.

Outside the window, the garden lay, empty of its seven black and stunted dwarf trees.

"Bianca," said the Queen.

The windows had been draped and gave no light. The light spilled from a shallow vessel, light in a sheaf, like pastel wheat. It glowed upon four swords that pointed east and west, that pointed north and south.

Four winds had burst through the chamber, and the grey-silver powders of Time.

The hands of the Witch Queen floated like folded leaves on the air, and

13

through dry lips the Witch Queen chanted:

"Pater omnipotens, mitere digneris sanctum Angelum tuum de Infernis."

The light faded, and grew brighter.

There, between the hilts of the four swords, stood the Angel Lucefiel, somberly gilded, his face in shadow, his golden wings spread and blazing at his back.

"Since you have called me, I know your desire. It is a comfortless wish. You ask for pain."

"You speak of pain, Lord Lucefiel, who suffer the most merciless pain of all. Worse than the nails in the feet and wrists. Worse than the thorns and the bitter cup and the blade in the side. To be called upon for evil's sake, which I do not, comprehending your true nature, son of God, brother of The Son."

"You recognize me, then. I will grant what you ask."

And Lucefiel (by some named Satan, Rex Mundi, but nevertheless the left hand, the sinister hand of God's design) wrenched lightning from the ether and cast it at the Witch Queen.

It caught her in the breast. She fell.

The sheaf of light towered and lit the golden eyes of the Angel, which were terrible, yet luminous with compassion, as the swords shattered and he vanished.

The Witch Queen pulled herself from the floor of the chamber, no longer beautiful, a withered, slobbering hag.

Into the core of the forest, even at noon, the sun never shone. Flowers propagated in the grass, but they were colorless. Above, the black-green roof hung down nets of thick green twilight through which albino butterflies and moths feverishly drizzled. The trunks of the trees were smooth as the stalks of underwater weeds. Bats flew in the daytime, and birds who believed themselves to be bats.

There was a sepulcher, dripped with moss. The bones had been rolled out, had rolled around the feet of seven twisted dwarf trees. They looked like trees. Sometimes they moved. Sometimes something like an eye glittered, or a tooth, in the wet shadows.

In the shade of the sepulcher door sat Bianca, combing her hair.

A lurch of motion disturbed the thick twilight.

The seven trees turned their heads.

A hag emerged from the forest. She was crook-backed, and her head was poked forward, predatory, withered and almost hairless, like a vulture's.

"Here we are at last," grated the hag, in a vulture's voice.

She came closer and cranked herself down on her knees and bowed her face into the turf and the colorless flowers.

Bianca sat and gazed at her. The hag lifted herself. Her teeth were yellow palings.

"I bring you the homage of witches, and three gifts," said the hag.

"Why should you do that?"

"Such a quick child, and only fourteen years. Why? Because we fear you. I bring you gifts to curry favor."

Bianca laughed. "Show me."

The hag made a pass in the green air. She held a silken cord worked curiously with a plaited human hair.

"Here is a girdle which will protect you from the devices of priests, from crucifix and chalice and the accursed holy water. In it are knotted the tresses of a virgin, and of a woman no better than she should be, and of a woman dead. And here —" a second pass and a comb was in her hand, lacquered blue over green —" a comb from the deep sea, a mermaid's trinket, to charm and subdue. Part your locks with this, and the scent of ocean will fill men's nostrils and the rhythm of the tides their ears, the tides that bind men like chains. Last," added the hag, "that old symbol of wickedness, the scarlet fruit of Eve, the apple red as blood. Bite, and the understanding of Sin, which the serpent boasted of, will be made known to you." And the hag made her last pass in the air and extended the apple, with the girdle and the comb, towards Bianca.

Bianca glanced at the seven stunted trees.

"I like her gifts, but I do not quite trust her."

The bald masks peered from their shaggy beardings. Eyelets glinted. Twiggy claws clacked.

"All the same," said Bianca, "I will let her tie the girdle on me, and comb my hair herself."

The hag obeyed, simpering. Like a toad she waddled to Bianca. She tied on the girdle. She parted the ebony hair. Sparks sizzled, white from the girdle, peacock's eye from the comb.

"And now, hag, take a little bit bite of the apple."

"It will be my pride," said the hag, "to tell my sisters I shared this fruit with you." And the hag bit into the apple, and mumbled the bite noisily, and swallowed, smacking her lips.

Then Bianca took the apple and bit into it.

Bianca screamed – and choked.

She jumped to her feet. Her hair whirled about her like a storm cloud. Her face turned blue, then slate, then white again. She lay on the pallid flowers, neither stirring nor breathing.

The seven dwarf trees rattled their limbs and their bear-shaggy heads, to no avail. Without Bianca's art they could not hop. They strained their claws and ripped at the hag's sparse hair and her

mantle. She fled between them. She fled into the sunlit acres of the forest, along the broken road, through the orchard, into a hidden passage.

The hag reentered the palace by the hidden way, and the Queen's chamber by a hidden stair. She was bent almost double. She held her ribs. With one skinny hand she opened the ivory case of the magic mirror.

"*Speculum, speculum. Dei gratia.* Whom do you see?"

"I see you, mistress. And all in the land. And I see a coffin."

"Whose corpse lies in the coffin?"

"That I cannot see. It must be Bianca."

The hag, who had been the beautiful Witch Queen, sank into her tall chair before the window of pale cucumber green and dark white glass. Her drugs and potions waited ready to reverse the dreadful conjuring of age the Angel Lucefiel had placed on her, but she did not touch them yet.

The apple had contained a fragment of the flesh of Christ, the sacred wafer, the Eucharist.

The Witch Queen drew her Bible to her and opened it randomly.

And read, with fear, the words: *Resurgat.*

It appeared like glass, the coffin, milky glass. It had formed this way. A thin white smoke had risen from the skin of Bianca. She smoked as a fire smokes when a drop of quenching water falls on it. The piece of Eucharist had stuck in her throat. The Eucharist, quenching water to her fire, caused her to smoke.

Then the cold dews of night gathered, and the colder atmospheres of midnight. The smoke of Bianca's quenching froze about her. Frost formed in exquisite silver scrollwork all over the block of misty ice which contained Bianca.

Bianca's frigid heart could not warm the ice. Nor the sunless green twilight of the day.

You could just see her, stretched in the coffin, through the glass. How lovely she looked, Bianca. Black as ebony, white as snow, red as blood.

The trees hung over the coffin. Years passed. The trees sprawled about the coffin, cradling it in their arms. Their eyes wept fungus and green resin.

Green amber drops hardened like jewels in the coffin of glass.

"Who is that, lying under the trees?" the Prince asked, as he rode into the clearing.

He seemed to bring a golden moon with him, shining about his golden head, on the golden armor and the cloak of white satin blazoned with gold and blood and ink and sapphire. The white horse trod on the colorless flowers, but the flowers sprang up again when the hoofs had passed. A shield hung from the saddle bow, a strange shield. From one side it had a lion's face, but from the other, a lamb's face.

The trees groaned and their heads split on huge mouths.

"Is this Bianca's coffin?" said the Prince.

"Leave her with us," said the seven trees. They hauled at their roots. The ground shivered. The coffin of ice-glass gave a great jolt, and a crack bisected it.

Bianca coughed.

The jolt had precipitated the piece of Eucharist from her throat.

In a thousand shards the coffin shattered, and Bianca sat up. She stared at the Prince, and she smiled.

"Welcome, beloved," said Bianca.

She got to her feet and shook out her hair, and began to walk toward the Prince on the pale horse.

But she seemed to walk into a shadow, into a purple room; then into a crimson room whose emanations lanced her like knives. Next she walked into a yellow room where she heard the sound of crying which tore her ears. All her body seemed stripped away; she was a beating heart. The beats of her heart became two wings. She flew. She was a raven, then an owl. She flew into a sparkling pane. It scorched her white. Snow white. She was a dove.

She settled on the shoulder of the Prince and hid her head under her wing. She had no longer anything black about her, and nothing red.

"Begin again now, Bianca," said the Prince. He raised her from his shoulder. On his wrist there was a mark. It was like a star. Once a nail had been driven in there.

Bianca flew away, up through the roof of the forest. She flew in at a delicate wine window. She was in the palace. She was seven years old.

The Witch Queen, her new mother, hung a filigree crucifix around her neck. "Mirror," said the Witch Queen. "Whom do you see?"

"I see you, mistress," replied the mirror. "And all in the land. I see Bianca."

Red as Blood
Chosen by Stephen Jones

Tanith Lee's story "Red as Blood" was first published in the July 1979 issue of Edward L. Ferman's *The Magazine of Fantasy and Science Fiction*. Not only was it nominated for a Nebula Award, but Lin Carter selected it for the sixth volume of his *The Year's Best Fantasy Stories* and it also became the title of the author's second collection from DAW Books, *Red as Blood or Tales from the Sisters Grimmer* (1983) – which is where I originally discovered it. Written at a time when re-imaginings of fairy tales were not as popular as they are today, the story is an atmospheric reversal of the *Snow White* legend – an idea that has since been (over)used in literature, movies and TV. But Tanith did it first and, as always, she did it better than most. From the subject matter, you may think that this is one of the author's superlative fantasy stories, and it is – to an extent. But it is also one of her equally superlative *horror* stories as well...

– Stephen Jones

Stephen Jones is one of Britain's most acclaimed horror and dark fantasy writers and editors. A multiple winner of the World Fantasy Award, Bram Stoker Award and British Fantasy Award, he has more than 135 books to his credit.

The Gorgon

The small island, which lay off the larger island of Daphaeu, obviously contained a secret of some sort, and day by day, and particularly night by night, began to exert an influence on me, so that I must find it out

Daphaeu itself (or more correctly herself, for she was a female country, voluptuous and cruel by turns in the true antique fashion of the Goddess), was hardly enormous. A couple of roads, a tangle of sheep tracks, a precarious, escalating village, rocks and hillsides thatched by blistered grass. All of which overhung an extraordinary sea, unlike any sea which I have encountered elsewhere in Greece. Water which might be mistaken for blueness from a distance, but which, from the harbour, or the multitude of caves and coves that undermined the island, revealed itself a clear and succulent green, like milky limes, or the bottle glass of certain spirits.

On my first morning, having come on to the natural terrace, the only recommendation of the hovellike accommodation, to look over this strange green ocean, I saw the smaller island, lying like a little boat of land moored just wide of Daphaeu's three hills. The day was clear, the water frilled with white where it hit the fangs in the interstices below the terrace. About the smaller island, barely a ruffle showed. It seemed to glide up from the sea, smooth as a mirror. The little island was verdant, also. Unlike Daphaeu's limited stands of stone-pine, cypress and cedar, the smaller sister was clouded by a still, lambent haze of foliage, that looked to be woods. Visions of groves, springs, a ruined temple, a statue of Pan playing the panpipes forever in some glade – where only yesterday, it might seem, a thin column of aromatic smoke had gone up – these images were enough, fancifully to draw me into inquiries about how the small island might be reached. And when my inquiries met first with a polite bevy of excuses, next with a refusal, lastly with a blank wall of silence, as if whomever I mentioned the little island to had gone temporarily deaf or mad, I became, of course determined to get to it, to find out what odd superstitious thing kept these people away. Naturally, the Daphaeui were not friendly to me at any time, beyond the false friendship one anticipates extended to a man of another nationality and clime, who can be relied on to pay his bills, perhaps allow himself to be overcharged, even made a downright monkey of in order to preserve goodwill. In the normal run of things, I could have had anything I wanted, in exchange for a pack of local lies, a broad local smile, and a broader local price. That I could not get to the little island puzzled me. I tried money, and I tried barter. I even, in a reckless moment, probably knowing I would not succeed, offered Pitos, one of the younger fishermen, the gold and onyx ring he coveted. My sister had made it for me, the faithful copy of an intaglio belonging to the house of Borgia, no less. Generally, Pitos could not pass the time of day with me without mentioning the ring, adding something in the nature of: "If ever you want a great service, any great service, I will do it for that ring." I half believe he would have stolen or murdered for it, certainly shared the bed with me. But he would not, apparently, even for the Borgia ring, take me to the little island.

"You think too much of foolish things," he said to me. "For a big writer, that is not good."

I ignored the humorous aspect of "big," equally inappropriate in the sense of height, girth or fame. Pitos' English was fine, and when he slipped into mild inaccuracies, it was likely to be a decoy.

"You're wrong, Pitos. That island has a story in it somewhere, I'd take a bet on it."

"No fish today," said Pitos. "Why you think that is?"

I refrained from inventing a tale for him that I had seen giant swordfish leaping from the shallows by the smaller island.

I found I was prowling Daphaeu, but only on the one side, the side where I would get a view, or views, of the small island. I would climb down into the welter of coves and smashed emerald water, to look across at the small island. I would climb up and stand, leaning on the sunblasted walls of a crumbling church, and look at the small island. At night, crouched over a bottle of wine, a scatter of manuscript, moths falling like rain in the oil lamp, my stare stayed fixed on the small island, which, as the moon came up, would seem turned to silver, or to some older metal, Nemean metal perhaps, sloughed from the moon herself.

Curiosity accounts for much of this, and contra-suggestiveness. But the influence I presently began to feel, that I cannot account for exactly. Maybe it was only the writer's desire to fantasize rather than to work. But every time I reached for the manuscript I would experience a sort of distraction, a sort of calling, uncanny, poignant, like nostalgia, though for a place I had never visited.

I am very bad at recollecting my dreams, but once or twice, just before sunrise, I had a suspicion I had dreamed of the island. Of walking there, hearing its inner waters, the leaves brushing my hands and face.

Two weeks went by, and precious little had been done in the line of work. And I had come to Daphaeu with the sole intention of working. The year before, I had accomplished so much in a month of similar islands — or had they been similar? — that I had looked for results of some magnitude. In all of fourteen days I must have squeezed out two thousand words, and most of those dreary enough that the only covers they would ever get between, would be those of the trash can. And yet, it was not that I could not produce work, it was that I knew, with blind and damnable certainty, that the work I needed to be doing sprang from that spoonful of island.

The first day of the third week I had been swimming in the calm stretch of sea west of the harbour, and had emerged to sun myself and smoke on the parched hot shore. Presently Pitos appeared, having scented cigarettes. Surgical and government health warnings have not yet penetrated to spots like Daphaeu, where filtered tobacco continues to symbolize Hollywood, or some other amorphous, anachronistic surrealism still hankered after and long vanished from the world beyond. Once Pitos had acquired his cigarette, he sprawled down on the dry grass, grinned, indicated the Borgia ring, and mentioned a beautiful cousin of his, whether male or female I cannot be sure. After this had been cleared out of the way, I said to him,

"You know how the currents run. I was thinking of a slightly more adventurous swim. But I'd like your advice."

Pitos glanced at me warily. I had had the plan as I lazed in the velvet water. Pitos was already starting to guess it.

"Currents are very dangerous. Not to be trusted, except by harbour."

"How about between Daphaeu and the other island? It can't be more than a quarter mile. The sea looks smooth enough, once you break away from the shoreline here."

"No," said Pitos. I waited for him to say there were no fish, or a lot of fish, or that his brother had got a broken thumb, or something of the sort. But Pitos did not resort to this. Troubled and angry, he stabbed my cigarette into the turf half-smoked. "Why do you want to go to the island so much?"

"Why does nobody else want me to go there?"

He looked up then, and into my eyes. His own were very black, sensuous, carnal, earthbound eyes, full of orthodox sins, and extremely young in a sense that had nothing to do with physical age, but with race, I suppose, the youngness of ancient things, like Pan himself, quite possibly.

"Well," I said at last, "are you going to tell me, or not? Because believe me, I intend to swim over there, today or tomorrow."

"No," he said again. And then: "You should not go. On the island there is a —" and he said a word in some tongue neither Greek nor Turkish, not even the corrupt Spanish that sometimes peregrinates from Malta.

"A *what?*'

Pitos shrugged helplessly. He gazed out to sea, safe sea without islands. He seemed to be putting something together in his mind, and I let him do it, very curious now, pleasantly unnerved by this waft of the occult I had already suspected to be the root cause of the ban.

Eventually he turned back to me, treated me once more to the primordial innocence of his stare, and announced:

"The cunning one "

"Ah," I said. Both irked and amused, I found myself smiling. At this, Pitos' face grew savage with pure rage, an expression I had never witnessed before – the façade kept for foreigners had well and truly come down.

"Pitos," I said, "I don't understand."

"*Meda,*" he said then, the Greek word, old Greek. "Wait," I said. I caught at the name, which was wrong, trying to fit it to a memory. Then the list came back to me, actually from Graves, the name which meant "the cunning" – Meda, Medea, Medusa "Oh," I said. I hardly wanted to offend him further by bursting into loud mirth. At the same time even while I was trying not to laugh, I was aware o the hair standing up on my scalp and neck. "You're telling me there is a gorgon on the island."

Pitos grumbled unintelligibly, stabbing the dead cigarette over and over into the ground.

"I'm sorry, Pitos, but it can't be Medusa. Someone cut her head off quite a few years ago. A guy called Perseus."

His face erupted into the awful expression again mouth in a rictus, tongue starting to protrude, eye flaring at me – quite abruptly I realized he wasn't raging, but imitating the visual panic-contortions of a man turning inexorably to stone. Since that is what the gorgon is credited with, literally petrifying men by the sheer horror of her countenance, it now seemed almost pragmatic of Pitos to be demonstrating. I was, too, a creditable facsimile of the sculpted gorgon's face sometimes used to seal ovens and jars. I wondered where he had seen one to copy it so well.

"All right," I said. "O.K., Pitos, fine." I fished in my shirt, which was lying on the ground, and took out some money to give him, but he recoiled. "I'm sorry," I said, "I don't think it merits the ring. Unless you'd care to row me over there after all."

The boy rose. He looked at me with utter contempt, and without another word, before striding off up the shore. The mashed cigarette protruded from the grass, and I lay and watched it, the tiny strands of tobacco slowly crisping in the heat of the sun, as I plotted my route from

Daphaeu.

Dawn seemed an amiable hour. No one in particular about on that side of the island, the water chill but flushing quickly with warmth as the sun reached over it. And the tide in the right place to navigate the rocks...

Yes, dawn would be an excellent time to swim out to the gorgon's island.

The gods were on my side, I concluded, as I eased myself out into the open sea the following morning. Getting clear of the rocks was no problem, their channels only half filled by the returning tide. While just beyond Daphaeu's coast I picked up one of those contrary currents that lace the island's edges and which, tide or no, would funnel me away from shore.

The swim was ideal, the sea limpid and no longer any more than cool. Sunlight filled in the waves and touched Daphaeu's retreating face with gold. Barely altered in a thousand years, either rock or sea or sun. And yet one knew that against all the claims of romantic fiction, this place did not look now as once it had. Some element in the air, or in time itself changes things. A young man of the Bronze Age falling asleep at sunset in his own era, waking at sunrise in mine, looking about him, would not have known where he was. I would swear to that.

Some thoughts I had leisure for in my facile swim across to the wooded island moored off Daphaeu.

As I had detected, the approach was smooth, virtually inviting. I cruised in as if sliding on butter. A rowboat would have had no more difficulty. The shallows were clear, empty of rocks, and if anything greener than the water off Daphaeu.

I had not looked much at Medusa's Island (I had begun jokingly to call it this), as I crossed, knowing would have all the space on my arrival. So I found myself wading in on a seamless beach of rare glycerine sand, and looking up, saw the mass of trees spilling from the sky.

The effect was incredibly lush, so much heavy green, and seemingly quite impenetrable, although the sun struck in glistening shafts, lodging like arrows in the foliage, which reminded me very intensely of huge clusters of grapes on a vine. Anything might lie behind such a barricade.

It was already beginning to be hot. Dry, I put on the loose cotton shirt, and ate breakfast packed in the same waterproof wrapper, standing on the beach impatient to get on.

As I moved forward, a bird shrilled somewhere ii its cage of boughs, sounding an alarm of invasion But surely the birds, too, would be stone, on Medusa's Island, if the legends were correct? And when stumbled across the remarkable stone carving of a man in the forest, I would pause in shocked amazement at its verisimilitude to the life. . . .

Five minutes into the thickets of the wood, I did indeed stumble on a carving, but it was of a moss-grown little faun. My pleasure in the discovery was considerably lessened, however, when investigation told me it was scarcely classical in origin. Circa 1920 would be nearer the mark.

A further minute and I had put the faun from my mind. The riot of waterfalling plants through which I had been picking my way broke open suddenly on an inner vista much wider than I had anticipated, while the focal point of the vista threw me completely. I cannot say what I had really been expecting. The grey-white stalks of pillars, some temple shrine, the spring with its votary of greenish rotted bronze, none of these would have surprised me. On the other hand, to find a house before me took me completely by surprise. I stood and looked at it in abject dismay, cursing its wretched normalcy, until I gradually began to see the house was not normal, in the accepted sense.

It had been erected probably at the turn of the century, when such things were done. An eccentric two-storeyed building, intransigently European, that is, the Europe of the north, with its dark walls and arched roofing. Long windows, smothered by the proximity of the wood, received and refracted no light. The one unique and startling feature – startling because of its beauty – was the parade of columns that ran along the terrace, in form and choreography for all the world like the columns of Knossos, differing only in colour. For these stems of the gloomy house were of a luminous sea-green marble, and shone as the windows did not.

Before the house was a stretch of rough-cut lawn, tamarisk, and one lost dying olive tree. As I was staring, an apparition seemed to manifest out of the centre of the tree. For a second we peered at each other, before he came from the bushes with a clashing of gnarled brown forearms. He might have been an elderly satyr; I, patently, was only a swimmer, with my pale foreigner's tan, my bathing trunks, the loose shirt. It occurred to me at last that I was conceivably trespassing. I wished my Greek were better.

He planted himself before me and shouted intolerantly, and anyone's Greek was good enough to get his drift. "Go! Go!" He was ranting, and he began to wave a knife with which, presumably, he had been pruning or mutilating something. "Go, you *go*!"

I said I had been unaware anybody lived on the island. He took no notice. He went on waving the knife, and his attitude provoked me. I told him sternly to put the knife down, that I would leave when I was ready, that I had seen no notice to the effect that the island was private property. Generally I would never take a chance like this with someone so obviously qualified to be a lunatic, but my position was so vulnerable, so ludicrous, so entirely indefensible, that I felt bound to act firmly. Besides which, having reached the magic grotto and found it was not as I had visualized, I was still very reluctant to abscond with only a memory of dark windows and sea-green columns to brood upon.

The maniac was by now quite literally foaming, due most likely to a shortage of teeth, but the effect was alarming, not to mention unaesthetic. As I was deciding which fresh course to take and if there might be one, a woman's figure came out on to the terrace. I had the impression of a white frock, before an odd, muffled voice called out a rapid — too rapid for my translation — stream of peculiarly accented Greek. The old man swung around, gazed at the figure, raised his arms, and bawled another foaming torrent to the effect that I was a bandit, or some other kind of malcontent. While he did so, agitated as I was becoming, I nevertheless took in what I could of the woman standing between the columns. She was mostly in shadow, just the faded white dress, with a white scarf at the neck, marking her position. And then there was an abrupt flash of warmer pallor that was her hair. A blonde Greek, or maybe just a peroxided Greek. At any rate, no snakes.

The drama went on, from his side, from hers. I finally got tired of it, went by him and walked toward the terrace, pondering, rather too late, if I might not be awarded the knife in my back. But almost as soon as I started to move, she leaned forward a little, and she called another phrase to him, which this time I made out, telling him to let me come on.

When I reached the foot of the terrace steps, I halted, really involuntarily, struck by something strange about her. Just as the strangeness of the house had begun to strike me, not its evident strangeness, the ill-marriage to location, the green pillars, but a strangeness of atmosphere, items the unconscious eye notices, where the physical eye is blind, and will not explain. And so with her. What was it? Still in shadow, I had the impression she might be in her early thirties, from her figure, her movements, but she had turned away as I approached, adjusting some papers on a wicker table.

"Excuse me," I said. I stopped, and spoke in English. For some reason I guessed she would be familiar with the language, perhaps only since it was current on Daphaeu. "Excuse me. I had no idea the island was private. No one gave me the slightest hint —"

"You are English," she broke in, in the vernacular, proving the guess to be correct.

"Near enough. I Find it easier to handle than Greek I confess."

"Your Greek is very good," she said, with the indifferent patronage of one who is multi-lingual. I stood there under the steps, already fascinated. Her voice was the weirdest I had ever heard, muffled, almost unattractive, and with the most incredible accent, if Greek at all. The nearest approximation I could come up with was Russian, but I could not be sure.

"Well," I said. I glanced over my shoulder a registered that the frothy satyr had retired into his shrubbery; the knife glinted as it slashed tamarisk in lieu of me. "Well, I suppose I should retreat Daphaeu. Or am I permitted to stay?"

"Go, stay," she said. "I do not care at all."

She turned then, abruptly, and my heart slammed into the base of my throat. A childish silly reaction yet I was quite unnerved, for now I saw what it w that had seemed vaguely peculiar from a distance. The lady on Medusa's island was masked.

She remained totally still, and let me have my reaction, neither helping nor hindering me.

It was an unusual mask, or usual — I am unfamiliar with the norm of such things. It was made some matte light substance that toned well with the skin of her arms and hands, possibly not so well with that of her neck, where the scarf provided camouflage. Besides which, the chin of the mask, this certain an extra to any mask I had ever seen, continued under her own. The mask's physiognomy was bland nondescriptly pretty in a way that was somehow gross insulting to her. Before confronting the mask, if had tried to judge the sort of face she would have, would have suspected a coarse, rather heavy beauty probably redeemed by one chiseled feature, a semi slender nose, perhaps. The mask, however, was vacuous. It did not suit her, was not true to her. Even after three minutes I could tell as much, or thought I could, which amounts to the same thing.

The blonde hair, seeming natural as the mask was not, cascaded down, lush as the foliage of the island. A blonde Greek, then, like the golden Greeks of Homer's time, when gods walked the earth in disguise.

In the end, without any help or hindrance from her, as I have said, I pulled myself together. As she had mentioned no aspect of her state, neither did I. I simply repeated what I had said before: "Am I permitted to stay?"

The mask went on looking at me. The astonishing voice said:

"You wish to stay so much; what do you mean to do here?"

Talk to you, oblique lady, and wonder what lies behind the painted veil.

"Look at the island, if you'll let me. I found the statue of a faun near the beach," elaboration implied I should lie: "Someone told me there was an old shrine here."

"Ah!" She barked. It was apparently a laugh. "No one," she said, "*told* you anything about this place."

I was at a loss. Did she know what she said? "Frankly then, I romantically hoped there might be."

"Unromantically, there is not. No shrine. No temple. My father bought the faun in a shop, in Athens. A tourist shop. He had vulgar tastes, but he knew it, and that has a certain charm, does it not?"

"Yes, I suppose it does. Your father —"

She cut me short again.

"The woods cover all the island. Except for an area behind the house. We grow things there, and we keep goats and chickens. We are very domesticated. Very sufficient for ourselves. There is a spring of fresh water, but no votary. No *genius loci*. I am *so* sorry to dash your dreams to pieces."

It suggested itself to me, from her tone of amusement, from little inflections in her shoulders, that she might be enjoying this, enjoying, if you like, putting me down as an idiot. Presumably visitors were rare. Perhaps it was even fun for her to talk to a man, youngish and unknown, though admittedly never likely to qualify for anyone's centrefold.

"But you have no objections to my being here," I pursued. "And your father?"

"My parents are dead," she informed me. "When I employed the plural, I referred to him," she gestured, a broad sweep of her hand, to the monster on the lawn, "and a woman who attends to the house. My servants, my unpaid servants. I have no money anymore. Do you see this dress? It is my mother's dress. How lucky I am the same fitting as my mother, do you not think?"

"Yes "

I was put in mind, suddenly, of myself as an ambassador at the court of some notorious female potentate, Cleopatra, say, or Catherine de Medici.

"You are very polite," she said, as if telepathically privy to my fantasies.

"I have every reason to be."

"What reason?"

"I'm trespassing. You treat me like a guest."

"And how," she said, vainglorious all at once, "do you rate my English?"

"It's wonderful."

"I speak eleven languages fluently," she, with off-handed boastfulness. "Three more I can read very well."

I liked her. This display, touching and magnificent at once, her angular theatrical gesturings, which now came more and more often, her hair, her flat-waisted figure in its 1940's dress, her large, well-made hands, and her

27

challenging me with the mask, saying nothing to explain it, all this hypnotised me.

I said something to express admiration, and she barked again, throwing back her blonde head and irresistibly, though only for a moment, conjuring Garbo's Queen Christina.

Then she walked down the steps, straight to me, demonstrating something else I had deduced, that she was only about an inch shorter than I.

"I," she said, "will show you the island. Come."

She showed me the island. Unsurprisingly, it was small. To go directly round it would maybe have taken less than thirty minutes. But we lingered, over a particular tree, a view, and once we sat down on the ground near the gushing milk-white spring. The basin under the spring, she informed me, had been added in 1910. A little bronze nymph presided over the spot, dating from the same year, which you could tell in any case from the way her classical costume and her filetted hair had been adapted to the fashions of hobble skirt and Edwardian coiffeur. Each age imposes its own overlay on the past.

Behind the house was a scatter of the meagre white dwellings that make up such places as the village on Daphaeu, now plainly unoccupied and put to other uses. Sheltered from the sun by a colossal cypress, six goats played about in the grass. Chickens, and an assortment of other fowl, strutted up and down, while a pig, or pigs, grunted somewhere out of sight. Things grew in strips and patches, and fruit trees and vines ended the miniature plantation before the woods resumed. Self-sufficiency of a tolerable kind, I suppose. But there seemed, from what she said, no contact maintained with any other area, as if the world did not exist. Postulate that a blight, or harsh weather, intervened, what then? And the old satyr, how long would he last to tend the plots? He looked two hundred now, which on the islands probably meant sixty. I did not ask her what contingency plans she had for these emergencies and inevitabilities. What good, after all, are most plans? We could be invaded from Andromeda tomorrow, and what help for us all then? Either it is in your nature to survive, somehow, anyhow, or it is not.

She had well and truly hooked me, of course. If I had met her in Athens, some sun-baked afternoon, I would have felt decidedly out of my depth, taken her for cocktails, and foundered before we had even reached the dinner hour. But here, in this pulsing green bubble of light and leaves straight out of one's most irrational visions of the glades of Arcadia, conversation, however erratic, communication, however eccentric, was happening. The most inexplicable thing of all was that the mask had ceased, almost immediately, to bother me. I cannot, as I look back, properly account for this, for to spend a morning, a noon, an afternoon, allowing yourself to become fundamentally engaged by a woman whose face you have not seen, whose face you are actively being prevented from seeing, seems now incongruous, to the point of perversity. But there it is. We discussed Ibsen, Dickens, Euripides and Jung. I remembered trawling anecdotes of a grandfather, mentioned my sister's jewellery store in St. Louis, listened to an astonishing description of wild birds flying in across a desert from a sea. I assisted her over rocky turf, flirted with her, felt excited by and familiar with her, all this with her masked face before me. As if the mask, rather than being a part of her, meant no more than the frock she had elected to wear, or the narrow-heeled vanilla shoes she had chosen to put on. As if I knew her face totally and had no need to be shown it, the face of her movements and her ridiculous voice.

But in fact, I could not even make out her eyes, only the shine in them when they caught the light, flecks of luminescence but not colour, for the eyeholes of the mask were long-lidded and rather small. I must have noticed, too, that there was no aperture in the lips, and this may have informed me that the mask must be removed for purposes of eating or drinking. I really do not know. I can neither excuse nor quite understand myself, seen in the distance there, with her, on her island. Hartley tells us that the past is another country. Perhaps we also were other people, strangers, yesterday. But when I think of this, I remember, too, the sense of drawing I had had, of being magnetised to that shore, those trees, the nostalgia for a place I had never been to. For she, it may be true to say, was a figment of that nostalgia, as if I had known her and come back to her. Some enchantment, then. Not Medusa's island, but Circe's.

The afternoon, even through the dapple *L'Apres Midi d'Un Faun* effect of the leaves, was a viridian furnace, when we regained the house. I sat in one of the wicker chairs on the terrace, and woke with a start of embarrassment to hear her laughing at me.

"You are tired and hungry. I must go into the house for a while. I will send Kleia to you with some wine and food."

It made a bleary sense, and when I woke again it was to find an old fat woman in the ubiquitous Grecian island black – demonstrably Kleia – setting down a tray of pale red wine, amber cheese and dark bread.

"Where is –" I realized I did not know the enchantress's name.

In any event, the woman only shook her head, saying brusquely in Greek: "No English. No English."

And when I attempted to ask again in Greek where my hostess had got to, Kleia waddled away leaving me unanswered. So I ate the food, which was passable, and drank the wine, which was very good, imagining her faun-buying father putting down an enormous patrician cellar, then fell alseep again, sprawled in the chair.

When I wakened, the sun was setting and the clearing was swimming in red light and rusty violet shadows. The columns burned as if they were internally on fire, holding the core of the sunset, it appeared, some while after the sky had cooled and the stars became visible, a trick of architectural positioning that won my awe and envy. I was making a mental note to ask her who had been responsible for the columns, and jumped when she spoke to me, softly and hoarsely, almost seductively, from just behind my chair – thereby promptly making me forget to ask any such thing.

"Come into the house, now. We will dine soon."

I got up, saying something lame about imposing on her, though we were far beyond that stage.

"Always," she said to me, "you apologise. There is no imposition. You will be gone tomorrow."

How do you know? I nearly inquired, but prevented myself. What guarantee? Even if the magic food did not change me into a swine, perhaps my poisoned dead body would be carried from the feast and cast into the sea, gone, well and truly, to Poseidon's fishes. You see, I did not trust her, even though I was somewhat in love with her. The element of her danger – for she *was* dangerous in some obscure way – may well have contributed to her attraction.

We went into the house, which in itself alerted me. I had forgotten a great curiosity I had had to look inside it. There was a shadowy unlit entrance hall, a sort of Roman atrium of a thing. Then we passed, she leading, into a small salon that took my breath away. It was lined, all over, floor, ceiling, walls, with the sea-green marble the columns were made of. Whether in good taste or bad I am not qualified to say, but the effect, instantaneous and utter, was of being beneath the sea. Smoky oil lamps of a very beautiful Art Nouveau design, hung from the profundity of the green ceiling, lighting the dreamlike swirls and oceanic variations of the marble, so they seemed to breathe, definitely to move, like nothing else but waves. Shoes on that floor would have squeaked or clattered unbearably, but I was barefoot, and now so was she.

A mahogany table, with a modest placing for eight, stood centrally. Only one place was laid.

I looked at it, and she said,

"I do not dine, but that will not prevent you."

An order. I considered vampires, idly, but mainly I was subject to an infantile annoyance. I had looked for the subtraction of the mask when she ate, without quite realizing it, and now this made me very conscious of the mask for the first time since I had originally seen it.

We seated ourselves, she two places away from me. And I began to feel nervous. To eat this meal while she watched me did not appeal. And now the idea of the mask, unconsidered all morning, all afternoon, stole over me like an incoming tide.

Inevitably, I had not dressed for dinner, having no means, but she had changed her clothes, and was now wearing a high-collared long grey gown, her mother's again, no doubt. It had the fragile look of age, but was very feminine and appealing for all that. Above it, the mask now reared, stuck out like the proverbial sore thumb.

The mask. What on earth was I going to do, leered at by the myopic soulless face which had suddenly assumed such disastrous importance.

Kleia waddled in with the dishes. I cannot recall the meal, save that it was spicey, and mostly vegetable. The wine came too, and I drank it. As I drank the wine, I began to consider seriously, for the first time (which seems very curious indeed to me now), the reason for the mask. What did it hide? A scar, a birthmark? I drank her wine, and I saw myself snatch off the mask, take in the disfigurement, unquelled, and behold the painful gratitude in her eyes as she watched me. I would inform her of the genius of surgeons. She would repeat, she had no money. I would promise to pay for the operation.

Suddenly she startled me by saying: "Do you believe that we have lived before?"

I looked in my glass, that fount of wisdom and possibility, and said, "It seems as sensible a proposition as any of the others I've ever heard."

I fancied she smiled to herself, and do not know why I thought that; I know now I was wrong.

Her accent had thickened and distorted further when she said,

"I rather hope that I have lived before. I could wish to think I may live again."

"To compensate for this life?" I said brutishly. I had not needed to be so obvious when already I had been given the implication on a salver.

"Yes. To compensate for this."

I downed all the wisdom and possibility left in my glass, swallowed an extra couple of times, and said, "Are you going to tell me why you wear a mask?"

As soon as I had said it, I grasped that I was drunk. Nor was it a pleasant drunkeness. I did not like the demanding tone I had taken with her, but I was angry at having allowed the game to go on for so long. I had no knowledge of the rules, or pretended I had not. And 1 could not stop myself. When she did not reply, I added on a note of ghastly banter, "Or shall I guess?"

She was still, seeming very composed. Had this scene been enacted before? Finally she said, "I would suppose you do guess it is to conceal something that I wear it."

"Something you imagine worth concealing, which, perhaps, isn't."

That was the stilted fanfare of bravado. I had braced myself, flushed with such stupid confidence.

"Why not," I said, and I grow cold when I remember how I spoke to her, "take the damn thing off. Take off the mask, and drink a glass of wine with me."

A pause. Then, "No," she said.

Her voice was level and calm. There was neither eagerness nor fear in it.

"Go on," I said, the drunk not getting his way, aware, (oh God), he could get it by the power of his intention alone, "please. You're an astounding woman. You're like this island. A fascinating mystery. But I've seen the island. Let me see you."

"No," she said.

I started to feel, even through the wine, that I had made an indecent suggestion to her, and this, along with the awful clichés I was bringing out increased my anger and my discomfort.

"For Heaven's sake," I said. "Do you know what they call you on Daphaeu?"

"Yes."

"This is absurd. You're frightened –"

"No. I am not afraid."

"Afraid. Afraid to let me see. But maybe I can help you."

"No. You cannot help me."

"How can you be sure?"

She turned in her chair, and all the way to face me with the mask. Behind her, everywhere about her. the green marble dazzled.

"If you know," she said, "what I am called on Daphaeu, are you not uneasy as to what you may see?"

"Jesus. Mythology and superstition and ignorance. I assure you, I won't turn to stone."

"It is I," she said quietly, "who have done that." Something about the phrase, the way in which she said it, chilled me. I put down my glass, and in that instant, her hands went to the sides of the mask and her fingers worked

32

at some complicated strap arrangement which her hair had covered.

"Good," I said, "good. I'm glad –"

But I faltered over it. The cold night sea seemed to fill my veins where the warm red wine had been. I had been heroic and sure and bold, the stuff of celluloid. But now I had my way, with hardly any preliminary, what *would* I see? And then she drew the plastic away and I saw.

I sat there, and then I stood up. The reflex was violent, and the chair scraped over the marble with an unbearable noise. There are occasions, though rare, when the human mind grows blank of all thought. I had no thought as I looked at her. Even now, I can evoke those long, long empty seconds, that lapse of time. I recollect only the briefest confusion, when I believe she still played some kind of hideous game, that what I witnessed was a product of her decision and her will, a gesture –

After all, Pitos had done this very thing to illustrate and endorse his argument, produced this very expression, the eyes bursting from the head, the jaw rigidly outthrust, the tendons in the neck straining, the mouth in the grimace of a frozen, agonised scream, the teeth visible, the tongue slightly protruding. The gorgon's face on the jar or the oven. The face so ugly, so demented, so terrible, it could petrify.

The awful mouth writhed.

"You have seen," she said. Somehow the stretched and distorted lips brought out these words. There was even that nuance of humour I had heard before, the smile, although physically, a smile would have been out of the question. "You have seen."

She picked up the mask again, gently, and put it on, easing the underpart of the plastic beneath her chin, to hide the convulsed tendons in her throat. I stood there, motionless. Childishly I informed myself that now I comprehended the reason for her peculiar accent, which was caused, not by some exotic foreign extraction, but by the atrocious malformation of jaw, tongue and lips, which somehow must be fought against for every sound she made.

I went on standing there, and now the mask was back in place.

"When I was very young," she said, "I suffered, without warning, from a form of fit, or stroke. Various nerve centres were paralysed. My father took me to the very best of surgeons, you may comfort yourself with that. Unfortunately, any effort to correct the damage entailed a penetration of my brain uncompromisingly delicate that it was reckon impossible, for it would surely render me an idiot Since my senses, faculties and intelligence were otherwise unaffected, it was decided not to risk this dire surgery, and my doctors resorted instead to alternative therapies, which, patently, were unsuccessful. As the months passed, my body adjusted to the unnatural physical tensions resulting from my facial paralysis. The pain of the rictus faded, or grew acceptable. I learned both how to eat, and how to converse, although the former activity is not attractive, and attend to it in private. The mask was made for me Athens. I am quite fond of it. The man who designed it had worked a great many years in the theatre, and could have made me a face of enormous beauty or character, but this seemed pointless even wasteful."

There was a silence, and I realized her explanation was finished.

Not once had she stumbled. There was neither hurt nor madness in her inflexion. There *was* something . . . at the time, I missed it, though it came me after. Then I knew only that she was far beyond my pity or my anguish, far away indeed from my terror.

"And now," she said, rising gracefully, "I will leave you to eat your meal in peace. Good night."

I wanted, or rather I felt impelled, to stay her with actions or sentences, but I was incapable of either. She walked out of the green marble room, and left me there. It is a fact that for a considerable space of time, I did not move.

I did not engage the swim back to Daphaeu that night, I judged myself too drunk, and slept on the beach at the edge of the trees, where at sunrise the tidal water woke me with a strange low hissing. Green sea, green sunlight through leaves. I swam away and found my course through the warming ocean and fetched up, exhausted and swearing, bruising myself on Daphaeu's fangs that had not harmed me when I left her. I did not see Pitos anywhere about, and that evening I caught the boat which would take me to the mainland.

There is a curious thing which can happen with human beings. It is the ability to perform for days or weeks like balanced and cheerful automata, when some substrata, something upon which our codes or our hopes had firmly rested has given way. Men who lose their wives or their God are quite capable of behaving in this manner, for an indefinite season. After which the collapse is brilliant and total. Something of this sort had happened to me. Yet, to fathom what I had lost, what she had deprived me of, is hard to say. I found its symptoms, but not the sickness which it was.

Medusa (I must call her that, she has no other name I know), struck by the extraordinary arrow of her misfortune, condemned to her relentless, uncanny, horrible isolation, her tragedy most deeply rooted in the fact that she was not a myth, not a fabulous and glamorous monster . . . For it came to me one night in a bar in Corinth, to consider if the first Medusa might

34

have been also such a victim, felled by some awesome fit, not petrifying but petrified, so appalling to the eyes, and, more significantly, to the brooding aesthetic spirit that lives in man, that she too was shunned and hated, and slain by a murderer who would observe her only in a polished surface.

I spent some while in bars that summer. And la much later, when the cold climate of the year's end closed the prospect of travel and adventure, I came afraid for myself, that dreadful writer's fear which has to do with the death of the idea, with inertia of hand and heart and mind. Like one of broken leaves, the summer's withered plants, I had dried. My block was sheer. I had expected a multitude of pages from the island, but instead I saw the unborn pages die on the horizon, where the beach met the sea.

And this, merely a record of marble, water plastic shell strapped across a woman's face, this is the last thing, it seems, which I shall commit to paper. Why? Perhaps only because she was to me such a lesson in the futility of things, the waiting fist of chance, the random despair we name World.

And yet, now and then, I hear that voice of hers I hear the way she spoke to me. I know now what heard in her voice, which had neither pain nor shame in it, nor pleading, nor whining, nor even a hint of the tragedy, the Greek tragedy, of her life. And what I heard was not dignity, either, or acceptance, nobleness. It was *contempt*. She despised me. She despised all of us who live without her odds, who struggle with our small struggles, incomparable hers. "Your Greek is very good," she said to me, with the patronage of one who is multi-lingual. And that same disdain she says, over and over to me "that you live is very good." Compared to her life, her existence, her multi-lingual endurance, what are my life, or my ambitions worth? Or anything.

It did not occur immediately, but still it occurred. In its way, the myth is perfectly accurate. I see it in myself, scent it, taste it, like the onset of inescapable disease. What they say about the gorgon is true. She has turned me to stone.

The Gorgon
Chosen by Vera Nazarian

Of all the shorter Tanith Lee works I've read, this one always comes to mind whenever I think of the entirety of her glittering oeuvre – brilliant as the sun-dappled cornucopia of the Greek islands themselves, and hoary as the verdant ancient shade concealed there. It's quintessential Lee, a strange mixture of the erotic unknown, visceral terror, and beautiful wonder, all put together in such a tempting siren call for the imagination. It is impossible to speak of Lee's work without using superlatives and committing imagery. But words quickly fail as the waking dream state takes over. You are caught and transported by the power of the ancient goddess, soon willingly lost in the examination of ancient truths, compelled to wander toward the inevitable end, to unmask the historical legend, and the mystery. "The Gorgon" is elegant yet prosaic, earthy and infinitely kaleidoscopic, a timeless myth brought forth and re-examined. The story of a nameless writer looking for solitude and inspiration in the Greek Islands, and stumbling upon a tantalizing, mysterious impossibility, is Tanith Lee at her poignant, insightful best.

– Vera Nazarian

Vera Nazarian is a two-time Nebula Award Finalist author, award-winning artist, publisher of Norilana Books, musician, philosopher, and creator of wonder.

Bite Me Not, or Fleur de Fur

Again, apparently, vampires lure me. This is a fairy-tale invented by me, in the mythic tradition of True (sexual) Love, for which all things may be required to be sacrificed.

For me, stained glass does seem to attend on vampires. But the pack of ravening angels flew out of the mind forest and surprised me, as such creatures often do.

And I confess the phrase Fleur de Fur *began as a love-name for my cat.*

I

In the tradition of young girls and windows, the young girl looks out of this one. It is difficult to see anything. The panes of the window are heavily leaded, and secured by a lattice of iron. The stained glass of lizard-green and storm-purple is several inches thick. There is no red glass in the window. The colour red is forbidden in the castle. Even the sun, behind the glass, is a storm sun, a green-lizard sun.

The young girl wishes she had a gown of palest pastel rose – the nearest affinity to red, which is never allowed. Already she has long dark beautiful eyes, a long white neck. Her long dark hair is, however, hidden in a dusty scarf, and she wears rags. She is a scullery maid. As she scours dishes and mops stone floors, she imagines she is a princess floating through the upper corridors, gliding to the dais in the Duke's hall. The Cursed Duke. She is sorry for him. If he had been her father, she would have sympathised and consoled him. His own daughter is dead, as his wife is dead, but these things, being to do with the cursing, are never spoken of. Except, sometimes, obliquely.

'*Rohise!*' dim voices cry now, full of dim scolding soon to be actualised.

The scullery maid turns from the window and runs to have her ears boxed and a broom thrust into her hands.

Meanwhile, the Cursed Duke is prowling his chamber, high in the East Turret carved with swans and gargoyles. The room is lined with books, swords, lutes, scrolls, and has two eerie portraits, the larger of which represents his wife, and the smaller his daughter. Both ladies look much the same with their pale egg-shaped faces, polished eyes, clasped hands. They do not really look like his wife or daughter, nor really remind him of them.

There are no windows at all in the turret, they were long ago bricked up

37

and covered with hangings. Candles burn steadily. It is always night in the turret. Save, of course, by night there are particular *sounds* all about it, to which the Duke is accustomed, but which he does not care for. By night, like most of his court, the Cursed Duke closes his ears with softened tallow. However, if he sleeps, he dreams, and hears in the dream the beating of wings . . . Often, the court holds loud revel all night long.

The Duke does not know Rohise the scullery maid has been thinking of him. Perhaps he does not even know that a scullery maid is capable of thinking at all.

Soon the Duke descends from the turret and goes down, by various stairs and curving passages, into a large, walled garden on the east side of the castle.

It is a very pretty garden, mannered and manicured, which the gardeners keep in perfect order. Over the tops of the high, high walls, where delicate blooms bell the vines, it is just possible to glimpse the tips of sun-baked mountains. But by day the mountains are blue and spiritual to look at, and seem scarcely real. They might only be inked on the sky.

A portion of the Duke's court is wandering about in the garden, playing games or musical instruments, or admiring painted sculptures, or the flora, none of which is red. But the Cursed Duke's court seems vitiated this noon. Nights of revel take their toll.

As the Duke passes down the garden, his courtiers acknowledge him deferentially. He sees them, old and young alike, all doomed as he is, and the weight of his burden increases.

At the furthest, most eastern end of the garden, there is another garden, sunken and rather curious, beyond a wall with an iron door. Only the Duke possesses the key to this door. Now he unlocks it and goes through. His courtiers laugh and play and pretend not to see. He shuts the door behind him.

The sunken garden, which no gardener ever tends, is maintained by other, spontaneous, means. It is small and square, lacking the hedges and the paths of the other, the sundials and statues and little pools. All the sunken garden contains is a broad paved border, and at its centre a small plot of humid earth. Growing in the earth is a slender bush with slender velvet leaves.

The Duke stands and looks at the bush only a short while.

He visits it every day. He has visited it every day for years. He is waiting for the bush to flower. Everyone is waiting for this. Even Rohise, the scullery maid, is waiting, though she does not, being only sixteen, born in the castle and uneducated, properly understand why.

The light in the little garden is dull and strange, for the whole of it is roofed over by a dome of thick smoky glass. It makes the atmosphere somewhat depressing, although the bush itself gives off a pleasant smell, rather resembling vanilla.

Something is cut into the stone rim of the earth-plot where the bush grows. The Duke reads it for perhaps the thousandth time. *O, fleur de feu -*

When the Duke returns from the little garden into the large garden, locking the door behind him, no one seems truly to notice. But their obeisances now are circumspect.

One day, he will perhaps emerge from the sunken garden leaving the door wide, crying out in a great voice. But not yet. Not today.

The ladies bend to the bright fish in the pools, the knights pluck for them blossoms, challenge each other to combat at chess, or wrestling, discuss the menagerie lions; the minstrels sing of unrequited love. The pleasure garden is full of one long and wary sigh.

Oh flurda fur

Pourma souffrance -

Sings Rohise as she scrubs the flags of the pantry floor.

Ned ormey par,

May say day mwar -

'What are you singing, you slut?' someone shouts, and kicks over her bucket.

Rohise does not weep. She tidies her bucket and soaks up the spilled water with her cloths. She does not know what the song, because of which she seems, apparently, to have been chastised, means. She does not understand the words that somehow, somewhere – perhaps from her own dead mother – she learned by rote.

In the hour before sunset, the Duke's hall is lit by flambeaux. In the high windows, the casements of oil-blue and lavender glass and glass like storms and lizards, are fastened tight. The huge window by the dais was long ago obliterated, shut up, and a tapestry hung of gold and silver tissue with all the rubies pulled out and emeralds substituted. It describes the subjugation of a fearsome unicorn by a maiden, and huntsmen.

The court drifts in with its clothes of rainbow from which only the colour red is missing.

Music for dancing plays. The lean pale dogs pace about, alert for titbits as dish on dish comes in. Roast birds in all their plumage glitter and die a second time under the eager knives. Pastry castles fall. Pink and amber fruits, and green fruits and black, glow beside the goblets of fine yellow wine.

The Cursed Duke eats with care and attention, not with enjoyment.

Only the very young of the castle still eat in that way, and there are not so many of those.

The murky sun slides through the stained glass. The musicians strike up more wildly. The dances become boisterous. Once the day goes out, the hall will ring to *chanson,* to drum and viol and pipe. The dogs will bark, no language will be uttered except in a bellow. The lions will roar from the menagerie. On some nights the cannons are set off from the battlements, which are now all of them roofed in, fired out through narrow mouths just wide enough to accommodate them, the charge crashing away in thunder down the darkness.

By the time the moon comes up and the castle rocks to its own cacophony, exhausted Rohise has fallen asleep in her cupboard bed in the attic. For years, from sunset to rise, nothing has woken her. Once, as a child, when she had been especially badly beaten, the pain woke her and she heard a strange silken scratching, somewhere over her head. But she thought it a rat, or a bird. Yes, a bird, for later it seemed to her there were also wings... But she forgot all this half a decade ago. Now she sleeps deeply and dreams of being a princess, forgetting, too, how the Duke's daughter died. Such a terrible death, it is better to forget.

'The sun shall not smite thee by day, neither the moon by night,' intones the priest, eyes rolling, his voice like a bell behind the Duke's shoulder.

'Ne moi mords pas,' whispers Rohise in her deep sleep. 'Ne mwar mor par, ne par mor mwar ...'

And under its impenetrable dome, the slender bush has closed its fur leaves also to sleep. O flower of fire, O fleur du fur. Its blooms, though it has not bloomed yet, bear the ancient name *Nona Mordica*. In light parlance they call it Bite-Me-Not. There is a reason for that.

II

He is the Prince of a proud and savage people. The pride they acknowledge, perhaps they do not consider themselves to be savages, or at least believe that savagery is the proper order of things.

Feroluce, that is his name. It is one of the customary names his kind give their lords. It has connotations with diabolic royalty and, too, with a royal flower of long petals curved like scimitars. Also the name might be the partial anagram of another name. The bearer of that name was also winged.

For Feroluce and his people are winged beings. They are more like a nest of dark eagles than anything, mounted high among the rocky pilasters and pinnacles of the mountain. Cruel and magnificent, like eagles, the sombre sentries motionless as statuary on the ledge-edges, their sable wings folded about them.

They are very alike in appearance (less a race or tribe, more a flock, an unkindness of ravens). Feroluce also, black-winged, black-haired, aquiline of feature, standing on the brink of star-dashed space, his eyes burning through the night like all the eyes along the rocks, depthless red as claret.

They have their own traditions of art and science. They do not make or read books, fashion garments, discuss God or metaphysics or men. Their cries are mostly wordless and always mysterious, flung out like ribbons over the air as they wheel and swoop and hang in wicked cruciform, between the peaks. But they sing, long hours, for whole nights at a time, music that has a language only they know. All their wisdom and theosophy, and all their grasp of beauty, truth, or love, is in the singing.

They look unloving enough, and so they are. Pitiless fallen angels. A travelling people, they roam after sustenance. Their sustenance is blood. Finding a castle, they accepted it, every bastion and wall, as their prey. They have preyed on it and tried to prey on it for years.

In the beginning, their calls, their songs, could lure victims to the feast. In this way, the tribe or unkindness of Feroluce took the Duke's wife, somnambulist, from a midnight balcony. But the Duke's daughter, the first victim, they found seventeen years ago, benighted on the mountainside. Her escort and herself they left to the sunrise, marble figures, the life drunk away.

Now the castle is shut, bolted and barred. They are even more attracted by its recalcitrance (a woman who says 'No'). They do not intend to go away until the castle falls to them.

By night, they fly like huge black moths round and round the carved turrets, the dull-lit leaded windows, their wings invoking a cloudy tindery wind, pushing thunder against thundery glass.

They sense they are attributed to some sin, reckoned a punishing curse, a penance, and this amuses them at the level whereon they understand it.

They also sense something of the flower, the *Nona Mordica*. Vampires have their own legends.

But tonight Feroluce launches himself into the air, speeds down the sky on the black sails of his wings, calling, a call like laughter or derision. This morning, in the 'tween-time before the light began and the sun-to-be drove him away to his shadowed eyrie in the mountain-guts, he saw a chink in the armour of the beloved refusing-woman-prey. A window, high in an old neglected tower, a window with a small eyelet which was cracked.

Feroluce soon reaches the eyelet and breathes on it, as if he would melt it. (His breath is sweet. Vampires do not eat raw flesh, only blood which is a perfect food and digests perfectly, while their teeth are sound of necessity.) The way the glass mists at breath intrigues Feroluce. But presently he taps at the cranky pane, taps, then claws. A piece breaks away, and now he sees how it should be done.

Over the rims and upthrusts of the castle, which is only really another mountain with caves to Feroluce, the rumble of the Duke's revel drones on.

Feroluce pays no heed. He does not need to reason, he merely knows, *that* noise masks *this* – as he smashes in the window. Its panes were all faulted and the lattice rusty. It is, of course, more than that. The magic of Purpose has protected the castle, and, as in all balances, there must be, or come to be, some balancing contradiction, some flaw . . .

The people of Feroluce do not notice what he is at. In a way, the dance with their prey has debased to a ritual. They have lived almost two decades on the blood of local mountain beasts, and bird-creatures like themselves brought down on the wing. Patience is not, with them, a virtue. It is a sort of foreplay, and can go on, in pleasure, a long, long while.

Feroluce intrudes himself through the slender window. Muscularly slender himself, and agile, it is no feat. But the wings catch, are a trouble. They follow him because they must, like two separate entities. They have been cut a little on the glass, and bleed.

He stands in a stony, small room, shaking bloody feathers from him, snarling, but without sound.

Then he finds the stairway and goes down.

There are dusty landings and neglected chambers. They have no smell of life. But then there comes to be a smell. It is the scent of a nest, a colony of things, wild creatures, in constant proximity. He recognises it. The light of his crimson eyes precedes him, deciphering blackness. And then other eyes, amber, green, and gold, spring out like stars all across his path.

Somewhere an old torch is burning out. To the human eye, only mounds and glows would be visible, but to Feroluce, the Prince of the vampires, all is suddenly revealed. There is a great stone area, barred with bronze and iron, and things stride and growl behind the bars, or chatter and flee, or only stare. And there, without bars, though bound by ropes of brass to rings of brass, three brazen beasts.

Feroluce, on the steps of the menagerie, looks into the gaze of the Duke's lions. Feroluce smiles, and the lions roar. One is the king, its mane like war-plumes. Feroluce recognises the king and the king's right to challenge, for this is the lions' domain, their territory.

Feroluce comes down the stair and meets the lion as it leaps the length

42

of its chain. To Feroluce, the chain means nothing, and since he has come close enough, very little either to the lion.

To the vampire Prince the fight is wonderful, exhilarating and meaningful, intellectual even, for it is coloured by nuance, yet powerful as sex.

He holds fast with his talons, his strong limbs wrapping the beast which is almost stranger than he, just as its limbs wrap him in turn. He sinks his teeth in the lion's shoulder, and in fierce rage and bliss begins to draw out the nourishment. The lion kicks and claws at him in turn. Feroluce feels the gouges like fire along his shoulders, thighs, and hugs the lion more nearly as he throttles and drinks from it, loving it, jealous of it, killing it. Gradually the mighty feline body relaxes, still clinging to him, its cat teeth bedded in one beautiful swanlike wing, forgotten by both.

In a welter of feathers, stripped skin, spilled blood, the lion and the angel lie in embrace on the menagerie floor. The lion lifts its head, kisses the assassin, shudders, let's go.

Feroluce glides out from under the magnificent dead weight of the cat. He stands. And pain assaults him. His lover has severely wounded him.

Across the menagerie floor, the two lionesses are crouched. Beyond them, a man stands gaping in simple terror, behind the guttering torch. He had come to feed the beasts, and seen another feeding, and now is paralysed. He is deaf, the menagerie-keeper, previously an advantage saving him the horror of nocturnal vampire noises.

Feroluce starts towards the human animal swifter than a serpent, and checks. Agony envelops Feroluce and the stone room spins. Involuntarily, confused, he spreads his wings for flight, there in the confined chamber. But only one wing will open. The other, damaged and partly broken, hangs like a snapped fan. Feroluce cries out, a beautiful singing note of despair and anger. He drops fainting at the menagerie-keeper's feet.

The man does not wait for more. He runs away through the castle, screaming invective and prayer, and reaches the Duke's hall and makes the whole hall listen.

All this while, Feroluce lies in the ocean of almost-death that is sleep or swoon, while the smaller beasts in the cages discuss him, or seem to.

And when he is raised, Feroluce does not wake. Only the great drooping bloody wings quiver and are still. Those who carry him are more than ever revolted and frightened, for they have seldom seen blood. Even the food for the menagerie is cooked almost black. Two years ago, a gardener slashed his palm on a thorn. He was banished from the court for a week.

But Feroluce, the centre of so much attention, does not rouse. Not until the dregs of the night are stealing out through the walls. Then some nervous instinct invests him. The sun is coming and this is an open place, he struggles through unconsciousness and hurt, through the deepest most bladed waters, to awareness.

And finds himself in a huge bronze cage, the cage of some animal appropriated for the occasion. Bars, bars all about him, and not to be got rid of, for he reaches to tear them away and cannot. Beyond the bars, the Duke's hall, which is only a pointless cold glitter to him in the maze of pain and dying lights. Not an open place, in fact, but too open for his kind. Through the window-spaces of thick glass, muddy sunglare must come in. To Feroluce it will be like swords, acids, and burning fire -

Far off he hears wings beat and voices soaring. His people search for him, call and wheel and find nothing.

Feroluce cries out, a gravel shriek now, and the persons in the hall rush back from him, calling on God. But Feroluce does not see. He has tried to answer his own. Now he sinks down again under the coverlet of his broken wings, and the wine-red stars of his eyes go out.

III

'And the Angel of Death,' the priest intones, 'shall surely pass over, but yet like the shadow, not substance –'

The smashed window in the old turret above the menagerie tower has been sealed with mortar and brick. It is a terrible thing that it was for so long overlooked. A miracle that only one of the creatures found and entered by it. God, the Protector, guarded the Cursed Duke and his court. And the magic that surrounds the castle, that too held fast. For from the possibility of a disaster was born a bloom of great value: now one of the monsters is in their possession. A prize beyond price.

Caged and helpless, the fiend is at their mercy. It is also weak from its battle with the noble lion, which gave its life for the castle's safety (and will be buried with honour in an ornamented grave at the foot of the Ducal family tomb). Just before the dawn came, the Duke's advisers advised him, and the bronze cage was wheeled away into the darkest area of the hall, close by the dais where once the huge window was but is no more. A barricade of great screens was brought, and set around the cage, and the top of it covered. No sunlight now can drip into the prison to harm the specimen. Only the Duke's ladies and gentlemen steal in around the screens and see, by the light of a candlebranch, the demon still lying in its trance of pain and bloodloss. The Duke's alchemist sits on a stool nearby, dictating many notes to a nervous apprentice. The alchemist, and the apothecary for that matter, are convinced the vampire, having drunk the lion almost dry, will recover from its wounds. Even the wings will mend.

The Duke's court painter also came. He was ashamed presently, and went away. The beauty of the demon affected him, making him wish to paint it, not as something wonderfully disgusting, but as a kind of superlative man, vital and innocent, or as Lucifer himself, stricken in the sorrow of his colossal Fall. And all that has caused the painter to pity the fallen one, mere artisan that the painter is, so he slunk away. He knows, since the alchemist and the apothecary told him, what is to be done.

Of course much of the castle knows. Though scarcely anyone has slept or sought sleep, the whole place rings with excitement and vivacity. The Duke has decreed, too, that everyone who wishes shall be a witness. So he is having a progress through the castle, seeking every nook and cranny, while, let it be said, his architect takes the opportunity to check no other window-pane has cracked.

From room to room the Duke and his entourage pass, through corridors, along stairs, through dusty attics and musty storerooms he has never seen, or if seen has forgotten. Here and there some retainer is come on. Some elderly women are discovered spinning like spiders up under the eaves, half blind and complacent. They curtsy to the Duke from a vague recollection of old habit. The Duke tells them the good news, or rather, his messenger, walking before, announces it. The ancient women sigh and whisper, are left, probably forget. Then again, in a narrow courtyard, a simple boy, who looks after a dovecote, is magnificently told. He has a fit from alarm, grasping nothing, and the doves who love and understand him (by not trying to) fly down and cover him with their soft wings as the Duke goes away. The boy comes to under the doves as if in a heap of warm snow, comforted.

It is on one of the dark staircases above the kitchen that the gleaming entourage sweeps round a bend and comes on Rohise the scullery maid, scrubbing. In these days, when there are so few children and young servants, labour is scarce, and the scullerers are not confined to the scullery.

Rohise stands up, pale with shock, and for a wild instant thinks that, for some heinous crime she has committed in ignorance, the Duke has come in person to behead her.

'Hear then, by the Duke's will,' cries the messenger. 'One of Satan's night-demons, which do torment us, has been captured and lies penned in the Duke's hall. At sunrise tomorrow, this thing will be taken to that sacred spot where grows the bush of the Flower of the Fire, and here its foul blood shall be shed. Who then can doubt the bush will blossom, and save us all, by the Grace of God.'

'And the Angel of Death,' intones the priest, on no account to be omitted, 'shall surely –'

'Wait,' says the Duke. He is as white as Rohise. 'Who is this?' he asks. 'Is it a ghost?'

The court stare at Rohise, who nearly sinks in dread, her scrubbing rag in her hand.

Gradually, despite the rag, the rags, the rough hands, the court too begins to see.

'Why, it is a marvel.'

The Duke moves forward. He looks down at Rohise and starts to cry. Rohise thinks he weeps in compassion at the awful sentence he is here to visit on her, and drops back on her knees.

'No, no,' says the Duke tenderly. 'Get up. Rise. You are so like my child, my daughter –'

Then Rohise, who knows few prayers, begins in panic to sing her little song as an orison:

Oh fleur de feu
Pour ma souffrance -

'Ah!' says the Duke. 'Where did you learn that song?'

'From my mother,' says Rohise. And, all instinct now, she sings again:

O flurda fur,
Pourma souffrance Ned ormey par
May say day mwar -

It is the song of the fire-flower bush, the *Nona Mordica*, called Bite-Me-Not. It begins, and continues: *O flower of fire, For my misery's sake, Do not sleep but aid me; wake!* The Duke's daughter sang it very often. In those days the shrub was not needed, being just a rarity of the castle. Invoked as an amulet, on a mountain road, the rhyme itself had besides proved useless.

The Duke takes the dirty scarf from Rohise's hair. She is very, very like his lost daughter, the same pale smooth oval face, the long white neck and long dark polished eyes, and the long dark hair. (Or is it that she is very, very like the painting?)

The Duke gives instructions, and Rohise is borne away.

In a beautiful chamber, the door of which has for seventeen years been locked, Rohise is bathed and her hair is washed. Oils and scents are rubbed into her skin. She is dressed in a gown of palest most pastel rose, with a girdle sewn with pearls. Her hair is combed, and on it is set a chaplet of stars and little golden leaves. 'Oh, your poor hands,' say the maids, as they trim her nails. Rohise has realised she is not to be executed. She has realised the Duke has seen her and wants to love her like his dead daughter. Slowly, an uneasy stir of something, not quite happiness, moves through Rohise. Now she will wear her pink gown, now she will sympathise with and console the Duke. Her daze lifts suddenly.

The dream has come true. She dreamed of it so often it seems quite normal. The scullery was the thing which never seemed real.

She glides down through the castle, and the ladies are astonished by her grace. The carriage of her head under the starry coronet is exquisite. Her voice is quiet and clear and musical, and the foreign tone of her mother, long unremembered, is quite gone from it. Only the roughened hands give her away, but smoothed by unguents, soon they will be soft and white.

'Can it be she is truly the princess returned to flesh?'

'Her life was taken so early – yes, as they believe in the Spice-Lands, by some holy dispensation, she might return.'

'She would be about the age to have been conceived the very night the Duke's daughter d--- That is, the very night the bane began –'

Theosophical discussion ensues. Songs are composed.

Rohise sits for a while with her adoptive father in the East Turret, and he tells her about the books and swords and lutes and scrolls, but not about the two portraits. Then they walk out together, in the lovely garden in the sunlight. They sit under a peach tree, and discuss many things, or the Duke discusses them. That Rohise is ignorant and uneducated does not matter at this point. She can always be trained. She has the basic requirements: docility, sweetness. There are many royal maidens in many places who know as little as she.

The Duke falls asleep under the peach tree. Rohise listens to the love-songs her own (her very own) courtiers bring her.

When the monster in the cage is mentioned, she nods as if she knows what they mean. She supposes it is something hideous, a scaring treat to be shown at dinnertime, when the sun has gone down.

When the sun moves towards the western line of mountains just visible over the high walls, the court streams into the castle and all the doors are bolted and barred. There is an eagerness tonight in the concourse.

As the light dies out behind the coloured windows that have no red in them, covers and screens are dragged away from a bronze cage. It is wheeled out into the centre of the great hall.

Cannons begin almost at once to blast and bang from the roof-holes. The cannoneers have had strict instructions to keep up the barrage all night without a second's pause.

Drums pound in the hall. The dogs start to bark. Rohise is not surprised by the noise, for she has often heard it from far up, in her attic, like a sea-wave breaking over and over through the lower house.

She looks at the cage cautiously, wondering what she will see. But she sees only a heap of blackness like ravens, and then a tawny dazzle, torchlight on something like human skin. 'You must not go down to look,' says the Duke protectively, as his court pours about the cage. Someone pokes between the bars with a gemmed cane, trying to rouse the nightmare which lies quiescent there. But Rohise must be spared this.

So the Duke calls his actors, and a slight, pretty play is put on throughout dinner, before the dais, shutting off from the sight of Rohise the rest of the hall, where the barbaric gloating and goading of the court, unchecked, increases.

IV

The Prince Feroluce becomes aware between one second and the next. It is the sound – heard beyond all others – of the wings of his people beating at the stones of the castle. It is the wings which speak to him, more than their wild orchestral voices. Besides these sensations, the anguish of healing and the sadism of humankind are not much.

Feroluce opens his eyes. His human audience, pleased, but afraid and squeamish, backs away, and asks each other for the two thousandth time if the cage is quite secure. In the torchlight the eyes of Feroluce are more black than red. He stares about. He is, though captive, imperious. If he were a lion or a bull, they would admire this 'nobility'. But the fact is, he is too much like a man, which serves to point up his supernatural differences unbearably.

Obviously Feroluce understands the gist of his plight. Enemies have him penned. He is a show for now, but ultimately to be killed, for with the intuition of the raptor he divines everything. He had thought the sunlight would kill him, but that is a distant matter, now. And beyond all, the voices and the voices of the wings of his kindred beat the air outside this room-caved mountain of stone.

And so Feroluce commences to sing, or at least, this is how it seems to the rabid court and all the people gathered in the hall. It seems he sings. It is the great communing call of his kind, the art and science and religion of the winged vampires, his means of telling them, or attempting to tell them, what they must be told before he dies. So the sire of Feroluce sang, and the grandsire, and each of his ancestors. Generally they died in flight, falling angels spun down the gulches and enormous stairs of distant peaks, singing.

48

Feroluce, immured, believes that his cry is somehow audible.

To the crowd in the Duke's hall the song is merely that, a song, but how glorious. The dark silver voice, turning to bronze or gold, whitening in the higher registers. There seems to be words, but in some other tongue. This is how the planets sing, surely, or mysteriously creatures of the sea.

Everyone is bemused. They listen, astonished.

No one now remonstrates with Rohise when she rises and steals down from the dais. There is an enchantment which prevents movement and coherent thought. Of all the roomful, only she is drawn forward. So she comes close, unhindered, and between the bars of the cage, she sees the vampire for the first time.

She has no notion what he can be. She imagined it was a monster or a monstrous beast. But it is neither. Rohise, starved for so long of beauty and always dreaming of it, recognises Feroluce inevitably as part of the dream-come-true. She loves him instantly. Because she loves him, she is not afraid of him.

She attends while he goes on and on with his glorious song. He does not see her at all, or any of them. They are only things, like mist, or pain. They have no character or personality or worth; abstracts.

Finally, Feroluce stops singing. Beyond the stone and the thick glass of the siege, the wing-beats, too, eddy into silence.

Finding itself mesmerised, silent by night, the court comes to with a terrible joint start, shrilling and shouting, bursting, exploding into a compensation of sound. Music flares again. And the cannons in the roof, which have also fallen quiet, resume with a tremendous roar.

Feroluce shuts his eyes and seems to sleep. It is his preparation for death.

Hands grasp Rohise. 'Lady — step back, come away. So close! It may harm you —'

The Duke clasps her in a father's embrace. Rohise, unused to this sort of physical expression, is unmoved. She pats him absently.

'My lord, what will be done?'

'Hush, child. Best you do not know.'

Rohise persists.

The Duke persists in not saying.

But she remembers the words of the herald on the stair, and knows they mean to butcher the winged man. She attends thereafter more carefully to snatches of the bizarre talk about the hall, and learns all she needs. At earliest sunrise, as soon as the enemy retreat from the walls, their captive will be taken to die lovely garden with the peach trees. And so to the sunken garden of the magic bush, the fire-flower. And there they will hang him up in the sun through the dome of smoky glass, which will be slow murder to him, but they will cut him, too, so his blood, the stolen blood of the vampire, runs down to water the roots of the fleur de feu. And who can doubt that, from such nourishment, the bush will bloom? The blooms are salvation. Wherever they grow it is a safe place. Whoever wears them is safe from the draining bite of demons. Bite-Me-Not, they call it; vampire-repellent.

Rohise sits the rest of the night on her cushions, with folded hands, resembling the portrait of the princess, which is not like her.

Eventually the sky outside alters. Silence comes down beyond the wall, and so within the wall, and the court lifts its head, a corporate animal scenting day.

At the intimation of sunrise the black plague has lifted and gone away, and might never have been. The Duke, and almost all his castle full of men, women, children, emerge from the doors. The sky is measureless and bluely grey, with one cherry rift in the east that the court refers to as 'mauve', since dawns and sunsets are never any sort of red here.

They move through the dimly lightening garden as the last stars melt. The cage is dragged in their midst.

They are too tired, too concentrated now, the Duke's people, to continue baiting their captive. They have had all the long night to do that, and to drink and opine, and now their stamina is sharpened for the final act.

Reaching the sunken garden, the Duke unlocks the iron door. There is no room for everyone within, so mostly they must stand outside, crammed in the gate, or teetering on erections of benches that have been placed around, and peering in over the walls through the glass of the dome. The places in the doorway are the best, of course; no one else will get so good a view. The servants and lower persons must stand back under the trees and only imagine what goes on. But they are used to that.

Into the sunken garden itself there are allowed to go the alchemist and the apothecary, and the priest, and certain sturdy soldiers attendant on the Duke, and the Duke. And Feroluce in the cage.

The east is all 'mauve' now. The alchemist has prepared sorcerous safeguards which are being put into operation, and the priest, never to be left out, intones prayers. The bulge-thewed soldiers open the cage and seize the monster before it can stir. But drugged smoke has already been wafted into the prison, and besides, the monster has prepared itself for hopeless death and makes no demur.

Feroluce hangs in the arms of his loathing guards, dimly aware the sun is near. But death is nearer, and already one may hear the alchemist's apprentice sharpening the knife an ultimate time.

The leaves of the *Noma Mordica* are trembling, too, at the commencement of the light, and beginning to unfurl. Although this happens every dawn, the court points to it with optimistic cries. Rohise, who has claimed a position in the doorway, watches it too, but only for an instant. Though she has sung of the fleur de fur since childhood, she had never known what the song was all about. And in just this way, though she has dreamed of being the Duke's daughter most of her life, such an event was never really comprehended either, and so means very little.

As the guards haul the demon forward to the plot of humid earth where the bush is growing, Rohise darts into the sunken garden, and lightning leaps in her hands. Women scream and well they might. Rohise has stolen one of the swords from the East Turret, and now she flourishes it, and now she has swung it and a soldier falls, bleeding red, red, *red*, before them all.

Chaos enters, as in yesterday's play, shaking its tattered sleeves. The men who hold the demon rear back in horror at the dashing blade and the blasphemous gore, and the mad girl in her princess's gown. The Duke makes a pitiful bleating noise, but no one pays him any attention.

The east glows in and like the liquid on the ground.

Meanwhile, the ironically combined sense of impending day and spilled hot blood have penetrated the stunned brain of the vampire. His eyes open, and he sees the girl wielding her sword in a spray of crimson as the last guards let go. Then the girl has run to Feroluce. Though, or because, her face is insane, it communicates her purpose, as she thrusts the sword's hilt into his hands.

No one has dared approach either the demon or the girl. Now they look on in horror and in horror grasp what Feroluce has grasped.

In that moment the vampire springs, and the great swanlike wings are reborn at his back, healed and whole. As the doctors predicted, he has mended perfectly, and prodigiously fast. He takes to the air like an arrow, unhindered, as if gravity does not any more exist. As he does so, the girl grips him about the waist, and slender and light, she is drawn upward too. He does not glance at her. He veers towards the gateway, and tears through it, the sword, his talons, his wings, his very shadow, beating men and bricks from his path.

And now he is in the sky above them, a black star which has not been put out. They see the wings flare and beat, and the swirling of a girl's dress and unbound hair, and then the image dives and is gone into the shade under the mountains, as the sun rises.

V

It is fortunate, the mountain shade in the sunrise. Lion's blood and enforced quiescence have worked wonders, but the sun could undo it all. Luckily the shadow, deep and cold as a pool, envelops the vampire, and in it there is a cave, deeper and colder. Here he alights and sinks down, sloughing the girl, whom he has almost forgotten. Certainly he fears no harm from her. She is like a pet animal, maybe, like the hunting dogs or wolves or lammergeyers that occasionally the unkindness of vampires have kept by them for a while. That she helped him is all he needs to know. She will help again. So when, stumbling in the blackness, she brings him in her cupped hands water from the cascade at the poolcave's back, he is not surprised. He drinks the water, which is the only other substance his kind imbibe. Then he smooths her hair, absently, as he would pat or stroke the pet she seems to have become. He is not grateful, as he is not suspicious. The complexities of his intellect are reserved for other things. Since he is exhausted he falls asleep, and since Rohise is exhausted she falls asleep beside him, pressed to his warmth in the freezing dark. Like those of Feroluce, as it turns out, her thoughts are simple. She is sorry for distressing the Cursed Duke. But she has no regrets, for she could no more have left Feroluce to die than she could have refused to leave the scullery for the court.

The day, which had only just begun, passes swiftly in sleep.

Feroluce wakes as the sun sets, without seeing anything in it. He unfolds himself and goes to the cave's entrance, which now looks out on a whole sky of stars above a landscape of mountains. The castle is far below, and to the eyes of Rohise as she follows him, invisible. She does not even look for it, for there is something else to be seen.

The great dark shapes of angels are wheeling against the peaks, the stars. And their song begins, up in the starlit spaces. It is a lament, their mourning, pitiless and strong, for Feroluce, who has died in the stone heart of the thing they prey upon.

The tribe of Feroluce do not laugh, but, like a bird or wild beast, they have a kind of equivalent to laughter. This Feroluce now utters, and like a flung lance he launches himself into the air.

Rohise at the cave mouth, abandoned, forgotten, unnoted even by the mass of vampires, watches the winged man as he flies towards his people. She supposes for a moment that she may be able to climb down the tortuous ways of the mountain, undetected. Where then should she go? She does not spend much time on these ideas. They do not interest or involve her. She watches Feroluce, and because she learned long ago the uselessness of weeping, she does not shed tears, though her heart begins to break.

As Feroluce glides, body held motionless, wings outspread on a down-draught, into the midst of the storm of black wings, the red stars of eyes ignite all about him. The great lament dies. The air is very still.

Feroluce waits then. He waits, for the aura of his people is not as he has always known it. It is as if he had come among emptiness. From the silence, therefore, and from nothing else, he learns it all. In the stone he lay and he sang of his death, as the Prince must, dying. And the ritual was completed, and now there is the threnody, the grief, and thereafter the choosing of a new Prince. And none of this is alterable. He is dead. Dead. It cannot and will not be changed.

There is a moment of protest, then, from Feroluce. Perhaps his brief sojourn among men has taught him some of their futility. But as the cry leaves him, all about the huge wings are raised like swords. Talons and teeth and eyes burn against the stars. To protest is to be torn in shreds. He is not of their people now. They can attack and slaughter him as they would any other intruding thing. *Go,* the talons and the teeth and the eyes say to him. *Go far off.*

He is dead. There is nothing left him but to die.

Feroluce retreats. He soars. Bewildered, he feels the power and energy of his strength and the joy of flight, and cannot understand how this is, if he is dead. Yet he *is* dead. He knows it now.

So he closes his eyelids, and his wings. Spear-swift he falls. And something shrieks, interrupting the reverie of nihilism. Disturbed, he opens his wings, shudders, turns like a swimmer, finds a ledge against his side and two hands outstretched, holding him by one shoulder, and by his hair.

'No,' says Rohise. (The vampire cloud, wheeling away, have not heard her; she does not think of them.) His eyes stay shut. Holding him, she kisses these eyelids, his forehead, his lips, gently, as she drives her nails into his skin to hold him. The black wings beat, tearing to be free and fall and die. 'No,' says Rohise. 'I love you,' she says. 'My life is your life.' These are the words of the court and of courtly love-songs. No matter, she means them. And though he cannot understand her language or her sentiments, yet her passion, purely that, communicates itself, strong and burning as the passions of his kind, who generally love only one thing, which is scarlet. For a second her intensity fills the void which now contains him. But then he dashes himself away from the ledge to fall again, to seek death again.

Like a ribbon, clinging to him still, Rohise is drawn from the rock and falls with him.

Afraid, she buries her head against his breast, in the shadow of wings and hair. She no longer asks him to reconsider. This is how it must be. *Love* she thinks again, in the instant before they strike the earth. Then that instant comes, and is gone.

Astonished, she finds herself still alive, still in the air. Touching so close, feathers have been left on the rocks, Feroluce has swerved away and upward. Now, conversely, they are whirling towards the very stars. The world seems miles below. Perhaps they will fly into space itself. Perhaps he means to break their bones instead on the cold face of the moon.

He does not attempt to dislodge her, he does not attempt anymore to fall and die. But as he flies, he suddenly cries out, terrible lost lunatic cries.

They do not hit the moon. They do not pass through the stars like static rain.

But when the air grows thin and pure there is a peak like a dagger standing in their path. Here, he alights. As Rohise lets go of him, he turns away. He stations himself, sentry-fashion, in the manner of his tribe, at the edge of the pinnacle. But watching for nothing. He has not been able to choose death. His strength and the strong will of another, these have hampered him. His brain has become formless darkness. His eyes glare, seeing nothing.

Rohise, gasping a little in the thin atmosphere, sits at his back, watching for him, in case any harm may come near him.

At last, harm does come. There is a lightening in the east. The frozen, choppy sea of the mountains below, and all about, grows visible. It is a marvellous sight, but holds no marvel for Rohise. She averts her eyes from the exquisitely pencilled shapes, looking thin and translucent as paper, the rivers of mist between, the glimmer of nacreous ice. She searches for a blind hold to hide in.

There is a pale yellow wound in the sky when she returns. She grasps Feroluce by the wrist and tugs at him. 'Come,' she says. He looks at her vaguely, as if seeing her from the shore of another country. 'The sun,' she says. 'Quickly.'

The edge of the light runs along his body like a razor. He moves by instinct now, following her down the slippery dagger of the peak, and so eventually into a shallow cave. It is so small it holds him like a coffin. Rohise closes the entrance with her own body. It is the best she can do. She sits facing the sun as it rises, as if prepared to fight. She hates the sun for his sake. Even as the light warms her chilled body, she curses it. Till light and cold and breathlessness fade together.

When she wakes, she looks up into twilight and endless stars, two of which are red. She is lying on the rock by the cave. Feroluce leans over her, and behind Feroluce his quiescent wings fill the sky.

54

She has never properly understood his nature: vampire. Yet her own nature, which tells her so much, tells her some vital part of herself is needful to him, and that he is danger, and death. But she loves him, and is not afraid. She would have fallen to die with him. To help him by her death does not seem wrong to her. Thus, she lies still, and smiles at him to reassure him she will not struggle. From lassitude, not fear, she closes her eyes. Presently she feels the soft weight of hair brush by her cheek, and then his cool mouth rests against her throat. But nothing more happens. For some while they continue in this fashion, she yielding, he kneeling over her, his lips on her skin. Then he moves a little away. He sits, regarding her. She, knowing the unknown act has not been completed, sits up in turn. She beckons to him mutely, telling him with her gestures and her expression *I consent. Whatever is necessary.* But he does not stir. His eyes blaze, but even of these she has no fear. In the end he looks away from her, out across the spaces of the darkness.

He himself does not understand. It is permissible to drink from the body of a pet, the wolf, the eagle. Even to kill the pet, if need demands. Can it be, outlawed from his people, he has lost their composite soul? Therefore, is he soulless now? It does not seem to him he is. Weakened and famished though he is, the vampire is aware of a wild tingling of life. When he stares at the creature which is his food, he finds he sees her differently. He has borne her through the sky, he has avoided death, by some intuitive process, for her sake, and she has led him to safety, guarded him from the blade of the sun. In the beginning it was she who rescued him from the human things which had taken him. She cannot be human, then. Not pet, and not prey. For no, he could not drain her of blood, as he would not seize upon his own kind, even in combat, to drink and feed. He starts to see her as beautiful, not in the way a man beholds a woman, certainly, but as his kind revere the sheen of water in dusk, or flight, or song. There are no words for this. But the life goes on tingling through him. Though he is dead, life.

In the end, the moon does rise, and across the open face of it something wheels by. Feroluce is less swift than was his wont, yet he starts in pursuit, and catches and brings down, killing on the wing, a great night bird. Turning in the air, Feroluce absorbs its liquors. The heat of life now, as well as its assertion, courses through him. He returns to the rock perch, the glorious flaccid bird danging from his hand. Carefully, he tears the glory of the bird in pieces, plucks the feathers, splits the bones. He wakes the companion (asleep again from weakness) who is not pet or prey, and feeds her morsels of flesh. At first she is unwilling. But her hunger is so enormous and her nature so untamed that quite soon she accepts the slivers of raw fowl.

Strengthened by blood, Feroluce lifts Rohise and bears her gliding down the moon-slit quill-backed land of the mountains, until there is a rocky cistern full of cold, old rains. Here they drink together. Pale white primroses grow in the fissures where the black moss drips. Rohise makes a garland and throws it about the head of her beloved when he does not expect it. Bewildered but disdainful, he touches at the wreath of primroses to see if it is likely to threaten or hamper him. When it does not, he leaves it in place.

Long before dawn this time, they have found a crevice. Because it is so cold, he folds his wings about her. She speaks of her love to him, but he does not hear, only the murmur of her voice, which is musical and does not displease him. And later, she sings him sleepily the little song of the fleur de fur.

VI

There comes a time then, brief, undated, chartless time, when they are together, these two creatures. Not together in any accepted sense, of course, but together in the strange feeling or emotion, instinct or ritual, that can burst to life in an instant or flow to life gradually across half a century, and which men call *Love*.

They are not alike. No, not at all. Their differences are legion and should be unpalatable. He is a supernatural thing and she a human thing, he was a lord and she a scullery sloven. He can fly, she cannot fly. And he is male, she female. What other items are required to make them enemies? Yet they are bound, not merely by love, they are bound by all they are, the very stumbling blocks. Bound, too, because they are doomed. Because the stumbling blocks have doomed them; everything has. Each has been exiled out of their own kind. Together, they cannot even communicate with each other, save by looks, touches, sometimes by sounds, and by songs neither understands, but which each comes to value since the other appears to value them, and since they give expression to that other. Nevertheless, the binding of the doom, the greatest binding, grows, as it holds them fast to each other, mightier and stronger.

Although they do not know it, or not fully, it is the awareness of doom that keeps them there, among the platforms and steps up and down, and the inner cups, of the mountains.

Here it is possible to pursue the airborne hunt, and Feroluce may now and then bring down a bird to sustain them both. But birds are scarce. The richer lower slopes, pastured with goats, wild sheep, and men – they lie far off and far down from this place as a deep of the sea. And Feroluce does not conduct her there, nor does Rohise ask that he should, or try to lead the way, or even dream of such a plan.

But yes, birds are scarce, and the pastures far away, and winter is coming. There are only two seasons in these mountains. High summer, which dies, and the high cold which already treads over the tips of the air and the rock, numbing the sky, making it brittle, as though the whole landscape might snap in pieces, shatter.

How beautiful it is to wake with the dusk, when the silver webs of night begin to form, frost and ice, on everything. Even the ragged dress – once that of a princess – is tinselled and shining with this magic substance, even the mighty wings – once those of a prince – each feather is drawn glittering with thin rime. And oh, the sky, thick as a daisy-field with the white stars. Up there, when they have fed and have strength, they fly, or Feroluce flies and Rohise flies in his arms, carried by his wings. Up there in the biting chill like a pane of ghostly vitreous, they have become lovers, true blind lovers, embraced and linked, their bodies a bow, coupling on the wing. By the hour that this first happened the girl had forgotten all she had been, and he had forgotten too that she was anything but the essential mate. Sometimes, borne in this way, by wings and by fire, she cries out as she hangs in the ether. These sounds, transmitted through the flawless silence and amplification of the peaks, scatter over tiny half-buried villages countless miles away, where they are heard in fright and taken for the shrieks of malign invisible devils, tiny as bats, and armed with the barbed stings of scorpions. There are always misunderstandings.

After a while, the icy prologues and the stunning starry fields of winter nights give way to the main argument of winter.

The liquid of the pool, where the flowers make garlands, has clouded and closed to stone. Even the volatile waterfalls are stilled, broken cascades of glass. The wind tears through the skin and hair to gnaw the bones. To weep with cold earns no compassion of the cold.

There is no means to make fire. Besides, the one who was Rohise is an animal now, or a bird, and beasts and birds do not make fire, save for the phoenix in the Duke's bestiary. Also, the sun is fire, and the sun is a foe. Eschew fire.

There begin the calendar months of hibernation. The demon lovers too must prepare for just such a measureless winter sleep, lined with feathers and withered grass. But there are no more flying things to feed them. Long, long ago, the last warm frugal feast, long, long ago the last flight, joining, ecstasy and song. So, they turn to their cave, to stasis, to sleep. Which each understands, wordlessly, thoughtlessly, is death.

What else? He might drain her of blood, he could persist some while on that, might even escape the mountains, the doom. Or she herself might leave him, attempt to make her way to the places below, and perhaps she could reach them, even now. Others, lost here, have done so. But neither considers these alternatives. The movement for all that is past. Even the death-lament does not need to be voiced again.

Installed, they curl together in their bloodless icy nest, murmuring a little to each other, but finally still.

Outside, the snow begins to come down. It falls like a curtain. Then the winds take it. Then the night is full of the lashing of whips, and when the sun rises it is white as the snow itself, its flame very distant, giving nothing. The cave mouth is blocked up with snow. In the winter, it seems possible that never again will there be a summer in the world.

Behind the modest door of snow, hidden and secret, sleep is quiet as stars, dense as hardening resin. Feroluce and Rohise turn pure and pale in the amber, in the frigid nest, and the great wings lie like a curious articulated machinery that will not move. And the withered grass and the flowers are crystallised, until the snows shall melt.

At length, the sun deigns to come closer to the earth, and the miracle occurs. The snow shifts, crumbles, crashes off the moutains in rage. The waters hurry after the snow, the air is wrung and racked by splittings and splinterings, by rushes and booms. It is half a year, or it might be a hundred years, later.

Open now, the entry to the cave. Nothing emerges. Then, a flutter, a whisper. Something does emerge. One black feather, and caught in it, the petal of a flower, crumbling like dark charcoal and white, drifting away into the voids below. Gone. Vanished. It might never have been.

But there comes another time (half a year, a hundred years), when an adventurous traveller comes down from the mountains to the pocki villages the other side of them. He is a swarthy cheerful fellow, would not take him for herbalist or mystic, but he has in a pot a plan found high up in the staring crags, which might after all contain anytl or nothing. And he shows the plant, which is an unusual one, ha' slender, dark, and velvety leaves, and giving off a pleasant smell vanilla. 'See, the *Nona Mordica*,' he says. 'The Bite-Me-Not. The flower that repels vampires.'

Then the villagers tell him an odd story, about a castle in another country, besieged by a huge flock, a menace of winged vampires, how the Duke waited in vain for the magic bush that was in his garden the Bite-Me-Not, to flower and save them all. But it seems there w curse on this Duke, who on the very night his daughter was lost, raped a serving woman, as he had raped others before. But this woman conceived. And bearing the fruit, or flower, of this rape, damaged her so she lived only a year or two after it. The child grew up unknowing, and in the end betrayed her own father by running away to the vampires, leaving the Duke demoralised. And soon after he went mad, and himself stole out one night, and let the winged fiends into his castle, so all there perished.

'Now if only the bush had flowered in time, as your bush flowers would have been well,' the villagers cry.

The traveller smiles. He in turn does not tell them of the heap peculiar bones, like parts of eagles mingled with those of a woman and man. Out of the bones, from the heart of them, the bush was rising, the traveller untangled the roots of it with care; it looks sound enough now in its sturdy pot, all of it twining together. It seems as if two separate plants are growing from a single stem, one with blooms almost black,and one pink-flowered, like a young sunset.

'Flur de fur,' says the traveller, beaming at the marvel, and his luck.

Fleur de feu. Oh flower of fire. That fire is not hate or fear, which makes flowers come, not terror or anger or lust, it is love that is the fire of the Bite-Me-Not, love which cannot abandon, love which cannot harm. Love which never dies.

Bite-me-Not or Fleur de Fur

Chosen by Freda Warrington and Cecelia Dart-Thornton

'In the tradition of young girls and windows, the young girl looks out of this one... The stained glass of lizard-green and storm-purple is several inches thick... The colour red is forbidden in the castle...Even the sun, behind the glass, is a storm sun, a green-lizard sun.'

In just a few words, Tanith Lee creates an atmosphere that pulls you straight into the story. That is her wondrous talent.

It hardly needs saying that the breadth of her imagination is amazing, her use of language astonishingly beautiful. Tanith was unique, creating endless kaleidoscopic visions that few writers, if any, have equalled. She breaks all those daft rules about not using adjectives and adverbs in glorious style, and the result is a spellbinding narrative that reads like poetry. I chose *Bite-Me-Not (or Fleur de Fur)* because the story embodies her skill at its most poignant. A household barricades itself into a vast, decaying castle, besieged by every night by flying vampires. These are no ordinary vampires but an alien race, incomprehensible to humans, proud and fierce. Yet an encounter between a wounded member of this race and a servant girl begins one of the most profound, chilling yet poignant love stories I've ever read.

Tanith's characters are often cold, unsentimental, even brutal. And yet, still a red flower blossoms out of the barren icy rock, love crosses impossible barriers, love is more important than power, love vanquishes death.

The result, in *Bite-Me-Not*, is ravishing. Tanith, we love you and miss you.

– Freda Warrington

Author of twenty-two fantasy books including Nights of Blood Wine, Freda was deeply inspired by Tanith Lee's incredible imagination. She contributed a story to Night's Nieces, the anthology published by Immanion Press in loving tribute to Tanith.

~

When I first read this gothic, strange, and richly gorgeous tale it became my favourite Lee short story. From the opening paragraph the reader is drawn into Tanith's universe of violent, exotic colours ("The stained glass of lizard-green and storm-purple is several inches thick") and mystery ("The colour red is forbidden in the castle" – *why?*) Synesthetically, even singing is expressed in colour: "The dark silver voice, turning to bronze or gold, whitening in the higher registers..." Tidal rainbows of colour swirl through Tanith's poetic prose, along

60

with her playfulness and wit – exemplified by the clever title, a pun that draws on a phonetic mistranslation of French into English and weaves itself into the story in many other ways. The reader cannot help but empathise with the protagonist from the very beginning; she's young, caring and downtrodden but wishes for more; she wistfully imagines herself as "...a princess floating through the upper corridors..." I was gripped, entranced and spellbound by the beautiful, sinister ambience of the castle of the Cursed Duke, and by the sound of powerful wings beating against the stones every night after dark... The way the story unfolds is unexpected. It soars and swoops among tall, sharp crags in a "...sky, thick as a daisy-field with the white stars..." until it reaches the apt, bittersweet, perfect conclusion.

– Cecelia Dart-Thornton

Cecilia Dart-Thornton is an Australian author responsible for numerous bestselling fantasy novels, notably the Bitterbynde Trilogy.

Jedella Ghost

That fall morning, Luke Baynes had been staying a night with his grandmother up on the ridge, and he was tramping back to town through the woods. It was about an hour after sun-up, and the soft level light was caught broadcast in all the trees, molasses-red and honey-yellow. The birds sang, and squirrels played across the tracks. As he stepped on to the road above the river, Luke looked down into the valley. There was an ebbing mist, sun-touched like a bridal veil, and out of this he saw her come walking, up from the river, like a ghost. He knew at once she was a stranger, and she was young, pale and slight in an old-fashioned long dark dress. Her hair was dark, too, hanging down her back like a child's. As she got closer he saw she was about 18, a young woman. She had, he said, not a pretty face, but serene, pleasing; he liked to look at her. And she, as she came up to him, looked straight at him, not boldly or rudely, but with an open interest. Luke took off his hat, and said, "Good morning." And the girl nodded. She said, "Is there a house near here?" Luke said there was, several houses, the town was just along the way. She nodded again, and thanked him. It was, he said, a lovely voice, all musi-cal and lilting upward, like a smile. But then she went and sat at the roadside, where a tree had been cut and left a stump. She looked away from him now, up into the branches. It was as if there was nothing more to say. He did ask if he could assist her. She answered at once, "No, thank you." And so, after a moment, he left her there, though he was not sure he should do. But she did not appear concerned or worried.

"She had the strangest shoes," he said.

"Her shoes?" I asked. Luke had never seemed a man for noting the footware of women, or of anyone.

"They were the colours of the woods," he said, "crim-son and gold and green. And – they seemed to me like they were made of glass."

"Cinderella," I said, "run off from the ball."

"But she had on both," he said, and grinned. After this we went for coffee and cake at Millie's.

I had no doubt he had seen this woman, but I thought perhaps he had made more of her than there was. Because I am a writer people sometimes try to work spells on me – Oh, John Cross, this will interest you. You can write about this. It does them credit, really, to make their imaginations work. But they should take up the pen, not I. Usually, I have enough ideas of my own. About ten, I went back to my room to work, and did not come out again until three. And then I too saw Luke's lady of the mist. She was standing in the square, under the old cobweb trees, looking up at the white tower of the church, on which the clock was striking the hour. People going about were glancing at her curiously, and even the old-timers on the bench outside the stables were eying her. She was a stranger, and graceful as a lily. And sure enough, she seemed to have on sparkling stained-glass shoes.

When the clock stopped, she turned and looked around her. Do any of us look about that way? Human things are cautious, circumspect – or conversely arrogant. And she was none of these. She looked the way a child does, openly, perhaps not quite at ease, but not on guard. And then she saw – evidently she saw – the old men on the bench, Will Marks and Homer Avary and Nut Warren. She became very still, gazing at them, until they in turn grew uneasy. They did not know what to do, I could see, and Nut, who was coming on for 90 years, he turned belligerent.

I stepped out and crossed the square, and came right up to her, standing between her and the old boys.

"Welcome to our town. My name's John Cross."

"I'm Jedella," she said at once.

"I'm glad to meet you. Can I help?"

"I'm lost," she said. I could not think at once what to say. Those that are lost do not speak in this way. I knew it even then. Jedella said presently, "You see, I've lived all my life in one place, and now – here I am."

"Do you have kin here?"

"Kin?" she said. "I have no kin."

"I'm sorry. But is there someone -?"

"No," she said. "Oh, I'm tired. I'd like a drink of water. To sit down."

I said, and I thought myself even then hard and cruel, "Your shoes."

"Oh. That was my fault. I should have chosen something else."

"Are they glass?"

"I don't know," she said.

I took her straight across to Millie's, and in the big room sat her at a table, and when the coffee came, she drank it down. She seemed comfortable with coffee, and I was surprised. I had already realized, maybe, that the things of civilized life were not quite familiar to her.

Hannah returned and refilled our cups – Jedella had refused my offer of food. But as Hannah went away, Jedella looked after her. The look was deep and sombre. She had eyes, Jedella, like the rivers of the Greek Hell – melancholy, and so dark.

"What's wrong with her?"

"With-?"

"With that woman who brought the coffee." Hannah was a robust creature, about 40. She was the wife of Abel Sorrensen, and had five children, all bright and sound – a happy woman, a nice woman. I had never seen her sick or languishing.

"Hannah Sorrensen is just fine."

"But-" said Jedella. She stared at me, then the stare become a gaze. "Oh, those men outside..."

"The old men on the bench," I said.

Jedella said, "I'm sorry, I don't mean to be impertinent." I said, squaring my shoulders, "I think you should see Doc McIvor. He's bound to have some plan of how to go on."

I had formed the impression she was a little mad. And, I confess, I wondered how she would react to the notion of a doctor.

But Jedella smiled at me, and then I saw what Luke had only heard in her voice. Her smile made her beautiful. For a moment I saw her as my muse. I wondered if I would fall in love with her, and feed upon her mystery. The writer can be selfish. But, in my own defence, I knew that here was something rare, precious – rich and strange.

"Of course I'll see him," she said. "I have no one, and nowhere to go. How kind you are."

What happens when the doctor is sick? An old adage to be sure. But Doc McIvor had gone to visit his niece in the city, who was expecting her first baby. Everyone knew but me. But then, I had only lived in the town for five years.

I did not want, I admit, to give Jedella, with her Lethe eyes and Cinderella shoes and heavenly smile, over to the law, so I took her to my rooming-house, and there Abigail Anchor came sweeping forth in her purple dress.

"I can give her that little room on the west side," said Abigail. "This girl has run away. I know it."

"Do you think so?" I asked.

"Oh, to be sure. Her daddy is some harsh man. Perhaps forcing her to marry. I won't sit in judgement, Mr Cross. Indeed, Mr Cross, you may know more than you say. But I won't ask it -"

"I don't know anything, Mrs Anchor." "That's as you say, Mr Cross."

I met Luke Baynes that night in the Tavern. We had a beer. He grinned at me again.

"They're talking. Your sweetheart's stashed away at Ma Anchor's."

"Yours and mine. You saw her first."

"Then it *is* the girl with glass shoes."

"A strange one," I said. "She keeps to herself. But when I came out tonight, she was at her window and the blind was raised. She was looking along the street."

Luke said, "Don't you know anything?"

"Not a thing. Abigail has sheltered her from the goodness of her heart. Her name's Jedella."

"I don't believe," said Luke, "she's real. She's a ghost." "I took her arm," I said. "She's real as you or I."

"What is it then?" he said.

"I think she's crazy. A little crazy. Probably someone will come after her. She can't have come far."

"But," he said, "she's — *wonderful*."

"Yes," I said. "A fascinating woman. The woman you can't have is always fascinating."

"You're too clever," he said. "I fancy going courting." "Don't," I said. I frowned into my drink. "Don't."

Two weeks passed, and Jedella lived in the room on the west side of the Anchor house. She gave no trouble, and I had had a word with Abigail about the rent. I believe Abigail helped with any female things that Jedella might have needed, and certainly, I was presented with a bill before too long. My trade had brought me mod-erate success, and I did not flinch.

Otherwise, I saw no reason to interfere. I gathered from Abigail that Jedella did not much wish to go out, yet seemed quite well. She ate her meals in private, and enjoyed the services of the house. Now and then I noted Jedella at her window, gazing along the street. Once I lifted my hand, but she did not respond. I let it go at that.

Of course, word had got around about the unknown young woman. I was sometimes pestered, but knowing next to nothing myself, could be of little assistance.

Did I want to draw Jedella out? Rather, I was inclined to avoid her. Real life that takes the form of a story, or appears to, is so often disappointing. Or, if one learns some gem, must one become a traitor who can no longer be trusted with anything? I prefer to invent, and that keeps me busy enough.

Luke did try to introduce himself to the woman on the west side. He took her flowers one afternoon, and a box of sweets in a green bow another. But, Jedella apparently seemed only amazed. She did not respond as a woman should, hopefully a flirtatious, willing woman. He was baffled, and retreated, to the relief of the two or three young ladies of the town who had such hopes of him, some day.

On the last Friday of that second week, just as I had finished a long story for the *Post*, I heard at Millie's that Homer Avory had died in his bed. He was nearly 80, which for the town is quite a youngster, and his daughter was in a rage, it seemed, for she had always loved him and had been planning a birthday dinner.

Everyone went to a funeral then, and presently I heard it was fixed for Tuesday. I looked out my black suit with a sensation of the droll and the sad. My father had once warned me, "You don't feel a death, John, not truly, till you start to feel your own." He was 50 when he said this, and he died two years after, so I may not argue. But I felt it was a shame about Homer, and about his daughter, who was 60 herself, and had lost her husband ten months before to a fever.

On Monday evening I was reading some books that had come in the mail, when a light knock sounded on my door.

It was not Abigail, evidently, who thundered, nor Luke, who burst in. I went to see, and there stood the apparition called Jedella, still in her dark dress, but with a new pair of simple shoes. Her hair was done up on her head.

"Good evening, Miss Jedella. Can I help you?"

"Mr Cross," she said, "something is happening tomorrow."

"Tomorrow? Oh, do you mean poor old Homer's funeral?"

"That," she said, "is what Abigail Anchor called it." "Abigail? Well, what else. A burial, a funeral." She stared straight at me. She said, still and low, "But what is that?"

Abigail had her rules, but it was just light. I drew Jedella into the room and left the door an inch ajar.

I made her sit down in my comfortable chair, and moved the books.

"How do you mean, Miss Jedella ?"

She seemed for a moment disturbed. Then she com-posed her pale face and said, "They say the – old man – has *died*."

"He has."

"Was he one of the three men I saw in the square that day?"

"Yes, just so."

"He has some terrible illness," she said. She looked about distractedly.

"Am I right?"

This unnerved me. I could not put it together. I recalled, I had thought her slightly insane. I said, quietly, "Unfortunately, he was old, and so he died. But, please believe, he had no ailment. He passed away peacefully in his sleep, I gather."

"But what do you mean?" she said.

"He's dead," I answered. "I'm afraid it happens." I had intended irony, but she gazed at me with such pathos, I felt myself colour, as if I had insulted her. I did not know what to say next. She spoke first.

"This funeral, what is it?"

"Jedella," I said firmly, "do you say you don't know what a funeral is?"

"No," said Jedella, "I have no idea."

If I had been three years younger, I suspect I would have thought myself the victim or some game. But peculiar things happen. Oddities, differences.

I sat down in the other chair.

"When a man dies, we put him in the earth. If you are religious, you reckon he waits there for the last trumpet, which summons him up to God."

"In the earth," she said. "But how can he stand it – is it some punishment?"

"He's dead," I replied, like stone. "He won't know." "How can he not know?"

In the window, the light of day was going out. And it came to me, as sometimes it did when a child, that per-haps this was the end, and the sun would never return.

In ten minutes or so, Abigail's boy would sound the bell for dinner. Jedella did not join the communal table.

"Jedella," I said, "I can't help you. It's too profound a question for me. Can I ask the minister to call on you?"

She said, "Why?"

"He may be able to assist you."

She said, looking at me, her countenance bewildered and yet serene even now, as if *she* had seen that I and all the world were mad – "This is a terrible place. I wish that I could help you, but I don't know how. How can you bear it, Mr Cross, when you witness such suffering?"

I smiled. "I agree, it can be difficult. But then, it could have been worse. We all come to it."

She said, "To what?"

The bell rang. Perhaps it was early, or I had misjudged. I said, "Well, you're very young, Jedella." Some phantom of my father's words, perhaps.

But Jedella went on looking at me with her Lethe eyes. She said, flatly,

"What does that mean?"

"Now this is silly. You keep asking me that. I mean that you're young. About 16, maybe."

I confess, I tried to flatter, making her a little less than she appeared to be. One should always be careful with a woman's age, one way or the other. In those days 16 was the dividing line; now it is more 20.

But Jedella, who Luke had thought a ghost, stared into my face. She was not flattered. She said, "Sixteen years do you mean? Of course not." "Sixteen, eighteen, whatever it may be."

Outside, my fellow boarders were going down the stairs; they would hear us talking and realize that John Cross had the woman in his room.

Jedella stood up. The last glimmer of light was behind her, and played about her slender shape, making her seem suddenly thin and despoiled. Abigail must have persuaded her to put up her hair. She was a shadow, and all at once, the shadow of someone else, as if I had seen through her – but to what?

"I am," she said, "sixty-five years of age."

I laughed. But it was a laugh of fright. For I could see her there like a little old lady, five years on from Homer's daughter.

"I'm going down to my meal, Jedella. Are you willing to come?"

"No," she said.

She turned, moved; the new lamplight from beyond the door caught her. She was eighteen. She went out on to the landing, and away up the house.

What we ate that night I have no notion. Someone – Clark, I think – regaled us with jokes, and everyone guffawed, but for Miss Pim, and Abigail, who did not approve. I chuckled too – but God knows why. Did I even hear what was said?

In the end we remembered, Homer was to go into the ground tomorrow, and a silence fell. I recall how Abigail lighted a candle in the window, a touching gesture, old superstition, but kind and sweet, to guide a soul home.

I had mentioned nothing of what Jedella had said to me, and no one had ventured to ask what she and I had had to converse on.

In my room, I walked about. I lit the lamp and picked up my books, and put them down.

Over in the west end of the house, she was, that girl with dark hair, who had come up from the morning mist, like a ghost.

In God's name, what had she been talking of? What did she suggest? What did she want?

I have said, if I had been a few years younger, I would have thought it a game. And, 40 years older, as now I am, I might have deemed it quite proper, to go across the house and knock on the door. Times change, and customs with them. It was not possible then.

At length I went to bed, and lay in the dark, with all the gentle quiet of that place about me, my haven from the city. But I could not rest. She said she did not know what a funeral was, she inquired how he could bear it, Homer, going into the ground. She told me she was 65 years old.

She was mad. She had come from the river in stained glass shoes, and she was crazy.

I dreamed I was at my father's burial, which once I had been, but no one else was there, save for Jedella. And she looked down into the pit of black earth, and she said to me, "Will you leave him here?"

I woke with tears on my face. I had not wanted to leave him there. Not my father, that lovable and good man, who had given me so much. But surely it had not been my father any more, down there in the dark?

The first light was coming, and I got up and sat by the window. The town was calm and the birds sang. Far off beyond the woods and the forests of pines, I could see, it was so clear, the transparent aurora of the mountains.

I knocked on Jedella's door about 9.30 in the morning, and when she opened it, I said, "Will you walk with me?" I wanted no more clandestine meetings in the rooms.

The funeral was at two. Outside there was nothing out of the ordinary going on. The trees had on their scalding full colour. The stores were open, and a dog or two were nosing down the street. Jedella looked at all this, in a sad, silent way. She reminded me of a widow.

We went into the square, and sat on the vacant bench under the cobweb trees.

"I want you to tell me, Jedella, where you come from. If you will."

She said, "Beyond the woods. Up in the pines. A house there."

"How far away?" I said. I was baffled.

"I don't know. It took me a day to reach this town. A day, and the night before."

"Why did you come here?"

"I didn't know what else to do. I didn't mean to come. I was only walking."

"Why then did you leave the house – the house in the pines?"

"They had all gone," she said. For a moment she looked the way I have only seen human things look after some great disaster, the wreck of a train, the random horror of a war. I did not know it then. What she spoke of was a terror beyond her grasp. It had hurt her, but it had no logic, like the acts of God.

"Who had gone?"

"The people who were there with me. Often they did, of course, but not all at once. The house was empty. I looked."

"Tell me about the house."

Then she smiled. It was the lovely, lilting smile. This memory made her happy.

"It was where I was, always."

"Where you were born?" I asked.

As if from far off, she smiled on at me. "The first thing I remember," she said.

She sat on the bench, and I realized absently that in her old-fashioned dress, she was clad as an old lady, like Homer's daughter or Elsie Baynes, or some other elder woman of our town. The air was sweet and crisp and summer had died. I said, "I'd like to hear."

"It's a big white house," she said, "and there are lots of rooms. I was usually in the upper house, though sometimes I went down. All around was a high wall, but I could see the tops of the trees. There were trees inside the garden too, and I walked there every day, except in winter. Then it was too cold, when the snow was down."

"Who was in the house with you?"

"Many people. Oh, lots of people, Mr Cross. They looked after me."

Curiously I said, as if encouraging a child. "Who did you like the best?"

"I liked them all – but you see, they didn't stay for long. No one ever stayed." She was sad once more, but in a deeper, softer way. She was indeed like a child, that was what I finally saw then, a child in an old lady's dress, which fitted. "When I was a girl," she said, oddly mimicking my thought, "I used to be upset by it, the going away. But in the end, I knew that it had to be."

"Why did it have to be?" I asked, blindly.

'That was their lives. But I remained. That was mine." "Tell me more about the house," I said.

"Oh, it was only a house. It was where I lived. Some of the rooms were large, and some, my bedroom, for example, quite small."

"What did you do there?"

"I read the books, and I painted on paper. And I played the piano. There was always something to do."

"Your father and mother," I said.

Jedella glanced at me. "What do you mean?"

The sun was warm on my face and hands, and yet the air was cool. A blue shadow descended from the tower of the church. Something had hold of me now, it held me back. I said, "Well, tell me about something that you enjoyed especially."

She laughed. Her laugh was so pretty, so truthful and young. "There were a great many things. I used to imagine places, places I'd never been – cities of towers from the books I'd read, and rivers and seas. And animals too. There are lions and tigers and bears, aren't there?"

"So I believe."

"Yes, I believe it too. Have you ever seen them?"

"In cages," I said.

She looked startled a moment. But then she brushed that away from her like a fallen leaf. "I longed to see them, and they said, one day."

I said, "Did they tell you when?"

"No. I suppose it was meant to be now. After I left the house."

"Then they told you you must leave?"

"Oh no. But when they were gone, the doors were all open. And the big door in the wall, that too."

I was trying now, quite hard, to follow along with her, not to delay or confuse by protestations. I thought how, when I had spoken of her being born, she had had that look of the polite guest at the party, when you say something he does not understand, but is too nice to debate on. "The door had never been open before?"

"No, never."

"Did – they – say why not?"

"I never asked, because, you see, it was the way I lived. I didn't need anything else."

She was young – or was she young? – yet surely there had been some yearning, like her wish to see the animals from the books. The young feel they are prisoners even when they are not, or not decidedly. Something came to me. I said, "Did you see pictures in your books of lion cubs?"

"Oh yes," she said.

I said, "And oncp, you were a child."

"Of course."

Above us the clock struck – it must have done so before. Now it was noon.

Jedella looked about her. She said, "Something's very wrong here. Can't you tell me what it is?"

"It's the way we are, the way we live," I said.

She sighed. She said, and there was that in her voice that filled me with a sort of primeval fear, "Is it like this everywhere?"

I said, intuitively, "Yes, Jedella."

Then she said, "Abigail Anchor brought some books up to me. It was a kindness. I didn't understand them."

"In what way?"

"Things happen in those books – that don't happen." I could have said this might be true of much poor fiction. But clearly she did not imply this. You had books in your house," I said. "What about those books?"

"Parts had been cut away," she said. I said nothing, but as if I had, she added, "I used to ask where those pieces were. But they said the books had been there a long time, that was all."

I said, blindly, as before, "For example, the lion cubs were there, and they grew up into lions. But you didn't know how they had arrived there." She was silent. I said, "And how long did the lions live, Jedella? Did the books say?"

Jedella the ghost, turned her dark eyes on me. She was no longer a temptation, not my muse. She said, "Always, of course. To live – is to live."

"For ever?"

She said and she did nothing. I felt my heart beat in a wild random crescendo, and all at once that peaceful square, that town where I had come to be quiet, was rushing all apart, like a jigsaw, broken. Then it settled. My heart settled.

"Will you come," I said, "to Homer's funeral?"

"If you think so," she said.

I got up and offered her my arm. "We'll take some lunch in Millie's. Then we'll go on."

Her hand was light on me, as a leaf of the fall.

She was quiet and nearly motionless all through the ceremony, and though she looked down at his old, creased, vacant, face, before the coffin was closed, she made no fuss about it.

But when everything was done, and we stood alone on the path, she said, "I used to watch the squirrels playing, in the trees and along the tops of the wall. They were black squirrels. I used to throw them little bits of cake. One day, John Cross, I saw a squirrel lying there on the grass in the garden. It didn't move. It was so still I was able to stroke its side. Then someone came from the house. I think it was a man called Orlen. And he picked up the squirrel. He said to me, 'Poor thing, it's fallen and stunned itself. Sometimes they do. Don't fret, Jedella. I'll take it back to its tree, and it will get better."

Over the lawn, Homer's daughter walked, leaning on the arm of her son. She was rubbing at her face angrily muttering about the meat dishes and the sweet pie she had been going to make for the birthday. Her son held his hat across his middle, head bowed, troubled the way we often are at grief we cannot share.

"So the squirrel was stunned," I said.

"Yes. And later he pointed it out to me, running along the wall."

"That same squirrel."

"He told me that it was."

"And you think now that Homer is only stunned, and we've thrown him down into the ground, and now they'll cover him with earth, so he can't get out."

We stood, two respectful and well-behaved figures. Her life had been an acceptance, and she was coming to accept even now the unacceptable.

"Jedella, will you describe for me very carefully the way you came here, from your house in the pines?"

"If you want."

"It would be a great help," I said. "You see, I mean to go there."

"I can't go back," she said.

I thought she was like Eve, cast out of Eden because she had failed to eat the forbidden fruit. "No, I won't make you, but I think I must. There may be some to all of this."

She did not argue with me. She had begun to accept also her utter indifference and that she was outnumbered. She guessed something had been done to her, as I did. She had ceased to debate, and would never resist.

When I first took up my life here, I went frequently to walk or ride in the wooded country. Then I got down to my work and adventured less. To ride out on this cold bright morning was no penance, though I had grown a little stiff, and guessed I should feel it later, which I did. The horse was a pretty mare by the name of May.

We went with care along the route Jedella had outlined, even drawing – she had a fair hand with a pencil – landmarks I might look for. Beyond the road we climbed nto the woods and so up the hill called Candy Crag, and over into the pines.

I was high up by nightfall, and I could feel the cold blowing down from the distant snow-lined mountains. I thought, as I made my camp, I might hear a wolf call up on the heights, but there was only stillness and the swarm of the stars. Such great calm is in those places and the sense of infinity. Some men can only live there, but for me, I should be lost. I like the little things. This was enough, a night or two, a day or two, up so close to the sky. At dawn I went on.

A couple of times I saw my fellow humans. A trapper with his gun, a man far down on the river. Both glimpsed me, and hailed me, and I them. For the rest, the wild things of the woods came and went, a porcupine, a deer, the birds, the insects. May stepped mildly through their landscape, her skin shining like a flame. I spoke to her now and then, and sang her a few songs.

I found the house with no trouble in the afternoon of that second day. Jedella had travelled more quickly than I, unless she had lost track of time.

You could see the mountains from there very well, a vast white battlement rising from the pelt of the pines. But near at hand, the forest was thick, so dense we had to pick our way. The house was in a clearing, as Jedella had told me, shut round with its tall white wall. It had a strange look, as if it had no proper architecture, no style of anywhere at all. Like boxes put together, and roofs put on, and windows set in. Something a child had made, but a child without fantasies.

The gate was open, and the sunlight slanted down through the trees and showed me a man standing there, on the path. He wore a white suit, and was smoking a cigarette. I had become used to the pipes and chewing-tobacco of my town. And somehow I had anticipated – God knows what. He was a very old man, too, but spare and upright, with a mane of thick, whitish hair, and eyebrows dark as bands of iron.

He lifted his hand, as he saw me. And this was not the lonely greeting of the trapper or the river man. I could see, he had expected me, or someone. Had he come there to wait for me?

I am not given to drama, except sometimes when I write, and can have it there on my own terms. But I eased myself off the horse and undid my saddlebag and took out the two brightly-coloured shoes that looked as if they were made of glass, and holding these out, I walked up to him.

"Jedella's slippers," he said. "Did she get so far in them?" "Quite far."

"They're not glass," he said, "something I fashioned, when I was younger. A sort of resin."

"I'd hoped," I said, "you would come and fetch her." "No, I can't do that. I haven't time now. It had to end, and she has to go on as best she can. She wouldn't know me now, in any case. She saw me for five or six years, when she was a child, and I was in my 20s."

"That would make her old," I said.

"Sixty-five is her age."

"So she said."

"And of course," he said, "it can't be, for she is 18 or 19, a girl."

Behind me, May shook her amber head, as if in warning, and a bird hammered a moment on the trunk of a tree.

"I came here," I said, "hoping to find out."

"Yes, I know it. And I shall tell you. I am Jedediah Goëste, and for now this house is mine. Will you step inside?"

I went with him up the path, leading May, who I settled in a sunny place. The trees were all around inside the wall, the trees where the black squirrels played. I had been struck by his name – Scandinavian, perhaps, and its affinity of sound to what Luke and I had come to call her: Miss Ghost. Jedediah, too, the father's name, and the daughter taking a feminized version, Jedella. Was it so simple? For yes, if he had been in his 20s, he would be near his 90s now, and she would be 65.

Inside the door was an open room, white-walled, quite pleasant, with ornaments and pictures, and with a large fireplace where some logs and cones were burning. Hot coffee stood on a table. Had he known the hour of my coming? No, that was too fanciful. It seemed to me I had better be as careful as I had been when riding through the denseness of the pines. Something strange there was, but not all of it could or need be.

A wide staircase ran up from the room and above was a sort of gallery. I noticed another man standing there, and Jedediah Goëste gestured to him quietly, and the man went away.

"My servant. He won't disturb us."

"Is that Orlen?" I said.

"Oh, no. Orlen is long gone. But Orlen was a avourite of Jedella's, I believe, when she was still a child. It was a pity they all had to leave her. She used to cry in the beginning. She cried when I left her. But later, they told me, she was philosophical. She had grown accustomed."

I had given him in turn my name, and he had taken the privilege of the old to call me at once John. We sat down in two large velvet armchairs, and I drank some of the coffee, hot and sweet and good.

"I have come back here," he said, "to die. It's comfortable for me here, and I have all I want. A few months, no more."

I said, "Then shouldn't you have kept her here?"

"She was given, implicitly, the choice. She might have remained, although I didn't think she would. If she had been here when I returned, I would, I think, have had to pretend to be someone else. And even then, the shock -"

"Your age. But it's your death that was the reason for letting her go."

"Yes. I can't anymore manage things, you see. The experiment is over."

"Experiment," I said.

"Come now," he said, "I believe you grasp it, John. I truly believe you do."

"I've read rather widely," I said. "Years ago, I came across the legend of the Buddha." Goëste folded his hands. He smiled his old strong teeth. "Buddha was originally a prince," I said, "and they resolved to keep all ugly things from him – poverty, disease, old age and death. He saw only beauty. Until one day something went wrong, and he found out the truth."

Jedediah Goëste said. "You see, John, I began to think of it even when I was quite young. From the start, everything comes our way. Even when they tell us lies, the facts are still before us. There is a moment when we must work it out. The old lady in the mauve dress with her hands crippled by rheumatics. The dead dog the cart ran over. The bird shot for the table. In Europe in the Middle Ages they fixed a skull over the church door. Under that skull was written, *Remember thou shall be as me.*" He leaned back. His eyes were black, like hers, but, paler with the watery encroachment of old age. "How does the infant learn?" he said. "He copies. The sounds from the mouths that become language. The gestures that become manners. The opinions that he will either adopt or rebel against. And he learns that the sun rises and sets, and as the days and the years go by, he grows, he changes. All around, the lesson is we grow to our fullness, but after that we decline. From the summit of that hill, the path leads downwards. Down to weakness and sickness, down to the first lines and wrinkles, the stiffening and the less-ening. Down to the bowed spine and the loss of teeth and sight and hearing. Down into the grave that awaits us all. *Remember thou shall be as me.* We are taught from the commencement, and reminded over and over."

He pointed at the rug before the fire, where I had laid the glass shoes that were not.

"I made those, to show it could be done. I've done many things like that. I had money, John, and time, and a brain. And, I confess, here and there I have experimented with living things – not to hurt them, never that. But to see. Always, to see."

"Jedella," I said, "was never told about old age, or death. Illness was for some reason mentioned, but as something that no longer existed. Pages were cut from books. The people of the house were always young and fit, and when it became likely they would cease to be, they were sent away. And when a squirrel died under her window, Orlen told her it was stunned, and took it back to its tree, and later he showed her the squirrel running on the wall."

"A girl came to me in the city," said Jedediah Goëste, "it was shocking, I had given her a child. She didn't want it. So she was paid, and I took the child to myself. That was Jedella. She was a baby – younger than Buddha, who I believe was twelve – too young to have learned anything at all. It was so perfect, John, and I had the means. I brought her here, and for those first years I was her friend. And after, of necessity, I had gone, those who came after me carried on my work. They were well-recompensed, and clever. There were no mistakes. She grew up in a world where no one sickened or aged or died. Where *nothing* died, and no death was seen, not even the dead animals for her food. Not even the leaves of the trees."

It was true. She had seen only the pines, renewal but not obvious slough – and then she had come from the open door and down into the woods of fall, where ruby and yellow and wine, the death descends from every tree.

"*Now* she sees it," I said. "She saw it as sickness to begin with. Or something that made no sense. But she's turning towards the terrible fact, Mr Goëste, that all things perish."

"Recollect," he said, "that she is 65 years old. She's like a girl. So many lessons, all the same. Can they be unlearned?"

I stood up. I was not angry, I have no word for what I was. But I could no longer sit in the chair before the fire nor drink the fragrant coffee, nor look in that old man's face that was so strong and sure.

"You've acted God, Mr Goëste."

"Have I? How can we presume to know how God has acted, or would act?"

"You think you've made her eternally young. You think you've made her *immortal*."

"I may have done," he said.

I answered him, "In a world where all things come to an end – what will become of her?"

"You will take care of her now," he said, so easily, so gently. "Your quiet little town. Good people. Kind people."

"But her pain," I said, "her *pain*."

Jedediah Goëste looked at me with her look. He was innocent, in her way. There was no chance against such innocence. "Pain, I think, is after all in the unfathomable jurisdiction of God. I've never been able to believe that mankind, for all its faults, could devise so horrible and so complex a thing."

"She never questioned?" I asked.

"Questions spring from doubt. Now she questions, I imagine?"

A log cracked in the fire. There was a small ache in my back I would not have had a year ago.

"If you wish, I should be happy for you to be my guest tonight, John."

I thanked him and made some excuse. Even then, even there, the etiquette of my father stayed with me. Those first lessons.

As I reached the door, Jedediah Goëste said one final thing to me: "I'm glad that she found her way to you."

But she had not found her way to me, nor to anyone, how could she? She had not found her way.

The years have passed in the town, and it has been faithful to Jedella. She has been protected as best we might. She has her little house behind the church, and her piano that we sent for from the city, her paints, her books – all kinds of books now. She reads for days on end, with her clear dark eyes. Sometimes she will read something out for me when even my glasses fail to help with the small print.

More people have come to the town with time, and for them she is a mystery that, largely, they are indifferent to. The new creatures of the world are very self-involved, and this has taken away some of the curiosity, the prying, that came to us so naturally. But then, the avalanches of war, and fear of war, the wonderful inven-tions that cause so much harm and confusion and noise, all these things change us, the children of this other world, much more so.

Luke died in a war. I have said elsewhere, and will not here, what I did there. Many were lost, or lost themselves. But others take those places. I was even famous for a year, and travelled in the cities and on other con-tinents, and grew tired and came home. And there the town was in its misty morning silence that the new cacophony cannot quite break.

That was a morning like this one, a fall morning, with the colours on the trees, and the new restaurant, where Millie's used to be, was having its windows washed.

But today the restaurant is old and familiar, and instead I passed Jedella's house, and she came out and I knew I should go in, just for an hour, maybe, and drink coffee, and eat her chocolate cake which she vaunts, and rightly so.

I went with caution over that road, for now there are sometimes motor-bikes upon it, and as I did I saw her waiting, pale and slender, a girl, with her hair cut short and permed and a touch of lipstick on her mouth.

She touched my arm at her door.

"Look, John," she said.

My eyes are not so good as I would like, but there in the pure, sheer sunlight, I did my best to see. She pointed at her cheek, and then, she put one finger to her hair.

"Is it your powder, Jedella? Yes, your hair looks grand." And then I did see, as she stood smiling up at me, her eyes full of the morning, of the new beginning of all things, I did see what she had found to show me with such pride. The little crease that had grown in her cheek. The single bright silver hair.

Jedella Ghost
Chosen by Sam Stone

I first read "Jedella Ghost" in a copy of *Interzone* many years ago. I was a regular subscriber in those days and it gave me an opportunity to sample the work of writers I hadn't heard of before. I was fascinated by the thought behind the concept of immortality that Tanith Lee depicted in this story. The idea that we age and die precisely because we know that aging and death are inevitable has always stayed with me. I later learned that Tanith had a wonderful ability for detailed imagery and thought-provoking, often reader-concept-changing, ideas that left you always with the outstanding belief that what she had written was entirely possible.

— Sam Stone

Sam Stone is an award winning British female genre writer. Her works can be found in paperback, ebook, audio and on screen. www.sam-stone.com

Medra

1

At the heart of a deserted and partly ruined city, an old hotel rose up eighty-nine storeys into the clear m sunset air. The hotel was not necessarily the tallest structure left in the city. It had been a very modern metropolis; many of its buildings were of great height. But it had happened that several of the blocks surrounding the hotel plaza had fallen, for one reason or another. Now the tiered, white architecture, like a colossal wedding cake, was visible from almost any vantage of the city, and from miles away, across the dusty dry plains of the planet beyond, the hotel could be seen.

This planet's sunset took a number of hours, and was quite beautiful. The hotel seemed softened in the filmy, rosy light. Its garlands and sprays of ornamentation, long-blunted by the wind, had over the years become the nesting-places of large climbing lizards. During the hours of sunfall they would emerge, crawling up and down the stem of the building, past the empty windows behind which lay empty rooms. Their armour blinked gold, their gargoyle faces stared away over the vistas of the city whose tall abandoned blocks flashed goldenly back at them. The big lizards were not foolish enough to mistake these skyscrapers for anything alive. The only dive thing, aside from themselves and occasional white skeletal birds which flew over, lived on the eighty-ninth floor. Sometimes the lizards saw the live thing moving about inside two layers of glass, and sometimes the throb of machineries, or music, ran down the limb of the hotel, so the stones trembled, and the lizards, clinging, trembled, listening with their fanlike swivelled ears.

Medra lived on the eighty-ninth floor. Through the glass portals she was frequently visible – a young Earth woman, by appearance, with coal-black hair that fell to her waist. She had a classical look, a look of calmness and restraint. Much of the day, and often for long intervals of the night, she would sit or lie perfectly still. She would not seem to move, not the flicker of a finger or quiver of an eyelid. It was just possible, after intense study, to see her breathing.

At such times, which actually occupied her on an average for perhaps twenty-seven hours in every thirty-six-hour diurnal-noc- turnal planetary period, Medra – lying motionless – experienced curious mental states. She would, mentally, travel a multiplicity of geographies, physical and nonphysical, over mountains, under oceans, even across and among galaxies. Through the flaming peripheries of stars she had passed, and through the cold reaches of a space where the last worlds hung tiny as specks of moisture on the window-panes of her rooms. Endless varieties of creatures came and went on the paths of Medra's cerebral journeys. Creatures of landscape, waterscape, airscape, and of the gaplands between the suns. Cities and other tumuli evolved and disappeared as simply as the forests and cultivation which ran towards her and away. She had a sense that all these visions concerned and incorporated her. That she wove something into them, from herself, if she did not actually form them, and so was a part of her own weaving, and of them. She threaded them all with love, lacking any fear, and when they drifted behind her she knew a moment's pang of gentle loss. But solely for that moment. It was only when she "woke" that Medra felt a true bereavement.

Her eyes would open. She would look around her. She would presently get up and walk about her apartment, which the hotel mechanisms kept for her scrupulously.

All the rooms were comfortable, and two or three were elegant. A hot-house with stained-glass walls projected from one side of the building. Enormous plants bloomed and fruited. There was a bath- room with a sunken bath of marble, in which it was feasible to swim. The literature and music, the art and theatre of many worlds, were plenteously represented. At the touch of a button, food of exquisite quality – in its day, the hotel had been renowned through twenty solar systems – would be served to Medra from out of the depths below.

She herself never went downstairs. Years ago, now and then, she had done so. She had walked the dusty riverbeds of the streets, or, getting into one of the small hover-cars, gone gliding between the walls, past the blank windows, over the bridges – and back again. At night, she had sat eighty-nine floors down on the hotel's decorated porch, sipping coffee or sherbet. The planet's stars were lustrous and thickly scattered. Slaves to their generators, a few lights still quickened in the city when sunset faded. She did not trouble to pretend that any life went on in those distant lighted buildings. Sometimes one of the lizards would steal up to her. They were very cautious, despite their size. She caressed those that came close enough and would allow it. But the lizards did not need her, and "waking," she did not understand them.

In recent years she stayed at the top of her tower. There was no purpose

84

in leaving her apartment. She accepted this.

But every so often, "waking," opening her eyes, sensing loss, she wept. She was alone and lonely. She felt the pain of it always, although always differently – sharp as a razor, insistent as a needle, dull as a healing bruise. "I'm alone," she said. Looking out from the balconied heights, she saw the lizards moving endlessly up and down. She saw the city and the dust haze far off which marked the plains beyond. The weaving of her dreams was her solace. But not enough.

"Alone," said Medra in a soft, tragic voice. She turned her back to the window.

And so missed a new golden spark that dazzled wildly over the sunset air, and the white feather of vapour which followed it down.

Jaxon landed his shuttle about half a mile from the city's outskirts. He emerged into the long sunset fully armed and, from force of habit, set the vessel's monitors on defensive. There was, almost certainly, nothing to defend against, out here. The planet had been thoroughly scanned by the mother-ship on the way in.

Jaxon began to stroll down to the city. He was an adventurer who would work for hire if the pay was good. What had tempted him to this outcast place, well-removed from the pioneer worlds and trade routes that generally supplied his living, was the connivance of a freelance captain whose ship now hung overhead. They had met in some dive on the rim of Lyra, Jaxon a figure of gold as he always was, but gold somewhat spoiled by the bloody nose and black eye gained at an adjacent fight.

"So thanks for saving my skin. What do you want?"

The captain showed him an old star-map and indicated a planet.

"Why?" said Jaxon.

The captain explained. It was, at that juncture, only a story, but stories sometimes led to facts. It would seem that a century before, a machine of colossal energy had been secreted on this small world. The planetary colony was promptly evacuated on the excuse of unstabilised earthquake activity. A whole city was abandoned. No one went there anymore. Out of bounds and off the current maps, the planet had by now been overlooked, forgotten. Only the story of the machine remained, and finally surfaced.

Very well, Jaxon would assume the captain wished that someone (Jaxon) would investigate. What capacity did the hidden machine have? There must be safeguards on it, which were? "It's presumably a war-machine. That's why it's been dumped. Whoever gets hold of it will be able to call the shots." ("Oh, nice," said Jaxon sarcastically, bleeding in his free drink.) "On the other hand, it may be nothing. But we'd like to follow the rumour up, without sticking our necks out too far."

"So you want to stick my neck out too far instead." The captain detailed the fee. Jaxon thought about it. It was not until he was aboard the ship that he asked again: "You still haven't given me specific answers to my two specific questions. What does this machine do? How's it protected?"

"All right. This is apocryphal, maybe. I heard it's an unraveller." Which was the slang name for something that had been a nightmare for decades, was condemned by all solar and galactic governments, could not, in any case, exist.

Jaxon said, "By which we're talking about a Matter-Displacement-Destructor?"

"Yes. And here's the punchline. Be ready to laugh. The only safeguard on the damn thing is one lone woman in a white hotel."

Legends abounded in space, birthed in bars and backlands, carried like seeds by the crazier shipping, planted in fertile minds, normally born to be nothing. But Jaxon, who had scented something frenetic behind the deal, was ultimately granted the whole truth. The freelance captain was a ruse. The entire run was government-based, the mission – to find and destroy that machine, if it existed. Anything else was a cover. A quasi-pirate on a joyride, a notorious adventurer looking for computer treasure – that was all it was to be. If the powers who had hidden the machine learned its fate and made a fuss, the event must fail to become a galactic confrontation. You didn't go to war because you'd been ripped off by a cat-burglar.

"Alternatively, someone may pulverise the cat-burglar."

"Or it may all be nothing. Tall stories. Lies. A storm in a teacup."

"You ever seen a storm in a teacup?" asked Jaxon. "I did, once. A trick some character pulled in a bar one night. It made a hell of a mess of the bar."

As he entered the city, framed between the sky-touching pylons of the bridge, Jaxon saw the hotel.

He stood and looked at it, and thought about the idea of one woman guarding there an MDD chaos device that could literally claw the fabric of everything – planets, suns, space itself – apart. If any of it were so, she would have to be a robot, or robo-android. He had a scanner of his own, concealed in the plain gold ring he always wore. This would tell him exactly what she was, if she existed, from a distance of three hundred feet from the building.

One of the hover-cars swam by. Jaxon hailed it and got in. It carried him swiftly towards the eccentric old hotel. Two hundred feet away from its royal icing facade, Jaxon consulted the ring. It told him promptly the woman did indeed exist and, as expected, exactly what she was. Her name had been planet-registered in the past; it was Medra. She was not a robot, an android, or even (present analysis) biologically tampered with. She was a young woman. She had black springing hair, pale amber skin, dark amber eyes. She weighed – "Just wait," said Jaxon. "More important, what about implants?" But there were no implants. The car was now only thirty feet from the building, and rising smoothly as an elevator up the floors, sixty, sixty-nine, seventy – "Check again," said Jaxon. The lizards glared at him with bulging eyes as he passed them, but he had already checked those – there were over two thousand of them dwelling in and on the building. They were saurian, unaggressive, obliquely intelligent, harmless, and nonmechanic. A bird flew over, a couple of hundred feet up. "And check *that*," snapped Jaxon, scowling at the lizards. But it was only a bird. Seventy-nine, eighty, eighty-nine – And the car stopped.

Jaxon beheld the woman called Medra. She was standing at a window, gazing out at him through a double thickness of glass. Her eyes were glorious, and wide.

Jaxon leaned forward, smiling, and mouthed; *Can I come in?*

He was made of gold. Golden skin, yellow-golden eyes, golden fleece of hair. The semi-uniform he wore was also of a tawny gleaming material. He seemed to blind what looked at him.

Medra retreated from the window and pressed the switch which let up the pressurised bubble over the balcony. The man stepped gracefully from the car to the balustrade and over. The bubble closed down again. Medra thought, should she leave him there, trapped and safe, an interesting specimen? But his presence was too powerful, and besides the inner glass was rather fragile and might be broken. She permitted the pane to rise, and golden Jaxon walked through into her room.

The selection of opening gambits was diverse. He had already decided what would be the most effective.

"Good evening," said Jaxon. "I gather the name by which you know yourself is Medra, M-E-D-R-A. Mine is usually Jaxon, J-A-X- O-N. I have been called other things. Your suite is charming. Is the service still good here? I'll bet it is. And the climate must be pleasant. How do you get on with the lizards?" He moved forward as he spoke. The woman did not back away. She met his eyes and waited. He paused when he was a couple of feet from her. "And the machine," he said, "where is that?"

She said, "Which machine? There are several."

"Now, you know which machine. Not the machine that makes the bed or tosses the salad or puts the music on. Not the city computer that keeps the cars running, or the generators that work the lights in the stores."

"There's nothing else," she said.

"Yes, there is. Or why are you here?"

"Why am I –?" She looked at him in astonishment.

All this time the ring was sending its tiny impulses through his skin, his finger joint, messages he had long ago learned to read quickly and imperceptibly. She is not lying. She is shocked by his arrival and so reacting unemotionally; presently emotion will break through. Her pulse ticks at this and this, rising now, faster. But she is not lying. (Brain-handled, then, not to know?) Possibly. Pulse rising, faster, and faster.

" – I'm here," she said, she gave a shaken little laugh, "because I stayed behind. That's all. The planet's core is unstable. We were told to leave. But I elected – to stay here. I was born here, you see. And all my family died here. My father was the architect who designed the hotel. I grew up in the hotel. When the ships lifted off I didn't go with them. There was nowhere else to go to. Nowhere tremors. The hotel is stabilised, although the other buildings sometimes – Only six months ago, one of the blocks across the plaza collapsed – a column of dust going up for half an hour. I'm talking too much," she said. "I haven't seen another human being for – I can't remember – I suppose – ten years?" The last was a question, as if he knew better than she and would tell her. She put her hands over her eyes and began to fall very slowly forwards. Jaxon caught her, and held her as she lay in his arms weeping. (No lies. Valid. Emotional impulse verified: the ring stung and tickled its information through to him.) It was also a long time for him since he had held any woman *this* way. He savoured it abstractedly, his thoughts already tracking in other directions, after other deductions. As if in the distance he took pleasure in the warm scent of her, the softness of her dark witch's hair; pleasure in comforting her.

II

There was time, all the time a world could give. For once, no one and nothing urging him to hurry. The only necessity was to be sure. And from the beginning he was sure enough, it was only a matter of proving that sureness, being certain of a certainty. Aside from the miniaturised gadgets he always carried with him, there were his own well-tuned senses. Jaxon knew, inside ten minutes, that there was nothing here remotely resembling the powerful technology of a fabled MDD. In other words, no key to nemesis. The government ship continued to cruise and to scan far overhead, tracking the hollows of the hills, the deep places underground, the planet's natural penthouses and basements. And he, striding through the city, riding through it in the ever-ready little cars, picked up no resonance of anything.

Yet, there was something. Something strange, which did not fit.

Or was that only his excuse for remaining here a fraction longer?

The first evening, as the sunset began at last to dissolve in night, she had said to him, "You're here, I don't know why. I don't understand you at all. But we'll have champagne. We'll open the ballroom." And when he grimaced with amusement she said, "Oh, be kind to us. Be kind to the hotel. It's pining for a guest."

And it was true, the hotel came alive at the touch of switches. It groomed and readied itself and put on a jewelry of lights. In the ballroom they ate off of the fine sercice, every plate, cup, napkin, and knife printed and embossed with the hotel's blazon. They drank from crystal goblets, and danced, on the crystal floor, the lazy sinuous contemporary dances of ten years ago, while music played down on them like a fountain. Sophisticated beyond his self-appointed station, Jaxon was not embarrassed or at a loss with any of this. Medra became a child again, or a very young girl. This had been her physical youth, which was happy, before – before the outsiders had come with their warnings, the death of the city, the going away of the ships and of everything.

But she was not a child. And though in her way she had the innocence of a very young girl, she was still a woman, moving against him when they danced, brushed by sequins from the lights. He was mostly accustomed to another kind of woman, hard, wise, sometimes even intellectual, the casual courtings, makings, and foregone departures amid the liquor-palaces he frequented on-planet, or in the great liners of deep space. This does not mean he had only ever known such women as these. There had been love affairs once or twice – that is, affairs of love. And Medra, her clever mind and her sweetness coming alive through the stimulus of this proximity – he was not immune to any of that. Nor to the obvious fact that, with a sort of primal cunning, she had trusted him, since she could do nothing else.

And for Medra? She fell in love with him the moment she saw him. It was inevitable, and she, recognising the cliché and the truth which underlay the cliché, and not being a fool, did not deny it.

After the first night, a first date, waited on and worshipped by the reborn glory of the hotel, they parted, went each to an allotted suite of rooms. As Jaxon revelled like a golden shark in the great bathroom, drew forth old brandies and elixirs from cabinets, eventually set up the miniaturised communicator and made contact with the ship, reporting nothing – as all this occurred, Medra lay on her bed, still clothed in her dancing dress, dreaming awake. The waking dream seemed superior to any other dream of stars and oceans and altitudes. The man who had entered her world – her planet, the planet of her awareness – he was now star, sun, ocean, and high sky-held peak. When she fell asleep, she merely slept, and in her sleep, dreamed of him.

Then the days began, extended warm days. Picnics in the ruins, where the dust made both carpet and parasol. Or lunches in the small number of restaurants which would respond, like the hotel, to a human request. Together they walked the city, explored its emptied libraries, occasionally finding some taped or crated masterpiece, which in the turmoil of evacuation had been overlooked.

In the stores, the mannequins, the solar Cadillacs, had combined to form curious sculptures of mutation.

Jaxon accompanied her everywhere, testing, on the lookout, alert for anything that would indicate the presence of the item he sought, or had come seeking. But the other level of him was totally aware of Medra. She was no longer in the distance. Every day she moved nearer. The search had become a backdrop, a prelude.

Medra wandered through the abandoned city, refinding it. She was full of pity and nostalgia. She had come to realise she would be going away. Although nothing had been said, she knew that when he left he would take her with him.

The nights were warm, but with a cooler, more fragrant warmth. The lizards came into the lighted plaza before the hotel, staring, their ears raised and opened like odd flowers. They fed from Medra's hands, not because they needed to, but because they recognised her, and she offered them food. It was almost a tradition between them. They enjoyed, but did not require the adventure. Jaxon they avoided.

Medra and Jaxon patrolled the nighttime city. (A beacon, the hotel glowed from many vantages.) In other high places, the soft wind blowing between them and the star-encrusted dark, he would put his arm around her and she would lean on him. He told her something of his life. He told her things that generally he entrusted to no one. Black things. Things he accepted in himself but took no pride in. He was testing her again, seeing now how she would respond to these facts; she did not dismiss them, she did not grow horrified and shut them out. She was coming to understand him after all, through love. He knew she loved him. It was not a matter of indifference to him. It crossed his mind he would not leave her here when he left the planet. In some other place, less rarified than this one, they would be far better able, each of them, to judge what was between them.

In the end, one night, travelling together in the elevator up towards the top floors of the hotel, Jaxon told her this: "This business I had here is settled. I'm leaving tomorrow."

Although she knew he would not go without her, even so she thought in this instant that of course he would go without her.

"I shall turn out all the lights," she said simply. "As your ship takes you away, you'll see a shadow spread across the city."

"You can watch that too," he said. "There's plenty of room in a shuttle for both of us. Unless you want to bring any of those damn lizards along."

The ritual completed, they moved together, not anymore to comfort, or to dance. Not as a test. He kissed her, and she returned his kiss.

They reached the eighty-ninth floor, and went into her apartment. On the bed where she had slept, and wandered among galaxies, slept and dreamed of him, they made love. About the bright whirlwind of this act, the city stood still as a stopped clock. The hotel was just a pillar of fire, with fiery gargoyles hotly frozen on its sides, and one solitary nova burning on the eighty-ninth floor.

III

A couple of hours before sunrise, Jaxon left his lover, Medra, sleeping. He returned to his rooms on the seventy-fourth floor and operated the communicator. He gave details to the mother-ship of his time of return. He told the government officer who manned the intercom that there would be a passenger on the shuttle. The officer was open-faced and noncommittal of tone, not discouraging. "She's the last of the colony," said Jaxon, reasonably, insidiously threatening. There would be no trouble over it. The story of the MDD had been run to ground and could be exploded. Spirits would be high, and Jaxon in favour. Maybe rich, for a short while. She would like that, the harmony money would produce for her, not the raw essentials of cash. . . .

Having switched off and dismantled the communicator into its compact travelling form, Jaxon lay back on his bed. He thought about the woman fifteen storeys above him, five minutes away. He thought about her as noncommittally and easily as the young man on the ship's bridge. But nevertheless, or perhaps sequentially, a wave of desire came in on him. Jaxon was about to leave the bed and go back to her, when he heard the door open and a whisper of silk. Medra had come to him.

She walked towards him slowly. Her face was very serious and composed. In the dimness of the one low lamp he had kept alight, her black hair gathered up the shadows and draped her with them. She was, no less than he, like a figure from a myth. No less than he. More so than he. And

91

then he saw – with a start of adrenalin that brought him to his feet – that the one low lamp was shining *through* her.

"What," he said, putting his hand to the small gun by the bed – uselessly – "is going on? A real ghost, or just an inefficient hologram? Who are you really, Medra? If von *are* Medra."

"Yes," she said. The voice was exactly hers, the same voice which, a handful of hours ago, had answered his in passion and insistence. "I'm Medra. Truly Medra. Not a hologram. I must approximate. Will you countenance an astral projection – the subconscious, free of the body?"

"Oh, fine. And the body? Let's not forget that. I'm rather fond of your body, Medra. Where is it?"

"Upstairs. Asleep. Very deeply asleep. A form of ultra-sleep it's well used to."

"If you're playing some game, why not tell me the rules?"

"Yes, I know how dangerous you are. *I* know, better than I do, that is, my physical self. I'm sorry," the translucent image of Medra said to him, most politely. "It can only be done this way. Please listen. You'll find that you do grasp everything I say to you. On some level, you've known all the time. The inner mind is always stronger and more resilient than the thinking process we have, desperately, termed the brain."

He sat down on the bed again. He allowed her to go on. At some point, he let the gun slide from his hand.

Afterwards, for the brief while that he remembered, he seemed to have heard everything in her voice, a conversation or dialogue. It was not improbable that she had hypnotised him in some manner, an aid to his acceptance.

She understood *(she,* this essence of Medra), why he had come to the planet, and the nature of the machine he had been pursuing. The legend of an MDD was merely that. Such a device did not, anywhere, exist. However, the story had its roots in a fact far more ambivalent and interesting. The enormous structure of the universe, like any vast tapestry, rubbed and used and much plundered, had come with the centuries to contain particular areas of weakness. In such spots, the warp and woof began to fray, to come apart – *fundamentally.* Rather than a mechanical destruction which could be caused to engender calamity, the macrocosm itself, wearing thin, created calamity spontaneously. Of course, this giving way of atoms was a threat both local and, in the long term, all- encompassing. A running tear in such a fabric – there could be only one solution. That every rent be mended, and thereafter monitored, watchfully held together; for eternity, if need be. Or at least until the last sentient life of the physical universe was done with it.

"You must picture then," she said, "guardians. Those who will remain at their posts for all time, as time is known to us. Guardians who, by a vast mathematical and esoteric weaving, constantly repair and strengthen the tissue of cosmic life. No, they are not computers. What upholds a living thing must itself be *alive*. We are of many galactic races. We guard many gates. This planet is one such gate, and I am one such guardian."

"You're a woman, an Earth woman," he recalled saying.

"Yes. I was born here, in the Terran colony, the daughter of an architect who designed one of the most glamorous hotels in twenty systems. When they came – those who search out the guardians are also sentient creatures, of course – they discovered that my brain, my intellectual processes, were suitable for this task. So they trained me. Here is one more reality: extended to its full range, the mind of a human being is greater, more complex, capable of more astounding feats, than any mechanism mankind has or will ever design. *I* am the computer you searched for, Jaxon. Not a force of chaos, but a blueprint for renewal and safety. For this reason I remained, for this reason I always must remain. Those who were evacuated were given a memory, a whole table of excellent reasons for leaving. You, also, will be given a reason. I will give it to you. There'll be no regrets. Despite all the joy you've brought me."

"I didn't arrive here alone," he said. "The sky up there is full of suspicious characters who may not believe –"

"Yes. They'll believe whatever you tell them. I've seen to it they will."

"Good God. So what are you? A human machine, the slave of some –"

"No slave. In the beginning I was offered a choice. I chose – this. But also to forget, as you will forget."

"You're still a woman, not –"

"Both. And yes, in her forgetfulness, sometimes the woman despairs and is bitterly sad. 'Awake,' she doesn't know what she is. Only 'sleeping,' she knows. Always to know, to know when 'awake' carries implications of power I don't trust myself with. Occasional sadness is better."

"Perhaps I don't accept any of this."

"Yes," she said. "All of it. As always happens. Dear love, you're not the first to alleviate my physical loneliness. When the time is right, I call and I'm answered. Who do you think drew you here?"

He swore. She laughed.

She said, "Don't be appalled. This episode is full of charm and amusement. Thank you again, so very much. Good-bye."

And she was gone. Into the air. The opening of the door, the whisper of material, they had been reassurances, and a ploy. He told himself he had been tricked. His nerves rioted with an impression of traps and subterfuge, but then these instincts quietened and the sullen protests ceased. It must be as she had said, on some level he did know and had accepted. There had been a joke once, God's a woman –

He fell asleep, sitting on the bed.

Jaxon drove the shuttle up into the pure air of sunrise, then beyond the sunrise into the inky night of space. He left it all behind him, the planet, the city, the hotel, and the woman. He felt bad about leaving her, but he had foreseen the pit before his feet. Living as she had, she would be a little mad, and certainly more than a little dependent. There was no room in his life for that; he would not be able to deal with it. Her fey quality had delighted him, but it was no grounds for perpetuity. Eventually she would have clung and he would have sloughed her in anger. It might have been expressive anger at that, beyond a cruel word, a cruel blow, and the hospitals were makeshift in the areas he most frequented. She wasn't for him, and it was better to finish on a note of pathos than in that kind of mess. Ships came by, she had told him. Someone else would rescue her, or not.

"Which woman?" he said to the captain of the mother-ship. "Fine. She didn't want to leave after all. Come on, you got what you wanted, I did your work for you. Now elaborate on the fee."

He had left her sleeping. Her hair had spread across the pillows, black breakers and rivulets of hair. Eyes like dark red amber closed by two petals of lids. He thought of the façades of empty buildings, the glitter of meaningless lights, the lizards who did not talk to her. He thought of the hot-house of coloured glass. He had a memory of strange wild dreams she had mentioned to him, which took the place of life. She was a difficult woman, not a woman to be lived with, and if loved, only for a little while. *I am half sick of shadows,* she said to him now, in his mind's ear. But that was a line from some antique poem of Earth, wasn't it? Somehow he didn't believe the phantom words. Those shadows were very real for Medra.

In the deserted, partly ruined city, on the eighty-ninth floor of the white hotel, Medra wept.

She wept with a terrible hurt, with despair, in her anguish of loss. And with shame. For she had trusted and moved forward openly, without camouflage, and the blow had crashed against her, breaking her, crippling her – as it seemed to her – forever. She had been misled. Everything had contrived to mislead her. His smile, his words, gestures of politeness and lust, meaning nothing. Even her planet had deceived her. The way in which the sunlight fell on particular objects, the way music sounded. The leaves that towered in the hot-house had misled her with their scent. And she, she was guilty too. Hope is a punishable offence. The verdict is always death; one more death of the heart.

Medra wept.

Later she wandered her rooms. And she considered, with a practical regard, the means to her absolute death. There were medicines which would ensure a civilised exit. Or cruder implements. She could even die in agony, if she wished, as if to curse with her pain's savageness the one who had betrayed her.

But all violent measures require energy, and she felt herself drained. Her body, a bell, rang with misery. After a prolonged stasis of insomnia, there was no other refuge but sleep.

Medra slept.

She slept, and so . . . she *slept*. Down, down, deeper and deeper, further and further. The chains of her physical needs, her pulses, sighs, hormones, were left behind as the golden shards of the city had been left behind, and as she herself had been left, by one she had decided to love. Then her brain, fully cognisant, trained, motivated, keyed to vast concepts and extraordinary parallels, then her *brain* woke up.

Medra moved outwards now, like a sky-flying bird, her wings bearing her strongly. Into the vistas, into the sheens and shades, murmurs and orchestrations. She travelled through a multiplicity of geographies, over mountains, under oceans, galaxies –

Through the periphery of suns she passed, the cold reaches of space. She wove the tapestry and was the tapestry. The pictures filled her with happiness. The universe was her lover. Here, then, in the mystery, the weaver heard some far-off echo, diminishing. She thought, It must stay between the glass. She saw herself, part of a pattern, and elsewhere, random, her life. She said to it, kindly, You are my solace, but you are not enough. The stars flowed by her, and her brain fashioned their fires and was fashioned by them. She thought: But this – *this* is enough.

Medra
Chosen by Allison Rich

Heartbreak is an unfortunate part of the human experience. Medra, on her planet of glass and steel and luxurious towers has faced her fair share, as well. We only read of Jaxon, who is only one of a long line of dashing men, treasure hunters, even, to visit her domain and be astounded by what he finds… and yet, like all the others, he does not stay.

Tanith's imagery in this story sweeps you up in a whirlwind of strange beauty. There are the ballrooms which open to serve only two human guests, glorious restaurants in which one can feast on delicacies, the well-appointed room in they can indulge in carnal pleasures. It all describes the frenzied and euphoric pleasures of new love and infatuation … which can only normalize into a more mundane and, perhaps, fraught realism.

We see Medra inconsolable after Jaxon leaves her. We feel her agonizing grief and pain. We can see her shut down in waves of almost unbearable anguish. And yet the other part of Medra, the practical one, informs Jaxon that *she* was the one who has lured *him* to the planet, and that he will not be the last. The "joke" has been on him and the sleeping girl in the tower of steel is the only *real* treasure on that planet, the most central part of the matrix.

Out of all of Tanith's stories, "Medra" is the one I read in order to feel a catharsis with the heartbreak and to connect with the inner warrior who will keep me strong and resilient. In the end we all stand alone. I am grateful to those inner guardians who protect our very own soul fortresses which not another single person will ever truly breach. We are strong and inviolate.

— Allison Rich

Allison Rich has been the webmistress of Daughter of the Night since 2004, which has become the official bibliography of the works of Tanith Lee.

The Ghost of the Clock

I don't believe in ghosts. Assuming there is a soul, why should it hang around here, if there is somewhere else it has to go? Oh, maybe there are recordings of past events that get left behind. Maybe even extreme emotions leave a kind of *colour*, like a stain. But that's it.

So, this isn't a ghost story. Although it has a ghost.

My name is Laura. And there came a time when clever Laura found herself in bad financial straits – unable to pay the rent on her so-called flat in London, (one room, and use of a bathroom down the hall), or for anything very much. My parents were long gone – my dad to that Somewhere Else I mentioned; my mother to southern France with her "New Bloke". She'd used him like camouflage and was virtually unfindable.

I ended up accepting the offer of a roof from my aunt.

Jennifer was my father's only sister. I'd seen her, once or twice, in childhood, but she had disliked my mother devotedly, so it hadn't been very often. I knew she had a house on the coast – I won't say where, but it was a good address. I'd been a bit surprised to get her letter.

It was a long journey, and the train stopped outside some picturesque country halt for about fifty minutes extra. My fellow passengers grumbled, but otherwise just carried on as usual, beetling over their ghastly twittering laptops, honking away into their bloody mobile phones. I went to the buffet and got a double gin and tonic. It was eleven thirty a.m., but what the hell.

In the afternoon, when I had arrived and was waiting for a taxi, what struck me was the light.

I've heard the light is different – better – in Greece. Having never been there, I don't know if that is true. But certainly the English light that curtained the seaside town was sheer and crystal *clean*, as if the sea cast it up fresh-spun. When we drove out of the station and off up the bumping, winding, narrow roads to the hills, I looked at all the May-green woods and fields burning in this light, and the birds darting over like arrows with gold-tipped flights, and then the vast sweep of the sea itself, bluer than the sky.

This was a beautiful spot. The sort of non-resort the sensitive, England-orientated rich go to, for their holidays. Only I wasn't on holiday. And decidedly I was not rich.

Soon, we saw the house.

"Fair old place, that," said the driver, who until then had been unchatty.

I felt embarrassed. I didn't want to say my aunt lived here. I toyed with the idea of telling him I'd applied for the job of scullery maid, but that would be about a century out of date. Secretary, then, or personal assistant?

Lamely, I said, "Yes, isn't it."

And he and I left it at that.

We went up a winding drive, and the house, which had appeared so dramatically on a hill-top, now vanished behind broad stands of oak, pine and hornbeam, and clouds of rhododendrons, blazing white and crimson.

Really, I suppose, it wasn't so big – not grounds or an estate, more a huge garden.

We passed under flowery terraces and roses, and then there was the house again, across a blank green oval of lawn.

It was a flat-fronted building, brown-skinned, with a large porch mounted on a little raised terrace, with a statue. I added up twelve windows along the top storey before I stopped counting.

All right, it wasn't a stately home, but it was much more than just a *home*.

There was a garden all round, but to one side the land dropped in terraces, and over there, through the boughs of a cedar-tree, the turquoise ocean appeared again, less than half a mile away.

The driver helped me with my bags, then left me. I watched the cab rattle off, as I stood at the door. I'd expected by now a servant in costume to come out to look down his nose at me. But no one had come, and when I finally jangled the old-fashioned bell, nothing happened either. Then I saw the electric bell hiding under the other one, and tried that.

Well, I did anticipate an employed door-opener of some sort at least.

But what eventually came was my Aunt Jennifer.

She looked at me with all the contempt of any imagined butler, before the falsest of false smiles oozed up her wrinkled face.

"Laura! How lovely. Do come in."

This was my aunt's big secret. She was mean. Wealthy people sometimes are, surprisingly so. It's how they stay wealthy, possibly. (I don't know how she was well-off when we hadn't been. I think it was from some kind of exclusive legacy.)

Really, if I'd thought, I'd have remembered enough from my childhood. I wasn't a stupid kid, less stupid probably than I've become since growing up. Twenty-five years back, when I was nine or so... That weird thing over the individual ice-cream, for example. "Just eat half, Laura, and save some for later. It will keep in the ice-box..." But my aunt was mean not only in the monetary sense, but in her ways.

She had hated my mother. And I was, after all, half my mother, even if, as far as I was concerned, I'd really only ever had one parent, and he was dead.

I loved my father. He was kind and gentle, a dreamer, who liked music, and silence. Death beglamoured him for me even more – after the agony went off. He had had a heart-attack the night before I was twenty.

Conceivably, I would have liked to get on with Jennifer, who had been his sister and so was, as I was, also partly him.

My bags got left in the wide walnut-brown hallway. We went into a sunny, rather dusty room, with long windows looking out over another lawn, the cedar and the sea. The windows weren't very clean. All that – the dust, the windows, startled me. I mean, I'd lived regularly in a tip, but I didn't expect that here – and definitely not amid this antique furniture and these Persian rugs.

The gardens too had been very well kept, trees neatly trimmed to proper *shapes*, and the lawns mowed to within an inch of their lives. So she *did* have a gardener.

My aunt told me I must sit down.

"You must sit down, Laura. You must be quite tired. But a cup of tea will put you right."

Then, another little shock. Jennifer crossed to an ornate eighteenth century sideboard and switched on an electric kettle roosting there. Next to this was set a covered tray. Presently, Jennifer brought everything to a coffee-table between the two white brocade sofas.

Unveiled, the tray held a plate of two dry chicken sandwiches, constructed perhaps in the early morning, two plain biscuits, and a banana past its first flush of youth. This feast was for me.

As she poured the boiled water on to the tea (bags of course) in the tarnished silver pot, I began to see the light. The garden she had kept up – for 'appearances'? But she had no help in the house, or very little. No one to dust or clean or shine up the silver, let alone open the door. No one came in to cook meals, either, or even make the poor old girl a cuppa.

She was sixty-seven by my reckoning. She looked older, having one of those faces that get easily creased.

"I've given you a west-facing room, Laura. It gets the last of the sun."

Fine, I thought. Chilly first thing and too hot on a summer's evening.

"Well, you must tell me all about yourself."

I glanced at her, and she sat there, like a slightly overweight Venus flytrap.

Shouldn't I think of her like that? Should I be sorry for her, all on her own, and not even able to afford, or too *afraid* to afford, despite her house, domestic help or even decent tea-bags? Had she fallen on hard times? Was she lonely? Did she truly want to know me? She must have known my whereabouts at least, because her letter had come straight to me. But before that, I hadn't seen or heard from her since the funeral.

"There's not much to say, Aunt Jennifer."

"But you've made a bit of a mess of your life, haven't you?"

Yes, Venus flytrap.

"Not really. Companies are folding all the time in London. Everywhere. It's the economic climate."

"I blame these computers," she said darkly. "This Internet thing."

"Works of the Devil," I heard myself mutter.

"Always wanting something for nothing," she concluded, as if I either hadn't said anything, or simply endorsed her own suspicions. "And this man – *Even*, was he called?"

"Eden."

I sensed she thought I'd had an affair with my boss.

"He let you down," she said.

"No, actually –"

"American," she appended scathingly. "Oh, they did plenty of that, letting girls down, I can tell you, in the last war."

I wondered what she'd got up to during the Blitz – to sound so pissed-off. She would have been a bit young, wouldn't she?

"Eden was great, and when the sh... when the trouble started, he did everything he could to put things right for all of us. It wasn't his fault. But if you mean did I sleep with him? No. He was very happily married."

"Oh yes," she said. She managed to look disgusted at my directness, and wisely aware I was lying, both at once. "However, you lost your flat and your job. And I gather you have no savings."

This was like an interview – perhaps by the police.

"I didn't have very much anyway. Living in London is very expensive."

"I'm sure it is. Well, never mind. You're here now. I'll take care of you."

I felt in that moment like a child – small, thirty-four-year-old orphan. I wanted to say, *Stuff it*. Get up and stalk out, perhaps throwing the half-dead banana at the dirty windows first. But I didn't. I had less than five hundred pounds in the bank and less than forty in my wallet. My three bags contained every scrap I owned that I hadn't sold for next to nothing. Because of my almost freelance status with the company, my tax situation was in a muddle. I wasn't highly skilled, had no tremendous talents, and for every job I was likely to seek, there would be at least fifteen other eager or desperate applicants. It used to be people over fifty who had difficulty getting work. Then it was forty. I'd begun to believe the age had recently fallen even lower. I'd been stacking shelves in the supermarket when Jennifer wrote to me.

If I wanted a breathing space, I would have to put up with her.

After all, it wasn't so bad, was it? The house was uncared for but lush, the gardens glorious, and the beach and swim-in-able sea just down the hill.

I said, I'm stupid now.

"Well, Laura, if you've finished your meal, perhaps you'd better take your bags up and settle into your room."

Dismissed.

"Okay. Thanks, I will." I rose and said, feeling I still had to, "It's very kind of you —"

The horrible creeping smile squeezed over her face again. She was all over-powdered and rosy like a girl gone quite wrong, and her hair was thick and old and coarse and too brown, so I knew it was from dye, and not a very good one either. Naturally.

Oh God, she made me sick. I was *allergic* to her.

She said, "That's all right, Laura. I know you had an unfortunate time with your mother, that can't have helped you. Anyway, pop upstairs now." She gave me directions to the room, with no intention of stirring herself to show me. Then: "I usually eat about seven. You'll find all the things ready for you in the kitchen. It's easy to find, the back-stair is just along from your room, on the left."

I checked.

"You mean the way to the kitchen?"

"Yes," she said.

Hold on, I thought. Am I hearing what I think? She plans for me to go down and fix dinner. Scullery maid, did I say? But no, it isn't that. She just means there's some sort of cold stuff ready, and I'm to bring it upstairs to save her aged legs.

"I'm afraid," she added, arch and acid, "I don't have a microwave. You'll have to manage the cooking without. I've never accepted those things are safe."

I found my room without problems. It wasn't a maid's room – those, if there were any, were up in the attics, I expect. But it could have won a prize for Smallest Guest Bedroom in Britain.

After I'd propped my bags against the single bed, I edged past a huge, bear-like wardrobe, and stared out of the window.

The view was good – inland, to fields and beech woods honey-spread by a westering sun. It was already almost five.

I knew that from my watch, not from any clock. The house *had* clocks – I'd passed one in the narrow side corridor, which led to this very room. But none in my bedroom. She had presumably anticipated I'd bring my own.

There was a bathroom to the right of the room, down an awkward step. It had bath and lavatory and so on, even a hand-held shower-attachment. There was some soap, (not new), and a couple of towels, and toilet-paper, bright green and rather cheap. The bathroom also had a tear in the lino floor-covering and some loose wall tiles. But the flush worked, and the water ran hot. Why complain? I'd lived with worse.

But after I'd showered and re-dressed, I sat on my lumpy bed, smouldering in my anger.

She wanted a skivvy. I knew it. Had I known before I came? No. There had been nothing in the letter to indicate any of this. Or... could I be wrong?

All right, then. Give it till tomorrow. And then, if necessary, take off. Because it would be better to do almost anything than become maid-of-all-work for my Aunt Jennifer. Oh – I could bloody murder her –

It was then that the clock clanged in the corridor.

So we come to the clock.

I'd barely looked at it on my way to the bedroom, but when I came out again to locate the kitchen stair, I first walked back the short distance down the corridor, and stared at the thing.

It was the ugliest clock, perhaps the most ugly piece of furniture I have ever seen.

It was about ten feet tall, made of some black old-looking wood that had a strong odour of must or rot to it, uncarved or decorated, except for a painting on its high-up face. A type of grandfather clock, I deduced, but the oddest thing was that, where in such a clock there's usually a glass panel to look through, and so observe the swinging pendulum – even a door that can be unlocked in order to adjust the mechanism – in this model there was not, only the closure of unrelieved wood. Nor did the clock make any working sound. None of that deep *tugk-tockk* you hear so much of in a good atmospheric period radio play. It had only made one noise, the single monstrous clang.

As I said, the face of the clock did have a decoration. First there were, in black, the Roman numerals. The hands were both firmly clamped to the VI, which was six all right – the actual time – but surely, if they had reached six and the clock had struck five minutes ago, the hands should now have moved on? I watched them awhile, and nothing happened. VI was all it was going to be.

To return to the decoration, though. The left side of the numerals was a woman's face done like a mask. The style was old-fashioned – it looked eighteenth century to me. It was also nasty in some way I couldn't quite determine – save that, since it *was* a mask, though it had smiling red lips, the eyes were gaps of black, and in the black of each gap was a tiny silver point, so little that, from that far below I couldn't see what it was – but they looked like *pins*.

On the other side of the clock-face was the image of something even less appealing. I took it for a monkey's head, this one wizened and evil-looking.

Having inspected the clock, I turned round and found the back stair, a twisting treacherous corkscrew lit by a couple of the narrowest windows. The kitchen was along a passage at the bottom.

Any doubts were cancelled. Everything was shoved on the big wooden table, ready for preparation, vegetables, potatoes, a (shop-made) fruit pie. Placed in the middle was a postcard with a view of the town, on the back of which were instructions about the stove, the cutlery and plates, and where the fridge- freezer was with the sausages.

Apparently my aunt had faith I could cook. But she also perhaps knew how ineptly, or why hadn't she wanted something more elaborate?

II

"This is all a little cold, Laura. Did you heat everything thoroughly?"

I said nothing, refusing now to play her game.

Before she started her critique of the food, (including its late arrival), she'd commented on the *size* of my meal – "*Two* sausages, Laura? And all those peas – Surely a young woman needs to watch her figure... and I thought I had left a cabbage out. The frozen peas were for Sunday."

Everything was fifth rate anyway. The sausages tasteless, the potatoes floury. Even the pie was flavoured mostly with chemicals and had about three apple slices in it.

We ate in the dining-room. This was another wide chamber, with windows giving on the lawn with the view of the sea. As daylight sank away, pink clouds and swallows came on, and then a high, blue-green dusk. By then I'd been back down for the apple-less pie, and down again to make instant coffee.

She didn't ask me to do this, she told me. And I obeyed.

And I kept thinking, I can't arrange a thing tonight. I'll sort all this out in the morning.

Am I spineless? Less that than rather tired.

The instant coffee, too, was not the kind that makes people alert, sexy and wise in the adverts. It was the kind you use to scare out the drains.

After dinner she opened the French doors, however, and said we should have an after-dinner stroll on the lawn.

Was she showing me what I would be missing if I rebelled and ran away?

The sea lay far out, adrift in the sky, dark now, and darker than the luminous dusk, just as it had been more blue than the sky, before. The air was fresh and pure and smelled of roses, clematis, and salt.

"Tomorrow," said Aunt Jennifer, "perhaps you should make an early start. I'm afraid everything has got very dirty. Perhaps you should begin downstairs. You won't forget to clean the windows, will you?"

I drew a breath of the beautiful air.

"Where in your letter to me," I said, "exactly, did you specify that if I came to stay in your house, I would automatically become your cook and cleaner?"

"Housekeeper, Laura."

"I see. Did you mention a fee, then, the wages I'd get for being your – er – housekeeper? I seem to have missed all that. "

"Oh, I can't afford to pay you. I can't afford that sort of luxury. But you're getting your keep, aren't you?"

I was, despite everything, dumbfounded by her relaxed demeanour. I thought, wildly, she's been dreaming this up, perhaps, for years. Why? To get at my *mother*? At me? What had *I* ever done to her?

We'd been walking along the lawn all this time. As if engrossed in the most ordinary, friendly dialogue.

Now, around the bushes, the drop opened before us, a sailing away of the hill in air and darkness, quite dramatic. And I thought, Shall I just push the old cow over? But naturally I would never do that.

And then she said, "Did you see the clock in the corridor near your door?"

"What has –?"

"Didn't you think it rather peculiar?"

I said nothing, less from stern resolve than an inability to keep up with this.

"It has a story. That clock."

She was, my aunt, a very dumpy, unattractive figure in her sensible jumper, skirt and shoes. Yet in the last of the twilight, she was melting to a shadow of her former self, a dumpy *solid* shadow, lit now and then by a smeary flash of eyes.

"This house was built about 1900, only about a hundred years ago. Some playwright owned it. Some homosexual creature. He used to collect eccentric bits of furniture. I'm sure I have no interest in him, or in them, and none of them remain. Apart from the clock. The clock was one of his finds, and it's always been in the house. Quite a curiosity. One can't move it, you see."

Despite myself, I reacted. "Why not?"

"Because it was nailed to the floor of the upper storey, and in such a way, it would mean all the floor-boards and the joists would have to come up, to pry it loose. I was warned about this. It's an eyesore, of course," she announced. "I don't imagine even you, Laura, with your extreme notions, would like it. At one time the previous tenants had it boarded up – but all that gave way, and well, I couldn't afford to have it done again."

"And besides, I added, "it's only in the corridor that leads to the back stairs."

"Yes, quite."

Dark now. Night had come. The swallows were finished and instead the odd bat was flitting over. I could just hear the sea, its slow sighing, so intimate, so eternally indifferent.

Jennifer said, "Did you see the two images painted on the face?"

"Yes."

"Youth and Age, they're called."

An explanation disconcertingly formed in my mind. The *mask* was youth – rather a quaint idea, I supposed – a hollow false face that didn't last and eventually had to come off to reveal what was truly there inside. Which was the evil-looking *monkey*? Yes, old age, the mischievous joker. It could make you ugly. *Animal.*

Was that precisely what was happening to Jennifer – mask ripped away, the mad beast beginning to show...?

But she said, "All a lot of nonsense, of course. The interesting part is about the main body of the clock, the area inside the wooden frame."

The day had been warm. It was getting chilly now. A stiff light wind, blowing in over cooling seas, iced down my arms and through my T-shirt, and between my sandalled toes crept the breaking dew.

"So?" I said. Why was I indulging her in this? What the hell was the matter with me? Tell her to fly off the hill, the old witch. Or I should. God, there must be a pub around here somewhere – light, warmth, sanity and booze –

Jennifer said, "It's haunted. The clock."

She said it with enormous relish. As if she was counting it, like her money.

"Oh I see."

"It's only a story, evidently," she glibly said, facile in her absolute certainty she was getting to me. Was she? I didn't believe in – "I found the history in an old book once, a library book, or I could show you – An unpleasant little tale. Most unpleasant."

"How do you know the clock in the book is the same clock?"

"Oh, the estate agent told me years ago, when I was buying the place. In case I found out, I imagine, and got ratty. Then when I read the story in the book, I recognised it was my clock, or rather the *house* clock. And the book gave a lot more details."

"You're obviously dying to tell me."

I tried to sound patronising, but really just wished I'd keep quiet.

She would tell me anyway.

But then Jennifer said, "Well, I don't know, Laura. At this late hour. I remember what a nervous child you were – I don't want to alarm you. It's not a nice story. It might keep you awake. And you'll need your sleep if you're to get an early start on the house in the morning."

And then – *then* – the foul old bag turned on her clumpy heel and marched away from me up the lawn, towards her economically faint-lit house. Leaving me with only the cold night and the indifferent sea, and the uneasy suspicion that if I didn't hurry after her, she might lock me out all night.

Had I been nervous as a child? Not especially. And yet there was a kind of something in me, always had been, a sort of feral awareness of – God knew what. Maybe that's why, in part, I don't believe in the supernatural. It's less that I don't than that I *won't*.

My father had been sensitive. Not afraid or cowardly, I don't mean that. But the rubbish of the world could get to him, truly upset him; reported cruelties in other countries, or my wretched mother... It was why he'd died, I think. Worry, and trying not to worry, or rather never passing the worry on to her, because he couldn't, to me because he wouldn't.

I *hated* thinking of him like this, now, sitting up in the awful bed, wondering – I couldn't help it – if Jennifer, who had been his elder by three years, had tried to frighten him when he was a little boy. They'd both been kids when the war started, and evacuated together to some farm. I had this picture of them in the unknown dark, he only about four or five, and *she* telling him horror stories.

All the time I sat there, I too was in the dark. There was no side-lamp, just the overhead bulb with the switch by the door. Another form of economy? Since, unless you wanted to sleep with the light full in your eyes, you had to turn it off before getting into bed.

Then the clock went off again. And I nearly jumped out of the house, let alone my skin.

This time, it clanged twice. But it was only just past midnight, according to my luminous alarm-clock.

I thought, (irrationally?) that's the other reason she's put me in here. So her damn clock can keep me awake.

Then, I heard the rustling sound.

Okay, I admit my hair stood on end. There I was in the spooky dark, alone, and here was this crepuscular little noise suddenly coming to join me, over there, by the door.

It's mice I decided.

So I switched on the torch I'd had the sense to bring, conjuring country lanes by night, and shone it full at the doorway, expecting to pick up two or more little bright mouse eyes.

It wasn't mice.

There, pushed in under the door, were some sheets of paper.

I gaped at them. Then I got out of bed, crossed the intervening three feet of room, and picked the papers up. Then I switched on the overhead light.

The papers were handwritten, and I knew the writing, over-ornamented and tightly cramped, as if nothing must slip between the words or letters. It was hers. I'd seen it on her letter.

Disbelieving, despite the rest, (and the obvious fact she must have crept soundless to my door in order to slot this under it), I read:

Laura, I remembered I had copied this from the library book I told you about. I thought you might be intrigued. I've pushed it under your door in order not to disturb you. Read it in the morning. No doubt, to your sophisticated mind, it will seem a very silly tale.

How was that for contradictory malice? Also, she *knew* I'd be 'disturbed', unless I was stone *deaf* and hadn't heard the clangs of the clock.

I sat down on one of the bed's rocky humps, and read the remainder of the hand-written pages, which detailed carefully the story of the clock. They did read as if these passages had come from a book.

The clock, the text informed me, dated back to 1768, and had been made in France. In those days it had had the normal glass window, through which the pendulum might be seen, and the whole front of the lower clock might be opened in order to reach the workings. The face, then and now, was decorated with a macabre motif then current in decadent Paris, and entitled *Youth and Age*, represented in either respective case by a mask and a distorted, monkey-like human head.

During the French Revolution, the clock reached England, brought over, for some inane reason, by fleeing aristocrats. And in 1820, it passed into the possession of an English family named Trente. They placed it in their country house, somewhere in the vicinity of Lathamfold.

Due to various reverses, there came in time to be only two females left to represent the Trente family, a young woman, Sabia Trente, and her elderly aunt, Eugenia. Both had experienced rather irksome lives, the old aunt unmarried and impoverished, dependant on her young niece, who, apparently no longer rich, and quite plain, was herself without hope of catching a suitable man.

The book, or Jennifer, omitted to say much about the existence they led together in their failing country mansion, rubbing each other up the wrong way all the while, since they didn't like each other at all, due to some quarrel in the family. Somewhat in the manner of an antique Cinderella, the aged aunt, (she was sixty-odd, which must have been more like eighty in those days), was soon consigned to the servants quarters, and required to carry out quite menial work uncomplimentary to her years and status. Sabia Trente, meanwhile, lost no opportunity to '*heap contumily*' on the old girl's head, and in the end they were deadly enemies.

By the year Sabia was thirty, youth's bloom gone and her last illusory chance of marriage with it, they occupied the mansion with only one actual servant. The grounds had run to seed and weed. Local farmers grazed their pigs and sheep on the meadows, and paid the Trentes a pittance to do it. The house was in bad repair, some of its roof down, and all its treasures sold.

All, that is, but for the French clock.

It would seem there was some sentimental or superstitious reason why Sabia Trente had *not* sold the clock, which might have brought a fair price as a curiosity, having become, of its kind, quite rare.

However, rather than be sold, something else happened with the clock.

One night, aunt and niece had a real falling out. For years they'd been arguing, but on this particular night it came to blows. Sabia struck first, slapping the old woman across the face and head so hard she fell down. It was then that Auntie Eugenia reached for a fire-iron. She in turn struck her niece a blow '*harsh enough it clove the brain-case in twain*'.

Skull fracture accomplished, Auntie, in the rational panic of the amateur turned professional, dragged her niece to the tall clock, standing handy, undid the door, and with the super-strength of fear and rage, stuffed Sabia inside. *Then*, Eugenia hauled the younger woman upright, propped her, (presumably smashed head lolling and bleeding) against the pendulum – which naturally at once stopped moving – slammed shut the door and locked it. She then flung the key in the fire, where the heat soon deformed and disguised it. Last of all, the inventive homicide pulled down one of the frowsty curtains and slung it right over the clock, draping it from top to toe, and thus hiding its new grisly contents from view.

Jennifer's library book calmly commented that the old servant woman, if she at all noticed the clock had been shrouded, paid no attention, being used to the 'eccentricities of her mistresses'. And when the dead body began to stink? The clock apparently held most of that safely inside. The occasional whiff was put down to dead rats in the wall, an occurrence of charming frequency.

Not even the disappearance of one of the Trentes was much noted. Both Sabia and Eugenia had long since ceased to frequent the village, or even the church. If the visiting pigs or farmers failed to see Sabia, trailing through the long grass of her estate in her ruined yellow gown, they doubtless only thought she had given up trailing, too, with her other renunciations .

As for the servant, '*she asked no questions*'.

Incredibly, if all this were a fact, Eugenia then lived on in the Trente house for five more years before she '*died of an apoplexy*'. The servant promptly left, stealing a few squalid items to assist her passage. Others came after the funeral, to clear and tidy the house. And that was when, of course, they found what was in the clock, a partly-mummified, partly-skeletal cadaver, held rigidly upright in its black-stained, pale yellow rags – which, once the curtain was fully off, was displayed as clearly as a mannequin in a shop window.

Some sort of investigation took place. It revealed, perhaps not amazingly, an account of what had actually happened, penned, (boastfully?), by Aunt Eugenia in her journal, and hidden in a concealed bureau drawer.

The clock meanwhile was broken open and the corpse removed and buried. A type of exorcism was reportedly performed. Exactly why was not specified. After that, the clock was sold at last, and went to unknown buyers.

Thereafter nothing was heard of it, until early in 1909, when it reappeared at an auction, boarded all round with plain wood, and said very definitely to be haunted. This was when the gay playwright, who had formerly inhabited Jennifer's house, saw the clock and collected it.

His name was Shelley Terrence, and he had enjoyed some stage successes during the Art Nouveau era, enough to set him up financially and leave him bored. At first he was *'fascinated'* by the clock, inviting his friends of all sexes down for weekends to see it. But then they, and he, changed their minds.

'*Terrence alleged,*' said Jennifer's book, '*that several of his guests had been woken at night in terror, on more than one occasion, by ghastly moans and cries issuing from the sealed-up stem of the clock. One of the guests, a certain Lady Devere Payne, claimed to have witnessed a pallid figure, in a yellow gown of the early Victorian years, lurching through the bedroom, from wall to wall – through both of which walls she passed unhindered – and wearing besides a scarlet, fringed turban that, the lady subsequently realised, was really a mass of wetly-matted hair and blood.*'

The guests fled, but worse was to follow.

Coming in late one evening, Terrence was standing talking with his manservant in the downstairs hall, when both men heard a *'creaking and groaning as of a ship at sea in high wind.'* Looking up, each man saw the same thing – the clock, which seemed to be moving quite rapidly across the top of the main staircase. It disappeared before reaching the stairs' opposite side, but not before they had also noticed shreds of yellowish material *'billowing'* from the spot where its door might have opened, had it still had one.

When they had gathered enough courage, Shelley and his man went to the room where the clock had originally been set down, and found it in a much altered position.

No surprise, another exorcism followed. After which, it seemed, Terrence was advised against ousting the clock, and instead recommended to have it ported to a back corridor, and there nailed down with long iron farriers' nails, right through the floor-boards and a joist.

This did seem to end the clock's personal activity. But by then a name had been given the ghost – the Woman in Yellow. And she herself did not leave Shelley Terrence entirely alone.

She would manifest at random awful moments, such as when he stood shaving, and saw her abruptly behind him in his mirror – a sight that so jolted him, he said, that he nearly cut off his ear. At last his nerves broke down, and he quit the house for America.

Thereafter another family, the pragmatic Jordans, lived there for a number of decades. It was they who had boarded up the clock entirely, but also they swore they did not credit ghosts, and experienced nothing unusual during their tenure.

And after the Jordans, though the book didn't mention her, came my aunt.

Perched on the hillock in the bed, I put the pages down, all this information meticulously copied, (or *invented?* – it didn't seem likely), by my own aunt.

That she was trying to frighten me, however, was pretty obvious. It was evidently all of a piece with her design for me here. To humiliate me and make me her unpaid servant – a curious reversal of Sabia and Eugenia Trente – wasn't sufficient. No, she wanted to give me nightmares, too.

Why did she have it in for me? I thought back, cautious. All I could recall was a dim, much younger version of Jennifer, making snide remarks about my mother's behaviour, Jennifer's nagging voice gnawing away at my father, and more sharply at child-me – "Don't do that, Laura. That grass will get your skirt dirty, and heaven knows, your mother won't have anything ready for you to change into." Oh, and Dad's funeral. When she stood there, dabbing her bright, dry, hard eyes, and I hadn't made time to talk to her, all wrapped up in my own misery, and not wanting anyone else to see. As if to grieve was a humiliation.

Was that enough to make her want to get at me so much? Maybe. She was slightly crazy.

More to the point, was her scheme working? I mean, was I scared?

I switched on the torch, then switched off the overhead light. I left the torch burning by my bed. I lay down, listening, and heard only the vague sounds of wood and plaster settling towards the cool of earliest morning.

Yes, I was, if not nervous, unnerved.

I didn't think I could sleep. Then I did. I dreamed, of course. Not about the Woman in Yellow. I was meeting Eden at Heathrow to fly to the U.S. with him, and I was very happy about this, and then I found my passport had vanished, but there was my father, grey and old, saying "I've got it here, Laura. It's all right." But we looked through the window of the caravan, which was suddenly there, and in which (in the dream) he'd been living, and it was full of *things* – *live* things – not really mice, more like ghastly little gingerbread figures – and they were eating the furniture –

And I woke up with my heart in my mouth, and it was light, 6 a.m., and the clock was striking ten.

III

I left the next morning.

Let me rephrase that. I tried to leave.

Having got up and dressed and herded my bags together, I bundled everything down the main stair to the hall.

It was by then only six-twenty, and there was no sign of Jennifer. Though I suspected she was an early riser, it seemed not *this* early.

My plan was to use the phone I'd noted yesterday in the drawing-room, and call the remembered number of the cab firm who'd brought me here.

When I walked into the room, the sunlight was cutting through it from the east-facing windows, and I could see the ocean glittering away below, never now to be reached. But when I lifted the old-fashioned receiver of the telephone, there was no dialling tone. I tried various things, nothing worked. I thought perhaps Jennifer unplugged the phone at night, and traced the wire around to its socket in the wall. But it was attached, and although I took it out and reconnected it, still the phone was dead.

Probably the machine itself had gone wrong and she frugally hadn't bothered to get it mended. Where then in the house would I find another phone that worked?

I searched the downstairs rooms, cursing myself now that I, abnormality among millions, had never invested in one of those mobiles I'd previously cursed on the train. Of course the one I'd used from the company had been recalled.

The rooms were all spacious, gracious, full of grand furniture and silk curtains, and all soiled and dusty and lit by sun. And phoneless.

I went to the kitchen then and made myself some of the foul coffee, double strength. Really I thought I knew where the one operational phone would be. It would be in Jennifer's bedroom.

As I stood there, in that dampish, still, shadowy, stone-floored vault, my body was prickling all over finally with a kind of fear. I *knew* I couldn't say to her, I am leaving now: Let me use the phone to call a cab.

She would somehow (how?) prevent it.

She wanted me here, she really did. To play with, to get back at for imagined trespasses. And did she hope for me something worse than humiliation and housework?

Jennifer and Eugenia – just how much, by now, did the two of them have in common?

Then I visualised lugging my bags through the winding twisty lanes, getting lost among fields and hedges, always glimpsing the sea and the way I should go, and not able to figure out physically how to get there. I thought of surly country folk, who would detest me and refuse me use of *their* phones, snarling dogs, bulls – the perfect layman's picture of the English Wild. Whatever else, it would be a long walk. It had taken the cab nearly an hour...

So I thought of a cunning plot. I'm a sort of survivalist. Up to a point, I'll do what I have to, to escape, evade, get by.

She came down at eight. By then I was cleaning the French windows of the drawing-room. The rest of the room was dusted and hoovered, though not polished. You don't, even if on an economy drive, polish wood like that with *Busy Bee* – which was all she had.

I heard her stop in the doorway. Was she thrilled? Triumphant? Or at all startled I'd actually given in?

"Hi," I said airily, only half turning. "Beautiful morning."

"Yes, it is," she said, grudgingly.

"I've almost done in here. I thought you'd like this room sorted out first."

"Yes." Then she said, "So you decided you'd do it."

"Oh, why not?" I said. "For a while, anyway. It's a great house, it's good to tidy it up." Then I turned round properly. There she was, in a rather grubby white wrap, with her dyed hair in curlers and a scarf. I said, "Just one thing, I'm really sorry. When I was hoovering, I knocked into that table with the phone and it fell off. When I picked it up I couldn't get the tone. I must have broken it. Of course, I'll pay for the repair."

She blinked. That was all. Then her dire little smile came out like a hiding slug. "That's all right, Laura. It doesn't work anyway. I don't use the telephone much."

I gawped, *astonished*, and anxiously said, "But miles up here, and you live alone – do you keep another phone for emergencies at least?"

"Oh yes."

That was all. I turned back as if completely satisfied. Whistling, I went on sparkling up the windows with newspaper. I *was* satisfied. She did have another phone. Just a matter of finding it.

Then, as I gave the last burnish to the panes, I saw in the glass that Jennifer was now advancing through the room towards me, and – well, this frightened me. Was she violent? For a second I pretended to go on obliviously rubbing the newspaper about, but keeping my eyes on her reflection. The image was virtually divided between outside and in, and she seemed to be passing through the cedar tree in sections, her stupid red scarf, wound over curlers, very vivid in the glass, and contrastingly, her wrapper looking rather like a long dress, and more yellow than white –

And then I knew what I was seeing.

It wasn't my Aunt Jennifer.

I whirled round, burning cold, in a terror the like of which I'd never ever felt – a sort of vertigo of fear. As if a hole had opened in the world and I was about to plunge through.

Nothing was in the room.

Not Jennifer. Nothing... else.

I made a noise, a silly noise.

After quite some time, I looked back at the window, and there was only the vague reflection of furniture held there among the branches of the cedar.

What do you do after something like that? If you're me, and you don't believe in ghosts, fairly quickly you put it down to hallucination caused by stress. And then you feel slightly better.

However, I was all the more keen to get out of the house.

She wanted breakfast, of course. Toast, cornflakes, marmalade – and tea, *not* coffee. I prepared that and she had it in the drawing-room, taking the opportunity, as she did so, to write down on a note-pad anything she thought I'd missed in my cleaning.

After all that, I explained I was just popping up to the loo. I guessed I'd get some comment about weak bladders or irregular bowels, but no.

Upstairs I went, but obviously not to the bathroom. I walked along the main upper hallway, and looked into the rooms until I found hers.

Her room was disgusting.

I have lived, I've said, in tips, but she really had no excuse. The bed was tightly made, otherwise there was mess and junk everywhere, old newspapers in stacks, magazines, boxes of sticky old orange powder and make-up dried in tubes. And worse than this, half-eaten packets of biscuits, sweets that *seemed* half-eaten, then taken out and *wrapped up again in their paper for future use* – Another defunct banana lay rotting in a turpentine reek on the windowsill, to the glee of several flies. The room stank of that, of many saccharine things going off. Of her.

I opened windows, and then I looked for the phone. And it wasn't there. Which was insane, for it was nowhere else and I truly didn't believe even crazy Jennifer wouldn't have one. She must have concealed it cleverly. Where?

Perhaps I was chicken, I didn't want to start rummaging around yet. I'd have to tell her I would do her room this afternoon, make it nice for her, some crap like that.

Then I went down to get on with the drudgery, and unlike me, *she* had found something – my bags, thrust in the hall cupboard.

"Whatever are these doing here? I said take them up."

"Oh, I will, when I sort them out later. They take up too much space in my room like this."

I can sometimes think on my feet.

But perhaps I wasn't fooling her. Had she been looking?

A curious day. I laboured like her slave. My arms began to ache, and my back from bending and stretching. With the mirrors and the windows, I whistled and sang Mozart and XTC extra loud, and saw nothing beyond what usually reflects in glass.

I made lunch, (canned pilchards), and ate some with her.

The pilchards seemed to give her a high. She started rambling on at me. I scarcely listened to her reminiscences – everything had been much better then, maybe for her it had – and diatribes against men in general, Lesbians in particular, the French, the Germans, the Americans, the Scottish, and those she chose to call "Negroes" (!), also workmen, all of them, and the money-grabbing, work-shy, n'ere-do-wells who had ruined the British economy, and perhaps included, unspoken, me.

I wanted to kill her. It's a fact. I felt I too was going mental. Didn't care what I might come to do.

Acting Oscar-earning well, I smarmily told her I'd decided to clean her bedroom.

"No, Laura, that can wait. There's still plenty to see to on this floor."

"Okay," I said.

Sod her. She wasn't going to stop me now.

The old witch had a rest after lunch, so she had told me, but not in her bedroom, in one of the downstairs rooms.

To this stroke of luck I replied I'd clean up in the kitchen, while she slept, so as not to disturb her.

"Oh, I don't sleep, Laura. I never sleep well."

"Just in case," Laura cheerily declared.

As I cleared the lunch things and went out, she was smiling to herself, a crafty slug smile. But this had gone far enough, and I meant to be out of this appalling house before nightfall. Even if I did have to walk all the way with my bags gripped in my teeth, and sleep on the beach when I got there.

Accordingly, all that afternoon I searched, mainly on the upper floor. I even got up into the attics by another narrow back stair – but they were such a shambles, and draped so thickly with cobwebs, I thought perhaps she hadn't herself gone up there in a decade. I didn't find a phone. I began to feel she had lied when she said she had another, just to get me running in circles. (Somehow, during all this circle-running, I'd managed to avoid going anywhere near the clock. I'd even used the other bathroom.)

The hot afternoon light was abruptly slanting. It was nearly five.

There she was, standing in the lower hall, glaring up at me.

"Why ever are you up there? I expected tea an hour ago."

"Sorry, I'll get it now," I heard myself say, still with vague self-amazement.

"I told you not to clean upstairs yet."

"I haven't. Sorry," I said again, "I took a nap."

Firmly I added, "I didn't have a great night."

She shrugged – placated? "Very well. We'll let it go. See to the tea now."

So I saw to the tea.

Inside me at last was a mindless – almost bestial – rising panic. I couldn't seem to pull myself around. I couldn't seem to confront her any more, or make up my mind what it was best for me to do. And in about three hours, the sun was going down, down into the land, leaving behind a darkness that would smother even that coal-blue sea, which looked as if it belonged in Africa, but had somehow washed up here. As had I, who might also – be smothered?

In the end what I did was drag all my bags down to the kitchen, (having found another way on to the back stair from the ground floor; I wouldn't return to my 'room' – or just wouldn't go by the clock.) In the kitchen, I sorted through them in the mode of life-boat intendees in movies. I was going to have to leave a lot behind; it would be too heavy to carry all that way.

At the finish, I had it all down to one single very heavy bag. This I then picked up, and walked upstairs again, as I hadn't been able to open the kitchen door to the outside, it was stuck – or locked.

In the lower hall, once more, I met her. She'd known, she must have done, all of it, even to my breaking point.

But "What are you doing, Laura?" she asked. She had put on lipstick, as if for a celebration.

I moved across, and paused facing her, at the foot of the main stair. She was between me and the front door. I put down my bag. I felt reckless.

"Sorry," I said again, "I just remembered I left the kettle on in London."

"You're leaving after all," she brilliantly fathomed.

"Sure am. I don't suppose you'll allow me to use the secret telephone to call a cab?"

"Certainly not, at this time of night," (it was about seven). "They wouldn't come out. Not all the way up here. If you really insist on going, then you must do it in the morning."

"No. I'm not spending another night here. Not with you, or your speciality ghosts."

116

She smiled. What a giveaway.

"Don't tell me a grown-up woman, even you, is frightened by a ghost story."

"I don't give a toss about ghost stories. I just don't like *you*, Aunt Jennifer, or your behaviour."

"It's mutual, then," she said. We stood there in the cup of the brown hall, dusted by me, and the tiled floor wiped to a gleam, as sunlight speared by in its death-throes. "Oh, don't think I ever could forget the way you used to behave to me. You, a child. I used to think she put you up to it, that slut of a mother of yours. But I don't think she would have bothered. She'd got *him* where she wanted him. And she was busy making a fool of him. She killed him with her goings-on."

"Shut up," I said, but almost listlessly, because I half agreed at least on that. She didn't take any notice anyway.

"But you were a dreadful little girl. I always saw you sneering at me behind my back, laughing at me. Always trying to get me to buy you things –"

"For God's sake I was a child –"

"She'd told you I was well-off, I suppose. And so it was: Can I have an ice-cream, can I go to the pictures, can I have that book on tigers –?"

"Well I didn't get them off you, did I? Oh, excuse me, I did get half an ice-cream once."

She shamed me. Had I been a whining, gift-grabbing kid? We hadn't had much, and Jennifer, then, used to flash her money. And she used to promise me things, too, presents, and at first I'd believed her, but I never got them. In me now, the panic was boiling into rage. The hall was stifling and turning red with it. Like her furious self-righteous face.

"Then the funeral," she announced. "My own brother, and your father, and there you were, and you couldn't say a word to me, just 'Hallo, Aunt'. And later I think you said good-bye. Both of us standing there over his grave, and you wouldn't say a word. You couldn't even spare me a drop of kindness."

"My father was dead," I said bitterly.

"My *brother* was dead," she cried. Her eyes flamed like slices of razor, and then they went up over my head, up to the top of the stairs, and she let out – not a scream – a sort of yelp.

At once the blood-red light in the hall seemed to darken. Something out there had got hold of the sun. Instantly, the nature of my turmoil changed. My back, my neck, my scalp, were covered by freezing ants.

I stared at her. "What is it?"

She didn't speak. She simply went on gazing up the stairway, and, still gazing, she began to back away, back through the door of the drawing-room, and now her lipstick mouth was hanging open.

I've no notion how, but I understood this was not part of the game.

As for me, for a moment I didn't think I *could* move. Then I knew I had to, because otherwise, if I just stayed there at the foot of the stairs, whatever – whatever was on them, coming down them, whatever that was – would soon be right where *I* was – and I didn't – no I *didn't* – want that –

So I somehow moved forward, to run after Jennifer through the drawing-room door, and at the same time, like Lot's misguided wife, I looked behind me –

And was turned, as she was, to an immovable pillar of volcanic salt.

Because what was standing still at the head of the stairs was the wooden clock, and what was coming *down* the stairs was Sabia Trente, not still at all, the skirts of her gown blowing round her, and her arms held up from the elbows, and her hands pointing with their grown-long finger-nails...

You see such things on a screen, a book-jacket, on the bloody Internet for God's sake, such images of gothic horror, these evocations of dynamic terror. It doesn't prepare you for the actual thing.

There she was. And she was worse than anything anyone could ever physically mock up, or imagine.

Her face was white, blue-white, and marked by the fringe of blood that was still unravelling down her right cheek, and yet never reached her already blood-stained gown or the stairs. Her forehead was red and also bruised black, and quills of bone stood out of her hair, (like a Spanish comb), which was otherwise clotted scarlet with blood. Her face had features, all sunken in and withered. It was a fallen monkey's face, yet too, like a mask – and in the place where her eyes had once been – were only two bruised black sockets of nothing, each secured in her head by a shining silver pin –

All I wanted was to run. It was the sum of my ambitions. And I couldn't do it. Could not move.

And so Sabia Trente came down the stair, and right up to me, and I smelled her stink worse than dead rats or rotting bananas, and then she passed directly through me, like a dank, dust-laden wind.

Perhaps I died for a split second when that happened. Perhaps my heart stopped. I don't know, can't remember.

It was just that suddenly she was past me, and I was still rooted there, watching her glide, as if she moved on ice-skates over a rink, through the drawing-room door.

Darkness had come, premature night. Once before I'd seen this creature move across the room, seen her in the window. Now I saw her from the back. Saw her so clearly, *solidly*, even the creases of her dress and the bones of her corset under it.

And I saw my Aunt Jennifer too, sprawled on a brocade sofa, screaming now, shrieking, and trying to bury her head in the cushions.

On which cue, Sabia Trente was raising up high a kind of stick, an iron thing like a wand with a strange glowing tip – she hadn't had it a moment ago – and I knew it was the poker from a fire that had been out for more than a century.

She was going to return the compliment of the cloven brain-case, not on her murderous, no longer available Aunt Eugenia, but on the skull of Jennifer.

I told you from the start, I don't believe in ghosts. I don't. I flatly refuse to. If I did, I think I would lose my mind for sure and for real and for good. And so, in those moments that lingered between Jennifer and me and the gates of Hell, I saw it all, what had truly happened, and *why* this thing was here, and what it was and what to do about it.

I was numb, had no feeling in my body, didn't really seem to be *in* it, except perhaps sitting tiny and high up behind my own eyes, like a lone passenger left on a train hurtling driverless to destruction.

For the train – me, driverless – was all at once rushing forward. It crashed headlong into the back of the stationary Sabia – I *felt* her – and I tore her apart with my hands, screaming myself now, over and over, "Go away – get lost – piss off – you don't exist –"

And she didn't exist. She was only air, and then she and her poker were gone. And at the head of the stairs the clock became a black cloud and then was gone too, back to its place in reality along the corridor.

I stood over Jennifer and I bawled at her now, "You made it up, didn't you, you fucking old bitch – *didn't* you?"

She whimpered. I struck her across the head. Not so hard. It was much better than a poker would have been. Then I pulled her to a sitting position and shouted abuse at her until she spoke. "I didn't – it was true – or at least in the book. Only not – not –"

"Not what, you cow?"

"Not that clock. Not *that* one."

She had wanted to pay me out for all my seven, nine and twenty-year-old transgressions against her. So she never quite lost track of me, and when the company folded, she was ready.

Yes, I was to have been her skivvy. For I must be punished. And, muddled as Jennifer had become, she had invested in the invented memory of me as a sensitive, nervy girl, ready to be dominated and scared witless by a contrived ghost story.

Although, as she'd said, the story was true – at least in a bona fide book, which carried the tale of the Trente murder and the haunted French clock. Even the piece about Shelley Terrence, though he had never lived in Jennifer's house – all these events had gone on somewhere else. For that reason she had had to copy out all the passages. To photocopy the printed text would have revealed too much and given the game away.

She had read the story one idle afternoon. And become obsessed enough to weave it into her retribution for me. And so mad, mad Aunt Jennifer, who wouldn't even pay to have her downstairs telephone repaired, forked out quite a sum to gain a rather poor reproduction of the Trente clock. This copy it was which was then placed – *unnailed* – in the corridor by my elected bedroom. She had even arranged for its random striking.

Well, she was off her head. And her loathing insanity and my allergic anger seem to have been enough. For yes, I take part of the blame. Without my side of it, I don't think it would have happened; she couldn't have done it on her own.

And what did happen?

Neither Jennifer nor I had ever had a child – in my case from choice, in hers I don't know. But we made a type of child between us, an *offspring* in that word's purest and most dreadful sense. For we fashioned the ghost of Sabia Trente between us, brought it to its unlife, and made it *run*.

If simply that, our projected hating energy, would have been sufficient to make the vengeful poker and its blow fatal – I've got no idea. Maybe. After all, I stopped it. I must have thought so then.

But, too, perhaps Jennifer and I merely hallucinated – visions of similar aspect experienced by more than one person at once, aren't uncommon in the annals either of the supernatural or science.

Whatever, as I said, this wasn't a ghost story, although it has a ghost.

And what happened *afterwards?* Soon told. She did a lot of cringing and crying her dry hard tears. But now I managed to make it clear I wouldn't stay another hour in her house.

I waited outside for the taxi, which took me away fast, so I just caught the nine-thirty-five train to London. The phone? I hardly believe it myself – she, the arch-reviler of modernity, had a weeny little mobile tucked in her handbag.

As I was going out of her door she came scurrying at me from the now thick-lit shadows of the house, and pushed a paper bag into my hand. I thought it probably contained some stale sandwiches to give me indigestion, or some already half-eaten sweets. I wanted to slap it to the ground, but something made me take it. Otherwise we parted without a touch, or another word. I didn't look at the paper bag until the train was drawing into London and I was going to throw it away.

Inside was a hundred pounds in tens, and a cheque for three thousand pounds. This was so obscene I felt nauseous. Or maybe that was only hunger, and the shock from everything else. I didn't throw up. I did cash and spend the money. And what does that make me?

I'm wondering though, if you wonder... if, despite the clock's being only a copy – yet somehow it did draw back the vengeance-seeking Sabia's dead remnant – and only my vaunted stupidity drove her off. No. However, your choice. Somebody said, it wasn't the dead you need to fear, but the living. Too damn right.

Since that night, I've heard nothing more from Jennifer. Years have elapsed. Now and then I ask myself what she does, alone, when it gets dark in that house.

The Ghost of the Clock
Chosen by Storm Constantine

I have so many favourite stories by Tanith Lee, it was a difficult task to pick one for this collection. To aid me, I decided to choose a tale from my favourite genre – ghost stories. Tanith wrote a lot of these, some of them with extremely unusual ghosts, and 'The Ghost of the Clock' has to be one of them.

The prose style of Tanith's fantasy tales was often exotic and voluptuous, but when she delved into contemporary supernatural stories she generally employed a different, more economical style – which was no less evocative of place and whatever spirits might be inhabiting it. This piece does what the best of traditional ghost stories used to do – captures a landscape and sets the scene for mystery. Not in an obvious or crude way, but as in the deft strokes of an artist's brush. In the classic ghost stories of the late nineteenth and early twentieth centuries, the landscapes and buildings – quite often big old houses – were as much characters in the story as those who were haunted. The setting itself added to the haunting.

In this story, Tanith plays with the familiar tropes of the genre. Very near the beginning, Laura, the narrator, states that she doesn't believe in ghosts. Many traditional ghost stories began that way, with the story-teller then going on to relate how their minds were changed. This story is different. As Laura says: "So this isn't a ghost story. Although it has a ghost."

Laura is in the position of having to throw herself upon the mercy of an aunt who lives in a big old house by the sea. Even Laura seems to think she might be in a story. She imagines that when she knocks upon the door, it will be opened by a servant from the last century, but of course there are no servants, and only her Aunt Jennifer to answer the door. The house she finds beyond the threshold is mysterious – and I won't go into detail here, so as not to spoil the plot – and Laura's life there becomes ever more peculiar.

Tanith clearly enjoyed playing with the genre and coming up with a tale so refreshing and intriguing. It's written in a beautiful, crisp style that matches the wit of the main character. A most delicious read.

– Storm Constantine

Storm Constantine is an author, editor, and publisher, founder of the independent imprint Immanion Press. The author of more than thirty books, her writing crosses many genres. She is best known for the ground-breaking Wraeththu series.

Cold Fire

From an idea by John Kaiine

We was ten mile out from Chalsapila, and it's a raw night. The sea mist brewing thick as wool. Then little tramp ship come alongside. I on the bridge with Cap'n. He my brother. Kinda. Jehosalee Corgen. Well. But sudden the tramper puts up her lights. She's got a lot of sail on for what she's at, maybee tracking tobaccer or hard liquor up and down. They take a need of that, in the little ports along Great Whale Sound.

– Fuckendam, say Corgen. – What this bitch go to want?

I shrug, don't I. How the hell I know. I amn't no sailor, I. Drunken, he picks me up at Chalsa, tooken me aboard. I can trim bit of sails, take a watch, that kinda stuff.

Now the tramper swim in close, making signal.

Across the black night water, Corgen and her cap'n speak.

Sounds threat-like ta me.

– What he say? ask Beau, the mate.

Afore I can offer, he goes up ter see.

Then so does I.

We stand there on the poop, with the great wing of foresails over, and lanterns flash, and I hear other cap'n tells Corgen – Hey, this good for ye and yor crew. Make lotta dolla.

– Don't need no more cargo, say Corgen.

– Nar, yer take this, no cargo, jus tow. Like horse with wagon.

– This gurl ain't no horse, say Corgen.

– Hey hey, she a good ship. Has the weight ta do it.

I think the guy on tramper he sound like a Rus. Looks too, big, goodlooken guy, and beard.

He say, – All ye do, tow dammen thing outa back and up. Get maybee nine hundred dolla. We given ye wodka too.

Shooting star is went over, like a silver angel spit.

Seems to me maybee guy on tramper is eying me real much. I go off. Then Beau too come back aways. – Govment, say Beau from mouth corner. – Seems we havta.

Corgen's busyness on sea never much legal. But govment boats turn a blind ey, ifn you make nice. So we'll do this, what so this is.

In a bit, tramper boys bring some stuff aboard, boxes, a crate, wodka in big cans like for kerosene. They gives ta Corgen where to go to pick up thing wants the towing, and he writes down careful. He sign a paper too. Then tramper turns off up the side of the night.

Boxes, stuff, full of food.

I hear Beau ask Corgen soon what the fuckdam we be go to carry.

– Chunk bludy ice, Corgen say. – Chunka ice and tow her up into bludy Artie.

– So high?

– Higher maybee. High as she go.

– For why in Christ's name?

Corgen shrug. – For nine hundred dolla.

Weather is clear, sea nearly smooth. Now we was sailing norard easterly, where the tramper say go. And all that pass as :s fisher boats for the codfish, and the faint shadow that come ire go of the land. First night ends and then a day, and when the sun low, making the sky red, Hammer up in look-out call he can see something new on the water. Men went go up rigging, to see, and so do I. Hanging there I can make out a kinda island, but it all put together of boats and rafts, with nets drifting, and there torchlights burn, so's as the red sea and sky getten black, this island what is no island, she go red.

– What there behind?

We crane forard like birds, stretch our necks. Behind the torch smokings stand something pale, like it was a misty pane of glass, so the darkness show through.

– A berg what that is.

– Nar. None of they here.

– A berg, I tells you. They come down this far, from Grenland. A great narrer one.

Like a piece of glass, like I say, so it is. A piece of the great ice, chipped offn sailing free, as the icebergs do.

Then come another ship, a big one she is, with no colours but with guns, and men on her deck all armed, officers and soldiers, only they ain't wearing any uniform, but you can see they are, the ways they's stood.

Corgen and Beau and Bacherly, they get rowed offn away.

We set ta wait. Don't go no closer.

Over on the island of boats men move around in the light and shadow, can't see what they do, that's all. The berg, if it a berg, none of us sure, goes fainter in the smokes.

Along of midnight, Corgen and the others they bring back.

Corgen has face like dried white fish. Other two ain't much pinker. They come up aboard. Corgen grabs me.

– Pete O Pete, say Corgen. – Christ. I never shoulda took this on. Thin luck, the days we leaves Chalsapila.

Then he puts his head down on my shoulder, like as when we was childa and ma was raw ter him.

The six other men on Corgen's bucket, they clusters around, and the over us sails nod, cos the wind's getting up from the south.

– Cap'n, what's to do?

He lifts his head. He look scared and sick.

– Never word'll come outa me, he say. – Shitten govment say we must, so we do. I can't tell you. You'll be to see it, morning come.

We stand round him, and his boys look like they have mutiny running in the back of their eyes. Then Corgen rechanges to his own self. He reach out and grip Hammer and Bacherly and shake pair of them so as the bones rattle under their clothes. – We got no choosing. Like birth and dying. No choosen. So we take it. Bruk the wodka out, Beau. We've a long haul to the North fuckdam pole.

Second night on the new course, two of Corgen's men jump over. You can see the land, can reach it if swim strong, and though that sea cold, men have their reasons.

Another man, Bacherly, he go over next night and not so lucky. Struck the side and stunned him. He's drunken, I guess. We pull him back aboard and empty him of water, but then he lie raving and shaken till Corgen speak to him. – I tell him, bite yer tongue or I'll throw ye back down.

Sight of land is gone by then. Bacherly is quiet, but sometimes he puke, or he cries.

The others is make to be brave. A coupla of them make pretend we don't tow no thing at all. Ando cusses a lot. He anyway allays do that.

None of them much goes aft to look. It don't matter if they looks, it amn't a danger – no moren towing it. They did tell us, when they brung it, and all the cables and chain was fixed and the hooks to hold all, they do tell us then, the ice on the berg is old and set so hard, thick as a stone wall, the officer say, ten feet forget it – this more twenty feet thick of ice. Can't stir. Can't break. This why it must be took to go upways north, to the Pole, this why. Though it came, officer believe, from the Southron Pole below, all the wide mile down at the earth's end. From there. And all this time, the ice held.

So now, cold as we go, now it shall never give way. He swears that too, on the Bible.

Since Chalsapila, when Corgen finds me in alley, I don't drink. Even the Rus blue and black wodka, sharp as spikes, I left it alone.

I saw to the work I can do, and I eat when others have their food, though they are keep back the food the tramper gave us for when this is done and over. Also I play them cards. Corgen gives me some money, so I can gamble on cards too and pay up when lose, which I do. Sometimes when I climb up to the yards, I tend the ties and canvas, but then I set a while, and look back along the ship to her stem, back to where the berg is. It is about half ship's length behind, seems to drift there. If was not for the iron cables, you should think it only followed us.

He said, the officer, the ice is twenty feet thick.

Yet I see through. Transpearant, the officer say, like crystal, this type of berg. Means nothing, still thick as five stone walls.

By see through it, I mean it's as like you look through frost on glass. I remember a gurl once, she wants her drink in a frost glass. Like that.

If any of the others see me, staring back, they never show at that time. Only Bacherly is sick, crying in the hold on his blankets. When I go to want to give him the hot soup he throws it down and he say I'm mad. to sail the ship. He say I never needed to go on, I coulda gone over side and ashore, I, like the other two that jumped over. He forget me that I can't swim.

But anyhow, strange though this is, 1 amn't afraid of it. What I am feeling as I look at it, I don't think to be fear. But each day or night then, either I'm up in the rigging, and watch toward the stem, or then I go up on the aft deck, and whoever is to be there at wheel, he give me a glance.

One say – Right glad I am that sail tween me and that
sea.

One say – You insane, Pete Corgen. I allays knew ye was. Is drink rottened yor brain.

As him he drink from wodka can.

But I go on by to rail, and I stood there, and I look. The first night I am doing it, the moon's up, and the biggest brightest of the stars. Shines right through the ice, like the electric light in the bar shone through that gurl's frost glass.

I never am mad, as that man say. I be have seen them as are mad. I am not.

Now it seems, that first time, never I see it so good, not when it come, and they tied it to the ship. Perhaps then I couldn't. As when you young, the first time you truly see a gurl, you canna look proper at her, though she is to be all you ever think on.

But first night in moon's shine. Well.

Christ. Like fire it is. But dull in frost. Frozened. Yet beautiful.

Beautiful.

Once saw a metal forged, was steel. It went go that colour, afore the cooling starts. But this, this is tween the heat and the cool. White red. Red silver. How can I say?

The shape.

Well.

I have see a lizard once. Yet this now not really like this lizard, which was only small, a kind creature.

And this ain't kind. Nor small.

Well.

How can I say?

Well, let me say, first time I fuck a gurl, when I have seen her nakd, and there she is, my heart in my throat she so sweet and so. There's no word.

And this, neither no word.

And still I must try explain.

Up in the column of the narrer ice the shape do stood, and it have the body of a lizard among the giant kind. The backbone is curving, flext like a curl of rope. And all covered with scale is it, like a great fish. And it is have wings. The wings are more like they of the butterfly. But tough, the wings, tough as sails, and have a pattern, but this like the kind of written book I canna read, the pattern. And it has legs, and forelegs like long arms, and on them like hands, both on the feet and the front feet, hands. And the hands do have to be with claws. Each claw look to be length my forearm. Then there is long neck, and the head.

What is head of it? Like horse, a little. But not like horse. No, like the lean head of race dog, long, and thin. It with two ears, set back. Ears are like dog ears. And the shut eyes like lizard's eyes.

I don't know what it is, this thing, in the ice. But I say to you, long afore I see this, I've look in some books. What books say want go hard for me, and the pictures too, and yet, piece by piece, sometime I will read then. This name I bring out. Dragon.

Dragon, dull red as burnt fire and cloved over frost white, wings spread like a moth against a lighted candle, and the eys shut. Shut eyes. No moving. Still like dead. Dragon. Dragon.

This we tow.

The weather it held, with the sea in pleats and slow, and soft gray sky that has sun like a lemon slice, and by night a moon like a ghost.

Porpus teem through water, wet slick speckle, like cats. Then is later, and the packs of the flat ice drifting by, and above over us black head tama flying.

All this while the dragon coil in the berg. No moving.

The twenty feet ice of the berg glister but never cracks. Each dayup, Corgen comes out with gun, and look over the berg ice, check.

1 try say to him about the dragon in the ice.

Corgen won't say back. Three times I try. Third time he slap me hard in the mouth so down I fall. Beau pulls me away, but as I not any drink in me, I feel no will ter do nothing on this, only sad, like as when I child.

Nights though, he, me and Beau we eat in the cabin. The wodka is still plenty. The guys from the tramper, they brung over a lot. Good best stuff, best than any ever drunk.

Only tastes bit of kerosene, Corgen say. Who care for that?

They drink, try to make me, laugh at me that I won't.

They sing some nights. So I with them.

In the ice it never moving. Eyes shut.

I think what eyes did it had behind the close, hot metal colour lids. Were they like fire? Was fire what it breathed as the book say?

As Corgen won't speak, I ask of Beau, what did the officers on the other ship say of the dragon, when first they make Corgen and he to see it.

– They come out talk of prehistry, say Beau. – Say this like elephant thing in Rus, that was trapt in hard old ice. This one some kind dynosar. But I see them dead dynosars in a show once. This out there nothing like them.

– Is it died? I say.

– For Christ, Pete, how fuck am I go to know? Looks well dead to me.

But the one who dies around then is Bacherly. I find him, as we was getting well up to north, toward the world's top.

Dense white mist that day, and we to go very slowly cos for of the ice drifts, which you hear grunt and creak and squeak now near, and now far off, but never see till close. And I go down with mess of meatpotato, and Bacherly is there and he's dead, with a red smear on chin.

Corgen come and kicks him to wake up. Bacherly don't take notice. We havta put him over side, and Ando say the prayer.

Some of the others have gutache too. But Corgen say they are all time drunken and that this is why, can't hold Rus wodka, it too good for them.

Then he say soft to me, – Or it that thing in there.

Meaning the dragon in the ice.

He say, – Some shitten disease carry on it. Those guys from the military, they jaw on, say too cold for any germ. How the fuck they knows? Couldna wait to get rid, and we the fuckfools to do muck work for them.

The stillness is like a dream.

When mist melts, I see three storms, three, four mile off north and east, boiling. But these never come up with Corgen's bucket. As if afraid to.

Tward northard, that a strange place. Never had I been up so high. A terrible white place, with islands of ice that look to anchor, so steady they are stuck on the water. And the land what seem ter go to want draw near, white land, bare as a cracked china plate, but it's ice. And now we was to see animals about, the lolling seals and walrus. One time there is two like swords flash, fish with horns that fight in the sea. – Narhl, say Corgen.

He was been here afore and know such beasts.

We is both to forard, us, when he tell me that. He never at back of ship, save when at helm, or when he checks the berg.

We be have long days on this travel. I forgetten how many.

Then one day, just like that one I have describe, Corgen and I is by the rail, when he lean over, and I hear he's throw up. When back he come, he have a smear of red on his lip.

One or two other of his men are sick now days on days, and all the rest belly rotten. Only I am not.

– Pete, Corgen say. – You never taste that filthy Rus piss muck, say you never?

– The wodka? Nar, Corgen. I swore I'd never, after Chalsapila.

– Thank Christ, say Corgen . – Listen now, it's got be medcin in.

– What medcin?

– Don't you be bludy fool. What medcin ya think? To fuckkill us all. Govment do it. We haul thing up here, and all while drinken, and it gets hold. No bludy nine hundred dolla for us, but poisoned. Done for, the boatload ofn us.

I start to cry. He hits me. Then we hug hard, like long ago.

– Why they do it? I say.

– To sew up our mouths. Christ know they want that thing us be to tow kept safe and froze and none to find.

I turn my head, canna help that, look all the way of the ship, to where the ghostly berg she float there still on her cables, as if she follow us. And in the yeller blubber white amba of the ice, the dragon not moving, curven, and I see.

— Corgen, I say. — Corgen.

— Now, say Corgen. — Listen close. The men and I are up to go the cabin. Have a final drunk of the piss muck, feel good one last, then I use the gun. Cap'n's job. And me the last.

— Christ. Nar, nar. We lay over tward the west, some settled place, get help.

— Too late, Peter. And beside, what to do of that in some settled place? That lizard. No, we go in cabin, we already done for. You'll hear some shots is all. Soon done. Leave it be. We two do say our god's bye here. Ye never had a stomache for a ruckus. Keep yor head, ad, you'll make shore. Leave bludy ship. Take the boat. Leave ship and us and the thing. Sea is very calm and slow. You will make ter shore.

I never have words. Now neither, they don't come. He wring me in his arms, and then go, and the other men appearing and they go after, some even lifting a hand to me, and Beau give me a sorry grin, as they are leaving like for a new ship. The cabin door shuts.

I stand alone.

Above, over I the sails swing and sigh, and every side the pack ice grind in the waves. There's shout and cussing and a can thrown behind the door which make it to shake.

I stand alone till and I hear the shots. One, two, three. Then a bit. Then four. Which is he, my brother.

I set down on the planks and cry, all the ice and water and empty around me. He were never my brother in blood. Ma's son she allays beat, and I only her died brother's boy she beat too, but never me so hard and cruel as he. Hated me he shoulda. Never done that. My brother, Corgen.

The dark by this time is to be coming, and never is quite dark, nor never now quite day. But I go down to ship's end, and stare at the dragon in the ice. And I saw as I had when I look ahind just before Corgen go in to die, that its eys are have come open, open wide.

Its eyes not like fire, no, they look like an old piece silver I once see in a church, pale but tarnish of black, and shine behind.

Very slow, slow as think, they seem to move. The rest dead still, no breath, no trembler of leg or head. But just these eyes move this way and that way.

All Corgen and crew be stark dead, they, and this have awaken sure, and not dead, there alive in the white amba of the ice.

And then its eyes look down, at me, so far down on the planks of the ship. The eys are to stare. And I know it have never, in all the time of its living days afore seen a thing like I am. As I, in all my living, never saw a thing like it but in a book I proper couldna read.

All around the dark drop like the snow.

When I have the things set right, I beginning what now I must.

So long a great while, the steel tooth works on the cabling, and the green sparks fly. I look up and they are reflect like thoughts in the old silver of the dragon's eyes.

All night I am take to cut the cords that bind the berg to the stern of Corgen's ship.

The big heat of cutting make me sweat, and make too the berg true sweat, and near the half dawn time, I see there are a crack all up the crystal ice, all splintery and furred white, and it leak, drip, drip, away in the cold sea.

The dragon watch all that.

No moving, but only the eys.

When part of the sky lift to the east, last of the iron cords smokes and screams off and crash down in the water. The berg shudder. There is wind now, blow fierce straight out of the sun, and drive Corgen's bucket over to larboard, to the west, and maybee we are to go to smash on the ice there. But I look back, and I see the berg drift now, free, and how the heat from the cutting I was made get ice to run down, and the sun catch on these flows, and sudden a chunk of the old, old ice fall out and into the water.

Then was a horrible circling tide that hides up in the ice packs, and hauls ship aways, with the wind too bending her, so she lie to her side, and the great berg go smaller and smaller. But I think of its eyes.

I go down in hold, where Bacherly died the first. I cover up me in his blude-mark blankets and sleep, for there's now no more of any kind I can be to do.

She run in, time later, on Spalt Island, where the codfishers have a camp town of huts, and they come take me from the ship to their fires. Later we bury my brother and his men in the deep inland snow. An old man he say words over them from the Bible. A young woman of the older peoples here, with hair black as oil, she rubs my hands in her square, hot, fat hands, to bring me warm. She's kind, the black haired woman.

The fishers go out and come in again in their boats with the nets thrashing with the codfish. But never have they to say that they see any odd thing.

Berg must of drift north and froze, or away again to south, or west or east, and burst like a frost glass on sharp wall of sun. Perhaps and too, what is in there maybee allays was dead, under the ice, its eyes only to open as sometimes a dead man's will, or he make groan or sigh, even though he dead as stone when you check him, but it's as you picken him up the final air go out. The men here say they have seen like this in shark. And too, it is like dead Beau done, yet he is rotten. But Corgen never did.

Long while since, I am on this island.

I am walking out to the land's edge, where ice thick as twenty feet. Stand there, I, and see the sky and the water. I think and think, but no word comes. Can such thing as a dragon come back from so far past? Such a thing as that, so pale metal red, so long shut in its prison of frost glass, just the sparks of the cutting free and the Artie sun's shine to warm it, just the tides to push it here or there, back into the cold on the world's roof, or down into the melt of the thaw. Or down otherways under the top of the sea.

The black haired woman kind to me, like they kind to the dead here. Ask no question.

I think all hour of all day. And night when I wait for to go sleep. Of Corgen shut in the snow and the dragon in the berg, and of that in me that is me. clove in the ice, gone out like a match. Forever and tomorrow and forever.

The black hair woman kind.

Cold Fire
Chosen by John Kaiine

Through fantasy, SF, horror, YA, contemporary, historical, gothic, lesbian/gay, plain old weird, detective, radio, television, there was only one thing Tanith couldn't write, and that was badly.

Of all her short stories, I have chosen this tale; *Cold Fire*. Her use of language here is phenomenal. ... *Shooting star is went over, like a silver angel spit.*

There is a word I am put in mind of when I read/hear this story – *Palimpsest*: a manuscript or piece of writing material on which later writing has been superimposed on effaced earlier writing. An unearthing of words written beneath sand, or in this case – Ice. A deciphering of an age-less artifact read aloud by any campfire.

It came about like most of her writing – we were eating dinner (knife, fork, pen) and a very strong but obvious idea came to mind – we talked about it and as usual she asked, "Are you writing this down?" By the following evening it was written. Tanith would always read her stuff to me and we would discuss it afterward. After she read it the first time, I asked her to read it again, it was so beautiful.

So enjoy the *voyage upways North with the berg, chipped offn sailing free. The Thin luck. The Wodka. White red and red silver in the ice. The shape, pattern. The This we tow.*

Forever and tomorrow and forever.

John Kaiine is an artist and author living on the English south coast. His work is often associated with Tanith Lee, to whom he was married.

The Crow

As by Judas Garbah

"Why in God's name did she call you that?"

"She hated me. I told you, she was always trying to lose me in the slums."

"Judas," said my companion, consideringly. His own name was Georges, a perfectly acceptable one. He could, if he wanted, link himself to whole calendars full of kings and saints. My name's fame, of course, came from the Iscariot family, all those years ago in Palestine. "Did you never think of changing it?"

"My father did. Once he'd extricated me from my mother's limp clutches."

"Oh? So tell me, what name did he give you?"

"Something ordinary and nondescript, a drab, paltry little name no one would remark or remember. What else but *Georges*?"

My companion then called me quite another sort of name. But presently got up and came to kiss me. A reasonably amiable lover, Georges. At least to begin with.

Soon after this, our lunch was finished. Despite the heat we rose and walked away from the terrace of the white-painted house, along the track of burnt earth that led up above the village.

A few miles off by train lay another country, and a surreal town constructed of stone vegetables, something magicked out of legend. We hadn't yet stirred ourselves to go there, too busy with ourselves and each other. But the village had begun to bore us. It was full, as all strange places are, of non-human aliens, acting out curious rituals and routines like automata. One is excluded, and anyway afraid to join in. One wishes one had gone there in disguise, able to speak in the proper local accent and dress and stink in the exact local way, so passing unobserved. But it's too late by then. One has been seen, heard, sniffed, catalogued. But then too, after all, everywhere is another planet until one has learned to know it, following which you finally understand you are *yourself* **the** alien, the unreal thing. Not merely uninitiated, but a monster.

Some dusty stunted olive trees cranked up the track beside us. Beyond lay emptied fields, brown vineyards already stripped of any harvest.

In a derelict poplar a cluster of black rags perched, and let out a raucous yell.

"Bloody crow," said Georges. He crouched quickly to the path, picked a shard and hurled it treeward. It seemed Georges was sullen now, not wanting this walk, but unable to decide on anything more inviting. The vegetable town, and I, the two previous attractions, must have dimmed together.

Up in the tree the crow, missed by the stone, hopped and throatily swore back at him.

Georges bent for another missile.

"Let it alone," I said, less from kindness than irritation. "It hasn't hurt you."

"I *hate* them, crows. They're bad luck." Off whirled the second stone. This one also missed. The crow however, lurched from the branches and flapped untidily off across the fields. It was old, or so it looked, its feathers dull and somehow misplaced, its chiding voice like a rusty rivet. "Go on, you devil! Get back to hell!" bellowed Georges, prancing about. He had gone mad, evidently. The red-black wine at lunch, the pale yellow spirit, the roast meat of a fresh-killed boar eaten last night, the leaky creaking house, myself, all these had driven him from his wits. My name, even, even that. How probable. Here he was, having fucked the betrayer of Christ. My God, he was doomed now all right.

At the top of the track about an hour later, we paused to regard the distant mountains, where Cathars had been hunted and tortured and burned in previous centuries. Their crime: the belief that the devil ruled the world, while God was a benign and powerless being, capable only of promising something nice after death.

Going on, appropriately perhaps, next minute a sort of wood evolved and closed in on us.

The trees were crookedly black and skeletal, strung with a bunting of dark desiccated leaves. Through their gaps the distance and its images appeared and retreated, like mosaics of vision in the henbane eaters temporary – or conclusive – blindness.

"What a spot," said Georges. "Like a witch-wood."

It was. Yet too it was the sort of terrain more normally found in northern Frankish literature. Here, it seemed a mistake. And besides, what was the type of wheedling witch who might emerge from it, to kidnap we two innocent children?

After a few more minutes of plodding on, Georges kicking at any plants on the woodland floor, the 'witch' appeared.

Georges let out a loud silly laugh. At this, the 'witch' turned all his power of attention on us. He was an old man. How old, I'm no longer certain. To me then he looked about a hundred. Very likely he was in his sixties. But in that climate, and in those days, both sexes were inclined to dry up and to desiccate, just like the distasteful leaves on the trees of the wood.

He was stooped over, very thin, all in faded black. Like the trees there, too. His hair was longish and grey. His eyes a filmy black. His nose seemed either hooked or oddly pointed. He glared at Georges, who backed away and turned to me in visible terror.

I said, in a poor facsimile of the local tongue and dialect, "Good day, señor."

At which the old bugger straightened himself, and drew from the corded belt at his waist a knife, sharp as a broken piece of glass.

Not very long ago, I was sitting on a bus in London. I do that now. Taxies are luxuries. It's Anna, sometimes Esther, who have money. Poor impoverished Judas gets by as he must, poor old dear.

But to get to the point. I found myself sitting behind another old man (I was the first) and in fact he was undoubtedly younger now than I am, in his early fifties, I'd think, maybe less.

The strangest thing instantly occurred to me. The back of his neck, the *shape* of his hair upon his head, his flat, well-made ears – these reminded me irresistibly of someone from my past, that is, my *far-off* past. A man too that I had never known well, yet somehow recalled in the most intense and – I supposed – accurate detail. For a brief while I wasn't sure whom he could be. But then gradually I remembered the witch-wood. Of course, it was none other than the 'witch' himself. Had I recorded him then, so intimately, from behind – this smooth strong neck, without what my sister Anna has sometimes referred to as the 'Westerner's Crank.' That is a neck with a dent along the back of it, which describes the passage of the spine into the skull. Among male Jews, according to Anna, this indentation is always absent. I must say I've seldom ever seen it, save in adolescent boys, and certainly the man on the bus did not have this *crank*. His neck was firm and rounded as a column, crisscrossed only two or three times by a few neat horizontal creases of gathering age.

His hair was dark, but greying. His ears, I decided, were very couth, not small but neatly aligned. Nor had the lobes elongated much.

From behind, he was curiously attractive, and he had besides an appealing odour of cleanness and health, only accentuated by some powdery hint of his age. Partly I wanted to bend forward and inhale him, the nape of his neck, his greying hair. I was – to be frank – for a second aroused, in the most absurd and romantic way.

And so I recalled the one he reminded me of.

In that second too, like an omen, the bastard turned and looked out of the bus window. Not a bad face, but not the face I had unconsciously primed myself to expect. He wasn't after all the 'witch' from the wood all those years before, and just above the Spanish border.

Georges screamed.

The knife in the old man's hand glittered perilously, a nasty slender penis of steel.

He stooped, and began to dig out, from under one of the trees, a clump of stiff spikes, each hosting a single indigo berry-like flower. These were, I thought, the flower known locally as *blue grape,* though I might well have mistranslated the name.

Georges tugged on my arm. "We must run away –"

"Rubbish. He isn't interested in us."

"He's mad – a madman."

The old man straightened up, at least as much as his bowed posture allowed. He shot us a glance from the drained ink of his eyes.

His free hand, which was brown and bony as a bunch of twigs, made a gesture to us. Surprisingly it was not obscene. He had beckoned. We were to follow him, somewhere. Yet his invitation seemed to give him no pleasure. He turned his back then, and stamped away among the trees.

I had spent so much of my life following unsuitable people about, often unavoidably, I immediately went after him.

Georges rambled to the rear, remonstrating, until I told him to be quiet. I thought he would leave me, believed he had, realized he had not, and partially forgot him. Our personal idyll certainly seemed to be reaching its end. Until quite mature, I tended always to expect advances – many excitable and usually unwanted – and in the same proportion, inevitable rejections. Anna used to say my own envisaging *caused* them to happen. Now I expect nothing very much, and seldom does anything come.

The sunlight burned holes through the trees, which were drawing together. Then a burnt sienna shadow, hot as a cauldron, filled the woody tunnel. Down which the old man quickly limped, illogically pursued by me (and Georges).

At the tunnel's end, a stark hillside opened out into a hole of air. Below, the wild land rolled off towards the mountains. On the brink, like something washed up by a wave, stood an old-fashioned house of some size and dilapidation. Before it was a yard, with chickens picking about, or squawking and flapping up on the broken wall. A line of red jars stood there, and fallen all around were bits of tiles from the roof. The old man, not once looking back, crossed the yard, cursing the chickens in thickly ornamental vernacular. He thrust at a wooden door, already ajar, and lurched on into the silent cavern of this palatial hovel.

"*Don't*," said Georges, running to catch me. "Don't be *stupid*, Judas."

I shook him off, navigated the chickens, and also walked straight into the house.

It was instantly underwater cool. So many of those places are like this inside their cave walls of stone. The space was wide, the floor also laid with tiles, also broken. A stair curved out of it, leading to the upper story. But a deeper shadow was in charge there, and the sickly honeyish smell of warmed rot drifted down.

Georges had now entered too, and fidgeted behind me.

"Those jars left outside are full of *piss*," he informed me.

"It's probably stale wine," I said. "Unless he's a tanner."

"Oh don't be such a fool, Judas. Let's get out."

The old man in black had disappeared, and there was a choice as to where he might have gone. Undoubtedly not up the stair so fast. But three closed doors marked the stained, veined empty walls, and a single archway, that gave on a steeply angled passage. Some sense of light was there.

A svelte lizard ran over the tiles on little clicking feet.

Georges now shrieked. He wasn't afraid of lizards.

I turned round, and saw a short round woman, covered up in the familiar drained black. She must have come in from outside as we had, and seemed furious rather than startled by our presence. At noisy Georges in particular she cast a baleful look, and spat directly on the floor, presumably either to ill wish him, or to render him invisible. As neither spell seemed to take, she briskly clumped across to one of the three doors, went through and slammed it.

Georges wailed as I progressed into the angled passage. Its crooked arm led out into another high-walled area, this roofless and lit by the open sky. It was a courtyard, once carefully planted, now becoming ruinous. Small stretched dead trees and roping brown vines webbed the walls, in some of them little mummified fruits, unrecognizable and black. A dry fountain had a noseless cherub pouring nothing from a shell. The floor was beaten earth, sun baked, and scattered by what looked like the torn-off wings of insects scorched in fire. He, the old man, sat on a stone bench against the wall. He too looked scorched, if not quite mummified.

He glanced at me again.

"*Ingles,*" he said.

I smiled. "No."

His eyes, tarnished mirrors. "*Judio,* he accurately decided.

I added, "*Mitad arabe.*"

He showed his tarnished teeth, a grin, or a primeval signal of rage, and lowered his gaze to the fistful of blue grape he was busy thrusting into soil.

The sun was slanting over. A ray struck suddenly down on the court, hitting the edge of the dead fountain. A strange noise sounded. I stared transfixed.

Very slowly, the wrecked cherub was splitting into two. As the two halves (perhaps like me, one half Jew, one half Arab) folded back, a peculiar black creature slid out. It most resembled a salamander, a tiny dragon from some bestiary. Huge barbs or spines ran along the ridge of its back. A pair of stiff black wings stiffly rose up, the hinged jaw undid and out came a violent hissing that made me jump. It wasn't I'd thought the thing was alive, I knew it must only be some mechanism, but the noise was vicious and I had no idea what to anticipate from it next. It showed me. Out of the clockwork jaws rushed a glittering stream of dirty fluid that splashed about the basin and over on to the earth below. The emission ceased. The mouth clapped shut with a clank.

The old man was laughing, presumably at me. I took no notice and went to inspect the salamander, now it was still. It seemed made of black iron. Had the sun shaft activated it? Maybe. Or else some trigger under the bench where the old man might tap it with his foot.

Behind me, back in the house, I could hear a murmur of voices. One seemed to belong to Georges, who had not come with me into the court.

"He is in no true danger from Marija," said the old man, in the local polyglot. I had begun to detect the more strident tones of a woman. Marija, then. She was welcome to Georges.

The old man had potted up the blue grape, and now, alarmingly, he came across the court towards me. He walked like a crab, arrogantly limping almost sideways. His face was made of brown pleatings. He leant past me and rapped the dragon on its snout. At which it raised itself all the way up on to its hind limbs, like a dog begging. It had eyes of mica that flashed. "Made of me. I am," the old man said to me, with a terrible, implacable pride, "Cuerca. Patxi Cuerca. Come, I will show you, in my room."

In the house, Georges was hysterically protesting in French, "*Non, non, madame —*"

But had he been in the court with us probably he would have clung to me, trying to anchor me to the spot, and save me from who knew what worse-than-death fate the old man was plotting.

Unimpeded, I accompanied Patxi Cuerca. And what sort of name was that, if I had even understood him? *Cuerca* – didn't that mean *crow*? Or no, perhaps not. Yet he was like a crow, like the eldritch crow in the tree the two stones missed.

The Room led directly off the court. Through the round-topped door we entered a windowless blank, where something seemed lurking in a smell of spice and mould. He struck a match and lit a lantern which hung just inside. I had not even seen it. Then, he shut us in.

A child somewhere – where? who? – had told me about the chamber in the rock where the robbers hid their treasure and Ali Baba found it. The child had not been Anna, though she was quite capable of that. But my sisters and I had never met when we were children.

The lantern, a huge ungainly object, swung for a few moments, then settled itself.

It was a filthy room, into which a rainbow had fallen, splashing everywhere, even into the webs of spiders.

With the erosion of time, which can eat at the edges even of the most visual memory, Cuerca's Room is difficult to describe, at least in logical terms. It acted instead on the optic nerve, the viscera.

What did I see first? There was a stripe of pure green that hung and blazed as if with green fire, and rippled as if with green water.

And over there, another stripe, this one orange, that did similar things. And there was a crimson square that kept immobile and glowed like the core of a hearth. And curves of deep blue and purple that twitched and waited, and a slinking manipulative yellow, like a leopard.

He didn't advise me. He let me find my own way. I began to see in greater depth.

He, it could only have been he, had painted shapes on the walls in vivid opaque colour. And over them and beside them and before them had been hung or slung, or nailed, or simply piled, objects that were of those same colours, either exactly, or in some corresponding colour-echo. A bunch of green enamel grapes suspended from a green cord before the green stripe, an emerald glass pitcher, its neck smashed off and instead surmounted with a green-painted egg, stood below, jade grapes on a plate of green faint enough to seem transparent. Against the red oblong rags of a tattered vermilion banner from some war, a red cup holding an artificial rose like blood. Where the yellow uncoiled, a piece of ochre ivory, shaped like the fretboard from some giant's guitar, nestled in a cascade of broken yellow glass. Against the blue a woman's blue shoe, its little heel caught in a sapphire comb. A cluster of dried oranges choked by necklaces of chipped amber melted into the orange circle...

The old man, Cuerca, went by me, and unceremoniously and unerringly shoved the purplish grape-flowers between the violet coloured jug without a handle and the chunk of raw amethyst beside the hoop of purple paint.

The expensive and the worthless clustered in each group as one. No hierarchies among these items, lost or abandoned, stolen or thrown out on rubbish heaps, all eventually pilfered by him, by Patxi Cuerca, brought here and each made part of its correct entity.

To outline all this is only to invite incomprehension and scorn. How could such an eccentric, *childish* medley convey anything? It did. No doubt the dark, flooded selectively by the big cracked lantern, caused some of the effect. But that hot day maybe my eyes had been thirsty. And now they drank.

The lamp flickered, some insect or cobweb dropping in there. I saw the yellow shape, crusted with its glisten, swing quietly sidelong to seize the blue shape – a woman, dancing – in its mouth. How gracefully she fell. But the red shape, stretching from oblong to square, and back to oblong, sprouted a thousand red roses, twining and knotting with their ruby thorns. The purple shape was a galleon's sail, marked with an indecipherable device. The orange shape was the ship's bodywork. They flowed together and sailed over the green shape of sea, which spangled and rioted with darting j'ade fish, spraying up the emerald foam –

But I thought of the spice and mould I could still smell, of drugs grown and harvested from the petrified courtyard, which formerly had been, had it, a Garden of Earthly Delights?

I blinked, once, twice. The shapes were static. Almost. Priceless and worthless. Unalive and living. They only shimmered a little, as the lamp had. Flicked a blue sequined eyelid or a sinuous tail. One last minuscule wave broke over the amber figurehead, who pursed her lips, before her face lapsed back to necklaces. The purple sail shivered as it flattened out against the wall. A single petal fell through the roses. Became again a broken red bead.

Quite suddenly then the old man, the magician, turned round, and the finale of his magic show was accomplished.

I saw him dazzling clear, meshed between the streams and orifices of colors. Like the salamander which had emerged from the chipped cherub, the real man now stepped free of his shell. Cuerca was young. He was straight, tall, lean, his shoulders back, his body planted as fluidly as an athlete's on his strong long legs. He wore his now inky clothes only in affectation, to match the ink-black feathers of his thick smooth hair, the jet stones of his eyes. His unlined face was handsome, nose aquiline, mouth long, slender and aloof. In his beautiful hands, articulately strong enough to rip out any beating heart, he held a burnished flame of knife. But you could not be afraid at this. You wanted all, and therefore anything and everything he might do. And he said to me, in perfect, only-slightly accented French (while the light glinted on his white teeth), "Go along now. Get out. You've seen. Go and rescue\your friend from Marija. *Remember*. I am Patxi Cuerca. Never *forget* you have seen me, and this room."

And then, weightless and careless, as if casting a paper, he tossed the knife over my head. It thunked into some soft place in the wall behind me.

Disarranged by its motion, the lamplight jumped again, the rainbow leapt, and all its pieces, with the shadow, came down on him, and covered him up. He was old once more, dirty and crippled, and crazy. So I turned and went out, and in the courtyard the dragon too had slid back into its stony carapace. The liquid it had spat was already dry.

Although I rescued him from Marija, Georges did not forgive me. She had been telling him he was her long lost son, it seemed, and threatening him with the rich (seventeen olive trees) betrothed he had deserted, telling him she would bring him wine and he must drink it.

Perhaps he *was* her son. After all, I had seen the Room, and I had seen Cuerca grow young again, and then old again. Metamorphosis riddled the place.

No doubt Cuerca's youth was only a trick of the light, as they say. Or drugs burning. Or the dazzling after-images of all the colours sprawled about in there.

Around thirteen years later – also long ago now – I saw a photograph of him as a young man, in a book to do with the art of that torrid southern region. For of course he had been an artist of repute, when young. Abstract paintings, sculptures and mechanical toys not for children, peculiar gardens even, were credited to his invention. He did, in the picture, look remarkably like what I'd glimpsed, or imagined, standing among his last creation, his Room. (The book did not mention, or did not know about, the Room.) But probably, even by the time I opened the book and saw him there, he was himself dead.

As Georges and I tramped back to our rented house in the ash of the afternoon, he swore at me and I at him. Any liking was gone, and any tenderness. Which wouldn't, naturally, prevent an orgy of famished coupling for another two days and three nights.

When we passed below the poplar tree, the crow had returned there. It sat far up, raising its dishevelled head to the over-gilded sky and rasping out a succession of caws.

Georges at once transferred his vitriol, or some of it, to the crow. "If I had a gun I'd shoot it!" And then to me, "I'd shoot you too, you damned Semite bugger."

But I only saw Cuerca's knife as if skimmed over my head; *Remember me. Remember me.*

Georges, immune to his own repetitions, was scrabbling for another stone. I pushed him hard so he fell flat on the track. When he got up, he followed me in rebellious docility.

"Bloody crow," he muttered. "Crow-crow-crow. Why do you want to protect it? What use is it? It's old and diseased and worthless. It's nothing."

The crow lifted itself out of the quills of the poplar. It spread its wings and sprang into the sky.

"Look, Georges," I said. "Do you see? It can fly."

From a fragmentary MS by Judas Garbah, collated and adapted by Anna Garber, his sister.

The Crow
Chosen by Craig Gidney

I met Tanith Lee only once, at Eastercon in 2008. But by then we had already had a long correspondence via email and post. When we met in person, it was like greeting an old friend.

I believe it was on a Sunday morning during that convention that Tanith told me about Judas, the brother of Esther Garber, the Jewish lesbian writer she channelled (see *Fatal Women: The Esther Garber Novellas*). Judas, she told me over a pint of cider she'd bought me, was Esther's half-brother. He was gay and lived in Egypt, and, like Esther, transmitted fiction to Tanith via spiritual channels. (By the way, Tanith was well aware of how this sounded and had a certain gallows humour about the process).

A year or less later, the plans to publish a follow up to *Fatal Women* fell through. At the time, I was volunteering for Lethe Press, who had published my debut, *Sea, Swallow Me and Other Stories*. I managed to broker a publication deal for the new collection, entitled *Disturbed By Her Song*, which was to feature short fiction by both the Garbers. "The Crow" is Judas Garbah's most Tanith-like piece in that collection, full of the menacing beautiful atmosphere she was a master at creating.

Craig Laurance Gidney is the author of the collections Sea, Swallow Me & Other Stories *(Lethe Press, 2008),* Skin Deep Magic *(Rebel Satori Press, 2014), the Young Adult novel* Bereft *(Tiny Satchel Press, 2013) and* The Nectar of Nightmares *(Dim Shores, 2015). He lives in his native Washington, DC. Website: craiglaurancegidney.com.*

White as Sin, Now

The initial notion behind this last novella was to form something like a pack of cards, brightly coloured sections that could almost be pulled out at random, and reshuffled in any order. Pretty soon, though, the story-line asserted itself, and drilled the pack into an ordered regiment.

Many of my obsessions have crowded into it, including queens and dwarfs, wolves and virgins and priests, deep snows, flowery meadows, ruins. The omnipresent forest appears again, also, in person, and in two distinct guises.

A last excursion then, into the wood.

The Dwarf (the Red Queen)

The dwarf Heracty balances on the rim of a frozen fountain, drawing pictures with his nails in the ice. His handsome face is set into the frame of a great leonine head applicable to a muscular man six feet tall. Heracty's form is that of an elf. But he has, too, an elfs eyes, long, aslant, and crystal-green.

Engaged on the scales of a mermaid, Heracty pauses, listening. His hearing is so acute, his ears sometimes hear noises that do not exist. He must decide now whether this sound physically belongs to the world, is a phantom, or a memory. Presently Heracty becomes sure that two narrow feet in shoes are descending a flight of cold stones.

He turns a little, looking sideways from his slanting eyes.

Held high in an archway over the stair are towers resembling a crown of thorns, on a half-disc of twilight. From that point, the Upper Palace drops like a cliff into a riverbed.

And from those heights she has again come down.

It is always at this hour, just as the sun goes away. In the ghostly 'tweentime, when all pale things pulse and stare . . . the white beasts of the fountain, the roses of snow across the gardens.

When she comes out suddenly from the arch at the bottom of the stair, she also is glimmering as if luminous.

She only looks straight ahead, beyond the fountain and the winter lawn, to a second arch, a second falling staircase. She does not see Heracty, has never seen him there, as she passes by like a sleepwalker.

The wide eyes of the Queen are so astute, Heracty knows, she sometimes glimpses things that do not exist.

As before, he slides from the fountain's rim, and silently follows her.

They then descend twenty flights of steps one after another, and the nineteen terraces between.

The Dwarf's First Interview with His Grandmother

On a bitter morning in spring, mother and son went to visit the grandmother in her marble house.

The woman was hardly more than thirty-five years of age, but with old, terrible, unhuman, alligator eyes.

To begin with she did not upbraid Heracty's mother, but only questioned her on domestic matters. The boy sat motionless and dumb on the rugs. He was very much aware of himself and of his mother's tense and trembling awareness of him. But his grandmother, by a slight flexing of her colossal will, had shut him out, so that he was not in the chamber at all. Until finally:

'It's a curse that struck you,' announced the grandmother to her daughter. 'I don't begin to guess who you wronged, to incur it. If I had my way, such things would be smothered as soon as their nature was evident.' Every syllable referred, of course, to Heracty.

The mother whispered, as she had done on many occasions, 'His father was normal. Straight, well-made –'

'Yes, yes,' said the grandmother, 'and between you, you managed this. A monster.' Now she bent her awful glance on the boy. 'I have come to a decision,' said Heracty's grandmother. His mother waited in abjection, and he in fear. 'The Prince collects freaks. He has got into his possession, so I hear, a two-headed dog, a unicorn, a gulon. And besides, six of *this* kind, half-men – though a pair are reckoned to be females, so I'm told.'

'You mean my son is to go up into the court of the Prince?' asked Heracty's mother, astonished.

'No. Into the Prince's menagerie.'

The Hunter (the Young Girl)

While the vampire lies sleeping, its soul, or what passes for it, roams the night, dreaming it is a wolf.

The season is winter, therefore snow covers the forests, hills and plains, and far away the mountains blackly glow upon a blacker sky where all the stars are out. Between the black and the white, the black wolf runs.

Presently there is a small stone house on the dark, with one lit pane.

The wolf runs among the fir trees. He raises himself up, something now between man and creature. His eyes of colourless mercury meet the image of a poor room, where a girl sits sewing by the hearth.

The wolf-soul does not see a girl. What it sees is a stream of living holy light far brighter than the dying wood on the fire, and an icon burning in it, as if in a cathedral window. There is a white hand containing red blood, plying the silver needle, a bending throat like the stem of a goblet of glass.

She puts her hair back from her cheek, and in that moment hears a noise outside, which is like the murmur of the trees, internalised, the rhythm of the sea in a shell.

Rising, the girl leaves her task. She has been stitching an altar-cloth for the church in the valley. But her eyes and hands, her shoulders, her very brain, are tired now. It is a relief for her to walk to the window of the room, to look out.

There is no moon. The forest stands against the door, and the wall of the dark. She beholds her own face reflected on the pane, transparent as a spirit. The strange noise comes again.

The girl lifts the latch of the door, and going out on the snow which so far is unmarked, prints it with the signature of her own bare feet. Forgotten, the door is left open behind her.

She thinks she sees for an instant a tall male figure against the fir trees, but it has the head of a wolf. Then there is also a pale-faced man, and two eyes of iron.

She moves forward, leaving her last message on the snow.

And abruptly the darkness engulfs her. She vanishes. Without a cry, she is gone for ever.

The Red Queen (the Lost Child)

Innocin, the Queen, has become conscious only gradually that something follows her. At first, she believes it to be a cat, then, later, a child. But the presence is subtly more imminent. Crossing through the deep shadows of pillared gullies, the Lower Palace, she realises that what is mysteriously on her track is nothing less – or more – than one of her stepson's pet dwarfs.

She wonders if the Prince himself has sent this spy. But surmise fades. Such matters have no interest.

In the shadows, the blood-red mantle of the Queen, limned with white ermine, her hair like red-bronze surrounding an ivory face, are elements of a female.

She enters a long corridor with a low ceiling, intricately carved. For all the hundreds of times she has traversed this thoroughfare, Innocin has never properly regarded the caving. She does not know what it represents although she has seen it over and over.

The was a day when she looked into her mirror. The light cut sharply as broken porcelain against one side of her face. She saw that she had lost her youth. It was then that she thought of a young girl, dressed in purest palest white, the sin of her husband, the dead King. Somewhere within the enormous labyrinth of the Palace, between the topmost towers and the deepest basements, the girl must have secreted herself. The afternoon had passed, and the sun gone down. But that sunset the Queen became, like a star, certain of her course.

She descended then the stairways to the terrace with the lawn and the great fountain. It had been autumn still, and sallow leaves lay adrift on the water of the basin.

Nothing disturbed the preoccupation of Innocin. She had crossed the terrace of the lawn and progressed down twenty further flights. She searched night after night, among decayed architecture, and neglected rooms, for the unmistakable, beautiful young girl.

So far, she has not found her.

Sometimes there is a glimpse or a clue – the white flicker of a skirt between two columns, a sigh that circles an upper gallery where no one seems to be and, on ascending, where no one is. Or a rose moulded from snow, poised in a hollow vase of ice.

The Hunter's Prey (the Dark Priest)

As a small child she had played about the cottage, a darling of the entire family. The truth was, the child did not belong to them at all. At midnight once, going out to make water, the man of the house had found an infant huddled in his doorway. It was late in summer, the nights not yet cold, but the child shivered and moaned. Conversely, although she could form noises, she had never apparently been taught human language. She could tell them nothing.

The woman had lost her baby some months before. This seemed the returns of heaven. Her husband was a woodcutter, quite prosperous, having three men in his employ, besides two strapping sons.

The household took in the girl-child, and gave her a village name.

Her origins she forgot instantly, except sometimes in nervous dreams. Then the woman would comfort her. 'Here is your mother,' the woman would confide, 'you're safe, my baby.' The man and the two boys brought her dolls and baubles from the town. Her childhood was happy and carefree.

However, about nine years old, by some arcane law, she had become a woman, and all was changed. She had work to do at which first she laboured diligently. But, as there was never respite when she grew bored or exhausted, her duties soon turned to drudgery. It did not occur to any of them, perhaps she had been born for something else.

While years sprang in flowers on the turf beyond the house, or fell in sculpted cones from the branches of the fir trees, the woodcutter's daughter also unremembered she had ever been a happy, carefree child.

She was the maidservant of her father and two brothers, and her mother's nurse, for the woman waxed sickly. The evening before the girl's fourteenth birthday – that is, the night-day of her discovery in the door of the stone house – her stepmother died.

'She shan't marry now,' said neighbours, down the valley in the village street. 'She must tend her own. She's got men enough to care for.'

A new priest had taken up his office at the church not long before. He was tall and slender, with a broad low brow, and his hair – untonsured, for this was a wild place – was black as the wing of a crow.

The young girl, seeing him stand above the coffin of her step-mother's corpse, dreamed a waking dream, which that night was translated. She believed she was a nun, gowned and coifed in snowy white. She served a dim altar where a tall crucifix gleamed, a man's pale body hammered on to it.

She would go to church every holy day, and often visited her stepmother's grave. She never approached the priest directly, but when he requested of his flock various attentions to the church, the young girl, though burdened by duties to home and kindred, gave her service.

The other women free to do so were mostly old, or else fat, sullen widows. The young girl felt herself shine strangely among them, a clear lily in withered reeds.

That was a terrible winter for wolves. They preyed on the sheepfolds and the byres, and several children were taken, or so it was supposed. One lean black wolf was seen frequently, but though the men scoured the forests round about, and laid snares, this animal was never trapped or killed.

The Dark Priest (the Wolfshead)

The priest elevates the Host, an offering and invitation to God. It is a moment of supreme sanctity, of supreme savagery even. Less substantially, he senses the consciousness of those persons who fill up the building, trailing from his lifted hands. A vast light, without tint or radiance, enspheres the church. And he is the arrow-head of the flight, fired out toward the celestial target of the omnipresent, awful, eternal, invisible, and actual, centre of all things. A ray of the sinking sun, unearthly and lemon-green, pierces through the window, penetrates the body of the priest – And at that instant the door of the church crashes wide.

The priest's awareness is smashed in pieces.

He turns, slowly lowering the sacred element. His black eyes give to him a scene of the sudden and the inappropriate. Whatever it may be proved to be – the onslaught of a local calamity, death, plague, or war, this interruption is to him only an unforgivable sacrilege.

A body of men stands in the nave, staring from side to side, in their hands some makeshift weapons. They are the inhabitants of outlying parts. They seldom enter the village save to get their ration of beer. Now it is not beer they want. The woodcutter's second son thrusts forward. He bellows insanely into the church: 'Out! Out! Demon! Out!' And swings up his axe.

'The Devil's hiding in your flock, shepherd,' says another man roughly, to the priest. 'It went by night and murdered his sister.'

The congregation starts to its feet, becomes a beast of many limbs and eyes and voices. The church is no longer a special place. The priest does not remonstrate. He sets down the precious Host, and feels keenly how it goes back into dust. The last of the vivid sunset is perishing round the feet of trampling peasants. There is nothing to be done, or said.

Arrogantly the priest watches from his altar as the mob, not finding after all the one suspected, blunders forth on to the greenly embered snow, bolts and plunges up an incline, collides with darkness at the entry of a hovel near the village cess-pit. Great blows shake the flimsy hut. Even from the church-door the priest hears them. He is very cold.

Shortly, a half-wit man who subsists in the hovel, the tender of the midden, is brought out on to the snow. The villagers search him, looking for marks of the Devil, tufts of feral hair, claws, certain lupine deformities of jaw, teeth and forehead. Presumably they uncover them all. While this goes on, the half-wit smiles courteously, and moves himself this way and that, in order to be helpful.

Next, still smiling and assisting them, he goes up the hill with the men, and the brother of the young girl – fifteen years of age, who, the night before, was found lying among the fir trees by her father's cottage, her throat torn open like a winter rose.

The crowd vanishes over the hill. Presently a scream sounds, shrill and sheer from the forest's edge above.

The priest does not make any gesture, except that, going back into the empty church, now closed already by shadow, he shuts and bars God's door.

Heracty's Second Interview with His Grandmother

Having reached the age of sixteen Heracty, the Prince's seventh dwarf, decided once again to visit his grandmother. This time he imagined he could do so on his own terms.

He dressed in a suit of clothes of wan green satin, a mulberry-red cloak, and wore in his ear a large pearl. He rode a most charming dappled pony, another of the Prince's gifts, and took with him for escort his little page not yet eight years old. Over the saddle of the pony, too, had been placed a couple of embroidered bags containing delicacies.

The gardens of the enormous eccentric Palace were equally vast and varied. Downhill lay the grandmother's marble box, a house given her decades before by an admirer (Heracty's unintentional grandfather), when she frequented the court. To get there first Heracty, the pony and page, must navigate an ornamental river. Then came a number of high floral steppes. Next they entered a mock forest, densely planted with pine, fir, rhododendron and cedar trees. Even at noon it was dusk in this forest, and here and there clockwork animals prowled and howled. At the turn of the track, a grey wolf pounced out on them, and the small page had hysterics.

'Hush,' said Heracty, who had been in the forest before. And he threw the clockwork wolf a peach from the bags, which it greedily and realistically ate, trotting *off* afterwards to bury the stone.

Beyond the forest lay an acre or two of modest meadows, and here the grandmother had her abode. As they got on to the path, the dwarf could see, across the shoulder of the landscape, the blurred valleys below where his mother had lived. But by this time she was dead.

The grandmother of Heracty was now not much over forty. Her complexion was nearly flawless as a girl's, her eyes had advanced from alligator to dragon.

'Well,' she said, looking her grandson over, satin, pearl, pony, page, and bags.

Heracty had the page distribute his presents. The grandmother fingered some of them and set them aside. The food and flasks of fine wine caused her short fits of harsh laughter.

'What a splendid fellow!' she jeered.

Heracty sat down, although, in her chairs, his feet hung in limbo far above the rugs.

'You did me a good turn, Granny,' said the dwarf, 'when you persuaded my mamma to send me into the Prince's service.'

'My idea was merely to get you out of the way and out of my sight.'

'Yet here I am again. What a sad nuisance.'

'Your tongue,' she said, 'has grown longer, if nothing else of you has. Or is it,' she amended, 'true? That which is said of the loins of your sort.'

The dwarf blushed, could not help it. But he had been well seasoned at the court, and he replied, 'Those few among the Prince's eldest servants who remember you always remark you had less manners than a pig. Naturally, I defend you, and only confess the sin of lying on holy days.'

The grandmother took one candied nut from the gifts and bit it in two. She then dropped both bites in the fireplace.

'What do you want, monster?'

'Tell me,' said Heracty immediately, 'about Innocin, the Red Queen.'

'When you hear so many remarks, how is it you never heard that?'

Heracty sat and waited. He made his face quite blank and his elf's body immobile. At last, the grandmother shifted.

'She was a slut in the kitchen, or something of that kind. He saw her, raised her, bedded her, became besotted, so married her. She's now Queen, but she was his second wife. The first died. When the King died himself, and his lechery with him, the Prince took power. It remains to be seen if he will ever get himself properly recognised, become King like his father. But for her, she's gone mad. So she wanders about, looking for a vanished daughter she had by the King.'

'A lost child?' said Heracty. He considered. 'Did it die at birth? Was the matter hidden?'

'How should I tell you?' asked the grandmother, 'What do I know?'

'Granny,' said the dwarf, 'in the basket of sugar-plums – I understand you're fond of them – is one sweet containing a potent and unpleasing purgative. Without harming you, it will cause you extreme discomfort.'

'Nasty little beast,' said his grandmother, bright-eyed. 'I'll eat none of them.'

'What a waste, and your favourites, too. The particular plum,' he added, 'is easy to identify, once I describe it.'

'Perhaps you are lying again. And perhaps any way, you'd indicate the wrong plum.'

'Perhaps. Or not.'

They sat then in silence some minutes, the dwarf a small elegant statue, she a lizard in a girl's skin.

Finally she said this:

'In the position I had at court, I learned that the Queen was to be thought of as barren. But it was not possibly the case. One infant, a girl, had certainly been born, but a portent made the Queen afraid of it, or her own shame at her low beginnings and bad blood. She sent it away into the forests, to be brought up among ignorant strangers.'

The dwarf sighed. 'Her lost child is,' he murmured, 'her own youth.' Granny threw all the sugar-plums in the fire.

The Menagerie (the Court)

Indeed, they live close to the Prince's menagerie. On calm nights, when the music from the Upper Palace is not too lively, they may hear the gulon catawaul and screech at the full moon, or the unicorn clicketing up and down on its gemmed hoofs, though the dog of two heads is generally reticent.

The dwarfs had been given their own town at the foot of the Palace. Each house is a doll's mansion, equipped with furnishings all the proper size, and with intelligent child servants always replaced in their tenth year. Rose gardens and knot gardens and gardens of topiary and water gardens, and so forth, make wondrous chessboard squares around the mansions. Everything is enclosed by a stout wall, whose gates are guarded at night by specially bred miniature mastiffs, who, introduced to the dwarfs as puppies, threaten to maul anyone who disturbs them. Only the prince himself, and his selected courtiers, can invade the sanctum whenever desired. But that is not often.

Heracty quickly became accustomed to the dwarfs' estate. He grasped how they were patronised, yet simultaneously, how could he dislike anything that so suited, and that rendered him so comfortable.

The four fellow male dwarfs were comely and alert, two with high boyish voices which, in one case, flowed out into a clear alto instrument for song, seemingly much prized by the Prince. The two dwarfesses were remarkable for their charms and accomplishments, one blonde, one dusky. The latter had wed her dwarf suitor – the wedding had been a fête at the Palace; the Prince gave the bride away – and it was said the union produced a child. But as the baby evinced every sign of growing up into an ordinary woman, it too was taken off, as a potential cause of future grief to the parents.

Heracty, sent among the dwarf community when it was established, expanding it into an uneven number: seven, though never made unwelcome, stayed an outsider. He became instead a student of men, the other species. When summoned to delight the Prince by his presence, handsomeness and wit, Heracty on his side narrowly observed everyone about him. He definitely supposed that he came of another race, human, but unadulterated. What he saw of fully formed human behaviour confirmed this opinion.

It was at a banquet that, initially, Heracty beheld the Red Queen, the dead King's widow.

She entered late, and the Prince rose graciously, and with ill- concealed boredom, to greet her. Seating herself, she stared about as if not knowing where she was, thinking it a dream. Occasionally she would take up some morsel from her plate, or begin to lift her goblet – but sustenance never reached her mouth, for obviously she forgot its purpose half-way. She wore a gown the shade of dying autumn, not a single jewel.

The Prince, comma demanding antics constantly that evening from Heracty, interrupted the dwarf's study a hundred times. Courteous and wise, Heracty never once displayed his annoyance.

The Queen left the feast before midnight. Heracty was not permitted to leave until the men lay drunken in their chairs, or over the tables.

When the dawn breaks, Heracty frequently goes into the menagerie. Adjacent to the dwarfs' enclosure, it is simple of access.

More often than not, the unicorn falls asleep at dawn, its muzzle laid on its flank, the curving horn, more swarthy than its hide, like the sinking crescent of the moon. The two-headed dog sits sadly, one head deep in thought and the other slumbering with the tongue hanging out.

But the gulon stalks its prettified pen, disdaining the luxury of its kennel. A fox-cat, it now looks most feline, but next second mostly canine, having strong features of both types. It is the colour of Queen Innocin's banquet gown, and her hair, and Heracty has been told that combings of its long damascened fur are sometimes woven to trim her mantles.

The eyes of the gulon are rather like Heracty's own, but lack any trace of courtly politeness or civilisation.

The gulon has been known to savage its keepers, one of whom lost an arm as a result. It is dissatisfied with its life and does not appreciate its uniqueness.

Heracty is wondering if Innocin the Queen has ever looked on the gulon.

When he witnessed her descent through the palace, sensed the wild, inane search, it fitted her like a costly necklace. It is a perfection. He could do no other thing.

He values it in her.

The Lost Child (the Palace)

The girl Idrel wakes like an early crocus.

She lifts her head and all about her lies the snow. Snow is her coverlet in a four-poster bed of ice. Slight wonder she dreamed she lay in coffin, but the coffin was of glass . . .

The girl gets to her feet. She does not feel the cold, only a deep desire to lie down again and sleep again – and this she believes is to be resisted. She is garbed only in a shift, and not, she guesses, her own. It covers her decently from neck to foot and even drags a little behind her as she walks. But for a shield against the winter it is useless. However, she is under protection. Feels it must be so. All the ways of the forest look alike to her. She consents to walk forward, in the direction she faced on walking, rising.

A stealthy umbra permeates the wood, it might be any time of day, though not of night. The snow is packed very hard and does not take an impression of the bare souls of Idrel. She expects wild animals lair among the firs and cedars, and perhaps will run out at her. Twiceshe catches a glimpse of some sinuous thing, the colour itself of the forest dusk – but this does not approach.

Sometimes a branch or bough cracks under the snow's weight, startling, like a whiplash. There are no other sounds but for the glacial ringing of silence itself,

How long the girl walks, in distance or time, she is unsure. But suddenly, the trees have thinned, and there ahead is a thick sky of grey nacre, and the terraces of a snow-hill cut into it.

Ghostly winds run on the hill, and blow the snow like white steam along the ground. Idrel climbs with three winds taking up her hair and throwing it to each other, and then down, clutching at her ankles, slapping her cheeks, and her eyes fill with slow tears. Then, at the summit, she discovers an odd road made all of solid ice.

Idrel steps on to the road of ice. Dimly, a reflection tapers from under her feet, and also there are objects caught there, mostly abstractions, though she begins to fancy statuary or frozen people are trapped in the glass coffin of it.

In a brief while, she perceives herself to have come in, almost unawares of the sameness of the snow, to a colossal ruin, maybe of a city. Tiles and parts of walls, doorways, roof-beams, arches, the skeletons of windows, have stolen round her, and high above a briary of knife-like of cruel towers hangs abandoned in heaven.

The sight of this abnormal edifice, or what there is left of it, causes Idrel, lost and alone, to question for the first time where she has come from, and who she is, and why she has travelled to such a place.

After an appreciable time, she mutters aloud, 'I shall remember, soon.'

And then she goes on, walking through the eroded architecture, down into dark avenues where pillars have collapsed and become static rollers of snow, and up stairways innumerable to her. And on her journey she passes only once something which touches her poignantly. This is an enormous flower, proportionally of stone but mostly of opaque, bluish ice. The shape of the flower is a rose, but this the lost girl fails to ascertain. Perhaps she never saw a rose before, in whatever spot she has come from.

At last – the sky is stained with a more foreboding twilight – the girl Idrel reaches a wide platform against a door which seems to be of iron. Icicles drip down it, with edges that are like razors. She is afraid to put her hand to the door.

She sits before it. Night now must find her here.

The desire to sleep returns, and there in the leaden sunset she shuts her eyes and knows no more.

The King (the Queen's First Sin)

It was not true, she had not been a slut of the kitchen, not even a scullery maid, Innocin – but neither had she been called, then, Innocin.

On a day in late spring, returning from a hunt, the King had passed across the rough meadows below the Palace. A few good houses stood about, with formal small gardens, and orchards. But on the meadowland the first poppies were blooming, and a girl was there, plucking them like the strings of the day-harp, gathering armfuls of fire. Her hair was like a soft fire, also, but not much in evidence, scraped back from her yellow-white face and confined in a long rat's tail of braid.

She was dressed like a servant and doubtless that was what she was.

The King, having glanced at her – attention caught by the blot of red among the redness of the poppies – rode on. Half a mile further, he reined in. He called someone, his steward, or some aristocratic companion. 'I spied a damsel in that last field. Have her got.'

This King had whims, now and then, and his court was not unaccustomed to them. An envoy was sent – but the girl had vanished from the meadow, perhaps frightened away by her vision of loud horsemen and the carcasses of deer.

He went back behind the great iron doors of his house, the King. He brooded. He was used to getting that which he chose to want. A dark man, big and bear-like, he began to think of delicate things, waist-chains of slender gold, satin stockings, tortoise-shell combs which, taken forth, let fall a light flood of hair . . .

Another whim came over him, and inside two days he had had made a slim dress of poppy-red velvet, and red-gold slippers with buckles printed by rubies. He had judged her measures; for the footwear, if it did not fit, he supposed she would make the best of things, the shoes being what they were.

He had the garments transported around the peripheries of the Palace, and out to the marble houses on the meadows. He did not go so far as to accompany the party in disguise. His only instruction was: 'Red hair, white face. And if these bits go on to her, then you have the proper animal.'

But the hunt did not turn up anything of the right looks, let alone the correct build to fill garments and slippers.

The King began to fret. He was not used to this, to not getting his way.

They said afterwards the management of temporal affairs suffered at that time, but in fact, by now, the King was no longer necessary in the manner of a ruler. The direction of such lands as were postulated to be his was under the sway of councils, assemblies and ministers. What matter if a scatter of minor papers went unsigned, or a town or two was spared a royal progress?

Months presented themselves and were spent.

Came a morning, sportively pretending to simplicity the King went out, on foot, with ten men and some dogs. He had almost forgotten the girl among the poppies, she was fading from him as the flowers had already had the grace to do. He would refer to how he had been cheated, occasionally, since he had stubbornly retained his dissatisfaction, the whiff of baulked romance, lose his temper then, or frown and call for music. This daybreak, it was quite out of his head.

There was a mist, mild and sweet, and in the mist suddenly he saw the girl, walking along, russet-cloaked, a basket on her arm.

She was going towards the ornamental woods out of which, further down, the King and his company had just emerged. In the mist, she seemed not to note eleven hunters and seven dogs. Perhaps her eyesight was poor, as others came later to believe.

Because she was slipping away into the shadows of the forest, the King motioned his men to silent stasis. He alone went back into the wood after her.

She had committed a kind of heresy against him. She had kept him waiting, and worse, vexed. He felt an entitlement now to do what he liked, although he would have done what he liked in any event.

The Blonde Dwarfess (the Beast in the Wood)

Heracty has been told that the flaxen dwarfess once had an adventure in the mock forest below the Palace.

He does not know whether to credit this. She herself has never told him anything of it, though she is far from reticent.

Apparently, she had gone down the floral steppes, and wandered, astray, among the trees. She was gathering flowers, and carried a basket. But she wore courtly finery, and a scarlet snood sewn with brilliants, a gift of the Prince's. No one had warned her of the clockwork animals in the forest. Or, if they ever had, she misunderstood. She had left her maid, a canny brat of six years, behind.

When something howled, the dwarfess took the noise for that of one of the Prince's hounds, which were sometimes exercised in a large enclosure at the other side of the steppes. It was a still afternoon, and sounds might travel.

Then, as she bent towards a clump of pale hyacinths, the dwarfess saw, in the midst of a bush, two narrow, gleaming and carnivorous eyes.

Next moment, a grey wolf slunk from the thicket.

The dwarfess curtsied to the wolf. Though she had not been informed, or had unremembered, clockwork, the etiquette of the Palace was by now ingrained in her. And at her curtsy, indeed, the wolf smiled, and prancing forward, capered all about her with expressions of amiability, so she was not in the least alarmed at it.

Presently the two walked on together. The wolf was helpful, nosing out for her absolute treasuries of flowers, aiding her in uprooting them. The dwarfess became fond of the smiling wolf, and on impulse placed her hand on his grey head.

No sooner had she done so than the wolf sprang and dashed her full-length on the ground. That done, it jumped on her, muddying her skirts and tearing them with its claws. It gave off bear-like roars, drooled and licked her, and sometimes bit her with excitement. Though these toothings were no more dangerous than the nips of an eager puppy, the lady in her terror imagined herself about to be devoured, eaten alive. She fainted.

On reviving, she found the wolf stretched heavily across her, using her pliant body and hair for a couch, fast asleep or certainly in the attitude of one grossly sleeping.

Not until the wolf awoke did she dare to stir. To her amazed relief, at her first cautious movement the beast quickly leapt away from her and darted into the forest.

The dwarfess, weeping, gathered up her slobbered skirts, and abandoning the spilled, crushed flowers, limped home.

At length, the gruesome tale was whispered to her consoeur, who pertly replied, 'Why, you should have thrown the brute an apple or a sweetmeat. That's all it wants.'

But the blonde dwarfess wished aloud, or so it was reported, that men might go and axe down the dreadful wood.

The Priest's Darkness (the Beauty)

Comfortless, the vampire dreams, while that which passes for its soul, a beast, lies snarling on the snow, pinned by hafts and staves. The cold is like a wound, felt all through the tangled blackness of the pelt, through to the scald of the blood, and snow burns on the lashes of the fiery eyes, which are not composed of pure ferocity but of questions, and lit by bewildered distress and pain. It cannot comprehend, this thing, why it has been pursued, brought down, is tortured now, solely for being, for living as what it is.

The speech of the hunters is a blur of successful hatred and successful fear. They are recalling an idiot, tender of a midden, whom in error they did to death for these crimes. Yet here is the culprit, caught in the act, the milk-white lamb in its jaws –

'But the other shape –!' one cries out now, frantic.

'That perishes too. See – what's done here, we'll go back and search the houses to find.'

'Somewhere the devil will be weltered in his own blood.'

They laugh. It is a laugh of utter fright.

And the black wolf writhes, grinning, also afraid.

Until it beholds an axe, glinting silver in the torchlight, the rays struck upward from the fevered snow, an axe of silver iron raised over all their heads.

161

The axe flashes and crashes down.

He experiences the impact, the *blow,* and starts up choking, blind and maddened, calling out to God, in the turmoil of a hard, thin bed.

But he is not killed, can breathe and see. And if he shouted aloud, beyond the walls his frozen village lies submissive enough, under the sterile quarter moon.

He has had this dream before, the priest. This dream, others. Once he would dream always that he led them, his flock, over the cliff of night into a valley of shadow, and there, as they entered the defile, he, the shepherd, seized them and sank his fangs into their throats. His dark priestly robe is a black pelt. He puts it on. Beware of me, he whispers, setting the wafer between their lips, giving them their sip of God's blood, as he aches for the beauty of their wine. He stalks them and can pull them down with pitiable ease. He has had so many. Is it only hundreds?

Now he sobs, kneeling before the window, which has no glass, only a broken shutter. There are no riches here. Only the love of God and the blessing of the Devil.

What is to be done?

He looks round wildly, but there is nothing to hand. Even the razor for shaving is blunt in its dish.

Besides, it is just an evil dream. Of course, he is so tired. This terrible place, when he had once thought of lofty cathedrals, of purity, dedication, and bliss.

The priest lies down again on the bony bed. He stares with open eyes at the beams in the roof, and disciplines himself to think of . . . beauty.

Now he stares with open, inner eyes. He sees an altar-cloth, a white dove ascending on gold; this becomes a window in a church which touches the sky. But then it is a white girl painted against flames, and in her hands is a poisoned apple, like red flesh, which she throws to him. There is the choice, to catch the apple, to allow it to go by. If it does so, another will catch it. The apple fills his hand. He senses its fragrance. He longs to shut his inner eyes, but to do so must open again the outer ones. The moon is in the window now. His lids are wet. He is ashamed.

Beauty in the Palace (the Vampire's Dream)

Somehow, perhaps by magic, the door has been opened. Icicles lie around Idrel on her platform. Within the doorway, a stair mounts into darkness. This is not inviting, yet seemingly it is an invitation, as sure as if a dark figure waited at the darkness' heart, calmly beckoning. Getting to her feet, the girl enters the doorway and climbs the stair.

The ruin is intent with strangeness, and the loud silence of snow and settled night.

Far beneath, in the blue ice-rose of a paralysed fountain, a mermaid had been trapped. Or, possibly, only drawn there with a dagger. And here, all at once, there are candelabra, with snow or wax heaped down their stems, but in their cups flames are beginning to burn up, like blossoms breaking too soon.

And then Idrel emerges high on the mountain of the wrecked enormous edifice, among its circlet of thorny towers. She is in a great hall, which has no roof and into which the towers seem to be gazing from huge eyes of dimly tinted glass. On the roofless walls hang lamps. As Idrel looks at them, they are being ignited, two or three at a time, by invisible tapers carried in unseen hands.

A cavern of pillared hearth has already flowered into fire. Instinctively, the young girl goes to it and stretches out her arms, flexes her fingers. The fire gives off heat. It warms her. It shows the crimson under her skin. Behind a curtain she finds a little closed chamber of some opulence, nested there in the ruin, and prepared for her, obviously for her.

A bath stands on silver feet, and from it rises scented steam, and a silver-framed table of vanities, mirrors, cosmetics, curling-tongs, and with jewellery littered about as if a princess had only just got up from it. Tall chests will offer her clothing. The unseen invisibles are pulling wide all the drawers and doors and trays, to demonstrate. While under its canopy, a bed has been aired with hot stones. It is a broad couch, the virgin notices, a marriage-bed, such as her foster parents shared. She senses, without nervousness or embarrassment, that someone may be watching her.

Idrel allows the sprites of the ruin to remove the shift of her village burial, steps into the soothing bath, and is laved so gently with unguents and water she cannot for an instant misinterpret the supernatural familiarities as anything human. She is made, and becomes, a beauty.

As she eats the dainty supper they have laid for her, the girl accepts the solution of her prior death, for this must be heaven and she is receiving her reward. As to the means of death, she cannot conjure any.

She inhabited one world, and now is here. She does not insult her condition by thinking she is dreaming. Perhaps, however, she is part of the dream of another.

That in mind, she ponders her pale hand with its new cuff of black, over both of which a coil of her hair has poured itself, in the firelight hectically coloured. A dramatic concoction for herself or any watcher: Black as ebony, red as blood, white as snow.

The Queen's Second Sin (the Dead King)

After he was done with her, the King lumbered to his feet, regarded her, and made as if to help her in turn to rise. Tumbled, her very downfall appealed to and enticed him. Provisions from her basket – she had been taking loaves and cakes to someone, somewhere – lay all over the turf. Candied cherries had bruised on her gown. Cherries, fulvous hair, maiden blood, a foam of petticoats. He was pleased by the artistic chaos he had created from her.

But she seemed to have lost her memory. He found that out when he had dragged her up. She had forgotten where she was going, where she had come from, even who she was. Her very name. He took it for a gambit, and guffawed. 'But you know who *I* am?' She thought, and shook her fragile head. 'Your King,' he told, her, not without pride. She looked at him in complete belief and pure uninterest. He felt then he could not leave such a simpleton at large. He would have her at home a day or so more. He ate her pastries like a hearty ploughboy as they went, having summoned the abortive hunt with a yell. They had only been waiting out of sight. 'A fine quarry, eh?' said the King, jostling his lackwit doll.

In the Palace, he soon grew used to her amnesia. It was rather novel. He gave her things instead, rooms, clothes. Even the dress and shoes he had bandied about. The slippers were in fact too small, and did not fit.

He had had a royal wife, once, who produced a viperish son, now being tutored, as was the vogue, elsewhere. The queen-mother next contracted a fatal plague during a pilgrimage she insisted on making, so it served her right. For himself the King did not foresee an era when he too, poisoned more slowly by various indulgences, would be gone, becoming in popular parlance 'Dead'.

What began as a clumsy snatch in a wood progressed to a merry hole-in-corner adventure, involving the game of secret passages and similar artifice.

Eventually, by accident, the King learned who it was probable he had abducted. An elderly aristocrat, living in a remote nook of the Palace grounds, which were considerable even in those days, had lost a child, a young, not quite legitimate daughter, fifteen years of age. It was suggested jealous older sisters of less beauty, the product of another union, had got rid of her. The description of the lost girl tallied sufficiently with that of the amnesiac now haunting the apartment of the King's favourite doxy.

Certain gifts were instigated. Vows of unspeaking were fashioned. The lady, garbed in her autumnal camouflage, was brought out and discovered to be, first, a duchess, and next, a queen. The ulcerous foot, and some other heralding ailments, had by now taken charge of the King. Virtue did not alleviate them.

Something else atrocious had meanwhile happened.

The Red Queen had ceased to be a girl, was not fifteen, not seventeen, not twenty, not thirty, any longer. Flourished in the harsh illumination of the public court, far from her shady room and fireglims, she revealed her decay into a woman.

There was a story she had conceived but not borne to term. If one had asked this Queen, to her face, she would not have dissembled, for she did not seem to know, even now, anything valid about herself.

She could not truly be said to know, even what she might be assumed to have realised – that she had been leapt on and vampirised, buried, dug out, thrust into the violent glare of an empty mirror which leered at, and insolently answered her, saying, Now you are old.

The King's bleared eyes, certainly, saw the etching of her bleak, icy face, as if it had been drawn on by a nail. It was unforgivable of her.

By the night of his summer death, he had, though, both forgiven and forgotten.

The son, fattened from viper to python, coming back, treated the madwoman Innocin with urbanity. He found it amusing so to do. After the amused period, it was established custom. Being very young, he thought her an antique. Such articles might keep their place, come and go as they wanted, wandering like a lost soul if no longer a lost child. Sometimes he would point her out to visitors, as another curio of his collection.

The Dwarf's Third Interview with His Grandmother

'Go away,' stridently commands Heracty's relative, as she sees him through her ice-locked window. In winter the marble houses are difficult to warm and tend to promote rheumatism. But the handsome dwarf, ignoring all temper of weather or woman, is already in, and standing by the hearth.

'What did I say to you?' snarls the grandmother.

'You welcomed me with tender cries,' says Heracty. 'And look at what I've brought you. A mantle trimmed by damascined fur combed from the Prince's gulon.'

The grandmother examines the item unkindly.

'There is no such animal as a gulon,' she remarks.

'The Red Queen,' says Heracty, musingly, 'has all her winter cloaks enhanced with gulon-fur, when not by ermine.'

'An ermine is only a weasel.'

'And what is a ghost?'

'The demon of a sickly stunted brain.'

'Wrong once more,' says Heracty. 'I'll tell you.' He seats himself by the fire, and props his boots on a stool. He notices today the grandmother looks ninety, and she that his legs seem to have grown longer. That is impossible. 'The Queen,' says Heracty, 'has visualised and hunted her lost youth so determinedly, it has taken on a shape. It has become a girl, lovely, clad in black velvet. But daylight or a lamp shine through her. She isn't substantial. And I believe, from the manner in which she gazes about, the Palace is just as unreal, in its way, to her. A ruin maybe is all she sees. Or else she exists in a previous or later time. Other dwarfs have met her. They say she lies down on their beds, with her feet and hair, both spangled, hanging over the ends. They say she wears slippers made of ice, or glass. The mastiffs fawn on her. The unicorn offers her rides. Even the two-headed dog turns one head. The gulon, naturally, spits and makes water. It's peevish. Have a honeyed almond? No? The gulon is very partial to them.'

'To hell with you, sir, your ghosts and gulons and honey and *legs*.'

'And here's a rose I found, after the phantom passed me on a stair.' Heracty extends it. 'A flower blooming in the snow.'

But, though exactly formed, the rose also is made of ice. Grandmother burns her fingers on it and, thrown at a wall, it smashes.

The Beast (the Bride)

The sumptuous bed, entombed by its curtains on which are sewn bizarre animals and birds, has invented a separate breathing. It had, of course, not been there when she lay down to sleep – but is now so close to her that, as she wakes, she partly believes the rhythm of breath is her own. Not, however, the smooth planes of flesh, the cool hands which take her face between them, the lips which press her mouth.

She is not afraid. It was so inevitable, this. Surely she has known these caresses before. She yields without a word, with all her self. And since this place is heaven, love too is unalloyed. She is spun away as if through a starry sky. She falls to earth uninjured, but completely changed.

The man who has shared with her the bed of the act of love, invisible to her in the dark as any of the magical servants, is held in her arms. She ventures only now to question him, because now it does not matter.

'You ask me for my name,' he responds. His voice is musical and low. 'Call me Lucander. He, Lucander, will be with you here, at night. But you will never see him.'

'But will I see you?'

'At these times, he and I are the same. Never.'

'Never?'

It is a ritual. It neither frightens nor convinces her, though she is prepared to honour its outer show. In the same way, in her former life, she would have cast spilt salt across one shoulder.

'Not once, Idrel. Never. Never attempt to see my face.'

'Why not? Why?'

'Light, and my face, can't agree together. Even the moon's my enemy. Especially that. Without doubt the sun.'

'But a single candle,' she says.

'Don't try to discover me. The revelation would drive you mad.'

'But why?'

'The beast stays to be found in man. The hunter which preys on the trusting sheep.'

'A beast.'

'The bestial joke of God. Monstrous.'

In the blinded blackness, the bride describes the face of her husband. Her fingertips learn only the mask of a human male, the brows and lashes, the lips and earlobes, the jaw with its masculine roughening. And the taste of him, of the fruits of the darkness.

'But by night you will be here with me?' She employs his name, 'Lucander.'

She is already, in his second embrace, planning for his future slumber, a tinder struck and the surprising candleflame.

Innocin's Ascent (the Queen's Last Sin)

Can it be her stepson's dwarf is continuing to follow her? No, surely, it is just her shadow compressed and thrown behind. For a new idea has occurred to Innocin. Not to descend in the twilight, but instead to seek higher, into the diadem of the Upper Palace, its tallest towers.

They are remote and neglected, and in the vast attics there perhaps a white skirt has often gone up and down, and pale feet have all this while been stepping.

As she ascends, the Queen considers the sin of her husband, a black sticky sin, or spotted red, the murder of her past amounting to an utter death. This sin it was that gave her to conceive the child clad in clement white.

The stairs are craning, spindly, thick with webs and dust. Yet far above in the air, a pastel eye beams on her, a window made encouraging by a lamp. Or only the moon in a cloud.

She crosses a passage, her cloak industriously sweeping up the dirt and old nests – once doves brooded here. The stars glint in broken bricks. The towers are very ancient. They belong to other, earlier, histories.

On a threshold, the Queen hesitates. It is now too dark for her to see anything, and the guiding light has vanished. Nevertheless, a sweet, slight voice is singing, the words indistinguishable, like a faint zephyr tingling through the bones of the tower.

Innocin sighs.

The voice she hears is like that of a child, but not a child lost and alone, bleeding or crying in the bitter cold. This is a found child, braiding her hair and playing with a rope of pearls. Roses unseasonably grow about her, a fire dances. There is food and wine. Slaves to serve, not to exact service. There is love.

Suddenly Innocin can see a cave of golden light, and a shining young woman going by through the yellow heart of it.

'Oh,' whispers the Red Queen. 'There she is.'

She smiles at the glamour and riches, all the nights and mornings, guessing the beloved is due to return. Not for the found daughter a wild beast in a forest, rending and blight.

The Queen smiles, and lets her soul go out of her.

The soul is gone.

Like an amber dove she falls from the tower-top, her mantle bearing her on its wing. She falls at Heracty's feet, where he stands in a court below.

Though her skeletal structure is dislodged at the impact, her body settles, resting her pristine on her back, her hands folded on her breast, her long lids closed, and her mouth still blossoming its flame of smile. Oh, she is yet saying, there she is. And the mirror has cracked, and set her free, at last.

The Wolf's Head (the Awakening)

There have been many nights and days. In the day, sometimes, led by the unseen slaves, Idrel explored the ruin, discovering its secret wonders. The labyrinth is full of ghosts. Frequently, the girl has witnessed, tiny in the telescoped lens of distant corridors, or courtyards five flights of stairs beneath, frantic scenes of another world, which plainly do not otherwise have substance. Idrel observes impartially games and feasts, courtings and quarrellings, aristocrats and unicorns and dwarfs.

But the nights are better for exploring.

In the snow-field of white sheets, her night-husband draws her away into the forest of desire – and abruptly the darkness engulfs her.

To these delights, the lingering tension of Idrel's plan has subtly been added.

Tonight she will carry it out.

Slipping from the bed, she fetches a candle. As she does this, a sigh seems to flutter round the chamber. The ruin is crammed with phantoms, and Idrel pays no heed.

Light is absent, the fire long-smothered and all the lamps doused before her lover's arrival. Carefully returning through screens and panes of blackness to the bed, she puts the candle down, strikes the tinder, lets the fire-bud drop on to the waxen branch where, like a canary, it beats its wings. When the flame steadies, holding it high, Idrel pulls aside a fold of the bed-curtain. She stares down at what lies sleeping on the white drift of the sheet.

Shadows and sheen combine to describe. Here are the lines of a man's body, which at the shoulders culminate in the head of a black wolf.

As soon as she sees it, she remembers, everything.

In that moment, too, perhaps alerted by the light and its flickering, or solely by the intensity of the watcher, the creature wakes. It growls softly, or, the muzzle of the wolf does so. Feral, human, lupine eyes glare up at the young girl standing there, pinning it with a stave of light, and clothed herself in her white nakedness, save where the same light blushes her apple-red.

'I look and I see,' says Idrel.

Her eyes say clearly: I knew all the time it was there, your black wolf. To live is to die. I'm dead, and here with you. You made me holy, taking my blood.

And leaning down, she kisses the wolf face, over and over, with quiet still kisses. And as she does this, the candle tilts and the burning hot wax sears and seals his skin, but he does not flinch at it. When Idrel lifts her head, she finds a man, with a man's skull and features, a broad low brow, hair black as crow's feathers, black-water eyes that regard her.

'There will be another bed,' he murmurs, 'with a dead wolf in it, or a living man – but not this one.'

'But you are Lucander. You are with me, here.'

The vampire, or supernatural spirit, whatever it is, has now fully recognised the soul, or ghost, of Idrel. That is, if Idrel ever existed beyond the brain of a red-haired queen.

They contemplate each other in the melting honey of the candle-gloom. When the candle finishes, who can say if they remain in the black night, or if they too have gone away.

Even the serene susurrus of their voices, which is yet to be distinguished, may not be real. Although more so, perhaps, than the stairs and galleries and towers of the preposterous Palace.

The Black Queen (the Seven Dwarfs)

Because he thinks of himself as an innovator, the Prince has had a strange new mausoleum built, on a hill three or four miles from the Palace. In the mausoleum lies the body of his stepmother, the dead Queen.

The view from the mausoleum is eloquent. Above, uncut meadows, woodland tapering to park, the mountain of the royal domicile. Below the sapphire basins of the valleys, the far-away forests which are not fakes, a thunder-cloud of trees, redolent and rowdy with every animal applicable to the clime.

The corpse of Innocin was come on at daybreak in a yard of the Upper Palace by some sozzled young nobles, who were startled but not astounded. It was decided she had toppled from a tower. The sin of suicide was not mentioned. Nevertheless the location of the new tomb was fortuitous, it did not require sacred ground. It could be erected as a monument. Somewhat to that end, the Prince had organised rather a peculiar funeral rite, which, repeated on and off in subsequent years, became known as the Masque of the Black Queen.

The title role was undertaken by the dusky dwarfess. Attired like midnight, with sables, and jets in her hair, she was drawn in a carriage by a team of plumed black greyhounds. The other six dwarfs, each got up allegorically, came behind, mounted or on foot as their character advised. Heracty had the part of Worldly Fame, his pony, a suit of cloth-of-gold, and the obligation of lugging on leash two ill-mannered peacocks. His brother dwarfs represented Modesty, Sloth, Rage and Joy. The blonde dwarfess, in butterfly costume, was asked to suggest Unearthly Apprehension. The dusky dwarfess, the Black Queen, was unarguably Lady Death.

Additional pets of the Prince's had work in the procession. The unicorn appeared wreathed in thorns as the Pardon Of Heaven. The gulon and dual-headed dog were excluded, however, as untrustworthy.

All this display, with the snuffling, labouring court plodding after, toiled out through heavy snow to the mausoleum, where dirges were sung, and flowers dyed black, or gilded, tossed on the ice. The mausoleum steps had gone to mirror, and the miraculous dome was topped again by a scoop of snow.

Months on, when the thaws of spring had manhandled the land and flung down the rime and snow from the slopes, the court would voluntarily visit the area, also the dwarfs. They would sit on the tomb-steps, and look pensively out into the valleys. Their reasons for doing so, particularly the reasons of the dwarfs, were banal. They liked the vista, thought it prudent to pretend respect, or relished the proof of the high brought low.

Heracty attends the tomb seldom. When giving the gulon exercise, as he now sometimes does, he will tend that way.

For its part, the fox-cat sniffs all about the mausoleum, trotting up the steps to peer with peridot eyes in at the transparent dome. Does the gulon recognise the bleached trimmings in which Innocin has been laid to rest? More likely, being fed on carrion, its interest is of that order.

The Tomb (the Spring)

The priest walks to the summit of a hill on an evening of late spring – and sees in front of him a curious monument.

The ordeal which he endured in a backward, superstitious village is over with. He has been recalled to the towns and cities of his earliest dreaming. Conversely, he has sloughed those dark nightmares that haunted his beginnings. The inner outcry for flesh, the carnal ravening, like hunger, these impediments are surpassed. He has wrestled with the subterranean angel, and triumphed.

Birds sing in the warm avenues of sky. The westering sun flies against a dome of glass, piercing it with a brilliant nail.

Having space, and peace, the young priest makes a detour and climbs the steps, and so concludes the monument is a tomb. Marble and granite, like a fist it grips an egg of sheer transparency. And in this oval mirror a woman lies composed, robed in creamy white, coifed like a nun, a circlet of gold binding her forehead. There is not a mark on her face. She would seem to be a girl. This aspect will be eternal. The sarcophagus has shut her fast in a vacuun, where no atmosphere can enter to corrupt. She will, therefore,

171

never grow old. She will never decay. Always her bones will be decently clad, until the Final Judgement.

The young man gazes in at the dead, seemingly sleeping girl. A kiss might awaken her.

It comes to him, how the Devil left him in the likeness of a black wolf, running off briskly along the roads of slumber. Of what is this dead girl dreaming, this white queen, as she lies in her shell of crystal for ever?

On the other side of the tomb, a blonde dwarf lady is seated at an aesthetic angle, but she too has gone to sleep. In a basket at her side are apples and peaches, one with a chunk bitten out of it.

Above, beyond, meadows, hillside, the winking of water, a wood where rhododendrons are flowering, some hint of towers or roofs.

A nonsensical beast like a large brown cat, or possibly a tabby fox, is eating poppies in the meadow-grass.

The priest walks on, leaving the tomb of glass for the sunset and the night.

Heracty's Omission of a Further Interview with His Grandmother

On the rim of the fountain, the seventh dwarf balances in the afterglow of summer sunfall, diving his hand into the water, making believe it is a fish. Then, removing his hand and knowing it again as the hand of an elf.

The creatures of the fountain loom over him, still tanned with pink day; great heat stays cosy in the stone. Roses have burst across the lawn.

Although she will never any more glide down the stair, cross this terrace, go by him sightlessly, sinking through the Palace, even so, sometimes he waits for her.

Heracty does not anticipate Innocin's ghost. A ghost cannot *become* a ghost. When a ghost dies, it springs to life.

It is years now since he went to call on his grandmother, but Heracty does think of her, for that old witch is waiting for him with malicious hope, but he will never go near her again. Her vigil is accordingly as pointless as this one he keeps on the fountain terrace.

Something stirs among the roses, and a shower of petals snows the dusk.

The moon is rising like a coin of breath, and the gulon, early, starts to yowl. The heart or soul of the gulon is rushing at liberty through a forest. And somewhere else, Heracty is a man with lion's hair, over six feet tall, his shoulders filling a doorway. Heracty knows this other life of his goes on. It is just there, or *there* — beneath an arch, behind a door. It takes only the brush of a feather to dislodge the barrier of iron between. He believes this, and knows this, and how simple it would be to do it. Heracty is puzzled, less dismayed than nonplussed, that he has never found the way.

White As Sin, Now
Chosen by Nadia van der Westhuizen

It is not an exaggeration to say that Tanith's work has profoundly shaped my life. From the first book I read (*The Book of the Damned*) I was irrevocably smitten: I knew even then that I would always work to celebrate her extraordinary writing in whatever way I could. The complexity of her stories inspired a passion for scholarship, and led me to pursue a career in academia. I always felt that Tanith's work never received the attention it deserved, and I was committed to redressing the imbalance as much as was possible. During my undergraduate and postgraduate studies I focused on Tanith's use of myth and folklore in her writing, and my PhD was entirely dedicated to her fairy tale adaptations. I continue to work on her folklore and fairy tale texts and, with that in mind, I wanted to choose a story for this collection which had a strong emphasis on that aspect of her writing. I didn't want to choose a relatively new story, or something out of the wonderful *Red as Blood* collection because that has recently been expanded and reprinted. I have therefore chosen an older story which not only shows Tanith's passion for fairy tale, but also her tremendous skill in manipulating the conventions of genre in order to create astonishing new forms. "White as Sin, Now" has always been one of my favourites and, as Tanith herself wrote, many of her "obsessions have crowded into it." It's a representation not only of Tanith's opulently rich Gothic aesthetic, which is arguably the element which most draws me to her work, but also of the person she was because it is one of those stories that really 'feels' like her – a phantasmagoric experience that alters you forever through its beauty and intensity.

Nadia van der Westhuizen works at UCL and Kingston University. She is currently assisting in editing The Fairy Tale World, a collection of essays for Routledge in their Routledge Worlds series.

After the Guillotine

In the 1980s I wrote a huge novel on the French Revolution – my only 'straight' historical novel to date.

Off shoots from that book gave me several ingredients for fantasy stories, of which this is one.

The characters are based on four actual people sent to the blade by Robespierre. In one case at least, the invented name casts a very thin veil over the original – Danton.

The men went to the scaffold singing the Marseillaise, or shouting, or in tears, or – all three. At any rate, they made a great deal of noise about death. The girl went sweetly and quietly, dressed like a bride. There was a reason for that. There were, of course, reasons for all of it.

To die at any time when you are not prepared to die is objectionable. To die when you are comparatively young, when there are things of paramount importance still to be accomplished, when, in dying, you will lose spring and hope, and those who love you, that also you love; these are fair causes for commotion. The famous figure, D'Antoine the Lion, however, did not roar *en route* to *la Guillotine*. He had done his roaring in the courtroom, and it had achieved very little good, and actually some harm. He had presently been 'legally' silenced, and that had shut up every one of them. D'Antoine's enemies were terrified of him, his speeches, his voice, his presence. Just as his friends loved him to distraction.

As the tumbrils jounced slowly along over the cobbles of Paris, (a form of traffic that had become quite banal), the Lion only occasionally grunted, or flexed his big body with bitter laughter. D'Antoine, bully, kingly master, charmer, conniver, atheist.

"I'm leaving things in a muddle," he had said after they condemned him. For himself, he reckoned on nothing, once the blade came down, hence his bitterness, and his lack of confusion. He was not afraid, or only very little. He had made his mark in the living world. "Show my head to the crowd," he would instruct the executioner. "It's worth looking at twice." Let us agree with that.

Héros, in the same cart, was one of those who sang, but rather negligently. The others who did so were mostly trying to keep their courage up, for while they sang, some of their terror and despair was held at bay. But Héros did not seem to be either depressed or afraid. His name, in this instance, is perfect for him, combination that it is of Hero and Eros. Lover and gallant, the image that comes to mind is appealing. One of the handsomest men of the era, he is everything one would wish to be at the hour of one's public death: beautiful, couth, composed. In his not-long career, he had enjoyed most of the sins and pleasures of his day. He had been in the beds of princesses, perhaps even of a prince or two. Aristocrat to his fingertips, he knew how to face this final couching. He sang melodiously. To the screaming rabble he was aloof, to his friends remotely kind. He kissed them farewell at the foot of the scaffold, and went up first to demonstrate how quick and easy it all was, not worth any show. Thereby offering a faultless one.

But in his heart, handsome peerless Héros had kept a seed of the Catholic faith, which refused to wither. He believed, in some subdued, shallow bottom of his brain, that he was bound for Hell hereafter. As he disdained to fuss over the loss of his elegant head, just so he would not throw a tantrum at a prospect of centuries of torment in the inferno. His coolness was therefore even more admirable. Let us pause a moment to admire him.

The third man we examine in the forward tumbril, Lucien, rather than being what one would wish to, on the day of one's public death, is more what one fears one would be. As some of his biographers politely put it, there had been some 'difficulty' in persuading him from the prison to the cart. Once installed, raw-eyed from weeping, only the neighbouring strength of the Lion kept him upright. Then, as the reeking, railing crowd pressed in, anger and terror mingled, and rather than sing Lucien began to shout. As the rabble screamed insults at him, so he screamed back. Ugly, where Héros was handsome and D'Antoine was grand, thin from prison, white and insane, and tearing his shirt in his struggles to escape the inescapable, or to be heard by the voluntarily deaf, he hurled charges and pleas until his voice, never strong, gave out. He had some justification. His was the spark that had initially fired the powder-keg of the Revolution. But no one listened now. The gist of all his words: *Remember what I did for you and set us free* – or, in short, *Let me LIVE!* – was entertaining, but no rallying point for the starving unanswered masses who, like vampires, had taken to existing on blood. There was, too, the matter of Lucien's wife, whom he adored, and who he feared, rightly, was on the same road to the guillotine as himself. To no avail, naturally, he was also trying to shout for her life.

We may be unpleasant here and say Lucien shouted his head off. Or we could say, journalist and pamphleteer that he was, that he wrote it off, by going into print with unwise assertions and demands.

As for an afterlife, he wrote, too, that he believed in the 'immortality of the soul'. So he did, but in a somewhat scattered, indefinite way. He had been anxious to impress, through his prison reading, the notion of continuance upon himself, as if he would need it where he would be going.

Let us, for the moment, stop talking about Lucien. And go on to that far more visual creature, his wife, the lovely Lucette.

There must have been something about Lucien. There he was, ugly, and there Lucette was – exquisite – and they were blissfully in love through several years of marriage. Maybe she preferred older men – he was ten years her senior. Or *younger* men – ten years her senior in age, he was in many other ways younger than everyone. The crime which sent Lucette to the scaffold was love. Because of love she had attempted to save her husband's neck, and thus proved troublesome to his powerful enemies. Thereafter it seemed to them she might become, through love, a focus for strife.

She made the journey to the guillotine some days after Lucien, Héros and D'Antoine. She travelled with an air of calm pleasure. She said, "Lucien is dead and there is nothing further I want from life. If these monsters hadn't murdered him, I would now thank them with tears of joy for sending me to join him in eternity." Lucette's inner secret was that she was by nature a priestess who had made Lucien her High Altar. She expected, after her sacrifice, to fall straight from the blade of the guillotine into her husband's arms. Despite, or because of, his rather Dionysian leanings – religions of music, drama, lilies in fields – Lucette believed in Heaven. That Lucien, regardless of his faults, was already there, she did not doubt.

So, in her white dress, her fleecy golden hair cut short, she went blithely up to the platform and lay down for the stroke, barely seeming to notice, they said, what the executioner was doing.

The guillotine is very swift and supposedly humane, but who knows? Stories are told of severed heads which winked malignly from the basket, and even of one that brokenly whispered a request for water. Doubtless the climate has an effect on an outdoor apparatus of this type – shrinking or swelling the metal parts; on some days it might do its work an iota more slowly, or more quickly, or more neatly, than on others. Nothing the crowd would notice, of course. And then the physique of the victim must be taken into account. A large neck makes its own demands, and the fact that long hair, collars and neck-cloths were removed indicates even such as these could throw the blade. Louis Capet required more than one stroke; an unreassuring if unusual occurrence. Nor should one forget the condition of the subject's nerves – as opposed merely to his nervousness. No two human things are quite alike. One ventures to suggest that there have been as many different sorts of death under the guillotine as there have been heads lopped by it.

D'Antoine, for example. Who could judge splendid powerful D'Antoine would experience that partitioning in the same way as anyone else?

It seemed, when it came, like a blow, the blow of a sledgehammer, but not quite hard enough – so there was an instant's appalled thought: *Those bloody fools have botched it!* Then the perspective altered. The eyes glimpsed the basket as the head fell into it, and other faces, already forgotten, looked up at it with anxiety as it came to meet them. After this, the light went, and there was only one odd final sensation, the head lying where it was, but the last reflexive relaxing spasms of the body eerily somehow communicated to it. *Is this what a chicken feels?* And a moment of horror, wondering how long one must endure this *this*. Followed by oblivion.

Oblivion of course, for D'Antoine the atheist had reckoned on Nothing. And here nothing was. All senses gone. The void. Blackness not even black, silence not even silence. *Sans* all.

There is a certain smugness attached to finding oneself perfectly right, even if one can no longer experience it.

Héros, who had been dispatched a short while before, *was* experiencing something similar.

In his case, the passage of the blade had been sheer. To use the analogy of hot knives through butter is in bad taste, but there. It is the best one. Stunned, Héros lost consciousness instantly. He may have expected to. When he opened his eyes again, everything was altered, but still he saw only what he expected.

The way to Hell was gaudy, festive almost; the lighting, to say the least, theatrical. Flames leaped crimson on the subterranean cliffs that lined the path, and a grotesquery of shadows danced with them. Héros was, on some unrecognised level, gratified to see that it had all the artistry of a good painting of the subject, indeed, some of it was so familiar that it filled him with a slight sense of *deja vu*. Presently, a masked devil swooped down at him on bat-wings, with a shriek. Héros, unprotesting, elegant, moved towards his punishment.

The bright entrance and the gradients beyond were littered by howling, pleading, rioting or bravely joking damned. Among them he caught sight of certain prior acquaintances, just those he would, in fact, have anticipated. He also partly expected to see D'Antoine arrive at any moment, ushered in behind him. D'Antoine, who had led a magnificently licentious life, had believed that only oblivion followed death. His friend would have been interested to see D'Antoine's face when he discovered he was wrong. On the whole. Héros did not think Lucien would make up the party. Although Lucien had done a thing or two that would doubtless disqualify him from eternal bliss, he had a sort of faun-like innocence that would probably keep him out of the ultimate basement area.

Occasionally goaded, though never prodded, by appalling devils, Héros walked on and found himself at length in a sort of waiting-room with broad open windows. These gazed out across incendiary lakes and lagoons, and mountains of anguished structure. Actual torments were visible from here, but, being in the distance, not very coherently. It was a subtle arrangement, threatening, but restrained. If questioned, Héros would have confessed that he approved of it. At a stone table in the waiting-room, a veiled figure sat dealing cards. Héros, who had been inclined to cards in life, sat down opposite and, without a word, they began to play a hand.

The game seemed to last a very long time. An extraordinarily long time. Abruptly, Héros came to from a kind of daze, and with a strange feeling to which he could assign no name – for he felt, absurdly, almost guilty. It appeared to him at that moment as if, rather than being kept waiting here, most cruelly, to learn his exact awful fate, he *himself* – but no, that was plainly ridiculous. Just precisely then, a tall flame burst through one of the windows, and out of the flame a demon stared at him with a cat's wild eyes. Beckoned, somewhat relieved, Héros abandoned the cards, and went towards the demon, which suddenly grasped him and bore him out into the savage landscape beyond the room. A backward glance showed the veiled figure had disappeared entirely.

They did not exchange small-talk, the demon and Héros. Hell spoke for itself. They passed over laval cauldrons in which figures swam and wailed, and emaciated moaning forms chained to the sides of mountains and tormented by various... *things*. Others of the condemned crawled about at the edges of retreating pools, croaking of thirst. Some toiled like ants, great boulders on their backs. Still others were being flayed or devoured by fiends, from the feet up. Allusions both historic and classical were nicely mingled. There was something, in a dreadful way, reassuring about it all.

At length, the demon chose to hover in mid-air close to a weird contraption, a kind of swing. Back and back it flung itself, then forth and forth, with a tireless pendulum motion, until about a mile away it plunged into a torrent of fire, and far off screaming was detectable. But now it was swinging back again. Seated in a froth of summery dresses – the height of Revolutionary French fashion – two young women, quite unscathed, toasted each other in white sparkling wine.

As they drew nearer, Héros noticed that there was room on the swing for one more person. Just then, the blonder of the two ladies glanced up and beheld him. "Why, it's Héros – Héros!" she cried; the darker girl joined in with: "We saved a place for you, Héros darling."

Héros smiled and greeted them. Both looked familiar, although he was not sure from where. Instead, each of them seemed like an amalgam of certain aspects of all the women he had known, the dark and the blonde, the coarse and the refined, aristo and plebeian – delightful. And no sooner had he concluded this, than his demon escort dropped him. There was no sensation of falling. One moment he was in the air, next moment in mid-flight on the swing, a girl either side, soft arms, warm lips, curly hair, and very good champagne being held for him to drink. "Knock it back quickly, lovely Héros. In a minute, we'll be into *that* again."

"The fire?" queried Héros. The swing had reached its furthest backward extent, paused, and now began once more to fly forward.

"Oh, the fire. The pain! The terror!"

"But it only lasts a moment," said her friend and, indeed, his.

"You get used to it."

They toasted the monarchy, something it had long since ceased to be sensible to do upstairs. Then they embraced.

The swing was broad and comfortable enough for almost... anything.

After a few extremely pleasant minutes, his two companions clutched at him with exclamations of fright and boiling red flames enveloped them. They all screamed with pain. Then the swing rushed out again and the pain vanished. They had not been burned, not even blistered. The champagne too retained its refreshing coolness, nor had any of it evaporated.

Héros relaxed amid the willing human cushions. Three seconds of agony against several minutes that were not agonising at all seemed an excellent arrangement. Of course one suffered. One was supposed to. But the ratio could only be described as – civilised.

The next time they went into the fire they were all singing a very lewd song of the proposed Republic. They screamed briefly, though in perfect tempo, and came out again on the succeeding verse.

In perfect tempo too, Lucien felt the pain of the guillotine's blade. It was swift and stinging, not unendurable, leaving an after-image of itself that grew in intensity, not to greater pain but to a terrible struggle. Physically, the guillotine had deprived him of sight, hearing and speech – but not totally of feeling. He hung there, formless, and for a long ghastly eternity fought to breathe, tried to swallow, and most of all to cry out.

When he broke from this, he did not know where he was, but that he was somewhere seemed self-evident. Still blind and deaf and dumb, he had convinced himself that he was now breathing, and because of this thought that he had somehow been rescued by the crowd, who must have pulled him clear of the crashing blade – by unimaginable means – at the last moment. But of course, there was no one near him, nothing. When he attempted to reach out, his hands found only emptiness, and besides, they were not hands. All *that* was done with. His body had been lost. Only he remained. And for a horrible second he was not even sure of that. But he held to himself grimly, to everything he could remember. This was the second struggle, and in the middle of it he managed to open his eyes, or at least, he began to see.

What he saw was not encouraging. It was truly a scene of total emptiness, a skyless desert made solely of the absence of things and yet there seemed to be matter in it. For example, to stare at something was to produce a sort of illusory smoky shape. And then again, there was nothing to be stared at in the first place. His feeling now was of depression, a fear and misery he had never known to such a degree even on the volatile emotional seesaw of his life. And of loneliness, which was the worst of all.

Somehow, he had survived death. Or had he? This seemed the most tenuous and precarious of survivals. *Limbo* was the notion that came to mind. If he still possessed a mind.

He found that he looked ceaselessly in all directions, but all directions were the same. He was searching for a method of escape, or a mode of return. His life was precious to him. He longed for it. He wanted to go back! There must be some way... And when this passionate yearning grew very strong, out of his confusion the desert seemed to fill with crowds and colour and noise. He was in a procession on horseback, or else watching one from the roadside. He heard the cannon booming over Paris or the day the Bastille fell; he heard – but these were only waking dreams. With an effort, each time he shook them off. The door to release was not to be found in this way.

It seemed then he rummaged about in the emptiness, or maybe hurried over it, or dug through it, all to no avail. And then, when he stopped, his thoughts grew very still and began gently to flow out from him. He was afraid to lose them, and himself. This fear was more dreadful than any of the others, more dreadful even than the fear of death had been.

There was anger too. None of this was what Lucien had believed would greet the 'immortal' soul. It was demonstrably useless to call on God. (He had done so.) Either God did not exist, or did not attend. There were also curious moments when it seemed to him that he, not God, had the key to all of this. But how could that be so?

Perched there in the depths of the waste, he huddled memories about him, warming himself at the recollections of beautiful Lucette, and crying over his child, or thinking that he cried. But the loneliness pressed down on him like an inexorable coffin-lid. Though he supposed he could people the colourless greyness, which was not even grey, with the figures of wife and friends, or with anything, he knew such toys were false, and useless.

Was everything he now experienced a punishment? Not the ridiculous Catholic Hell, but some more deadly state, where he must wander for ever, weighted by depression, alone, until his own self was worn away as time washes smooth a stone? Lucette – Lucette...

Lucette, desiring her freedom so much, was already partly out of her body as the blade fell. She heard, and felt the stroke, but from some way off. Then the multitude, the blood-soaked guillotine, all Paris, the very world, dashed away beneath her. She rose into a sky almost cloudless and utterly blue. Whole and laughing and lovely, she entered Heaven with the lightest step, in her white dress, her hair already long again.

It was all so beautiful. It was as she had dreamed of it when a child. Balanced on their clouds of cirrus, the streets of gold, the pearly dazzling palaces, the handsome people smiling and brave, the little animals that made free of every step and cornice, the birds and the kind angels that flew overhead, about the level of the fourth-floor windows... She ran along, crying with pleasure, at every crossroads expecting to meet Lucien – probably sitting writing something, and so engrossed, he had momentarily forgotten the time of her arrival. But she did not find him. And at last, there in the golden sunlight of endless day, Lucette paused.

A stately woman in white robes came down the boulevard, and Lucette approached her. "Madame, excuse me, but I should like to ask your advice."

The woman looked at her, gently smiling.

"I'm searching for my husband. He died some days ago, and I expected he would be here before me..."

The woman went on smiling.

"Madame – I can't find him."

"Then perhaps he is not here."

"There is nowhere else he could be," said Lucette firmly.

"Ah, my dear, there are numerous other places. He could be in any one of them."

Lucette frowned and her fine eyes flashed. Was this woman daring to suggest...? "Where?" said Lucette. It was a challenge. One did not live next to a fighter such as Lucien without some of the trademarks rubbing off.

But enigmatically, the woman only said, "Seek and ye shall find." And so passed on down the street.

Lucette sat under a portico to pet a pair of white rabbits. She told them about Lucien, and once about the child they had had to leave behind them, and then she wept. The rabbits were patient and dried her tears on their fur.

Eventually Lucette rose and went on alone, determined to search every street and park, every room and cupboard of Heaven. She did so. Up stairs she hurried, over bridges, under which ran the sapphire streams of Paradise, scattered with flowers and ducks. Into high bell-towers she went, and from the tallest roofs of all she gazed into rosy distances, between the flight paths of the angels. She did not grow tired. There could be no tiredness. But she grew unsure, she grew uneasy. Now and then she asked someone. Once, she even asked an angel, who stood calmly on a pillar some feet over her head. But no one could aid her. Lucien? Who was Lucien? She was accustomed, was Lucette, to being married to a famous man. It added to her sense of outrage and sadness that they did not know him.

Though there was no time, yet her search of Heaven took a lot of it. In the end, it seemed to her she had visited every inch. Finally, she sought a gate, and walked out of it into the clouds. She turned her back on Bliss. It was not bliss, if her love was not to be there with her.

An infinity of sky stretched away and away. Lucette moved across it, still searching, and the glow of the ethereal city faded behind her. Like an... illusion.

On the astral plain, though illusions may be frequent, one does not sleep, let alone turn in one's sleep; neither does one do so in annihilation. Nevertheless, in a manner of speaking, D'Antoine did 'turn' in his 'sleep'.

It was as if, determined to wake up at a particular hour, he now partly surfaced from deep slumber to ask himself, drowsily, unwillingly, "Is it time, yet?" But apparently it was not yet time. With a – metaphorical – grunt, the Lion, who no longer remembered he had been the Lion, sank down once more into the cosy arms of oblivion, burrowed, nestled, and was gone again.

The demon whose turn it was on the spit with Héros stared at him quizzically.

"Don't you find all this," said the demon, "a bit samey?"

"Being tortured, do you mean? I suppose, as torturer, *you* might find it so. We can swap places if you like."

"You miss the point," said the demon.

Héros eyed the demon's pitchfork. "Not always."

As it had turned out, the lascivious fiery swing was not the only appliance to which Héros had been subjected. He had suffered many more stringent punishments. Although strangely enough, only when he himself began to consider the lack of them. But doubtless that was merely the prescience of guilt. Strangely too, more strangely in fact, even the worst of the tortures seemed rather hollow. This one, for example, of being slowly roasted alive, stabbed the while at suitable junctures by the pitchfork – somehow it was difficult to retain the sense of agony. One's mind unaccountably wandered. One had to *remember* to writhe. It was not that it did not hurt. It hurt abominably. And yet…

"I apologise," said Héros, "if I don't seem properly attentive. No fault of yours, I assure you."

"Perhaps," said the demon, "yours?"

"Oh, undoubtedly mine."

"Perhaps," said the demon, "you shouldn't be here."

The spit had stopped revolving. The roasting flames grew pale.

"I can't think where else."

"Try," said the demon.

Héros frowned. Now one thought of it, this was the first occasion one of the minions of Hell had held a conversation with one. Since his bonds had disappeared, Héros sat up and looked about him. Hell seemed oddly inactive, and dull, as if it were cooling down, a truly appalling idea. Weary spirals of old smoke, as if from something as mundane as burnt pastry, crawled upwards from the cold grey obsidian rocks. Nothing else moved. When Héros turned to the communicative demon, it too was gone.

The fires of Hell went out, and Héros sat alone there. No friend, no enemy, for whom to exhibit courage, no audience for whom to shine.

After a long time, a feeling of discomfort, *spiritual* malaise, drove him to his feet. He walked along the shelving greynesses, searching for something, unable to realise what. And as he did so he ceased to walk, began simply to progress.

Calm arrived suddenly. It was like letting drop a ton weight you had been holding onto for years; it was wonderful. And almost immediately on the lightening and the calm began a quickening of interest, a dramatic, pervasive excitement…

Lucien started up – and in that instant was aware he was no longer Lucien, was no longer even *he* – and that it did not matter. That it was actually a great relief.

Simultaneously all the greyness went away. The desert went. Instead...
Here one is presented with the problem of describing a rainbow to those
blind from birth, when one is, additionally, oneself as blind. But there is that
marvellous beast again, the analogy. Analogously, then. The small bit of
psychic fibre, which had been, a few seconds or years ago, the young man
Lucien, passionate revolutionary, first-class writer, fairly consistent hysteric,
and post-guillotinee, was all at once catapulted out of its self-constructed
prison of terrors and miseries, into a garden of sun and flowers and birdsong.
No, not Heaven. But so glorious the garden was, and limitless, it would have
put Heaven to shame. And over there were mountains to be climbed, and
over there seas to be swum, and up there, a library of wisdom with wide-
open doors. And most charming of all, drifting here and there in earnest
discussion with each other, or merely quietly reposing together, or quite
alone yet *still* together – others, who were family and friends, thousands of
them, the closest and the best; old rivals to be tussled with, familiar loves to
be embraced. And imbuing it all a spirit of gladsome and determined,
ferocious curiosity. Of course, it was not like this. Not at all. Yet, it was.
Suffice it to say that the soul, which had last been Lucien, dashed into it with
the psychic equivalent to a howl of joy, and was welcomed. And here is one
more analogy. Imagine you were rendered voluntarily amnesiac, (absurd, but
imagine it), and came to believe you were a small wooden post located in a
cellar. And as the time went by, you saw the advantages of being a small
wooden post, began, adaptable creature that you were, to like it, and so to
dislike the idea of being anything else. And then the cellar door opened. And
then the amnesia lifted.

Somewhere on the edges of the analogous garden, the soul that had been
Lucien met the soul that had been peerless, assured Héros, entering in a
bemused, nervous sort of way. And the two souls greeted each other, and
reassured each other that everything was all right, before dashing off to
discover all the things they were now so eager to find out about.

While somewhere close by, close as the bark to the inside of a tree, yet
totally distanced, D'Antoine 'turned' again in his 'sleep', muttered
something, metaphorically, and nodded off into oblivion once more.

That oblivion of his was turning out rather easy. Had she known,
Lucette might have envied it. But as it was, her own sleepless journey
reminded her of the tasks of Psyche in the Greek myth, a story Lucien had
once told her, at the Luxembourg Gardens, and which had retained for her
ever after the shattering poignancy of that time. In this way, it sometimes
seemed a malign fate, even a malign goddess, hindered her.

Sometimes, the perimeter of her vision conveyed the image of a flock of fierce golden sheep with terrible teeth, or else she seemed to be kneeling, sorting grains on the ground. Eventually, she toiled with a pitcher up a steep, featureless hill. The sky was misty now, no longer blue but a colourless almost-grey. She too had entered the region of *limbo,* though she did not know it. She did know she must fill the pitcher at the black stream of Lethe, which brought forgetfulness, which, in effect, took all awareness of self away. Only by filling the pitcher, fulfilling the task, could she ever hope to find Lucien.

Unlike the myth, there was no opposition at the stream. As she bent towards the water, Lucette saw her reflection, just as she had seen it, living, in so many mirrors, even in a mirror that had also, once, reflected the face of Marie Antoinette. And in that moment, Lucette felt a pang of compassion for all lovely young discarded bodies, the white skin, the sunlit hair − for they were of no more use, nor hers to her, and now she understood as much.

Next time, she thought. But, *next time,* what? Then, letting fall the pitcher, and letting it vanish, too, she lifted a handful of the black water of forgetfulness, and with a last wistful thought of love, she drank it.

The incorporeal state did not seem quite right to the one who had been Lucette. She − it − was young, yet old enough that intimations reached through of one day when incorporeality would seem pleasant and informative, and another day, centuries in the future, when incorporeality would be yearned for. Meanwhile, these conditions were imperfect, yet they were not, after all, alien. Then, the young soul advanced or circled or perhaps did not move at all, and in doing so found the soul which had been Lucien.

Though neither was as they had been, no longer Lucien, no longer Lucette, no longer male or female, even so, the aura of love and kindness they had shared still bonded them, attracted them both to the other's vicinity. But there were many such bonds now open to each of them. They came together now, and would come together often, and touch in the way souls do touch, which is naturally the rainbow and the blind again. But since there was no loneliness and no rejection and no anguish where now they were, they did not need to cling together, a single unit of two, against a hostile environment. For this environment was benign, and it and they were one.

In this story, you see, the lovers do not join for ever to violin accompaniment on a cloud of mortal love. The lovers are no longer mortal, and there are no violins, no clouds. It is difficult not to experience annoyance or mournfulness, or even fear, that individual liaisons do not need to persist, in frantic intensity, *there* where the love is all-pervasive, calm and unconditional. We must try not to lament or to be irritated by them. Only note how happy they are, even if 'happy' is an analogous word.

While, somewhere close as a hand to a glove, D'Antoine 'turns' over and finally wakes, and is no longer D'Antoine. The lengthy sleep of nothingness has acted like a sponge, and wiped away physical identity. Though the emerging soul remembers it, of course, as all of them remember who they have been, plan who they *will* be, (no unfinished business is ever left unfinished; there will be other work, other loves, other springs), it is now a garment held in the hands, not the substance of the self. The true self is quite free. It leaps forward into liberty with an analogous roar of delight and resolution.

The resonance of such roars is a commonplace of the astral. Just as the sound of tears, the cry of pain, and the falling crash of the guillotine are a commonplace, here.

After the Guillotine

Chosen by Mavis Haut
And Kari Sperring

Tanith Lee has been much admired for the beauty and originality of her prose, her psychological and emotional acuity, her humour and much besides. Perhaps less visited, is the less visible arena of Lee's responses to abstract ideas. Lee's cornucopia is huge and I have so many favourite stories, I have selected one which examines her ability to understand material in a subjective form.

Lee's imagination is never kept at arm's length. She absorbs outer events as if she had experienced them for herself subjectively. Her characters, times, places, each with its own quirks, odours and echoes, can seem to have emerged from actual encounters. Even the smallest scraps aren't wasted. She plunges in, enveloping herself in them, apparently transforming what she observes into her own, lived experiences, and seeming to close the gap between subject and object. This intuitive approach must exist to some degree in all acts of reading and writing, but Lee practices it with sometimes startling proximity. She has a sort of double vision, both subjective and objective. She is never judgemental in her search to take in the *experiences* of the other vicariously and her reinventions all primarily respect the subjective experiences of other beings. She is only borrowing them – or possibly they invade her. She has described herself as the bus, not the driver.

This story (like the novel, *The Gods are Thirsty*, and, more obliquely, the novella *Madame Two Swords*) relates to the French Revolution. All of them focus on the lives and deaths of a small group of revolutionaries, each crucial in the early shaping of the revolution, but all destined for the guillotine.

Lee crosses the boundary between life and death with seamless lightness. We meet the four men on their way to the scaffold, follow them through their executions and on into their afterlives. Their experiences of life after death depend entirely on each one's expectations. The results vary greatly as Lee moves through death's different landscapes as if in a series of elaborate dance steps. She steps easily into her own writerly shoes with lines such as, "But there is that marvellous beast again, the analogy." "Allusions both historical and classical were nicely observed." The wife of one takes on Psyche's labours to reach reunion with her beloved husband. Another dismisses the "ridiculous Catholic Hell", while in the sleep of death the sceptic half-awakes "With a – metaphorical – grunt", then "burrowed, nestled and was gone again."

The entire story can be read as an extended excursion into the uses of metaphor. Lee studies the process of transformation through metaphor with microscopic care. She openly displays how metaphor can transform abstract ideas into narrative, and then confronts death, identity, epistemology, faith and

– perhaps her own favourite subject – the nature of true love. Lee, the writer, remarks on true love's ineffability, but she never seeks to tell it. Nor does she ever abandon the delicate subjectivities of other first persons to the naked cold of objective vision.

– Mavis Haut

Mavi Haut was one of Tanith Lee's dearest friends.

~

I'm a historian. I did not set out to be, but it's where I ended up and, by and large, it sits well with me. But historians and histories (and I mean histories, for there is no one universal History, but rather many overlapping and equal valid histories) have this in common. They are inclined to look at events sideways, to wonder about roads not travelled and to seek journeys into other minds. In that sense, we are a lot like writers. 'After the Guillotine' is a story Tanith wrote inspired by her novel *The Gods are Thirsty,* which is set during and about the French Revolution. That latter is a key event in the histories of western Europe and the development of new systems of government. It occupies a lot of space in the minds of many historians, philosophers, economists and political thinkers. *The Gods Are Thirsty* is a historical novel. But in 'After the Guillotine', however, Tanith added a new motif to her theme and looked at the revolution, several of its central figures and their actions sidelong, asking what if, how come and if only.

It's a lovely reflection on death and guilt and our conception of what might happen after. And it's a powerful commentary on history.

The historian in me loves it. So does the writer.

– Kari Sperring

Kari Sperring is an academic mediaeval historian, and author of five books on early Welsh, Irish, and Scandinavian history. Her fantasy novel Living with Ghosts *won the 2010 Sydney J Bounds Award and was shortlisted for the William L Crawford Award.*

Taken at His Word

1

Olvero the Scholar left the Governor's court, intending to kill himself by drinking the poisonous ink from his ink-well. It was not long before sunrise. The sky was black as the intended ink, slit by one prescient, envenomed slash of red.

Consumed by self-pity Olvero leaned on a wall, and wept.

Yet, even while weeping, he heard the simultaneous nagging of that stern, pure, obdurate voice of his mind. Though he might have every justification for pitying himself, he must resist. Self-pity was useless. Just as suicide, in this instance, was despicable. Others had a right to both self-pity and self-destruction, but Olvero (Olvero admonished himself) had not. He was young, strong, healthy, not ugly, and though his last cash had gone, still not entirely without potential funds. For could he not sell most of his possessions and so gain enough to support himself, at least another month? What, after all, did he need with the silver ring his adulterous mother had left him in place of herself? Or the little blue glass goblet he had rescued from a court official's banquet, where all else was being drunkenly smashed? Why too did Olvero need a quiet apartment with white walls and having a view of tall trees in which birds sang, at dawn and sunfall? Or, come to that, a supportive chair? A mattress? A roof? For God's sake, let him lose all and wander in rags and weather. See what gems he could write *then*, damn all his enemies to Hell.

Ah. The stern voice, as had been the weeping voice, was now subsumed in a raging one.

It was the City Governor's fault. *He* had deigned, after three months of the scholar's life spent in unaffordable bribes and waiting, to consider an epic drama the scholar had written. Tonight, however, the Governor had rejected the drama, having himself kept the scholar waiting thirteen months. This was done during a supper, to which the scholar had been summoned, and placed at a very low table. The rejection was staged just before the meat course when, having invited the scholar to stand up, the Governor and his courtiers regaled him with their censure and ridicule and – worse – 'disappointment' in the 'poorness' of his work.

191

"My last meal in a nest of ignorant vipers!" *Oh, God*, thought the scholar, wiping his eyes on his sleeve, *if I begin to write now as tritely as I speak – I deserve no better than a dose of poisoned ink.*

The birds were singing beautifully when he reached his room.

He stood by the window and stared at sun rising from river, turning the foliage of all the framing trees, and all the feathers of the flying birds, to gold, carmine and amber.

Then he poured himself a cup of chocolate. It was the very last cup.

On the desk he spread his scorned epic, leafed through its pages, read here and there a line or two. His heart leapt. Though he would never claim perfection for any of his work, Olvero had known, since his eighteenth year, that what he did was of worth; was worthy too of notice. For it was not, really, *his*. That is, it was *given* him. It was a *gift* to him – or perhaps some *reward* he had earned by other work, in some other mystical and forgotten world inhabited before this one. Its glories came from *there*, that higher source, God, or gods, or angels – or even non-malignant demons possibly – which possessed him whenever he sat to the paper and dipped a quill into ink. Any flaws, of course, were due to his own misunderstanding – or mishearing – of the silent yet omniscient guidance which thereafter fired his brain and moved his hand.

He had been blessed. Olvero knew it. And yet if some vast power had chosen him as an imperfect yet acceptable conduit, the mortal power of men now spurned him. More, it seemed set to obliterate him.

At the thought, rage towered up again in Olvero, potent as lust. But he stamped upon the rage. He shut it in his heart, tightly bound it, locked on it the doors of his mind. For rage would interfere with the mediumistic process of his work. As indeed could great sorrow – the memory of his mother's departure, the later loss of a young woman he had deeply loved, who had fallen away from love of him . . . or extreme physical pain – as when he had been beaten by a gang of thieves for not having enough money to satisfy their rapacity. ..(also let it be said, for defending himself and breaking a pair of their noses).

Nevertheless, of these three distractions – rage, sorrow, pain – rage seemed the worst. It blocked and muddied the receptive channel. It must not break loose again. However many deserters, thieves, governors, *monsters* he was compelled to confront.

And so he sat down and closed the manuscript of his epic and drew towards him a piece of fresh paper – one of the hundred final sheets he had.

His urge was only to write a short piece, perhaps even a poem to praise the birds in the dawn. To bid them farewell, for the approaching day when he must leave his apartment.

But instead his mind slipped strangely askew. He thought first of a ghost story he had heard only yesterday, in the small tavern where sometimes he took a glass of wine. But the story was old now that he considered it. Then his mind – was it fumbling? After all still too dismayed to seek true dreams and images? – his mind slewed like a sailed craft to the wind. Olvero stared in vague surprise at an inner procession of odd, uncanny freaks. After the predatory ghost, a ghoul, said for years to prey on the burial ground of the city's cathedral. Next, an undine who lurked in a village well, drawing young men to their deaths. A murderous witch came after, with rats in her hair... a stone-inflicting gorgon whose own hair comprised snakes... a devil of the Eastern lands that danced in a sand storm, with ready teeth as pointed as awls.

Olvero stood up. He thrust away from the table.

To work with such nonsense was absurd.

He should sleep.

Yet even as he moved towards the mattress in the alcove, Olvero turned about again. He recrossed the room, leaned over the paper and, with the quill fresh dipped, wrote there very large and black, and with many curlicues of the sort he seldom if ever employed, one word. *Vampire*.

Stepping back once more, he regarded this effort.

He swore, both amused and disgusted. Best leave it all, go sleep, awake refreshed. Evidently, he could do nothing legitimate till then.

The Scholar Olvero sold his winter coat, (it was not yet autumn) a jacket reserved for grand occasions; (such as the Governor's disgraceful dinner); his boots, the blue goblet, one of the pillows from his mattress-bed... There were also things of lesser value. They all went. And with their unopulent returns, he kept himself in cheap lamp-oil, cheap ink, cheap food, dull husk-filled coffee and watered wine. His rent though seemed likely to plunge into arrears. Olvero borrowed from a usurer. (Leeches, all he dealt with, yet no worse than the Governor.)

During this while, a matter of eighteen days, Olvero found he could not write a single word.

Or, ultimately and bizarrely, that was all he *could* write.

Coming back to his desk on the very evening following his return from the Governmental palace, he had seated himself to construct the brief simple ode previously considered. Now to sunset birds, carrolling a sinking disc.

The trees were falling into deep black, and stars scorching through them, when Olvero flung up from the table. He had written only gibberish, he believed. Masses of half-formed, unpunctuated sentences, verbs lacking nouns, and adjectives lacking meaning, and all of it with letters left out – things similar to *carlet* for scarlet, or *rung* for running, *ght* for night and *inggni* for singing.

Olvero thought he had gone mad, and became afraid. He set himself to write at least one word carefully, readably. And found he wrote again the word **Vampire**. Then he attempted the word *God* and instead wrote *Bark*. Next *Howl*.

After this he drank the last of his good wine, two cups. Then he wrote a prosaic list of things he must do – buying more cheap bread, stopping up a mouse-hole – and this all came out quite sensibly, spelled in the usual way and coherent.

But nothing else other than such lists *would* come. He could not even describe the darkness of the night, nor the narrow lighted windows across the street, nor a fisherman's fire on the river bank. This was like a horrible attack of lexicological hiccups or incurable stammering. Oh, he had known his ill-treatment by the Governor, (and by all those through the years who had belittled and tried to deny – or better, ruin – his gift) had harmed him. But surely not to such a pitch as to rob him of his true *life*, his ability to *work*.

In the end, drunk on the last of the strong wine, he sat and wrote over and over the one word he could now pen. *Vampire*. **Vampire**. **VAMPIRE**. And each time he ornamented it more and more. He draped it in coils and spirals, dots, slots, festoons of calligraphic decoration. Until, eventually, it seemed less a word than a briar-clump, or curving wall of thorns worthy of some fairy-tale imprisonment, that both shut in and shut out, threatening mutilation and death to any trying to get through it either way.

Next day then, and for seventeen days after, waking generally late, Olvero the Scholar wrote angrily across two, three, even four whole sheets of paper. He wrote over and over and only the ghastly and primitive word for a nightmare creature in which he, his enlightened self, did not believe. *Vampire*. **Vampire**. **VAMPIRE**. Vampire.

Then, not even pausing to sip water, he encumbered the word with swathes of inky ornament. He went out only reluctantly and after noon, in order to sell one or other more possession, or to visit the usurious establishment.

On the eighteenth day, Olvero did not leave his room.

He had nothing left to sell. Even his mother's ring was sold. Most of his paper was gone, too. Only one little stoop of ink remained.

Not even, now, enough to poison himself.

Perhaps, instead, he might eat the papers with their inky alphabetic briar forests of *vampire vampire vampire.*

The birds sang heartlessly at the dying sun.

Birds did not care for the sun's nightly death. Nor its morning birth-agonies. Nor would they care at all if Olvero, a mere human, could not sit and look at them, nor praise their voices. Another would do as well at the window. Or none at all.

By flickering, fading lamplight, **Vampire** wrote Olvero with enormous attention and in the last ink, across the height and width of a single sheet of paper.

Tomorrow he would wheedle another small loan, leaving his shoes as surety. He would then get drunk in the tavern on weak beer, next drowning himself in the river. Make the birds sing for that!

Vampire: deceiver, cheat, criminal, parasite, perpetrator of violence, adversary having implacable and undeserved powers, anti-god, un-thing, mindless drainer of blood and life...

Olvero dreamed he was still scribbling the word on and on. Yet there was a difference. Before, he had written **Vampire** first, then ensconced it in draperies of ink. Now in the dream, he *commenced* with a proliferation of inked coils and curls and curdles, and out of these gradually if remorselessly the letters of the word **Vampire** grew. Like a serpent it rose from two hundred score of looping, swirling talons.

The scholar opened his eyes. He was awake?

His room, in darkness after he had blown out the lamp, was now lit with a soft creamy radiance. Perhaps the moon had risen, and shone in at the window. No, it had not. The sky beyond the glass was black with latest night or most premature morning. The moon was dead. It would never shine again.

In here, however –

The pages covered with the word (**Vampire**) had somehow been dislodged and scattered in a loose heap on the floor. These were what gave off the glow, being now mostly pure white, unspoiled by marks. Instead the inked and thorn-like curlicues had also risen straight up, just as in the dream, right off the paper. In the white-lit air now the darkly molten spiky spiral hedges knotted and unreeled, embracing each other, *strangling* each other with wet-gleaming and spiny tentacles and feelers.

Olvero stared. He had become only eyes.

With those he watched what next emerged from the dance of the separated Word.

The shape was elongate and thin. Yet instantly solid, opaque and actual as marble and ebony. It also swayed and wriggled its long body, which while seeming legless as that of a huge worm, still displayed arms and hands, a neck, a face, a torrent of spooling hair, all of which wove and rippled in restless, ceaseless gesturings. The constant, almost tidal *flux* of it, having once formed, nevertheless retained a basic hardness and permanence. Nowhere was this more evident than in the awful *face*. It was a dead-white mask, equipped with all required features – but formed of a sort of – living? – alabaster. And where its eyes burned between the white lids they were only black – black as ink. And the lips were wet-black too, and between them showed a wet-ink-black mouth and an ink-black pointed tongue. And from the upper jaw extruded two extended canine teeth, the whitest things of all, and glittering.

Even as Olvero watched, this structure of animated writing folded suddenly as a closing fan. All motion stopped. Balanced on its black tail, the creature now represented utter stasis. Only the black tongue flicked once across the black lips, and the ink pools of the eyes were shut for a split second in a white-lidded blink.

Either it smiled at Olvero, or that was the thing's habitual expression in repose.

On the floor, the sheets of paper lay sodden and limp, not a single written mark on them. (Tomorrow the pages would have fallen to pieces. The ink-well – and the air – would be empty of darkness).

But now the creature hovered, elevated maybe an inch or so above the floor. It was quite impossible to tell if it had either or any gender. As for intelligence, it was not to be said. Yet intent it did seem to have. It smiled at Olvero, or *through* Olvero, a few more moments, during which the scholar, who had become only eyes, felt himself also adrift in the atmosphere of the room. Then the Vampire gathered itself together like a vast skein of black and snow-white wool. Mobile once more, it spun into itself, flattened, compressed, became like a twisted stalk of salty bitumen – and vanished.

At once all light was gone. All dark, too.

Olvero dropped away down miles of nothingness, and did not come back to himself again until light had refilled his window, and the rent-collecting landlord hammered on his door.

2

There was plague in the city. Everyone spoke of it.

A man would, in the day, be healthy and about his business or pleasures as usual. Come next birdsong dawn, someone or other would find him – on the open street, tucked behind some wall of the tavern, in his own chamber, flung across floor or bed – a chalk-white corpse already stenchful and turning rotten, covered with peculiar lesions and wounds that were dryly black, since no blood remained in his body. Or *her* body; women were often victims too.

What kind of plague was it then? Most citizens knew the name for it but in the first days none would mention that name. Then they did, almost all of them. *Vampire*.

"Vampire," they said, whispered, muttered, shrieked, and hurried to the churches and cathedrals for blessed objects and holy water. None of these things did any good. It seemed the plague creature was not itself religious, had not the intellectual wit to reverence the might of God or gods – nor even demons – for counter-spells did no good either.

None had seen the *Vampire*. Or, only the dead had done so. (A wife, say, rousing from a sickening deathly sleep more like a trance, would wake beside her husband to find him a corpse. It would seem the night-fiend was selective, had *chosen* between them – while she had been spared any sight of it, or what it did).

It preyed everywhere, through all strata of society, from the lowest to the highest. Although... a certain partiality, aside even from its tendency to *choose*, might have been observed in its – what could one call it? – diet.

Fathers who bullied and whipped their sons, mothers who abandoned their sons while still children, girls who rejected their young suitors, tutors who scorned their pupils, thieves who beat those they robbed, officials who took bribes and patronizingly prevaricated... usurers, evicting landlords, tavern-keepers who refused an old customer a little beer gratis... Such were the feasts of the vampire. On these it supped, and left them whiter than their own bones, colder than winter, and riddled all over with black coils and curlicues of wounds, almost like a devilish scrivening.

3

Veranilla the Courtesan went to the Governor 's palace, intending to provide him with sex, as their customary bargain was. It was late in the afternoon and the sky was rosy as a peach. Only the east showed a single hint of shadow.

Quite satisfied with her life, the courtesan felt neither unease nor resentment. She had been well-trained since her fourteenth year, and never used unkindly by her mother (also of the sorority) nor her early patrons. By the time she encountered any patrons of the rougher sort she was established, and able to make them rue the day they were born.

Having left her carriage, Veranilla entered the palace by a discreet way which led through charming gardens. In the vestibule she made her arrival known to a chamberlain, and was presently installed in a nice supper-room. Here she dined, as on her previous two visits, alone with the Governor.

She always found the Governor, the most powerful man in the city aside from the Bishop (whom she had also accommodated on several occasions), quite affable company. Descended from a mercantile family, the Governor was respectful of all the creative trades, including in his favour both artists and prostitutes. "But how I wish Heaven would spare me," he told her, as they reached the stage of sweets and fruit, "these bloody writers! Are they all quite mad? I don't refer to our popular playwrights, who so please the people – naturally not – nor those that work for the opera. But these others, the ones who wish only to entertain themselves with inept over-purpled gibberish, and may take seventeen stanzas of dross to reach some paltry climax – worthy only of putting on in a wine-shop latrine!"

The Governor did not once mention the plague. Let alone any plebeian chatter of a supernatural night-beast. The Governor, Veranilla suspected, did not even privately believe in the Supreme Being, but frequently alluded to the present age as an enlightened one. Men should, the Governor averred, have by now outgrown silly fancies.

That evening the sunset was prolonged and vivid and, just before the Governor went through into his bedroom, he and she paused to admire the crimsoning sky through a window of fine glass. Many small birds were flying over the garden trees, looking like swarms of bees against the red dusk, and Veranilla stayed to watch them, while the Governor stepped into the other room. Here he preferred to undress first and climb into the bed, sitting to observe as Veranilla took off her clothes. He left the door partly ajar, however, as normal. And so she heard at once when he let out a sudden wavering cry of what sounded like extreme terror.

Despite the relative reasonableness of her life so far, Veranilla had also been trained to be cautious.

She therefore turned from the window and walked softly in her satin shoes to the barely open door. Here she looked cautiously around its panelling and into the chamber beyond.

It too possessed long windows, and was filled by a deep wine-red brilliance. By this the young woman saw all, very clearly.

The Governor stood bolt upright by the bed, still in his shirt and breeches. He was transfixed. As well he might be. For there, in the middle of the floor, a million streaming jet-black muscular filaments circled and poured upward. They had come from nowhere, Veranilla surmised – for even as she stared, more and more of them evolved, apparently from nothing, to thicken and entwine the bristling mass already writhing on the tiles. It reminded her instantly of something: a sea-monster she had as a child once been shown, in a tank during carnival. Yet this apparition was the nastier, and much larger too. And all the while it swelled, rose upward, *grew*.

Veranilla did not scream. Nor did she remonstrate, not even calling out to the plainly panic-stricken Governor. *His* face was a study in insane horror. Hers in iron self-control.

All this time the fiery light, rather than dim, had intensified – as if the sun, just now down under the earth's edge, had exploded there like gunpowder.

Accordingly the Courtesan Veranilla was in no doubt when, from the tumult of thrashing thorny tentacles, a form began to consolidate itself. This form, not of a man, was of a creature. A creature like a black worm; with a black unspecified torso – less human than resembling the thorax of a giant insect. And from that came out the death-white arms and skinny hands and neck like a fungus stem and face like a mask, everything caught in a whirl of viper-like hairs, and other extended fringes, these all a liquid, poisonous black.

Just then the creature turned its head. Its flattish plate-like mask demonstrated a fixation with the casement. In this position also Veranilla was able to note the ink-pool of a single eye, the gleaming black lips and pointed tongue, the fangs. She was ready to hide herself more thoroughly should the obscene head turn further in her direction, but instead the creature's interest was, for that second, only in the window. Or rather, in the last flights of the birds beyond, as they went singing and settling to their roosts. She was to say later that she sensed a terrible hatred the creature had for these innocent birds. As if it resented their careless song and ability to fly. And Veranilla was glad that, being a monster of darkness, it might not manifest earlier in the day – and certainly not in the open sunset – to snatch any of them. Men though were to be snared both day and night.

At the hour, she nevertheless forgot about the birds, for next moment the *Vampire* (it was now to prove its title) sprang and dazzled through the air straight upon the Governor. Trapped in the thorns and tines, immediately borne to the ground beneath it, the Governor was able only to let out one deep, loud scream. Before the *Vampire* silenced him.

Veranilla had seen certain unpalatable events. But this surpassed them all.

At the theatrical maelstrom of ripped flesh and other bodily fragments, lit by sprays of scarlet that rivalled and then outshone the dying light, she did not look very long. In a minute, noiseless as a ghost herself, she fled through the outer room and into the corridor beyond.

As she had thought, the Governor's guards were seated some way off, playing cards. Any outcries they might have heard they would have put down to sensual transports, for the Governor had been inclined to voice his joys. No more, Veranilla believed. She knew but too well both guards must witness, as she had done, the awful scene in the bedroom. Or might she herself not be suspect? Might she still be, even should any think she had wrought the act through evil magic?

4

The apartment where the scholar now lived lay two-thirds below the level of the street. Part of an old cellar, it had stayed cold, damp, fusty, dark, and redolent of wines long since drunk. A small hole provided a sort of window, but it was above Olvero's head. Along with admitting grudging daylight, the hole enabled rubbish sometimes to be kicked or pushed through into the cell, out of sheer malice.

In other areas of this establishment persons made raucous noise at all and any hour. That would have disturbed Olvero, had he had the inspiration to work. But he had none, let alone the means; paper, ink were gone. To get any money at all now he must carry out menial tasks, such as the porting of night-soil. He was unskilled in any craft save writing. He had in fact supposed at first he might be employed penning letters or other stuff for those unable to write at all. But obviously, as a general rule, those who could not write or read had acquaintances similarly unequipped. The one oaf who hired Olevro, to construct a note to a creditor, refused to pay until said creditor ceased his harrying. Worse, when the creditor read the note and continued merciless, the oaf returned and attacked Olvero. (Curiously, the oaf was discovered dead of the blood-draining plague only a night or so after.)

The scholar anyway had lost not only the knack for writing, but for living. He sat in his cellar-cell most of the time brooding on his ill-fortune. From the beginning, he had put down his sight of a **Vampire** rising from its written name as a dream or hallucination, brought on by anger and despair. That the paper had been made soggy and broken up in shreds the scholar attributed to some spillage, or to rain or dew somehow seeping through the unopened window of his former room.

The scholar did not believe in vampires.

Even when he heard the stories and affright from the lower city, the tally of 'vampiric' murders, Olvero dismissed them. He was a man of an Enlightened Era – if ironically too a genius persecuted by the lightless ignorance of fools. What could be more perfect in the cruel balance of existence?

He had been going on in this manner for a couple of months. A chill fall had meanwhile entered the city, hennaing the trees prior to shearing them, hanging early icicles from roofs, to provoke winter against the talented amateurism of autumn.

Olvero woke one morning with the foul taste of hunger in his mouth, and drank some stagnant water that did not relieve it.

When fists thundered on the door, he recalled the last landlord, who had demanded rent then slung him in the street. But the cell was in a ruin, it was free. The scholar thought those who knocked might, if left alone, depart.

But soon the door was broken down. Several of the Governor's soldiers came in.

"We have been searching for you," said one, with a grimace.

A wild hope gripped the scholar. He gaped at the men and half-remembered some tale he had heard a while before – when was that? – that the Governor had fallen sick. Could it be illness had slashed the veil from the Governor's eyes? The man now grasped that Olvero was a god-gifted writer, and so had sent to find and raise him from the mud to gold and glory?

Foolishly perhaps then, Olvero did not question the soldiers. Yet probably in any case it would not have mattered.

Olvero's dungeon cell was not so different from the cellar.

In fact it had certain superiorities. For example, the window could be looked through despite the bars. It afforded a glimpse of sky now and then blue. Nor was it accessible from the public road. Besides, food was provided and, if hardly tempting to a connoisseur, at least it was, fairly regularly, there. The water was no dirtier or more unhealthy than that available at the cellar.

Wretchedly Olvero told himself that, once freed (obviously, his imprisonment was an error), he would have much material to use in some future ode, epic or saga. Secretly he did not think he would ever be able to use it, however. His genius had died within him. Either that, or the gods had withdrawn their gift from him.

Eventually he was taken out and, to his dreary, added horror, chained. Up into an elegant cold room he was dragged. A great many officials and men of the Governor's court sat about, also priests in their own finery, each of whom glared at him with concentrated attention. The Governor himself was not present.

Olvero had no means of deducing that the Governor was dead – had been stone-dead indeed, from the first smiting of the *Vampire*. Few in the city had learned this. Only the Governor's immediate circle, his council, the Bishop, seven priests, three or four soldiers, and one woman knew. The murder was concealed, and the rumour of the Governor's sickness substituted, in order that the crime's perpetrator might not escape. Nevertheless, it took some while for any to find him. Since Olvero (for by then the perpetrator was known to be himself) had vanished from his accustomed lodging. The soldiers who next hunted for him, arrested and jailed him, had been given beforehand special safeguards from the Bishop. They had not known why. Nor luckily that, if put to the test, they would have been no use at all.

But Olvero the Scholar was not privy to any of this, either.

Now he stared about, blinking at the brightness of the room. And an official stood up and began to pronounce.

"Sirs, your Grace, my lord the Bishop, here then the felon is before us. In broad day, when alone we are secure from the vile beast he has conjured. Some thirty-seven significant persons of the city have by now perished through his midnight acts, and God knows how many of the lower orders, who inevitably have gone uncounted."

At this Olvero glanced around, wondering – *a felon?* – to whom they referred. Then it came to him that they meant none other than he. The scholar laughed bitterly, just as he had when the Governor had publically reviled him those months before.

"Hark," exclaimed the official, "he jeers at us, he is so certain of Satan's care of him. Come, let us get on. Bring in the woman Veranilla."

Then the doors were undone and the courtesan entered. Olvero gazed at her without much comprehension; though she was beautiful, she reminded him of no woman he had ever met.

Veranilla wore mourning, however, and seeing it Olvero came to realise quite abruptly that all save the priests did so. Therefore he was not very startled at the official's next words: "Now, Veranilla, inform us, if you will, of what occurred on the evening of the Governor's death."

The courtesan remained respectfully subdued, cool and self-possessed. As with much of what she did, she had rehearsed herself carefully in this monologue. She was blameless, and meant to be found so. Olvero, undeniably the culprit, must suffer solo for his disgusting deeds.

After a moment she spoke.

She explained that she had been visiting the Governor on an occasion of business, for he had graciously consented to offer her advice about a mercantile venture. (This, it went without saying, was a politeness, for only a mere handful were not aware of the true nature of their transaction. There would be other little politenesses and euphemisms in her account. Some to uphold decorum. Others, more personal to herself, were employed to make sure that she appeared quite beyond reproach.)

Veranilla told them how the Governor had gone into an adjoining room to fetch a book he wished to refer to. Presently she heard an awful cry. Rushing to the door she saw the *Vampire* already evolved from nothing – for there was no way in at all, the outer door and all the windows shut. More, it had already felled the Governor, slain him, and was busy ripping him wide open with its long white nails and teeth, and lashes of its black, whip-like tentacles of hair. Even the inky pointed tongue, Veranilla vowed (with the most sensitive yet couth shudder), sliced the flesh like a knife. Blood flew everywhere. They might have seen it – most of those present had – sprayed about the walls of the bedroom, as if the ghastly crimson sunset had permanently stained them. The *Vampire* by then guzzled amid the carnage on the Governor's wounds. Powerless to help the poor dead gentleman, yet herself unnoted by the creature, Veranilla had run to fetch the guard. Thereafter the three of them witnessed the final horror.

The courtesan was at pains to stress that the *Vampire* had also the skill of beglamouring bystanders with a sort of deathly trance. It was because of that no other survivor had ever seen the beast, so she believed, even when it supped on their closest companion or spouse in the very same chamber, or even the same bed. But as things had this time happened, the *Vampire* had itself not at first seen Veranilla. (This aspect of her account was demonstrably true). Now though, she added, when she and the brave guardsmen reached the doorway, the creature, even while engaged in its grisly feast, did detect them and cast on them an immobilising spell. Only the absorption of the monster in its supper presumably prevented it from rendering them fully unconscious. Therefore they had seen, but been forced to stand like statues, unable to move hand or limb. (In actuality, this was another of Veranilla's little lies. The guards, on viewing the Vampire had certainly become frozen – with utter terror. But she had no intention of telling the officials of the court such a thing. She had even convinced the guards themselves that they had all the while been straining to leap to the Governor's aid, and only ill-magic had held them back. It had never been her task to make enemies among those who might be useful).

In the end, Veranilla continued, total night consumed the world. And at last the ***Vampire*** rose from its victim. A curious glow played about it, revealing how the creature seemed to unwind from itself, like a knot of serpentine vines untwisting from a stock. These fell away into the dark, sizzled out, and all illumination ceased. The fiend had vanished into thin air. Only then were any of the three able to move once more.

At once lights were kindled. And so they beheld the dreadful remains of the Governor, and saw, each one of them, what no other ever had: the freshness of the marks and wounds, and through that freshness, what they portended. For in every other previous case the drained bodies had dried and sunk upon themselves before they were discovered, thus distorting what was, in the first one or two hours, entirely visible. An alarm was next raised. Certain others were brought in haste into the room, among them even his Grace the Bishop himself.

Vampires – such did not exist. All these people had lost their minds. Olvero gazed superciliously upon them. And they, in turn, glared venomously at *him*.

"You are a male witch," announced the official. "You will not even merit cleansing torture, nor the offer that you recant, and beg God's forgiveness. For you, Olvero, such amenities are valueless. Your own creature, the Vampire, has itself betrayed you to the gallows."

Olvero finally felt a wave of fear.

He rose from it gasping, as a man briefly might when drowning in an icy river.

"Betrayed me – what lunacy is this? Such a demon does not exist. So how – *betray*?"

The official composed himself to granite. He replied in a voice of steel.

"The marks upon the body of our lord, the Governor, were closely examined. Drawings even were made of them by two of the leading artists of the city. Other bodies then, previously killed by your conjuration, were exhumed and studied, and the type of their wounds, decipherable in the light of this *later* evidence, displayed infallibly that *you* were the sole instigator. The monster is *your* creation – *yours* the will behind the wicked butchery – *yours* the despicable sorcery. You are damned. God will have *no* pity on your soul. Our work is only to expunge you, for your creature too will perish with you. That has been made plain by its own method."

Olvero blinked. He felt greatly tired, and the chains weighed him to the earth, or to Hell perhaps. He knew at last he was guilty, yes, he must know it. Why else had his genius abandoned him?

Humbly; or simply brokenly, he asked, "Still I fail to grasp – what *method*?

What was the *type* of the wounds? How – did they reveal my – guilt?"

"Their pattern."

"I fail still –"

"He has gone mad," said the official. "The weight of his own infamy already destroys him. Show him one of the drawings," he added to a clerk. "Be aware, Olvero, each corpse we have found is signed the same."

In this way, just before they took him from the room, and so that very afternoon to his execution, Olvero saw drawn in ink on artist's paper a sketch of the body of the slaughtered Governor. The corpse seemed covered in black curlicues and chirographic decorations – and these were the slashes, punctures, slicing, bites and tears the **Vampire** had performed. While entangled in their centre – with slight effort Olvero came to perceive three words, which were also made of wounds, and also ornamentally defined. They were black as blackness, and might be discerned by any seeing, literate eye. **Olvero the Scholar**, they read.

Time passes. Some one hundred and forty years after, various manuscripts of Olvero's were accidentally located. They caused a sensation and shot to fame. To this day several of his plays are still performed, if necessary in translation, in many of the great theatres of the world. His poetry is included in erudite volumes, and quoted by modern writers of acknowledged talent; even taught in universities. Certain sources claim his two unfinished novels have had nearly as many reprintings as the most popular of the wonderful works of Defoe.

As to the stories that surround Olvero's defamation and death, they are ascribed to superstition and moronic inanity. The slow will always try to pull down the faster runner. In this instance, seemingly, they succeeded.

And the Word was made flesh
Gospel of John, Ch.1, V. 14.

Taken At His Word
Chosen by Ian Whates

Trying to select a favourite Tanith Lee story is one of those impossible choices designed to stump an AI or flummox the Sphynx. It's a bit like asking me to choose a favourite beer, or cheese, or author... There are so *many* excellent options. In the end, I resolved the dilemma by being selfish; I chose a story that mattered to me, for reasons that will mean little to anyone else but a very great deal to yours truly.

You see, back in 2009 it was announced that World Horrorcon was coming to the UK, Brighton to be precise. To mark the occasion, I decided to put together an anthology of original vampire stories, *The Bitten Word*. John Kaiine and Les Edwards provided two brilliant and very different images for the front and back covers, and all manner of very talented authors contributed stories – several of whom (Storm, Freda, Sarah, Sam) have subsequently contributed to this book. Then, of course, there was Tanith.

In compiling *The Bitten Word* I was seeking to deliver a collection of stories that gave a twist to the vampire myth, confounding the reader's expectations while adhering to the central tenet. Most of the stories did precisely that, but none managed to do so quite as Tanith's did. Here was an author who had written so many vampire stories, how could she possibly have anything fresh or different to say on such a familiar theme?

When I finished reading "Taken at His Word" I was grinning from ear to ear, delighted with the piece: a story about a thwarted writer whose very words become the vampire. In one deft stroke Tanith delivered a play on the book's title that reworked the classic trope with panache and joyful wickedness, bringing a whole new dimension to the project.

So wonderful, so delicious, so Tanith.

– Ian Whates

The Isle is Full of Noises

... and if you gaze into the abyss, the abyss gazes also into you.

— Nietzsche

1

It is an island here, now.

At the clearest moments of the day – usually late in the morning, occasionally after noon, and at night when the lights come on – a distant coastline is sometimes discernible. This coast is the higher area of the city, that part which still remains intact above water.

The city was flooded a decade ago. The Sound possessed it. The facts had been predicted some while, and various things were done in readiness, mostly comprising a mass desertion.

They say the lower levels of those buildings which now form the island will begin to give way in five years. But they were saying that too five years back.

Also there are the sunsets. (Something stirred up in the atmosphere apparently, by the influx of water, some generation of heat or cold or vapour.) They start, or appear to do so, the sunsets, about three o'clock in the afternoon, and continue until the sun actually goes under the horizon, which in summer can be as late as seven forty-five.

For hours the roof terraces, towerettes and glass-lofts of the island catch a deepening blood-and-copper light, turning to new bronze, raw amber, cubes of hot pink ice.

Yse lives on West Ridge, in a glass-loft. She has, like most of the island residents, only one level, but there's plenty of space. (Below, if anyone remembers, lies a great warehouse, with fish, even sometimes barracuda, gliding between the girders.)

Beyond her glass west wall, a freak tree has rooted in the terrace. Now nine years old, it towers up over the loft, and the surrounding towers and lofts, while its serpentine branches dip down into the water. Trees are unusual here. This tree, which Yse calls Snake (for the branches), seems un-phased by the salt content of the water. It may be a sort of willow, a willow crossed with a snake.

Sometimes Yse watches fish glimmering through the tree's long hair that floats just under the surface. This appeals to her, as the whole notion of the island does. Then one morning she comes out and finds, caught in the coils of her snake-willow, a piano.

Best to describe Yse, at this point, which is not easy. She might well have said herself, (being a writer by trade but also by desire) that she doesn't want you to be disappointed, that you should hold on to the idea that what you get at first, here, may not be what is to be offered later.

Then again, there is a disparity between what Yse seems to be, or is, and what Yse *also seems* to be, or *is*.

Her name, however, as she has often had to explain, is pronounced to rhyme with 'please' – more correctly, *pleeze:*

Eeze. Is it French? Or some sport from Latin-Spanish? God knows.

Yse is in her middle years, not tall, rather heavy, dumpy. Her fair, greying hair is too fine, and so she cuts it very short. *Yse* is also slender, taller, and her long hair, (still fair, still greying) hangs in thick silken hanks down her back. One constant, grey eye.

She keeps only a single mirror, in the bathroom above the wash basin. Looking in it is always a surprise for Yse: Who on earth is that? But she never lingers, soon she is away from it and back to herself. And in this way too, she deals with Per Laszd, the lover she has never had.

Yse had brought the coffee-pot and some peaches on to the terrace. It is a fine morning, and she is considering walking along the bridge-way to the boat-stop, and going over to the cafés on East Heights. There are always things on at the cafés, psychic fairs, art shows, theatre. And she needs some more lamp oil.

Having placed the coffee and fruit, Yse looks up and sees the piano.

*"Oh, "*says Yse, aloud.

She is very, very startled, and there are good reasons for this, beyond the obvious oddity itself.

She goes to the edge of the terrace and leans over, where the tree leans over, and looks at the snake arms which hold the piano fast, tilted only slightly, and fringed by rippling leaves.

The piano is old, huge, a type of pianoforte, its two lids fast shut, concealing both the keys and its inner parts.

Water swirls round it idly. It is intensely black, scarcely marked by its swim.

And has it been swimming? Probably it was jettisoned from some apartment on the mainland (the upper city). Then, stretching out its three strong legs, it set off savagely for the island, determined not to go down.

Yse has reasons, too, for thinking in this way.

She reaches out, but cannot quite touch the piano.

There are tides about the island, variable, sometimes rough. If she leaves the piano where it is, the evening tide may be a rough one, and lift it away, and she will lose it.

She *knows* it must have swum here.

Yse goes to the table and sits, drinking coffee, looking at the piano. As she does this a breeze comes in off the Sound, and stirs her phantom long heavy soft hair, so it brushes her face and neck and the sides of her arms. And the piano makes a faint twanging, she thinks perhaps it does, up through its shut lids that are like closed eyes and lips together.

"What makes a vampire seductive?" Yse asks Lucius, at the Cafe Blonde. "I mean, irresistible?"

"His beauty," says Lucius. He laughs, showing his teeth. "I knew a vampire, once. No, make that twice. I met him twice."

"Yes?" asks Yse cautiously. Lucius has met them all, ghosts, demons, angels. She partly believes it to be so, yet knows he mixes lies with the truths; a kind of test, or trap, for the listener. "Well, what happened?"

"We walk, talk, drink, make love. He bites me. Here, see?" Lucius moves aside his long locks (luxurious, but greying, as are her own). On his coal-dark neck, no longer young, but strong as a column, an old scar.

"You told me once before," says Yse, "a shark did that."

"To reassure you. But it was a vampire."

"What did you do?"

"I say to him, Watch out, monsieur."

"And then?"

"He watched out. Next night, I met him again. He had yellow eyes, like a cat."

"He was undead?"

"The undeadest thing I ever laid."

He laughs. Yse laughs, thoughtfully. "A piano's caught in my terrace tree."

"*Oh* yeah," says Lucius, the perhaps arch liar.

"You don't believe me."

"What is your thing about vampires?"

"I'm writing about a vampire."

"Let me read your book."

"Someday. But Lucius – it isn't their charisma. Not their beauty that makes them irresistible –"

"No?"

"Think what they must be like . . . skin in rags, dead but walking. Stinking of the grave –"

"They use their hudja-magica to take all that away."

"It's how they make *us* feel."

"Yeah, Yse. You got it."

"What they can do to *us*."

"Dance all night," says Lucius, reminiscent. He watches a handsome youth across the cafe, juggling mirrors that flash unnervingly, his skin the colour of an island twilight.

"Lucius, will you help me shift the piano into my loft?"

"Sure thing."

"Not tomorrow, or next month. I mean, could we do it today, before sunset starts?"

"I love you, Yse. Because of you, I shall go to Heaven."

"Thanks."

"Shit piano," he says. "I could have slept in my boat. I could have paddled over to Venezule. I could have watched the thought of Venus rise through the grey brain of the sky. Piano huh, piano. Who shall I bring to help me? That boy, he looks strong, look at those mirrors go."

The beast had swum to shore, to the beach, through the pale, transparent urges of the waves, when the star Venus was in the brain-grey sky. But not here.

There.

In the dark before star-rise and dawn, more than two centuries ago. First the rifts, the lilts of the dark sea, and in them these mysterious thrusts and pushes, the limbs like those of some huge swimmer, part man and part lion and part crab – but also, a manta ray.

Then, the lid breaks for a second through the fans of water, under the dawn star's piercing steel. Wet as black mirror, the closed lid of the piano, as it strives, on three powerful beast- legs, for the beach.

This Island is an island of sands, then of trees, the sombre sullen palms that sweep the shore. Inland, heights, vegetation, plantations, some of coffee and sugar and rubber, and one of imported kayar. An invented island, a composite.

Does it crawl on to the sand, the legs still moving, crouching low like a beast? Does it rest on the sand, under the sway of the palm trees, as a sun rises?

The Island has a name, like the house which is up there, unseen, on the inner heights. Bleumaneer.

(Notes: Gregers Vonderjan brought his wife to Bleumaneer in the last days of his wealth ...)

The piano crouched stilly at the edge of the beach, the sea retreating from it, and the dark of night falling away ...

It's sunset.

Lucius, in the bloody light, with two men from the Café Blonde from the (neither the juggler), juggle the black piano from the possessive tentacles of the snake-willow.

With a rattle, a shattering of sounds (like slung cutlery), it, fetches up on the terrace. The men stand perplexed, looking at it. Yse watches from her glass wall.

"Broke the cock thing."

"No way to move it. Shoulda tooka crane."

They prowl about the piano, while the red light blooms across its shade.

Lucius tries delicately to raise the lid from the keys. The lid does not move. The other two, they wrench at the other lid, the piano's top (pate, shell). This too is fastened stuck. (Yse had made half a move, as if to stop them. Then her arm fell lax.)

"Damn ol' thing. What she wan' this ol' thing for?"

They back away. One makes a kicking movement. Lucius shakes his head; his long locks jangle across the flaming sky.

"Do you want this, girl?" Lucius asks Yse by her glass.

"Yes." Shortly. "I said I did."

"'S all broke up. Won't play you none," sings the light-eyed man, Carr, who wants to kick the piano, even now his loose leg pawing in its jeans.

Trails of water slip away from the piano, over the terrace, like chains.

Yse opens her wide glass doors. The men carry the piano in, and set it on her bare wooden floor.

Yse brings them, now docile as their maid, white rum, while Lucius shares out the bills.

"Hurt my back," whinges Carr the kicker.

"Piano," says Lucius, drinking, "pian – o – O pain!"

He says to her at the doors (as the men scramble back into their boat), "That vampire I danced with. Where he bit me. Still feel him there, biting me, some nights. Like a piece of broken bottle in my neck. I followed him, did I say to you? I followed him and saw him climb in under his grave just before the sun came up. A marble marker up on top. It shifted easy as breathe, settles back like a sigh. But he was beautiful, that boy with yellow

211

eyes. Made me feel like a king, with him. Young as a lion, with him. *Old* as him, too. A thousand years in a skin of smoothest suede."

Yse nods.

She watches Lucius away into the sunset, of which three hours are still left.

Yse scatters two bags of porous litter-chips, which are used all over the island, to absorb the spillages and seepages of the

Sound, to mop up the wet that slowly showers from the piano. She does not touch it. Except with her right hand, for a second, flat on the top of it.

The wood feels ancient and hollow, and she thinks it hasn't, perhaps, a metal frame.

As the redness folds over deeper and deeper, Yse lights the oil lamp on her work-table, and sits there, looking forty feet across the loft, at the piano on the sunset. Under her right hand now, the pages she has already written, in her fast untidy scrawl.

Piano-o. O pain.

Shush, says the Sound-tide, flooding the city, pulsing through the walls, struts and girders below.

Yse thinks distinctly, suddenly – it is always this way – about Per Laszd. But then another man's memory taps at her mind.

Yse picks up her pen, almost absently. She writes:

'Like those hallucinations which sometimes come at the edge of sleep, so that you wake, thinking two or three words have been spoken close to your ear, or that a tall figure stands in the corner... like this, the image now and then appears before him.

'Then he sees her, the woman, sitting on the rock, her white dress and her ivory-coloured hair, hard-gleaming in a post-storm sunlight. Impossible to tell her age. A desiccated young girl, or unlined old woman. And the transparent sea lapping in across the sand ...

'But he has said, the Island is quite deserted now.'

2: *Antoinette's Courtship*

Gregers Vonderjan brought his wife to Bleumaneer in the last days of his wealth.

In this way, she knew nothing about them, the grave losses to come, but then they had been married only a few months. She knew little enough about him, either.

Antoinelle was raised among staunch and secretive people. Until she was fourteen, she had thought herself ugly, and after that, beautiful. A sunset revelation had put her right, the westering glow pouring in sideways to paint the face in her mirror, on its slim, long throat. She found too she had shoulders, and cheekbones. Hands, whose tendons flexed in fans. With the knowledge of beauty, Antoinelle began to hope for something. Armed with her beauty she began to fall madly in love – with young officers in the army, with figures encountered in dreams.

One evening at a parochial ball, the two situations became confused.

The glamorous young man led Antoinelle out into a summer garden. It was a garden of Europe, with tall dense trees of twisted trunks, foliage massed on a lilac northern sky.

Antoinelle gave herself. That is, not only was she prepared to give of herself sexually, but to give herself up to this male person, of whom she knew no more than that he was beautiful.

Some scruple – solely for himself, the possible consequences – made him check at last.

"No – no –" she cried softly, as he forcibly released her and stood back, angrily panting.

The beautiful young man concluded (officially to himself), that Antoinelle was 'loose', and therefore valueless. She was not rich enough to marry, and besides, he despised her family.

Presently he had told his brother officers all about this girl, and her 'looseness'.

"She would have done anything," he said.

"She's a whore," said another, and smiled.

Fastidiously, Antoinelle's lover remarked, "No, worse than a whore. A whore does it honestly, for money. It's her work. This one simply does it."

Antoinelle's reputation was soon in tatters, which blew about that little town of trees and societal pillars, like the torn flag of a destroyed regiment.

She was sent in disgrace to her aunt's house in the country.

No one spoke to Antoinelle in that house. Literally, no one. The aunt would not, and she had instructed her servants, who were afraid of her. Even the maid who attended Antoinelle would not speak, in the privacy of the evening chamber, preparing the girl for the silent evening supper below, or the lumpy three-mattressed bed.

The aunt's rather unpleasant lap-dog, when Antoinelle had attempted, unwatched, to feed it a marzipan fruit, had only turned its rat-like head away. (At everyone else, save the aunt, it growled.)

Antoinelle, when alone, sobbed. At first in shame – her family had already seen to that, very ably, in the town. Next in frustrated rage. At last out of sheer despair.

She was like a lunatic in a cruel, cool asylum. They fed her, made her observe all the proper rituals. She had shelter and a place to sleep, and people to relieve some of her physical wants. There were even books in the library, and a garden to walk in on sunny days. But language – *sound* – they took away from her. And language is one of the six senses. It was as bad perhaps as blindfolding her. Additionally, they did not even speak to each other, beyond the absolute minimum, when she was by – coarse-aproned girls on the stair stifled their giggles, and passed with mask faces. And in much the same way too, Antoinelle was not permitted to play the aunt's piano.

Three months of this, hard, polished months, like stone mirrors which reflected nothing.

Antoinelle grew thinner, more pale. Her young eyes had hollows under them. She was like a nun.

The name of the aunt who did all this was Clemence – which means, of course, clemency – mild, merciful. (And the name of the young man in the town who had almost fucked Antoinelle, forced himself not to for his own sake, and then fucked instead her reputation, which was to say, her *life*... His name was Justus.)

On a morning early in the fourth month, a new thing happened.

Antoinelle opened her eyes, and saw the aunt sailing into her room. And the aunt, glittering with rings like knives, *spoke* to Antoinelle.

"Very well, there's been enough of all this. Yes, yes. You may get up quickly and come down to breakfast, Patice will see to your dress and hair. Make sure you look your best."

Antoinelle lay there, on her back in the horrible bed, staring like the dead newly awakened.

"Come along," said Aunt Clemence, holding the awful little dog untidily scrunched, "make haste now. What a child!" As if Antoinelle were the strange creature, the curiosity.

While, as the aunt swept out, the dog craned back and chattered its dirty teeth at Antoinelle.

And then, the third wonder, Patice was chattering, breaking like a happy stream at thaw, and shaking out a dress.

Antoinelle got up, and let Patice see to her, all the paraphernalia of the toilette, finishing with a light pollen of powder, even a fingertip of rouge for the matte pale lips, making them moist and rosy.

"Why?" asked Antoinelle at last, in a whisper.

"There is a visitor," chattered Patice, brimming with joy.

Antoinelle took two steps, then caught her breath and dropped as if dead on the carpet.

But Patice was also brisk; she brought Antoinelle round, crushing a vicious clove of lemon oil under her nostrils, slapping the young face lightly. Exactly as one would expect in this efficiently cruel lunatic asylum.

Presently Antoinelle drifted down the stairs, lightheaded, rose-lipped and shadow-eyed. She had never looked more lovely or known it less.

The breakfast was a ghastly provincial show-off thing. There were dishes and dishes, hot and cold, of kidneys, eggs, of cheeses and hams, hot breads in napkins, brioches, and chocolate. (It was a wonder Antoinelle was not sick at once.) All this set on crisp linen with flashing silver, and the fine china normally kept in a cupboard.

The servants flurried round in their awful, stupid (second-hand) joy. The aunt sat in her chair and Antoinelle in hers, and the man in his, across the round table.

Antoinelle had been afraid it was going to be Justus. She did not know why he would be there – to castigate her again, to apologise – either way, such a boiling of fear – or something – had gone through Antoinelle that she had fainted.

But it was not Justus. This was someone she did not know.

He had stood up as she came into the room. The morning was clear and well-lit, and Antoinelle had seen, with a dreary sagging of relief, that he was old. Quite old. She went on thinking this as he took her hand in his large one and shook it as if carelessly playing with something, very delicately. But his hand was manicured, the nails clean and white-edged. There was one ring, with a dull colourless stone in it.

Antoinelle still thought he was quite old, perhaps not so old as she *had* thought.

When they were seated, and the servants had doled out to them some food and drink, and gone away, Antoinelle came to herself rather more.

His hair was not grey but a mass of silvery blond. A lot of hair, very thick, shining, which fell, as was the fashion then, just to his shoulders. He was thick-set, not slender, but seemed immensely strong. One saw this in ordinary, apparently unrelated things – for example the niceness with which he helped himself now from the coffee-pot. Indeed, the dangerous playfulness of his handshake with a woman; he could easily crush the hands of his fellow men.

Perhaps he was not an old man, really. In his forties, (which would be the contemporary age of fifty-five or -six.) He was losing his figure, as many human beings do at that age, becoming either too big or too thin. But if his middle had spread, he was yet a presence, sprawled there in his immaculately white ruffled shirt, the broad-cut coat, his feet in boots of Spanish leather propped under the table. And to his face, not much really had happened. The forehead was both wide and high, scarcely lined, the nose aquiline as a bird's beak, scarcely thickened, the chin undoubled and jutting, the mouth narrow and well-shaped. His eyes, set in the slightest rouching of skin, were large, a cold clear blue. He might actually be only just forty (that is, fifty). A fraction less.

Antoinelle was not to know, in his youth, the heads of women had turned for Gregers Vonderjan like tulips before a gale. Or that, frankly, now and then they still did so.

The talk, what was that about all this while? Obsequious pleasantries from the aunt, odd anecdotes he gave, to do with ships, land, slaves and money. Antoinelle had been so long without hearing the speech of others, she had become nearly word-deaf, so that most of what he said had no meaning for her, and what the aunt said even less.

Finally the aunt remembered an urgent errand, and left them.

They sat, with the sun blazing through the windows. Then Vonderjan looked right at her, at Antoinelle, and suddenly her face, her whole body, was suffused by a savage burning blush.

"Did she tell you why I called here?" he asked, almost indifferently.

Antoinelle, her eyes lowered, murmured childishly, thoughtlessly, "No – she – she hasn't been speaking to me –"

"Hasn't she? Why not? Oh," he said, "that little business in the town."

Antoinelle, to her shock, began to cry. This should have horrified her – she had lost control – the worst sin, as her family had convinced her, they thought.

He knew, this man. He knew. She was ashamed, and yet unable to stop crying, or to get up and leave the room.

She heard his chair pushed back, and then he was standing over her. To her slightness, he seemed vast and overpowering.

He was clean, and smelled of French soap, of tobacco, and some other nuance of masculinity, which Antoinelle at once intuitively liked. She had scented it before.

"Well, you won't mind leaving her, then," he said, and he lifted her up out of her chair, and there she was in his grip, her head drooping back, staring almost mindlessly into his large, handsome face. It was easy to let go. She did so. She had in fact learnt nothing, been taught nothing by the whips and stings of her wicked relations. "I called here to ask you," he said, "to be my wife."

"But ..." faintly, "I don't know you."

"There's nothing to know. Here I am. Exactly what you see. Will that do?"

"But more faintly still, ""why would you want me?" "You're just what I want. "But," nearly inaudible, "I was – disgraced.""

"We'll see about that. And the old she-cunt won't talk to you, you say?"

Antoinelle, innocently not even knowing this important word (which any way he referred to in a foreign argot), only shivered. "No. Not till today."

"Now she does because I've bid for you. You'd better come with me. Did the other one, the soldier-boy, have you? It doesn't matter, but tell me now."

Antoinelle threw herself on the stranger's chest – she had not been told, or heard his name. "No – no –" she cried, just as she had when Justus pushed her off.

"I must go slowly with you then," said this man. But nevertheless, he moved her about, and leaning over, kissed her.

Vonderjan was an expert lover. Besides, he had a peculiar quality, which had stood him, and stands others like him, in very good stead. With those he wanted in the sexual way, providing they were not unwilling to begin with, he could spontaneously communicate some telepathic echo of his needs, making them theirs. This Antoinelle felt at once, as his warm lips moved on hers, his hot tongue pierced her mouth, and the fingers of the hand which did not hold her tight, fire-feathered her breasts.

In seconds her ready flames burst up. Businesslike, Vonderjan at once sat down, and holding her on his lap, placed his hand, making nothing of her dress, to crush her centre in an inexorable rhythmic grasp, until she came in gasping spasms against him, wept, and wilted there in his arms, his property.

When the inclement aunt returned with a servant, having left, she felt, sufficient time for Vonderjan to ask, and Antoinelle sensibly to acquiesce, she found her niece tear-stained and dead white in a chair, and Vonderjan drinking his coffee, and smoking a cigar, letting the ash fall as it wished on to the table linen.

"Well then," said the aunt, uncertainly.

Vonderjan cast her one look, as if amused by something about her.

"Am I to presume – may I – is everything –"

Vonderjan took another puff and a gout of charred stuff hit the cloth, before he mashed out the burning butt of the cigar on a china plate.

"Antoinelle," exclaimed the aunt, "what have you to say?"

Vonderjan spoke, not to the aunt, but to his betrothed. "Get up, Anna. You're going with me now." Then, looking at the servant (a look the woman said after was like that of a basilisk), "Out, you, and put some things together, all the lady will need for the drive. I'll supply the rest. Be quick."

Scarlet, the aunt shouted, "Now sir, this isn't how to go on."

Vonderjan drew Antoinelle up, by his hand on her elbow. *He* had control of her now, and she need bother with nothing. She turned her drooping head, like a tired flower, looking only at his boots.

The aunt was ranting. Vonderjan, with Antoinelle in one arm, went up to her. Though not a small woman, nor slight like her niece, he dwarfed her, made of her a pygmy.

"Sir – there is her father to be approached – you must have a care –"

Then she stopped speaking. She stopped because, like Antoinelle, she had been given no choice. Gregers Vonderjan had clapped his hand over her mouth, and rather more than that. He held her by the bones and flesh of her face, unable to pull away, beating at him with her hands, making noises but unable to do more, and soon breathing with difficulty.

While he kept her like this, he did not bother to look at her, his broad body only disturbed vaguely by her flailing, weak blows. He had turned again to Antoinelle, and asked her if there was anything she wished particularly to bring away from the house.

Antoinelle did not have the courage to glance at her struggling and apoplectic aunt. She shook her head against his shoulder, and after a little shake of his own (at the aunt's face) he let the woman go. He and the girl walked out of the room and out of the house, to his carriage, leaving the aunt to progress from her partial asphyxia to hysterics.

He had got them married in three days by pulling such strings as money generally will. The ceremony did not take place in the town, but all the town heard of it. Afterwards Vonderjan went back there, without his wife, to throw a lavish dinner party, limited to the male gender, which no person invited dared not attend, including the bride's father, who was trying to smile off, as does the deathshead, the state it has been put into.

At this dinner too was Justus. He sat with a number of his friends, all of them astonished to be there. But like the rest, they had not been able, or prepared, to evade the occasion.

Vonderjan treated them all alike, with courtesy. The food was of a high standard – a cook had been brought from the city – and there were extravagant wines, with all of which Gregers Vonderjan was evidently familiar. The men got drunk, that is, all the men but for Vonderjan, who was an established drinker, and consumed several bottles of wine, also brandy and schnapps, without much effect.

At last Vonderjan said he would be going. To the bowing and fawning of his wife's relatives he paid no attention. It was Justus he took aside, near the door, with two of his friends. The young men were all in full uniform, smart as polish, only their bright hair tousled, and faces flushed by liquor.

"You mustn't think my wife holds any rancour against you," Vonderjan announced, not loudly, but in a penetrating tone. Justus was too drunk to catch himself up, and only idiotically nodded. "She said, I should wish you a speedy end to your trouble."

"What trouble's that?" asked Justus, still idiotically.

"He has no troubles," added the first of his brother officers, "since you took that girl off his hands."

The other officer (the most sober, which was not saying much – or perhaps the most drunk, drunk enough to have gained the virtue of distance), said, "Shut your trap, you fool. Herr Vonderjan doesn't want to hear that silly kind of talk."

Vonderjan was grave. "It's nothing to me. But I'm sorry for your Justus, naturally. I shouldn't, as no man would, like to be in his shoes."

"What shoes are they?" Justus belatedly frowned.

"I can recommend to you," said Vonderjan, "an excellent doctor in the city. They say he is discreet."

"*What?*"

"What is he saying –?"

"The disease, I believe they say, is often curable, in its earliest stages."

Justus drew himself up. He was almost the height of Vonderjan, but like a reed beside him. All that room, and waiters on the stair besides, were listening. "I am not – I have no – *disease* –"

Vonderjan shrugged. "That's your argument, I understand. You should leave it off perhaps, and seek medical advice, certainly before you consider again any courtship. Not all women are as soft-hearted as my Anna."

"What – what?"

"Not plain enough? From what you showed her she knew you had it, and refused you. Of course, you had another story."

As Vonderjan walked through the door, the two brother officers were, one silent, and one bellowing. Vonderjan half turned, negligently. "If you don't think so, examine his prick for yourselves."

Vonderjan did not tell Antoinelle any of this, but a week later, in the city, she did read in a paper that Justus had mysteriously been disgraced, and had then fled the town after a duel.

Perhaps she thought it curious.

But if so, only for a moment. She had been absorbed almost entirely by the stranger, her strong husband.

On the first night, still calling her Anna, up against a great velvet bed, he had undone her clothes and next her body, taking her apart down to the clockwork of her desires. Her cry of pain at his entry turned almost at once into a wavering shriek of ecstasy. She was what he had wanted all along, and he what she had needed. By morning the bed was stained with her virginal blood, and by the blood from bites she had given him, not knowing she did so.

Even when, a few weeks after, Vonderjan's luck began to turn like a sail, he bore her with him on his broad wings. He said nothing of his luck. He was too occupied wringing from her again and again the music of her lusts, forcing her arching body to contortions, paroxysms, screams, torturing her to willing death in blind red afternoons, in candlelit darkness, so that by daybreak she could scarcely move, would lie there in a stupor in the bed, unable to rise, awaiting him like an invalid or a corpse, and hungry always for more.

3

Lucius paddles his boat to the jetty, lets it idle there, looking up.

Another property of the flood-vapour, the stars by night are vast, great liquid splashes of silver, ormolu.

The light in Yse's loft burns contrastingly low.

That sweet smell he noticed yesterday still comes wafting down, like thin veiling, on the breeze. Like night-blooming jasmine, perhaps a little sharper, almost like oleanders.

She must have put in some plant. But up on her terrace, only the snake tree is visible, hooping over into the water.

Lucius smokes half a roach slowly.

Far away the shoreline glimmers, where some of the stars have fallen off the sky.

"What you doing, Yse, Yse-do-as-she-please?"

Once he'd thought he saw her moving, a moth-shadow crossing through the stunned light, but maybe she is asleep, or writing.

It would be simple enough to tie up and climb the short wet stair to the terrace, to knock on her glass doors. (How are you, Yse? Are you fine?) He had done that last night. The blinds were all down, the light low, as now. But through the side of the transparent loft he had beheld the other shadow standing there on her floor. The piano from the sea. No one answered.

That flower she's planted, it is sweet as candy. He'd never known her do a thing like that. Her plants always died, killed, she said, by the electrical vibrations of her psyche when she worked.

Somewhere out on the Sound a boat hoots mournfully.

Lucius unships his paddles, and wends his craft away along the alleys of water, towards the cafés and the bigger lights.

Whenever she writes about Per Laszd, which, over twenty-seven years, she has done a lot, the same feeling assails her: slight guilt. Only slight, of course, for he will never know. He is a man who never reads anything that has nothing to do with what he does. That was made clear in the beginning. She met him only twice, but has seen him, quite often, then and since, in newspapers, in news footage, and on network TV. She has been able therefore to watch him change, from an acidly, really too- beautiful young man, through his thirties and forties (when some of the silk of his beauty frayed, to reveal something leaner and more interesting, stronger and more attractive), to a latening middle age, where he has gained weight, but lost none of his masculine grace, nor his mane of hair which – only perhaps due to artifice – has no grey in it.

She was in love with him, obviously, at the beginning. But it has changed, and become something else. He was never interested in her, even when she was young, slim and appealing. She was not, she supposed, his 'type'.

In addition, she rather admired what he did, and how he did it, with an actor's panache and tricks.

People who caught her fancy she had always tended to put into her work. Inevitably Per Laszd was one of these. Sometimes he appeared as a remote Figure, on the edge of the action of other lives. Sometimes he took the centre of the stage, acting out invented existences, with his perceived actor's skills.

She had, she found though, a tendency to punish him in these roles. He must endure hardships and misfortunes, and often, in her work, he was dead by the end, and rarely of old age.

Her guilt, naturally, had something to do with this – was she truly punishing him, not godlike, as with other characters, but from a petty personal annoyance that he had never noticed her, let alone had sex with her, or a single real conversation. (When she had met him, it had both times been in a crowd. He spoke generally, politely including her, no more than that. She was aware he had been arrogant enough, if he had wanted to, to have demandingly singled her out.)

But really she felt guilty at the liberties she took of necessity, with him, on paper. How else could she write about him? It was absurd to do otherwise. But describing his conjectured nakedness, both physical and intellectual, even spiritual (even supposedly 'in character'), her own temerity occasionally dismayed Yse. How dared she? But then, how dare ever to write anything, even about a being wholly invented.

A mental shrug. *Alors*... well, well. And yet...

Making him Gregers Vonderjan, she felt, was perhaps her worst infringement. Now she depicted him (honestly) burly with weight and on-drawing age, although always hastening to add the caveat of his handsomeness, his power. Per himself, as she had seen, was capable of being majestic, yet also mercurial. She tried to be fair, to be at her most fair, when examining him most microscopically, or when condemning him to the worst fates. (But, now and then, did the pen slip?)

Had he ever sensed those several dreadful falls, those calumnies, those *deaths?* Of course not. Well, well. There, there. And yet ...

How wonderful that vine smells tonight, Yse thinks, sitting up in the lamp-dusk. Some neighbour must have planted it. What a penetrating scent, so clean and fresh yet sweet. It was noticeable last night, too. Yse wonders what the flowers are, that let out this aroma. And in the end, she stands up, leaving the pen to lie there, across Vonderjan and Antoinelle.

Near her glass doors, Yse thinks the vine must be directly facing her, over the narrow waterway under the terrace, for here its perfume is strongest.

But when she raises the blinds and opens the doors, the scent at once grows less. Somehow it has collected instead in the room. She gazes out at the other lofts, at a tower of shaped glass looking like ice in a tray. Are the hidden gardens there?

The stars are impressive tonight. And she can see the hem of the star-spangled upper city.

A faint sound comes.

Yse knows it's not outside, but in her loft, just like the scent.

She turns. Looks at the black piano.

Since yesterday (when it was brought in), she hasn't paid it that much attention. (Has she?) She had initially stared at it, tried three or four times to raise its lids – without success. She had thought of rubbing it down, once the litter-chips absorbed the leaking water. But then she had not done this. Had not touched it very much.

Coming to the doors, she has circled wide of the piano.

Did a note sound, just now, under the forward lid? How odd, the two forelegs braced there, and the final leg at its end, more as if it balanced on a tail of some sort.

Probably the keys and hammers and strings inside are settling after the wet, to the warmth of her room.

She leaves one door open, which is not perhaps sensible. Rats have been known to climb the stair and gaze in at her under the night blinds, with their calm clever eyes. Sometimes the criminal population of the island can be heard along the waterways, or out on the Sound, shouts and smashing bottles, cans thrown at brickwork or impervious, multi-glazed windows.

But the night's still as the stars.

Yse goes by the piano, and through the perfume, and back to her desk, where Per Laszd lies helplessly awaiting her on the page.

4: *Bleumaneer*

Jeanjacques came to the Island in the stormy season. He was a mix of black and white, and found both peoples perplexing, as he found himself.

The slave-trade was by then defused, as much, perhaps, as it would ever be. He knew there were no slaves left on the Island, that is, only freed slaves remained. (His black half lived with frenzied anger, as his white half clove to sloth. Between the two halves, he was a split soul.)

There had been sparks on the rigging of the ship, and all night a velour sky fraught with pink lightning. When they reached the bay next morning, it looked nearly colourless, the sombre palms were nearly grey, and the sky cindery, and the sea only transparent, the beaches white.

The haughty black master spoke in French.

"They call that place *Blue View.* "

"Why's that?"

"Oh, it was for some vogue of wearing blue, before heads began to roll in Paris."

Jeanjacques said, "What's he like?"

"Vonderjan? A falling man."

"How do you mean?"

"Have you seen a man fall? The instants before he hits the ground, before he's hurt – the moment when he thinks he is still flying."

"He's lost his money, they were saying at Sugarbar." "They say so."

"And his wife's a girl, almost a child."

"Two years he's been with her on his Island."

"What's she like?"

"White."

"What else?"

"To me, nothing. I can't tell them apart."

There had been a small port, but now little was there, except a rotted hulk, some huts and the ruins of a customs house, thatched with palm, in which birds lived.

For a day he climbed with the escorting party, up into the interior of the Island. Inside the forest it was grey-green-black, and the trees gave off sweat, pearling the banana leaves and plantains. Then they walked through the wild fields of cane, and the coffee trees. Dark figures still worked there, and tending the kayar. But they did this for themselves. What had been owned had become the garden of those who remained, to do with as they wanted.

The black master had elaborated, telling Jeanjacques how Vonderjan had at first sent for niceties for his house, for china and Venetian glass, cases of books and wine. Even a piano had been ordered for his child-wife, although this, it seemed, had never arrived.

The Island was large and overgrown, but there was nothing, they said, very dangerous on it.

Bleumaneer, *Blue View*, the house for which the Island had come to be called, appeared on the next morning, down a dusty track hedged by rhododendrons of prehistoric girth.

It was white walled, with several open courts, balconies. Orange trees grew along a columned gallery, and there was a Spanish fountain (dry), on the paved space before the steps. But it was a medley of all kinds of style.

"Make an itinerary and let me see it. We'll talk it over, what can be sold."

Jeanjacques thought that Vonderjan reminded him most of a lion, but a lion crossed with a golden bull. Then again, there was a wolf-like element, cunning and lithe, which slipped through the grasslands of their talk.

Vonderjan did not treat Jeanjacques as what he was, a valuer's clerk. Nor was there any resentment or chagrin. Vonderjan seemed indifferent to the fix he was in. Did he even care that such and such would be sorted out and taken from him – that glowing canvas in the salon, for example, or the rose-mahogany cabinets, and all for a third of their value, or less, paid in banknotes that probably would not last out another year. Here was a man, surely, playing at life, at living. Convinced of it and of his fate, certainly, but only as the actor is, within his part.

Jeanjacques drank cloudy orjat, tasting its bitter orange-flowers. Vonderjan drank nothing, was sufficient, even in this, to himself.

"Well. What do you think?"

"I'll work on, and work tonight, present you with a summary in the morning."

"Why waste the night?" said Vonderjan.

"I must be ready to leave in another week, sir, when the ship returns."

"Another few months," said Vonderjan, consideringly, "and maybe no ship will come here. Suppose you missed your boat?"

He seemed to be watching Jeanjacques through a telescope, closely, yet far, far away. He might have been drunk, but there was no smell of alcohol to him. Some drug of the Island, perhaps?

Jeanjacques said, "I'd have to swim for it."

A man came up from the yard below. He was a white servant, shabby but respectable. He spoke to Vonderjan in some European gabble.

"My horse is sick," said Vonderjan to Jeanjacques. "I think I shall have to shoot it. I've lost most of them here. Some insect, which bites."

"I'm sorry."

"Yes." Then, light-heartedly, "But none of us escape, do we."

Later, in the slow heat of the afternoon, Jeanjacques heard the shot crack out, and shuddered. It was more than the plight of the unfortunate horse. Something seemed to have hunted Vonderjan to his Island and now picked off from him all the scales of his world, his money, his horses, his possessions.

The clerk worked at his tally until the sun began to wester about four in the evening. Then he went up to wash and dress, because Vonderjan had said he should dine in the salon, with his family. Jeanjacques had no idea what he would find. He was curious, a little, about the young wife – she must by now be seventeen or eighteen. Had there been any children? It was always likely, but then again, likely too they had not survived.

At five, the sky was like brass, the palms that lined the edges of all vistas like blackened brass columns, bent out of shape, with brazen leaves that rattled against each other when any breath blew up from the bay. From the roof of the house it was possible also to make out a cove, and the sea. But it looked much more than a day's journey off. Unless you jumped and the wind blew you.

Another storm mumbled over the Island as Jeanjacques entered the salon. The long windows stood wide, and the dying light flickered fitfully like the disturbed candles.

No one took much notice of the clerk, and Vonderjan behaved as if Jeanjacques had been there a year, some acquaintance with no particular purpose in the house, neither welcome nor un.

The 'family', Jeanjacques saw, consisted of Vonderjan, his wife, a housekeeper, and a young black woman, apparently Vrouw Vonderjan's companion.

She was slender and fine, the black woman, and sat there as if a slave-trade had never existed, either to crucify or enrage her. Her dress was of excellent muslin, ladyishly low cut for the evening, and she had ruby ear-drops. (She spoke at least three languages that Jeanjacques heard, including the patois of the Island, or house, which she exchanged now and then with the old housekeeper.)

But Vonderjan's wife was another matter altogether.

The moment he looked at her, Jeanjacques' blood seemed to shift slightly, all along his bones. And at the base of his skull, where his hair was neatly tied back by a ribbon, the roots stretched themselves, prickling.

She was not at all pretty, but violently beautiful, in a way far too large for the long room, or for any room, whether spacious or enormous. So pale she was, she made her black attendant seem like a shadow cast by a flame. Satiny coils and trickles of hair fell all round her in a deluge of gilded rain. Thunder was the colour of her eyes, a dark that was not dark, some shade that could not be described visually but only in other ways. All of her was a little like that. To touch her limpid skin would be like tasting ice-cream. To catch her fragrance like small bells heard inside the ears in fever.

When her dress brushed by him as she first crossed the room, Jeanjacques inadvertently recoiled inside his skin. He was feeling, although he did not know it, exactly as Justus had felt in the northern garden. Though Justus had not known it, either. But what terrified these two men was the very thing which drew other men, especially such men as Gregers Vonderjan. So much was plain.

The dinner was over, and the women got up to withdraw. As she passed by his chair, Vonderjan, who had scarcely spoken to her throughout the meal (or to anyone), lightly took hold of his wife's hand. And she looked down at once into his eyes.

Such a look it was. Oh God, Jeanjacques experienced now all his muscles go to liquid, and sinking, and his belly sinking down into his bowels; which themselves turned over heavily as a serpent. But his penis rose very quickly, and pushed hard as a rod against his thigh.

For it was a look of such explicit sex, trembling so colossally it had grown still, and out of such an agony of suspense, that he was well aware these two lived in a constant of the condition, and would need only to press together the length of their bodies, to ignite like matches in a galvanic convulsion.

He had seen once or twice similar looks, perhaps. Among couples kept strictly, on their marriage night. But no, not even then.

They said nothing to each other. Needed nothing to say. It had been said.

The girl and her black companion passed from the room, and after them the housekeeper, carrying a branch of the candles, whose flames flattened as she went through the doors on to the terrace. (*Notes:* This will happen again later.)

Out there, the night was now very black. Everything beyond the house had vanished in it, but for the vague differential between the sky and the tops of the forest below. There were no stars to be seen, and thunder still moved restlessly. The life went from Jeanjacques' genitals as if it might never come back.

"Brandy," said Vonderjan, passing the decanter. "What do you think of her?"

"Of whom, sir?"

"My Anna." (Playful; who else?)

Jeanjacques visualized, in a sudden unexpected flash, certain objects used as amulets, and crossing himself in church.

"An exquisite lady, sir."

"Yes," said Vonderjan. He had drunk a lot during dinner, but in an easy way. It was evidently habit, not need. Now he said again, "Yes."

Jeanjacques wondered what would be next. But of course nothing was to be next. Vonderjan finished his cigar, and drank down his glass. He rose, and nodded to Jeanjacques. "Bon nuit."

How could he even have forced himself to linger so long? Vonderjan demonstrably must be a human of vast self- control.

Jeanjacques imagined the blond man going up the stairs of the house to the wide upper storey. An open window, drifted with a gauze curtain, hot, airless night. Jeanjacques imagined Antoinelle, called Anna, lying on her back in the bed, its nets pushed careless away, for what bit Vonderjan's horses to death naturally could not essay his wife.

"No, I shan't have a good night," Jeanjacques said to Vonderjan in his head. He went to his room, and sharpened his pen for work.

In the darkness, he heard her. He was sure that he had. It was almost four in the morning by his pocket watch, and the sun would rise in less than an hour.

Waveringly she screamed, like an animal caught in a trap. Three times, the second time the loudest.

The whole of the inside of the house shook and throbbed and scorched from it.

Jeanjacques found he must get up, and standing by the window, handle himself roughly until, in less than thirteen seconds, his semen exploded on to the tiled floor.

Feeling then slightly nauseous, and dreary, he slunk to bed and slept gravely, like a stone.

Antoinelle sat at her toilette mirror, part of a fine set of silver-gilt her husband had given her. She was watching herself as Nanetta combed and brushed her hair.

It was late afternoon, the heat of the day lying down but not subsiding.

Antoinelle was in her chemise; soon she would dress for the evening dinner.

Nanetta stopped brushing. Her hands lay on the air like a black slender butterfly separated in two. She seemed to be listening.

"More," said Antoinelle.

"Yes." The brush began again.

Antoinelle often did not rise until noon, frequently later. She would eat a little fruit, drink coffee, get up and wander about in flimsy undergarments. Now and then she would read a novel, or Nanetta would read one to her. Or they would play cards, sitting at the table on the balcony, among the pots of flowers.

Nanetta had never seen Antoinelle do very much, and had never seen her agitated or even irritable.

She lived for night.

He, on the other hand, still got up mostly at sunrise, and no later than the hour after. His man, Stronn, would shave him. Vonderjan would breakfast downstairs in the courtyard, eating meat and bread, drinking black tea. Afterwards he might go over the accounts with the secretary. Sometimes the whole of the big house heard him shouting (except for his wife, who was generally still asleep). He regularly rode (two horses survived), round parts of the Island, and was gone until late afternoon, talking to the men and women in the fields, sitting to drink with them, rum and palm liquor, in the shade of plantains. He might return about the time Antoinelle was washing herself, powdering her arms and face, and putting on a dress for dinner.

A bird trilled in a cage, hopped a few steps, and flew up to its perch to trill again.

The scent of dust and sweating trees came from the long windows, stagnant yet energizing in the thickening yellow light.

Nanetta half turned her head. Again she had heard something far away. She did not know what it was.

"Shall I wear the emerald necklace tonight?" asked Antoinelle, sleepily. "What do you think?"

Nanetta was used to this. To finding an answer.

"With the white dress? Yes, that would be effective."

"Put up my hair. Use the tortoiseshell combs."

Nanetta obeyed deftly.

The satiny bright hair was no pleasure to touch, too electric, stickily clinging to the fingers – full of each night's approaching storm. There would be no rain, not yet.

Antoinelle watched as the black woman transformed her. . Antoinelle liked this, having only to be, letting someone else put her together in this way. She had forgotten by now, but never liked, independence. She wanted only enjoyment, to be made and remade, although in a manner that pleased her, and which, after all, demonstrated her power over others.

When she thought about Vonderjan, her husband, her loins clenched involuntarily, and a frisson ran through her, a shiver of heat. So she rationed her thoughts of him. During their meals together, she would hardly look at him, hardly speak, concentrating on the food, on the light of the candles reflecting in things, hypnotizing herself and prolonging, unendurably, her famine, until at last she was able to return into the bed, cool by then, with clean sheets on it, and wait, giving herself up to darkness and to fire.

How could she live in any other way?

Whatever had happened to her? Had the insensate cruelty of her relations pulped her down into a sponge that was ultimately receptive only to this? Or was this her true condition, which had always been trying to assert itself, and which, once connected to a suitable partner, did so, evolving also all the time, spreading itself higher and lower and in all directions, like some amoeba?

She must have heard stories of him, his previous wife, and of a black mistress or two he had had here. But Antoinelle was not remotely jealous. She had no interest in what he did when not with her, when not about to be, or actually in her bed with her. As if all other facets, both of his existence and her own, had now absolutely no meaning at all.

About the hour Antoinelle sat by the mirror, and Vonderjan, who had not gone out that day, was bathing, smoking one of the cigars as the steam curled round him, Jeanjacques stood among a wilderness of cane fields beyond the house.

That cane was a type of grass tended always to amaze him, these huge stripes of straddling stalks, rising five feet or more above his head. He felt himself to be a child lost in a luridly unnatural wood, and besides, when a black figure passed across the view, moving from one subaqueous tunnel to another, they now supernaturally only glanced at him, cat-like, from the sides of their eyes.

Jeanjacques had gone out walking, having deposited his itinerary and notes with Vonderjan in a morning room. The clerk took narrow tracks across the Island, stood on high places from which (as from the roof), coves and inlets of the sea might be glimpsed.

The people of the Island had been faultlessly friendly and courteous, until he began to try to question them. Then they changed. He assumed at first they only hated his white skin, as had others he had met, who had refused to believe in his mixed blood. In that case, he could not blame them much for the hatred. Then he understood he had not assumed this at all. They were disturbed by something, afraid of something, and he knew it.

Were they afraid of her — of the white girl in the house? Was it that? And why were they afraid? Why was he himself afraid — because afraid of her he was. Oh yes, he was terrified.

At midday he came to a group of hut-houses, patchily colour-washed and with palm-leaf roofs, and people were sitting about there in the shade, drinking, and one man was splitting rosy gourds with a machete, so Jeanjacques thought of a guillotine a moment, the red juice spraying out and the *thunk* of the blade going through. (He had heard they had split imported melons in Marseilles, to test the machine. But he was a boy when he heard this tale, and perhaps it was not true.)

Jeanjacques stood there, looking on. Then a black woman got up, fat and not young, but comely, and brought him half a gourd, for him to try the dripping flesh.

He took it, thanking her.

"How is it going. Mother?" he asked her, partly in French, but also with two words of the patois, which he had begun to recognize. To no particular effect.

"It goes how it go, monsieur."

"You still take a share of your crop to the big house?" She gave him the sidelong look. "But you're free people, now."

One of the men called to her sharply. He was a tall black leopard, young and gorgeous as a carving from chocolate. The woman went away at once, and Jeanjacques heard again that phrase he had heard twice before that day. It was muttered somewhere at his back. He turned quickly, and there they sat, blacker in shade, eating from the flesh of the gourds, and drinking from a bottle passed around. Not looking at him, not at all.

"What did you say?"

A man glanced up. "It's nothing, monsieur."

"Something came from the sea, you said?"

"No, monsieur. Only a storm coming."

"It's the stormy season. Wasn't there something else?"

They shook their heads. They looked helpful, and sorry they could not assist, and their eyes were painted glass.

Something has come from the sea.

They had said it too, at the other place, further down, when a child had brought him rum in a tin mug.

What could come from the sea? Only weather, or men. Or the woman. She had come from there.

They were afraid, and even if he had doubted his ears or his judgment, the way they would not say it straight out, that was enough to tell him he had not imagined this.

Just then a breeze passed through the forest below, and then across the broad leaves above, shaking them. And the light changed a second, then back, like the blinking of the eye of God.

They stirred, the people. It was as if they saw the wind, and the shape it had was fearful to them, yet known. Respected.

As he was walking back by another of the tracks, he found a dead chicken laid on a banana leaf at the margin of a field. A propitiary offering? Nothing else had touched it, even a line of ants detoured out on to the track, to give it room.

Jeanjacques walked into the cane fields and went on there for a while. And now and then other human things moved through, looking sidelong at him.

Then, when he paused among the tall stalks, he heard them whispering, whispering, the stalks of cane, or else the voices of the people. Had they followed him? Were they aggressive? They had every right to be, of course, even with his kind. Even so, he did not want to be beaten, or to die. He had invested such an amount of his life and wits in avoiding such things.

But no one approached. The whispers came and went.

Now he was here, and he had made out, from the edge of this field, Vonderjan's house with its fringe of palms and rhododendrons (Blue View), above him on the hill, only about half an hour away.

In a full hour, the sun would dip. He would go to his room and there would be water for washing, and his other clothes laid out for the dinner.

The whispering began again, suddenly, very close, so Jeanjacques spun about, horrified.

But no one was there, nothing was there.

Only the breeze, that the black people could see, moved round among the stalks of the cane, that was itself like an Egyptian temple, its columns meant to be a forest of green papyrus.

"It's black," the voices whispered. "Black."

"Like a black man," Jeanjacques said hoarsely.

"Black like black."

Again, God blinked his eyelid of sky. A figure seemed to be standing between the shafts of green cane. It said, "Not black like men. So black we filled with terror of it. Black like black of night is black."

"Black like black."

"Something from the sea."

Jeanjacques felt himself dropping, and then he was on his knees, and his forehead was pressed to the powdery plant- drained soil.

He had not hurt himself. When he looked up, no one was in the field that he could see.

He got to his feet slowly. He trembled, and then the trembling, like the whispers, went away.

The storm rumbled over the Island. It sounded tonight like dogs barking, then baying in the distance. Every so often, for no apparent reason, the flames of the candles flattened, as if a hand had been laid on them.

There was a main dish of pork, stewed with spices. Someone had mentioned there were pigs on the Island, although the clerk had seen none, perhaps no longer wild, or introduced and never wild.

The black girl, who was called Nanetta, had put up her hair elaborately, and so had the white one, Vonderjan's wife. Round her slim pillar of throat were five large green stars in a necklace like a golden cake-decoration.

Vonderjan had told Jeanjacques that no jewellery was to be valued. But here at least was something that might have seen him straight for a while. Until his ship came in. But perhaps it never would again. Gregers Vonderjan had been lucky always, until the past couple of years.

A gust of wind, which seemed to do nothing else outside, abruptly blew wide the doors to the terrace.

Vonderjan himself got up, went by his servants, and shut both doors. That was, started to shut them. Instead he was standing there now, gazing out across the Island.

In the sky, the dogs bayed.

His heavy bulky frame seemed vast enough to withstand any night. His magnificent mane of hair, without any evident grey, gleamed like gold in the candlelight. Vonderjan was so strong, so nonchalant.

But he stood there a long while, as if something had attracted his attention.

It was Nanetta who asked, "Monsieur — what is the matter?"

Vonderjan half turned and looked at her, almost mockingly, his brows raised.

"Matter? Nothing."

She has it too, Jeanjacques thought. He said, "The blacks were saying, something has come from the sea."

Then he glanced at Nanetta. For a moment he saw two rings of white stand clear around the pupil and iris of her eyes. But she looked down, and nothing else gave her away.

Vonderjan shut the doors. He swaggered back to the table. (He did not look at his wife, nor she at him. They kept themselves intact, Jeanjacques thought, during proximity, only by such a method. The clerk wondered, if he were to find Antoinelle alone, and stand over her, murmuring Vonderjan's name, over and over, whether she would fall back, unable to resist, and come, without further provocation and in front of him. And at the thought, the hard rod tapped again impatiently on his thigh.)

"From the sea, you say. What?"

"I don't know, sir. But they were whispering it. Perhaps Mademoiselle knows?" He indicated Nanetta graciously, as if giving her a wanted opening.

She was silent.

"I don't think," said Vonderjan, "that she does."

"No, monsieur," she said. She seemed cool. Her eyes were kept down.

Oddly — Jeanjacques thought — it was Antoinelle who suddenly sprang up, pushing back her chair, so it scraped on the tiles.

"It's so hot," she said.

And then she stood there, as if incapable of doing anything else, of refining any desire or solution from her own words.

Vonderjan did not look at her, but he went slowly back and undid the doors. "Walk with me on the terrace, Anna."

And he extended his arm.

The white woman glided across the salon as if on runners. She seemed weightless — *blown*. And the white snake of her little narrow hand crawled round his arm and out on to the sleeve, to rest there. Husband and wife stepped out into the rumbling night.

Jeanjacques sat back and stared across the table at Nanetta.

"They're most devoted," he said. "One doesn't often see it, after the first months. Especially where the ages are so different. What is he, thirty, thirty-two years her senior?"

Nanetta raised her eyes and now gazed at him impenetrably, with the tiniest, most fleeting smile.

He would get nothing out of her. She was a lady's maid, and he a jumped-up clerk, but both of them had remained slaves. They were calcined, ruined, defensive, and armoured.

Along the terrace he could see that Vonderjan and the woman were pressed close by the house, where a lush flowering vine only partly might hide them. Her skirts were already pushed askew, her head thrown sideways, mouth open and eyes shut. He was taking her against the wall, thrusting and heaving into her.

Jeanjacques looked quickly away, and began to whistle, afraid of hearing her cries of climax.

But now the black girl exclaimed, "Don't whistle, don't do that, monsieur!"

"Why? Why not?"

She only shook her head, but again her eyes – the black centres were silver-ringed. So Jeanjacques got up and walked out of the salon into Vonderjan's library across the passage, where now the mundane papers concerning things to be sold, lay on a table.

But it has come, it has come through the sea, before star-rise and dawn, through the rifts and fans of the transparent water, sliding and swimming like a crab.

It has crawled on to the sand, crouching low, like a beast, and perhaps mistaken for some animal.

A moon (is it a different moon each night? Who would know?), sinking, and Venus in the east.

Crawling into the tangle of the trees, with the palms and parrot trees reflecting in the dulled mirror of its lid, its carapace. Dragging the hind limb like a tail, pulling itself by the front legs, like a wounded boar.

Through the forest, with only the crystal of Venus to shatter through the heavy leaves of sweating bronze.

Bleumaneer, La Vue Bleu, Blue Fashion, Blue View, seeing through a blue eye to a black shape, which moves from shadow to shadow, place to place. But always nearer.

Something is in the forest.

Nothing dangerous. How can it hurt you?

5

Yse is buying food in the open air market at Bley. Lucius had seen her, and now stands watching her, not going over.

She has filled her first bag with vegetables and fruit, and in the second she puts a fish and some cheese, olive oil and bread.

Lucius crosses through the crowd, by the place where the black girl called Rosalba is cooking red snapper on her skillet, and the old poet paints his words in coloured sand.

As Yse walks into a liquor store, Lucius follows.

"You're looking good, Yse."

She turns, gazing at him – not startled, more as if she doesn't remember him. Then she does. "Thank you. I feel good today."

"And strong. But not *this* strong. Give me the vegetables to carry, Yse."

"Okay. That's kind."

"What have you done to your hair?"

Yse thinks about this one. "Oh. Someone put in some extra hair for me. You know how they do, they hot-wax the strands on to your own."

"It looks fine."

She buys a box of wine bottles.

"You're having a party?" Lucius says.

"No, Lucius. I don't throw parties. You know that."

"I know that."

"Just getting in my stores. I'm working. Then I needn't go out again for a while, just stay put and write."

"You've lost some weight," Lucius says, "looks like about twenty-five pounds."

Now she laughs. 'Wo. I wish. But you know I do sometimes, when I work. Adrenaline."

He totes the wine and the vegetables, and they stroll over to the bar on the quay, to which fresh fish are being brought in from the Sound. (The bar is at the top of what was, once, the Aquatic Museum. There are still old cases of bullet-and-robber- proof glass, with fossils in them, little ancient dragons of the deeps, only three feet long, and coelacanths with needle teeth.)

Lucius orders coffee and rum, but Yse only wants a mineral water. Is she dieting? He has never known her to do this. She has said, dieting became useless after her forty-third year.

Her hair hangs long, to her waist, blonde, with whiter blonde and silver in it. He can't see any of the wax-ends of the extensions, or any grey either. Slimmer, her face, hands and shoulders have fined right down. Her skin is excellent, luminous and pale. Her eyes are crystalline, and outlined by soft black pencil he has never seen her use before.

She says sharply, "For a man who likes men, you surely know how to look a woman over, Lucius."

"None better."

"Well don't."

"I'm admiring you, Yse."

"Well, still don't. You're embarrassing me. I'm not used to it any more. If I ever was."

There is, he saw an hour ago — all across the market — a small white surgical dressing on the left side of her neck. Now she absently touches it, and pulls her finger away like her own mother would do. They say you can always tell a woman's age from her hands. Yse's hands look today like those of a woman of thirty-five.

"Something bite you, Yse?"

"An insect. It itches."

"I came by in the boat," he says, drinking his coffee, leaving the rum to stand in the glass. "I heard you playing that piano."

"You must have heard someone else somewhere. I can't play. I used to improvise, years ago. But then I had to sell my piano back then. This one... I haven't been able to get the damn lid up. I'm frightened to force it in case everything breaks."

"Do you want me to try?"

"Thanks — but maybe not. You know, I don't think the keys can be intact. How can they be? And there might be rats in it."

"Does it smell of rats?"

"Oddly, it smells of flowers. Jasmine, or something. Mostly at night, really. A wonderful smell. Perhaps something's growing inside it."

"In the dark."

"Night-blooming Passia," Yse says, as if quoting.

"And you write about that piano," says Lucius.

"Did I tell you? Good guess then. But it's not about a piano. Not really. About an Island."

"Where is this island?"

"Here." Yse sets her finger on a large note-book that she has already put on the table. (Often she will carry her work about with her, like a talisman. This isn't new.)

But Lucius examines the blank cover of the book as if scanning a map. "Where else?" he says.

Now Yse taps her forehead. *(In my mind.)* But somehow he has the impression she has also tapped her left ear, directly above the bite — as if the island was in there too. *Heard* inside her ear. Or else, heard, felt — inside the *bite*.

"Let me read it," he says, *not* opening the note-book. "You can't."

"Why not?"

"My awful handwriting. No one can, until I type it through the machine and there's a disc."

"You write so bad to hide it," he says.

"Probably."

"What's your story really about?"

"I told you. An Island. And a vampire."

"And it bit you in the neck."

Again, she laughs. "*You're* the one a vampire bit, Lucius. Or has it gone back to being a shark that bit you?"

"All kinds have bit me. I bite them, too."

She's finished her water. The exciting odour of cooking spiced fish drifts into the bar, and Lucius is hungry. But Yse is getting up.

"I'll carry your bag to the boat-stop."

"Thanks, Lucius."

"I can bring them to your loft."

"No, that's fine."

"What did you say about a vampire," he asks her as they wait above the sparkling water for the water-bus, "not what they are, what they *do* to you – what they make you feel?"

"I've known you over five years, Lucius –"

"Six and a half years."

"Six and a half then. I've never known you very interested in my books."

The breeze blows off the Sound, flattening Yse's shirt to her body. Her waist is about five inches smaller, her breasts formed, and her whole shape has changed from that of a small barrel to a curvy egg-timer. Woman-shape. Young woman-shape.

He thinks, uneasily, will she begin to menstruate again, the hormones flowing back like the flood of the Sound tides through the towers and lofts of the island? Can he scent, through her cleanly-showered, soap and shampoo smell, the hint of fresh blood?

"Not interested, Yse. Just being nosy."

"All right. The book is about, among others, a girl, who is called Antoinelle. She's empty, or been made empty, because what she wants is refused her – so she's like a soft, flaccid, open bag, and she wants and wants. And the soft wanting emptiness pulls him – the man – inside. She drains him of volition, and of his good luck. But he doesn't care. He also wants this. Went out looking for it. He explains that in the next section, I think ..."

"So she's your vampire."

"No. But she makes a vampire possible. She's like a blue-print – like compost, for the plant to grow in. And the heat there, and the decline, that lovely word *desuetude*. And empty spaces that need to be continually *filled*. Nature abhors a vacuum. Darkness abhors it too, and rushes in. Why else do you think it gets dark when the sun goes down?"

"Night," he says flatly.

"Of course not." She smiles. "Nothing so ordinary. It's the black of outer space rushing to fill the empty gap the daylight filled. Why else do they call it *space?*""

She's clever. Playing with her words, with quotations and vocal things like that.

Lucius can see the tired old rusty boat chugging across the water.

(Yse starts to talk about the planet Vulcan, which was discovered once, twice, a hundred or a hundred and fifty years ago, and both times found to be a hoax.)

The bus-boat is at the quay. Lucius helps Yse get her food and wine into the boat. He watches as it goes off around this drowned isle we have here, but she forgets to wave.

In fact, Yse has been distracted by another thought. She had found a seashell lying on her terrace yesterday. This will sometimes happen, if an especially high tide has flowed in.

She's thinking about the seashell, and the idea has come to her that, if she put it to her left ear, instead of hearing the sound of the sea (which is the rhythm of her own blood, moving), she might hear a piano playing.

Which is how she might put this into the story.

By the time the bus-boat reaches West Ridge, sunset is approaching. When she has hauled the bags and wine to the doors of her loft, she stands a moment, looking. The snake-willow seems carved from vitreous. The alley of water is molten. But that's by now commonplace.

Even out here, before she opens her doors, she can catch the faint overture of perfume from the plant which may – must – be growing in the piano.

She dreamed last night she followed Per Laszd for miles, trudging till her feet ached, through endless lanes of shopping mall, on the mainland. He would not stop, or turn, and periodically he disappeared. For some hours too she saw him in conversation with a slender, dark-haired woman. When he vanished yet again, Yse approached her. "Is he your lover?" *"No, "* chuckled the incredulous woman. *"Mine? No. "* In the end Yse had gone on again, seen him ahead of her, and at last given up, turned her back, walked away briskly, not wanting him to know she had pursued him such a distance. Then only did she feel his hands thrill lightly on her shoulders –

At the shiver of memory, Yse shakes herself.

She's pleased to have lost weight, but not so surprised. She hasn't been eating much, and change is always feasible. The extensions cost a lot of money. Washing her hair is now a nuisance, and probably she will have them taken out before too long.

However, seeing her face in the mirror above the wash basin, she paused this morning, recognizing herself, if only for a moment.

A red gauze cloud drifts from the mainland.

Yse undoes her glass doors, and in the shadow, there that other shadow stands on its three legs. It might be anything but what it is, as might we all.

6: *Her Piano*

On the terrace below the gallery of orange trees, above the dry fountain, Gregers Vonderjan stood checking his gun.

Jeanjacques halted. He felt for a moment irrationally afraid – as opposed to the other fears he had felt here.

But the gun, plainly, was not for him.

It was just after six in the morning. Dawn had happened not long ago, the light was transparent as a window-pane.

"Another," said Vonderjan enigmatically. (Jeanjacques had noticed before, the powerful and self-absorbed were often obscure, thinking everyone must already know their business, which of course shook the world.)

"... Your horses."

"My horses. Only two now, and one on its last legs. Come with me if you like, if you're not squeamish.

I am, extremely, Jeanjacques thought, but he went with Vonderjan nevertheless, slavishly.

Vonderjan strode down steps, around corners, through a grove of trees. They reached the stables. It was vacant, no one about but for a single man, some groom.

Inside the stall, two horses were together, one lying down. The other, strangely uninvolved, stood aloof. This upright one was white as some strange pearly fish-animal, its eyes almost blue, Jeanjacques thought, but perhaps that was a trick of the pure light. The other horse, the prone one, half lifted its head, heavily.

Vonderjan went to this horse. The groom did not speak. Vonderjan kneeled down.

"Ah, poor soldier –" then he spoke in another tongue, his birth-language, probably. As he murmured, he stroked the streaked mane away from the horse's eyes, tenderly, like a father, caressed it till the weary eyes shut, then shot it, quickly through the skull. The legs kicked once, strengthlessly, a reflex. It had been almost gone already.

Jeanjacques went out and leaned on the mounting-block. He expected he would vomit, but did not.

Vonderjan presently also came out, wiping his hands, like Pilate.

"Damn this thing, death," he said. The anger was wholesome, *whole*. For a moment a real man, a human being, stood solidly by Jeanjacques, and Jeanjacques wanted to turn and fling his arms about this creature, to keep it with him. But then it vanished, as before.

The strong handsome face was bland – or was it *blind?*

"None of us escape death."

That cliché once more, masking the *horror* – but what *was* the horror? And was the use of the cliché only acceptance of the harsh world, precisely what Vonderjan must have set himself to learn?

"Come to the house. Have a brandy," said Vonderjan.

They went back, not the way they had come, but using another flight of stairs. Behind them the groom was clearing the beautiful dead horse like debris or garbage. Jeanjacques refused to look over his shoulder.

Vonderjan's study had no light until great storm-shutters were undone. It must face, like the terrace, towards the sea.

The brandy was hot.

"All my life," said Vonderjan, sitting down on his own writing-table, suddenly unsolid, his eyes wide and unseeing, "I've had to deal with fucking death. You get sick of it. Sick to death of it."

"Yes."

"I know you saw some things in France."

"I did."

"How do we live with it, eh? Oh, you're a young man. But when you get past forty. Christ, you feel it, breathing on the back of your neck. Every death you've seen. And I've seen plenty. My mother, and my wife. I mean, my first wife, Uteka. A beautiful woman, when I met her. Big, if you know what I mean. White skin and raven hair, red-gold eyes. A Viking woman."

Jeanjacques was mesmerized, despite everything. He had never heard Vonderjan expatiate like this, not even in imagination.

They drank more brandy.

Vonderjan said, "She died in my arms."

"I'm sorry –"

"Yes. I wish I could have shot her, like the horses, to stop her suffering. But it was in Copenhagen, one summer. Her people everywhere. One thing, she hated sex."

Jeanjacques was shocked despite himself.

"I found other women for that," said Vonderjan, as if, indifferently, to explain. The bottle was nearly empty. Vonderjan opened a cupboard and took out another bottle, and a slab of dry, apparently stale bread on a plate. He ripped off pieces of the bread and ate them.

It was like a curious Communion, bread and wine, flesh, blood. (He offered none of the bread to Jeanjacques.)

"I wanted," Vonderjan said, perhaps two hours later, as they sat in the hard stuffed chairs, the light no longer window- pane pure, "a woman who'd take that, from me. Who'd want me pushed and poured into her, like the sea, like they say a mermaid wants that. A woman who'd take. I heard of one. I went straight to her. It was true."

"Don't all women…" Jeanjacques faltered, drunk and heart racing, "take…?"

"No. They give. Give, give, give. They give too bloody much."

Vonderjan was not drunk, and they had consumed two bottles of brandy, and Vonderjan most of it.

"But she's – she's taken – she's had your *luck* –" Jeanjacques blurted.

"Luck. I never wanted my luck."

"But you –"

"Wake up. I had it, but who else did? Not Uteka, my wife. Not my wretched mother. I hate cruelty," Vonderjan said quietly. "And we note, this world's very cruel. We should punish the world if we could. We should punish God if we could. Put Him on a cross? Yes. Be damned to this fucking God."

The clerk found he was on the ship, coming to the Island, but he knew he did not want to be on the Island. Yet of course, it was now too late to turn back. Something followed through the water. It was black and shining. A shark, maybe.

When Jeanjacques came to, the day was nearly gone and evening was coming. His head banged and his heart galloped. The dead horse had possessed it. He wandered out of the study (now empty but for himself) and heard the terrible sound of a woman, sick-moaning in her death-throes: Uteka's ghost. But then a sharp cry came; it was the other one, Vonderjan's second wife, dying in his arms.

As she put up her hair, Nanetta was thinking of whispers. She heard them in the room, echoes of all the other whispers in the house below.

Black – it's black – not black like a man is black… black as black is black …

Beyond the fringe of palms, the edge of the forest trees stirred, as if something quite large were prowling about there. Nothing else moved.

She drove a gold hairpin through her coiffure.

He was with her, along the corridor. It had sometimes happened he would walk up here, in the afternoons. Not for a year, however.

A bird began to shriek its strange stupid warning at the forest's edge, the notes of which sounded like *J'ai des lits! J'ai des lits! "*

Nanetta had dreamed this afternoon, falling asleep in that chair near the window, that she was walking in the forest, barefoot, as she had done when a child. Through the trees behind her something crept, shadowing her. It was noiseless, and the forest also became utterly still with tension and fear. She had not dared look back, but sometimes, from the rim of her eye, she glimpsed a dark, pencil-straight shape, that might only have been the ebony trunk of a young tree.

Then, pushing through the leaves and ropes of a wild fig, she saw it, in front of her not at her back, and woke, flinging herself forward with a choking gasp, so that she almost fell out of the chair.

It was black, smooth. Perhaps, in the form of a man. Or was it a beast? Were there eyes? Or a mouth?

In the house, a voice whispered, "Something is in the forest."

A shutter banged without wind.

And outside, the bird screamed *I have beds! I have beds!*

The salon: it was sunset and thin wine light was on the rich man's china, and the Venice glass, what was left of it.

Vonderjan considered the table, idly, smoking, for the meal had been served and consumed early. He had slept off his brandy in twenty minutes on Anna's bed, then woken and had her a third time, before they separated.

She had lain there on the sheet, her pale arms firm and damask with the soft nap of youth.

"I can't get up. I can't stand up."

"Don't get up. Stay where you are," he said. "They can bring you something on a tray."

"Bread," she said, "I want soft warm bread, and some soup. And a glass of wine."

"Stay there," he agreed again. "I'll soon be back."

"Come back quickly," she said. And she held out the slender, strong white arms, all the rest of her flung there and limp as a broken snake.

So he went back and slid his hand gently into her, teasing her, and she writhed on the point of his fingers, the way a doll would, should you put your hand up its skirt.

"Is that so nice? Are you sure you like it?"

"Don't stop."

Vonderjan had thought he meant only to tantalize, perhaps to fulfil, but in the end he unbuttoned himself, the buttons he had only just done up, and put himself into her again, finishing both of them with swift hard thrusts.

So, she had not been in to dine. And he sat here, ready for her again, quite ready. But he was used to that. He had, after all, stored all that, during his years with Uteka, who, so womanly in other ways, had loved to be held and petted like a child, and nothing more. Vonderjan had partly unavoidably felt that the disease, which invaded her body, had somehow been given entrance to it because of this omitting vacancy, which she had not been able to allow him to fill – as night rushed to engulf the sky once vacated by a sun.

This evening the clerk looked very sallow, and had not eaten much. (Vonderjan had forgotten the effect brandy could have.) The black woman was definitely frightened. There was a type of magic going on, some ancient fear-ritual that unknown forces had stirred up among the people on the Island. It did not interest Vonderjan very much, nothing much did, now.

He spoke to the clerk, congratulating him on the efficiency of his lists and his evaluation, and the arrangements that had been postulated, when next the ship came to the Island.

Jeanjacques rallied. He said, "The one thing I couldn't locate, sir, was a piano."

"Piano?" Puzzled, Vonderjan looked at him.

"I had understood you to say your wife – that she had a piano –"

"Oh, I ordered one for her years ago. It never arrived. It was stolen, I suppose, or lost overboard, and they never admitted to it. Yes, I recall it now, a pianoforte. But the heat here would soon have ruined it anyway."

The candles abruptly flickered, for no reason. The light was going, night rushing in.

Suddenly something, a huge impenetrable shadow, ran by the window.

The woman, Nanetta, screamed. The housekeeper sat with her eyes almost starting out of her head. Jeanjacques cursed. *What was that?*

As it had run by, fleet, leaping, a mouth gaped a hundred teeth – like the mouth of a shark breaking from the ocean. Or had they mistaken that?

Did it have eyes, the great black animal which had run by the window? Surely it had eyes –

Vonderjan had stood up, and now he pulled a stick from a vase against the wall – as another man might pick up an umbrella, or a poker – and he was opening wide the doors, so the women shrank together and away.

The light of day was gone. The sky was blushing to black. Nothing was there.

Vonderjan called peremptorily into the darkness. To Jeanjacques the call sounded meaningless, gibberish, something like *Hooh! Hoouah!* Vonderjan was not afraid, possibly not even disconcerted or intrigued.

Nothing moved. Then, below, lights broke out on the open space, a servant shouted shrilly in the patois.

Vonderjan shouted down, saying it was nothing. "Go back inside." He turned and looked at the two women and the man in the salon. "Some animal." He banged the doors shut.

"It – looked like a lion," Jeanjacques stammered. But no. It had been like a shark, a fish, which bounded on two or three legs, and stooping low.

The servants must have seen it too. Alarmed and alerted, they were still disturbed, and generally calling out now. Another woman screamed, and then there was the crash of glass.

"Fools," said Vonderjan, without any expression or contempt. He nodded at the housekeeper. "Go and tell them I say it's all right."

The woman dithered, then scurried away – by the house door; avoiding the terrace. Nanaetta too had stood up and her eyes had their silver rings. They, more even than the thing which ran across the window, terrified Jeanjacques.

"What was it? Was it a wild pig?" asked the clerk, aware he sounded like a scared child.

"A pig. What pig? No. Where could it go?"

"Has it climbed up the wall?" Jeanjacques rasped.

The black woman began to speak the patois in a singsong and the hair crawled on Jeanjacques' scalp.

"Tell her to stop it, can't you."

"Be quiet, Nanette," said Vonderjan.

She was silent.

They stood there.

Outside the closed windows, in the closed dark, the disturbed noises below were dying off.

Had it had eyes? Where had it gone to?

Jeanjacques remembered a story of Paris, how the guillotine would leave its station by night, and patrol the streets, searching for yet more blood. And during a siege of antique Rome, a giant phantom wolf had stalked the seven hills, tearing out the throats of citizens. These things were not real, even though they had been witnessed and attested, even though evidence and bodies were left in their wake. And, although unreal, yet they existed. They grew, such things, out of the material of the rational world, as maggots appeared spontaneously in a corpse, or fungus formed on damp.

The black woman had been keeping quiet. Now she made a tiny sound. They turned their heads.

Beyond the windows – dark blotted dark, night on night.

"It's there."

A second time Vonderjan flung open the doors, and light flooded, by some trick of reflection in their glass, out across the place beyond.

It crouches by the wall, where yester eve the man carnally had his wife, where a creeper grows, partly rent away by their movements.

"In God's sight," Vonderjan says, startled finally, but not afraid.

He walks out, straight out, and they see the beast by the wall does not move, either to attack him or to flee.

Jeanjacques can smell roses, honeysuckle. The wine glass drops out of his hand.

Antoinelle dreams, now.

She is back in the house of her aunt, where no one would allow her to speak, or to play the piano. But she has slunk down in the dead of night, into the sitting-room, and rebelliously lifted the piano's lid.

A wonderful sweet smell comes up from the keys, and she strokes them a moment, soundlessly. They feel... like skin. The skin of a man, over muscle, young, hard, smooth. Is it Justus she feels? (She knows this is very childish. Even her sexuality, although perhaps she does not know this, has the wanton ravening quality of the child's single-minded demands.)

There is a shell the inclement aunt keeps on top of the piano, along with some small framed miniatures of ugly relatives.

Antoinelle lifts the shell, and puts it to her ear, listens to hear the sound of the sea. But instead, she hears a piano playing, softly and far off.

The music, Antoinelle thinks, is a piece by Rameau, for the harpsichord, transposed.

She looks at the keys. She has not touched them, or not enough to make them sound.

Rameau's music dies away.

Antoinelle finds she is playing four single notes on the keys, she does not know why, neither the notes, nor the word they spell, mean anything to her.

And then, even in the piano-dream, she is aware her husband, Gregers Vonderjan, is in the bed with her, lying behind her, although in her dream she is standing upright.

They would not let her speak or play the piano – they would not let her have what she must have, or make the sounds that she must make.

Now *she* is a piano.

He fingers her keys, gentle, next a little rough, next sensually, next with the crepitation of a feather. And, at each caress, she sounds, Antoinelle, who is a piano, a different note. His hands are over her breasts. (In the dream too, she realizes, she has come into the room naked.) His fingers are on her naked breasts, fondling and describing, itching the buds at their centres. Antoinelle is being played. She gives off, note by note and chord by chord, her music.

Still cupping, circling her breasts with his hungry hands, somehow his scalding tongue is on her spine. He is licking up and up the keys of her vertebrae, through her silk-thin skin.

Standing upright, he is pressed behind her. While lying in the bed, he has rolled her over, crushing her breasts into his hands beneath her, lying on her back, his weight keeping her pinned, breathless.

And now he is entering her body, his penis like a tower on fire.

She spreads, opens, melts, dissolves for him. No matter how large, and he is now enormous, she will make way, then grip fierce and terrible upon him, her toothless springy lower mouth biting and cramming itself full of him, as if never to let go-

They are swimming strongly together for the shore.

How piercing the pleasure at her core, all through her now, the hammers hitting with a golden quake on every nerve- string.

And then, like a beast (a cat? A lion?), he has caught her by the throat, one side of her neck.

As with the other entry, at her sex, her body gives way to allow him room. And, as at the very first, her virgin's cry of pain changes almost at once into a wail of delight.

Antoinelle begins to come (to enter, to arrive).

Huge thick rollers of deliciousness, purple and crimson, dark and blazing, tumble rhythmically as dense waves upwards, from her spine's base to the windowed dome of her skull.

Glorious starvation couples with feasting, itching with rubbing, constricting, bursting, with implosion, the architecture of her pelvis rocks, punches, roaring and spinning in eating movements and swallowing gulps –

If only this sensation might last and last.

It lasts. It lasts.

Antoinelle is burning bright. She is changing into stars. Her stars explode and shatter. There are greater stars she can make. She is going to make them. She does so. And greater. Still she is coming, entering, arriving.

She has screamed. She has screamed until she no longer has any breath. Now she screams silently. Her nails gouge the bed-sheets. She feels the blood of her virginity falling drop by drop. She is the shell and her blood her sounding sea, and the sea is rising up and another mouth, the mouth of night, is taking it all, and she is made of silver for the night which devours her, and this will never end.

And then she screams again, a terrible divine scream, dredged independently up from the depths of her concerto of ecstasy. And vaguely, as she flies crucified on the wings of the storm, she knows the body upon her body (its teeth in her throat), is not the body of Vonderjan, and that the fire-filled hands upon her breasts, the flaming stem within her, are black, not as black is black, but black as outer space, which she is filling now with her millions of wheeling, howling stars.

7

The bird which cries *Shadily! Shadily!* flies over the island above the boiling afternoon lofts, and is gone, back to the upper city mainland, where there are more trees, more shade.

In the branches of the snake-willow, a wind-chime tinkles, once.

Yse's terrace is full of people, sitting and standing, with bottles, glasses, cans, and laughing. Yse has thrown a party. Someone, drunk, is dog-paddling in the alley of water.

Lucius, in his violet shirt, looks at the people. Sometimes Yse appears. She's slim and ash-pale, with long, shining hair, about twenty-five. Closer, thirty-five, maybe.

"Good party, Yse. Why you throw a party?"

"I had to throw something. Throw a plate, or myself away. Or something."

Carr and the fat man, they got the two lids up off the piano by now.

It won't play, everyone knew it wouldn't. Half the notes will not sound. Instead, a music centre, straddled between the piano's legs, rigged via Yse's generator, uncoils the blues.

And this in turn has made the refrigerator temperamental. Twice people have gone to neighbours to get ice. And in turn these neighbours have been invited to the party.

A new batch of lobsters bake on the griddle. Green grapes and yellow pineapples are pulled apart.

"I was bored," she says. "I couldn't get on with it, that vampire story."

"Let me read it."

"You won't decipher my handwriting."

"Some. Enough."

"You think so? All right. But don't make criticisms, don't tell me what to do, Lucius, all right?"

"Deal. How would *I* know?"

He sits in the shady corner (*Shadily!* the bird cried mockingly (*J'ai des lits*) from Yse's roof), and now he reads. He can read her handwriting, it's easier than she thinks.

Sunset spreads an awning.

Some of the guests go home, or go elsewhere, but still crowds sit along the wall, or on the steps, and in the loft people are dancing now to a rock band on the music centre.

"Hey this piano don't play!" accusingly calls Big Eye, a late learner.

Lucius takes a polite puff of a joint someone passes, and passes it on. He sits thinking.

Sunset darkens, claret colour, and now the music centre plays Mozart.

Yse sits down by Lucius on the wall.

"Tell me, Yse, how does he get all his energy, this rich guy. He's forty, you say, but you say that was like fifty, then. And he's big, heavy. And he porks this Anna three, four times a night, and then goes on back for more."

"Oh that. Vonderjan and Antoinelle. It's to do with obsession. They're obsessive. When you have a kink for something, you can do more, go on and on. Straight sex is never like that. It's the perversity — so-called perversity. That revs it up."

"Strong guy, though."

"Yes."

"Too strong for you?"

"Too strong for me."

Lucius knew nothing about Yse's 'obsession' with Per Laszd. But by now he knows there is something. There has never been a man in Yse's life that Lucius has had to explain to that he, Lucius, is her friend only. Come to that, not any women in her life, either. But he has come across her work, read a little of it – never much – seen this image before, this big blond man. And the sex, for always, unlike the life of Yse, her books are full of it.

Lucius says suddenly, "You liked him but you never got to have him, this feller."

She nods. As the light softens, she's not a day over thirty, even from two feet away.

"No. But I'm used to that."

"What is it then? You have a bone to pick with him for him getting old?"

"The real living man you mean? He's not old. About fifty-five, I suppose. He looks pretty wonderful to me still."

"You see him?" Lucius is surprised. "I see him on TV. And he looks great. But he was – well, fabulous when he was younger. I mean actually like a man out of a fable, a myth." She's forgotten, he thinks, that she never confided like this in Lucius. Still though, she keeps back the name.

Lucius doesn't ask for the name.

A name no longer matters, if it ever did.

"You never want to try another guy?"

"Who? Who's offering?" And she is angry, he sees it. Obviously, he is no use to her that way. But then, did she make a friendship with Lucius for just that reason?

"You look good, Yse."

"Thank you." Cold. Better let her be. For a moment. A heavenly, unearthly scent is stealing over the evening air.

Lucius has never seen the plant someone must have put in to produce this scent. Nothing grows on the terrace but for the snake-willow, and tonight people, lobster, pineapple, empty bottles.

"This'll be a mess to get straight," he says.

"Are you volunteering?"

"Just condoling, Yse."

The sunset totally fades. Stars light up. It's so clear, you can see the Abacus Tower, like a Christmas tree, on the mainland.

"What colour are his eyes, Yse?"

"... Eyes? Blue. It's in the story."

"No, girl, the other one."

"Which –? Oh, *that* one. The vampire. I don't know. Your vampire had yellow eyes, you said."

"I said, he made me feel like a king. But the sex was good, then it was over. Not as you describe it, extended play."

"I did ask you not to criticise my work."

"No way. It's sexy. But tell me his eyes' colour?"

"Black, maybe. Or even white. The vampire is like the piano."

"Yeah. I don't see that. Yse, why is it a piano?"

"It could have been anything. The characters are the hotbed, and the vampire grows out of that. It just happens to form as a piano – a sort of piano. Like dropping a glass of wine, like a cloud – the stain, the cloud, just happen to take on a shape, randomly, that seems to resemble some familiar thing."

"Or is it because you can play it?"

"Yes, that too."

"And it's an animal."

"And a man. Or male. A male body."

"Black as black is black. Not skin-black."

"Blacker. As black as black can be."

He says quietly, "La Danse aux Vampires."

A glass breaks in the loft and wine spills on the wooden floor – shapelessly? Yse doesn't bat an eyelash.

"You used to fuss about your things."

"They're only things."

"We're all only things, Yse. What about the horses?" "You mean Vonderjan's horses. This is turning into a real interrogation. All right. The last one, the white one like a fish, escapes, and gallops about the Island."

"You don't seem stuck, Yse. You seem to know plenty enough to go on."

"Perhaps I'm tired of going on."

"Looked in the mirror?"

"What do you mean?"

"Look in the mirror, Yse."

"Oh that. It's not real. It won't last."

"I never saw a woman could do that before, get fifteen years younger in a month. Grow her hair fifty times as thick and twenty times longer. Lose forty pounds without trying, and nothing *loose*. How do you *feel*, Yse?"

"All right."

"But do you feel good?"

"I feel all right."

"It's how they make you feel, Yse. You said it. They're not beautiful, they don't smell like flowers or the sea. They come out of the grave, out of beds of earth, out of the cesspit shit at the bottom of your soul's id. It's how they make you feel, what they can do to change you. Hudja-magica. Not them. What they can do to *you*. "

"You are crazy, Lucius. There've been some funny smokes on offer up here tonight."

He gets up.

"Yse, did I say, the one I followed, when he went into his grave under the headstone, he say to me, *You come in with me, Luce. Don't mind the dark. I make sure you never notice* it."

"And you said no."

"I took to my hot heels and ran for my fucking life."

"Then you didn't love him, Lucius."

"I loved my fucking life."

She smiles, the white girl at his side. Hair and skin so ivory pale, white dress and shimmering eyes, and who in hell is she?

"Take care, Yse."

"Night, Lucius. Sweet dreams."

The spilled wine on the floor has spilled a random shape that looks like a screwed-up sock.

Her loft is empty. They have all gone.

She lights the lamp on her desk, puts out the others, sits, looking at the piano from the Sound, forty feet away, its hind lid and its fore lid now raised, eyes and mouth.

Then she gets up and goes to the piano, and taps out on the keys four notes.

Each one sounds.

D, then E, then A. And then again D.

It would be *mort* in French, *dood* in Dutch, *tod* in German. Danish, Czech, she isn't sure . . . but it would not work.

I saw in the mirror.

PianO. O, pain.

But, it doesn't hurt.

8: *Danse Macabre*

A wind blew from the sea, and waxy petals fell from the vine, scattering the lid of the piano as it stood there, by the house wall.

None of them spoke.

Jeanjacques felt the dry parched cinnamon breath of Nanetta scorching on his neck, as she waited behind him. And in front of him was Vonderjan, examining the thing on the terrace.

"How did it get up here?" Jeanjacques asked, stupidly. He knew he was being stupid. The piano was supernatural. It had run up here.

"Someone carried it. Hew else?" replied Vonderjan.

Did he believe this? Yes, it seemed so.

Just then a stifled cry occurred above, detached itself and floated over them. For a moment none of them reacted to it; they had heard it so many times and in so many forms.

But abruptly Vonderjan's blond head went up, his eyes wide. He turned and strode away, half running. Reaching a stair that went to the gallery above, he bounded up it.

It was the noise his wife made, of course. But she made it when he was with her (inside her). And he had been here –

Neither Nanetta nor Jeanjacques went after Gregers Vonderjan, and neither of them went any nearer the piano.

"Could someone have carried it up here?" Jeanjacques asked the black woman, in French.

"Of course." But as she said this, she vehemently shook her head.

They moved away from the piano.

The wind came again, and petals fell again across the blackness of its carapace.

Jeanjacques courteously allowed the woman to precede him into the salon, then shut both doors quietly.

"What is this?"

She looked up at him sleepily, deceitfully.

"You called out."

"Did I? I was asleep. A dream ..."

"Now I'm here," he said.

"No," she said, moving a little way from him. "I'm so sleepy. Later."

Vonderjan stood back from the bed. He gave a short laugh, at the absurdity of this. In the two years of their sexual marriage, she had never before said anything similar to him. (And he heard Uteka murmur sadly, "Please forgive me, Gregers. Please don't be angry.")

"Very well."

Then Antoinelle turned and he saw the mark on her neck, glowing lushly scarlet as a flower or fruit, in the low lamplight.

"Something's bitten you." He was alarmed. He thought at once of the horses dying. "Let me see."

"Bitten me? Oh, yes. And I scratched at it in my sleep, yes, I remember."

"Is that why you called out, Anna?"

She was amused and secretive.

Picking up the lamp, he bent over her, staring at the place.

A little thread, like fire, still trickled from the wound, which was itself very small. There was the slightest bruising. It did not really look like a bite, more as if she had been stabbed on purpose by a hat-pin.

Where he had let her put him off sexually, he would not let her do so now. He went out and came back, to mop up the little wound with alcohol.

"Now you've made it sting. It didn't before."

"You said it itched you."

"Yes, but it didn't worry me."

"I'll close the window."

"Why? It's hot, so hot –"

252

"To keep out these things which bite."

He noted her watching him. It was true she was mostly still asleep, yet despite this, and the air of deception and concealment which so oddly clung to her, for a moment he saw, in her eyes, that he was old.

When her husband had gone, Antoinelle lay on her front, her head turned, so the blood continued for a while to soak into her pillow.

She had dreamed the sort of dream she had sometimes dreamed before Vonderjan came into her life. Yet this had been much more intense. If she slept, would the dream return? But she slept quickly, and the dream did not happen.

Two hours later, when Vonderjan came back to her bed, he could not at first wake her. Then, although she seemed to welcome him, for the first time he was unable to satisfy her. She writhed and wriggled beneath him, then petulantly flung herself back. "Oh finish then. I can't. I don't want to."

But he withdrew gently, and coaxed her. "What's wrong, Anna? Aren't you well tonight?"

"Wrong? I want what you usually give me."

"Then let me give it to you."

"No. I'm too tired."

He tried to feel her forehead. She seemed too warm. Again, he had the thought of the horses, and he was uneasy. But she pulled away from him. "Oh, let me sleep, I must sleep."

Before returning here, he had gone down and questioned his servants. He had asked them if they had brought the piano up on to the terrace, and where they had found it.

They were afraid, he could see that plainly. Afraid of unknown magic and the things they beheld in the leaves and on the wind, which he, Vonderjan, could not see and had never believed in. They were also afraid of a shadowy beast, which apparently they too had witnessed, and which he thought he had seen. And naturally, they were afraid of the piano, because it was out of its correct situation, because (and he already knew this perfectly well), they believed it had stolen by itself out of the forest, and run up on the terrace, and *was* the beast they had seen.

At midnight, he went back down, unable to sleep, with a lamp and a bottle, and pushed up both the lids of the piano with ease.

Petals showered away. And a wonderful perfume exploded from the inside of the instrument, and with it a dim cloud of dust, so he stepped off.

As the film cleared, Vonderjan began to see that something lay inside the piano. The greater hind lid had shut it in against the piano's viscera of dulcimer hammers and brass-wire strings.

When all the film had smoked away, Vonderjan once more went close and held the lamp above the piano, leaning down to look, as he had with his wife's bitten throat.

An embalmed mummy was curled up tight in the piano.

That is, a twisted knotted thing, blackened as if by fire, lay folded round there in a preserved and tarry skin, tough as any bitumen, out of which, here and there, the dull white star of a partial bone poked through.

This was not large enough, he thought, to be the remains of a normal adult. Yet the bones, so far as he could tell, were not those of a child, nor of an animal.

Yet, it was most like the burnt and twisted carcass of a beast.

He released and pushed down again upon the lid. He held the lid flat, as if it might lunge up and open again. Glancing at the keys, before he closed them away too, he saw a drop of vivid red, like a pearl of blood from his wife's neck, but it was only a single red petal from the vine.

Soft and loud. In his sleep, the clerk kept hearing these words. They troubled him, so he shifted and turned, almost woke, sank back uneasily. *Soft and loud* – which was what *Pianoforte* meant ...

Jeanjacques' mother, who had been accustomed to thrash him, struck him round the head. A loud blow, but she was soft with grown men, yielding, pliant. And with him, too, when grown, she would come to be soft and subserviently polite. But he never forgot the strap, and when she lay dying, he had gone nowhere near her. (His white half, from his father, had also made sure he went nowhere near his sire.)

Nanetta lay under a black, heavily-furred animal, a great cat, which kneaded her back and buttocks, purring. At first she was terrified, then she began to like it. Then she knew she would die.

Notes: The black keys are the black magic. The white keys are the white magic. (Both are evil.) Anything black, or white, must respond.

Even if half-black, half-white.

Notes: The living white horse has escaped. It gallops across the Island. It reaches the sea and finds the fans of the waves, snorting at them, and canters through the surf along the beaches, fish-white, and the sun begins to rise.

Gregers Vonderjan dreams he is looking down at his dead wife (Uteka), in the rain, as he did in Copenhagen that year she died. But in the dream she is not in a coffin, she is uncovered, and the soil is being thrown on to her vulnerable face. And he is sorry, because for all his wealth and personal magnitude, and power, he could not stop this happening to her. When the Island sunrise wakes him at Bleumaneer, the sorrow does not abate. He wishes now she had lived, and was here with him. (Nanetta would have eased him elsewhere, as she had often done in the past. Nanetta had been kind, and warm-blooded enough.) (Why speak of her as if she too were dead?)

Although awake, he does not want to move. He cannot be bothered with it, the eternal and repetitive affair of getting up. shaving and dressing, breakfasting, looking at the accounts, the lists the clerk has made, his possessions, which will shortly be gone.

How has he arrived at this? He had seemed always on a threshold. There is no time left now. The threshold is that of the exit. It is all over, or soon will be.

Almost all of them had left. The black servants and the white, from the kitchen and the lower rooms. The white housekeeper, despite her years and her pernickety adherences to the house. Vonderjan's groom – he had let the last horse out, too, perhaps taken it with him.

Even the bird had been let out of its cage in Antoinelle's boudoir, and had flown off.

Stronn stayed, Vonderjan's man. His craggy indifferent face said, *So, have they left?*

And the young black woman, Nanetta, she was still there, sitting with Antoinelle on the balcony, playing cards among the Spanish flowers, her silver and ruby earrings glittering.

"Why?" said Jeanjacques. But he knew.

"They're superstitious," Vonderjan, dismissive. "This sort of business has happened before."

It was four in the afternoon. Mornings here were separate. They came in slices, divided off by sleep. Or else, one slept through them.

"Is that – is the piano still on the terrace? Did someone take it?" said Jeanjacques, giving away the fact he had been to look, and seen the piano was no longer there. Had he dreamed it?

"Some of them will have moved it," said Vonderjan. He paced across the library. The windows stood open. The windows here were open so often, anything might easily get in.

The Island sweated, and the sky was golden lead.

"Who would move it?" persisted Jeanjacques.

Vonderjan shrugged. He said, "It wasn't any longer worth anything. It had been in the sea. It must have washed up on the beach. Don't worry about it."

Jeanjacques thought, if he listened carefully, he could hear beaded piano notes, dripping in narrow streams through the house. He had heard them this morning, as he lay in bed, awake, somehow unable to get up. (There had seemed no point in getting up. Whatever would happen would happen, and he might as well lie and wait for it.) However, a lifetime of frantic early arising, of hiding in country barns and thatch, and up chimneys, a lifetime of running away, slowly curdled his guts and pushed him off the mattress. But by then it was past noon.

"Do they come back?"

"What? What did you say?" asked Vonderjan.

"Your servants. You said, they'd made off before. Presumably they returned."

"Yes. Perhaps."

Birds called raucously (but wordlessly) in the forest, and then grew silent.

"There was something inside that piano," said Vonderjan, "a curiosity. I should have seen to it last night, when I found it."

"What – what was it?"

"A body. Oh, don't blanch. Here, drink this. Some freakish thing. A monkey, I'd say. I don't know how it got there, but they'll have been frightened by it."

"But it smelled so sweet. Like roses –"

"Yes, it smelled of flowers. That's a funny thing." "Sometimes the dead do smell like that. Just before the smell changes."

"I never heard of that."

"No. It surprised me years ago, when I encountered it myself. Something fell through the sky – an hour. And now it was sunset.

Nanetta had put on an apron and cooked food in the kitchen. Antoinelle had not done anything to assist her, although, in her childhood, she had been taught how to make soups and bake bread, out of a sort of bourgeois pettiness.

In fact, Antoinelle had not even properly dressed herself. Tonight she came to the meal, which the black woman had meticulously set out, in a dressing-robe, tied about her waist by a brightly-coloured scarf. The neckline drooped, showing off her long neck and the tops of her round young breasts, and the flimsy improper thing she wore beneath. Her hair was also undressed, loose, gleaming and rushing about her with a water-wet sheen.

Stronn too came in tonight, to join them, sitting far down the table, and with a gun across his lap.

"What's that for?" Vonderjan asked him.

"The blacks are saying there's some beast about on the Island. It fell off a boat and swam ashore."

"You believe them?"

"It's possible, mijnheer, isn't it. I knew of a dog that was thrown from a ship at Port-au-Roi, and reached Venice."

"Did you indeed."

Vonderjan looked smart, as always. The pallid topaz shone in his ring, his shirt was laundered and starched.

The main dish they had consisted of fish, with a kind of ragoût, with pieces of vegetable, and rice.

Nanetta had lit the candles, or some of them. Some repeatedly went out. Vonderjan remarked this was due to something in the atmosphere. The air had a thick, heavy saltiness, and for once there was no rumbling of thunder, and constellations showed, massed above the heights, once the light had gone, each star framed in a peculiar greenish circle.

After Vonderjan's exchange with the man, Stronn, none of them spoke.

Without the storm, there seemed no sound at all, except that now and then, Jeanjacques heard thin little rills of musical notes.

At last he said, "What is that I can hear?"

Vonderjan was smoking one of his cigars. "What?"

It came again. Was it only in the clerk's head? He did not think so, for the black girl could plainly hear it too. And oddly, when Vonderjan did not say anything else, it was she who said to Jeanjacques, "They hang things on the trees – to honour gods – wind gods, the gods of darkness."

Jeanjacques said, "But it sounds like a piano."

No one answered. Another candle sighed and died.

And then Antoinelle – *laughed*.

It was a horrible, terrible laugh. Riling and tinkling like the bells hung on the trees of the Island, or like the high notes of any piano. She did it for no apparent reason, and did not refer to it once she had finished. She should have done, she should have begged their pardon, as if she had belched raucously.

Vonderjan got up. He went to the doors and opened them on the terrace and the night.

Where the piano had rested itself against the wall, there was nothing, only shadow and the disarrangement of the vine, all its flower-cups broken and shed.

"Do you want some air, Anna?"

Antoinelle rose. She was demure now. She crossed to Vonderjan, and they moved out on to the terrace. But their walking together was unlike that compulsive, gliding inevitability of the earlier time. And, once out in the darkness, they *only* walked, loitering up and down.

She is mad, Jeanjacques thought. This was what he had seen in her face. That she was insane, unhinged and dangerous, her loveliness like vitriol thrown into the eyes of anyone who looked at her.

Stronn poured himself a brandy. He did not seem unnerved, or particularly *en garde*, despite the gun he had lugged in.

But Nanetta stood up. Unhooking the ruby ear-drops from her earlobes, she placed them beside her plate. As she went across the salon to the inner door, Jeanjacques noted her feet, which had been shod in city shoes, were now bare. They looked incongruous, those dark velvet paws with their nails of tawny coral, extending long and narrow from under her light gown; they looked lawless, in a way nothing of the rest of her did.

When she had gone out, Jeanjacques said to Stronn, "Why is she barefoot?"

'Savages."

Old rage slapped the inside of the clerk's mind, like his mother's hand. Though miles off, he must react. "Oh," he said sullenly, "barbaric, do you mean? You think them barbarians, though they've been freed."

Stronn said, "Unchained is what I mean. Wild like the forest. That's what it means, that word, savage – forest."

Stronn reached across the table and helped himself from Vonderjan's box of cigars.

On the terrace, the husband and wife walked up and down. The doors stayed wide open.

Trees rustled below, and were still.

Jeanjacques too got up and followed the black woman out, and beyond the room he found her, still in the passage. She was standing on her bare feet, listening, with the silver rings in her eyes.

"*What can you hear?* "

"You hear it too."

"Why are your feet bare?"

"So I can go back. So I can run away."

Jeanjacques seized her wrist and they stood staring at each other in a mutual fear, of which each one made up some tiny element, but which otherwise surrounded them.

"What —" he said.

"Her pillow's red with blood," said Nanetta. "Did you see the hole in her neck?"

"No."

"No. It closes up like a flower – a flower that eats flies. But she bled. And from her other place. White bed was red bed with her blood."

He felt sick, but he kept hold of the wand of her wrist.

"There *is* something."

"You know it too."

Across the end of the passageway, then, where there was no light, something heavy and rapid, and yet slow, passed by. It was all darkness, but a fleer of pallor slid across its teeth. And the head of it one moment turned, and, without eyes, as it had before, it gazed at them.

The black girl sagged against the wall, and Jeanjacques leaned against and into her. Both panted harshly. They might have been copulating, as Vonderjan had with his wife.

Then the passage was free. They felt the passage draw in a breath.

"Was in my room," the girl muttered, "was in my room that is too small anything so big get through the door. I wake, I see it there."

"But it left you alone."

"It not want me. Want *her.*"

"The white bitch."

"Want her, have her. Eat her alive. Run to the forest," said Nanetta, in the patois, but now he understood her, "run to the forest." But neither of them moved.

"No, please, Gregers. Don't be angry."

The voice is not from the past. Not Uteka's. It comes from a future now become the present.

"You said you have your courses. When did that prevent you before? I've told you, I don't mind it."

"No. Not this time."

He lets her go. Lets go of her.

She did not seem anxious, asking him not to be angry. He is not angry. Rebuffed, Vonderjan is, to his own amazement, almost relieved.

"Draw the curtains round your bed. Anna. And shut your window."

"Yes, Gregers."

He looks, and sees her for the first time tonight, how she is dressed, or not dressed.

"Why did you come down like that?"

"I was hot... does it matter?"

"A whore in the brothel would put on something like that." The crudeness of his language startles him. (Justus?) He checks. "I'm sorry, Anna. You meant nothing. But don't dress like that in front of the others."

"Nanetta, do you mean?"

"I mean, of course, Stronn. And the Frenchman."

Her neck, drooping, is the neck of a lily drenched by rain. He cannot see the mark of the bite.

"I've displeased you."

Antoinelle can remember her subservient mother (the mother who later threw her out to her aunt's house), fawning in this way on her father. (Who also threw her out.)

But Vonderjan seems uninterested now. He stands looking instead down the corridor.

Then he takes a step. Then he halts and says, "Go along to your room, Anna. Shut the door."

"Yes, Gregers."

In all their time together, they have never spoken in this way, in such platitudes, ciphers. Those things used freely by others.

He thinks he has seen something at the turn of the corridor. But when he goes to that junction, nothing is there. And then he thinks, of course, what *could* be there?

By then her door is shut.

Alone, he walks to his own rooms, and goes in.

The Island is alive tonight. Full of stirrings and displacements.

He takes up a bottle of Hollands, and pours a triple measure.

Beyond the window, the green-ringed eyes of the stars stare down at Bleumaneer, as if afraid.

When she was a child, a little girl, Antoinelle had sometimes longed to go to bed, in order to be alone with her fantasies, which (then), were perhaps 'ingenuous'. Or perhaps not.

She had lain curled up, pretending to sleep, imagining that she had found a fairy creature in the garden of her parents' house.

The fairy was always in some difficulty, and she must rescue it – perhaps from drowning in the bird bath, where sparrows had attacked it. Bearing it indoors, she would care for it, washing it in a tea-cup, powdering it lightly with scented dust stolen from her mother's box, dressing it in bits of lace, tied at the waist with strands of brightly coloured embroidery silk. Since it was seen naked in the tea-cup, it revealed it was neither male nor female, lacking both breasts and penis (she did not grossly investigate it further), although otherwise it appeared a full-grown specimen of its kind. But then, at that time, Antoinelle had never seen either the genital apparatus of a man or the mammalia of an adult woman.

The fairy, kept in secret, was dependent totally upon Antoinelle. She would feed it on crumbs of cake and fruit. It drank from her chocolate in the morning. It would sleep on her pillow. She caressed it, with always a mounting sense of urgency, not knowing where the caresses could lead – and indeed they never led to anything. Its wings she did not touch. (She had been told, the wings of moths and butterflies were fragile.)

Beyond Antoinelle's life, all Europe had been at war with itself. Invasion, battle, death, these swept by the carefully closed doors of her parents' house and by Antoinelle entirely. Through a combination of conspiracy and luck, she learned nothing of it, but no doubt those who protected her so assiduously reinforced the walls of Antoinelle's self-involvement. Such lids were shut down on her, what else was she to do but make music with herself – *play* with herself.. .

Sometimes in her fantasies, Antoinelle and the fairy quarrelled. Afterwards they would be reconciled, and the fairy would hover, kissing Antoinelle on the lips. Sometimes the fairy got inside her nightdress, tickling her all over until she thought she would die. Sometimes she tickled the fairy in turn with a goose-feather, reducing it to spasms identifiable (probably) only as hysteria.

It never flew away.

Yet, as her own body ripened and formed, Antoinelle began to lose interest in the fairy. Instead, she had strange waking dreams of a flesh-and-blood soldier she had once glimpsed under the window, who, in her picturings, had to save her – not from any of the wild armies then at large – but from an escaped bear. .. and later came the prototypes of Justus, who kissed her until she swooned.

Now Antoinelle had gone back to her clandestine youth. Along, in the room, its door shut, she blew out the lamp. She threw wide her window. Standing in the darkness, she pulled off her garments and tossed them down.

The heat of the night was like damp velvet. The tips of her breasts rose like tight buds that wished to open.

Her husband was old. She was young. She felt her youngness, and remembered her childhood with an inappropriate nostalgia.

Vonderjan had thought something might get in at the window. She sensed this might be true.

Antoinelle imagined that something climbed slowly up the creeper.

261

She began to tremble, and went and lay down on her bed.

She lay on her back, her hands lying lightly over her breasts, her legs a little apart.

Perhaps after all Vonderjan might ignore her denials and come in. She would let him. Yes, after all she had stopped menstruating. She would not mind his being here. He liked so much to do things to her, to render her helpless, gasping and abandoned, his hands on her making her into his instrument, making her utter sounds, noises, making her come over and over. And she too liked this best. She liked to do nothing, simply to be made to respond, and so give way. In some other life she might have become the ideal fanatic, falling before the Godhead in fits whose real, spurious nature only the most sceptical could ever suspect. Conversely, partnered with a more selfish and less accomplished lover, with an ignorant Justus, for example, she might have been forced to do more, learned more, liked less. But that now was hypothetical.

A breeze whispered at the window. (What does it say?)

That dream she had had. What had that been? Was it her husband? No, it had been a man with black skin. But she had seen no one so black. A blackness without any translucence, with no blood inside it.

Antoinelle drifted, in a sort of trance.

She had wandered into a huge room with a wooden floor. The only thing in it was a piano. The air was full of a rapturous smell, like blossom, something which bloomed yet burned.

She ran her fingers over the piano. The notes sounded clearly, but each was a voice. A genderless yet sexual voice, crying out as she touched it – now softly, excitedly, now harsh and demanding and desperate.

She was lying on the beach below the Island. The sea was coming in, wave by wave – glissandi – each one the ripples of the wire harp-strings under the piano lid, or keys rippling as fingers scattered touches across them.

Antoinelle had drained Gregers Vonderjan of all he might give her. She had sucked him dry of everything but his blood. It was his own fault, exalting in his power over her, wanting to make her a doll that would dance on his fingers' end, penis's end, *power's* end.

Her eyes opened, and, against the glass windows, she saw the piano standing, its lids lifted, its keys gleaming like appetite, black and white.

Should she get up and play music on it? The keys would feel like skin.

Then she knew that if she only lay still, the piano would come to *her*. She was *its* instrument, as she had been Vonderjan's.

The curtain blew. The piano shifted, and moved, but as it did so, its shape altered. Now it was not only a piano, but an animal.

(*Notes:* Pianimal.)

It was a beast. And then it melted and stood up, and the form it had taken now was that of a man.

Stronn walked around the courtyard, around its corners, past the dry Spanish fountain. Tonight the husks of flowers scratched in the bowl, and sounded like water. Or else nocturnal lizards darted about there.

There was only one light he could see in Gregers Vonderjan's big house, the few candles left undoused in the salon.

The orange trees on the gallery smelled bitter-sweet. Stronn did not want to go to bed. He was wide awake. In the old days, he might have had a game of cards with some of the blacks, or even with Vonderjan. But those times had ceased to be.

He had thought he heard the white horse earlier, its shod hoofs going along the track between the rhododendrons. But now there was no sign of it. Doubtless one of the people on the Island would catch the horse and keep it. As for the other animal, the one said to have escaped from a passing ship, Stronn did not really think it existed, or if it did, it would be something of no great importance.

Now and then he heard the tinkling noise of hudja bells the people had hung on the banana trees. Then a fragment like piano music, but it was the bells again. Some nights the sea breathed as loudly up here as in the bay. Or a shout from one of the huts two miles off might seem just over a wall.

He could hear the vrouw, certainly. But he was used to hearing that. Her squeaks and yowls, fetching off as Vonderjan shafted her. But she was a slut. The way she had come in tonight proved it, in her bedclothes. And she had never given the meester a son, not even tried to give him a child, like the missus (Uteka) had that time, only she had lost it, but she was never very healthy.

A low thin wind blew along the cane fields, and Stronn could smell the coffee trees and the hairy odour of kayar.

He went out of the yard, carrying his gun, thinking he was still looking for the white horse.

A statue of black obsidian might look like this, polished like this.

The faint luminescence of night, with its storm choked within it, is behind the figure. Starlight describes the outline of it, but only as it turns, moving towards her, do details of its forward surface catch any illumination.

Yet too, all the while, adapting to the camouflage of its environment, it grows subtly more human, that is, more recognizable.

For not entirely – remotely – human is it.

Does she comprehend?

From the head, a black pelt of hair waterfalls away around it, folding down its back like a cloak –

The wide flat pectorals are coined each side three times. It is six-nippled, like a panther.

Its legs move, columnar, heavily muscled and immensely vital, capable of great leaps and astonishing bounds, but walking, they give it the grace of a dancer.

At first there seems to be nothing at its groin, just as it seems to have no features set into its face ... except that the light had slid, once, twice, on the long rows of perfect teeth.

But now it is at the bed's foot, and out of the dark it has evolved, or made itself whole.

A man's face.

The face of a handsome Justus, and of a Vonderjan in his stellar youth. A face of improbable mythic beauty, and opening in it, like two vents revealing the inner burning core of it, eyes of grey ice, which each blaze like the planet Venus.

She can see now, it has four upper arms. They too are strong and muscular, also beautiful, like the dancer's legs.

The penis is large and upright, without a sheath, the black lotus bulb on a thick black stem. No change of shade. (No light, no inner blood.) Only the mercury-flame inside it, which only the eyes show.

Several of the side teeth, up and down, are pointed sharply. The tongue is black. The inside of the mouth is black. And the four black shapely hands, with their twenty long, flexible fingers, have palms that are black as the death of light.

It bends towards Antoinelle. It has the smell of night and of the Island, and of the sea. And also the scent of hot-house flowers, that came out of the piano. And a carnivorous smell, like fresh meat.

It stands there, looking at her, as she lies on the bed.

And on the floor, emerging from the pelt that falls from its head, the long black tail strokes softly now this way, now that way.

Then the first pair of hands stretch over on to the bed, and after them the second pair, and fluidly it lifts itself and *pours* itself forward up the sheet, and up over the body of the girl, looking down at her as it does so, from its water-pale eyes. And its smooth body rasps on her legs, as it advances, and the big hard firm organ knocks on her thighs, hot as the body is cool.

He walked behind her, obedient and terrified. The Island frightened him, but it was more than that. Nanetta was now like his mother (when she was young and slim, dominant and brutal). Once she turned, glaring at him, with the eyes of a lynx. *'Hush.* ' "But I —" he started to say, and she shook her head again, raging at him without words.

She trod so noiselessly on her bare feet, which were the indigo colour of the sky in its darkness. And he blundered, try as he would.

The forest held them in its tentacles. The top-heavy plantains loomed, their blades of black-bronze sometimes quivering. Tree limbs like enormous plaited snakes rolled upwards. Occasionally, mystically, he thought, he heard the sea.

She was taking him to her people, who grasped what menaced them, its value if not its actual being, and could keep them safe.

Barefoot and stripped of her jewels, she was attempting to go back into the knowingness of her innocence and her beginnings. But he had always been over-aware and a fool.

They came into a glade of wild tamarinds — could it be called that? A *glade?* It was an aperture among the trees, but only because trees had been cut down. There was an altar, very low, with frangi-pani flowers, scented like confectionary, and something killed that had been picked clean. The hudja bells chimed from a nearby bough, the first he had seen. They sounded like the sistra of ancient Egypt, as the cane fields had recalled to him the notion of a temple.

Nanetta bowed to the altar and went on, and he found he had crossed himself, just as he had done when a boy in church.

It made him feel better, doing that, as if he had quickly thrown up and got rid of some poison in his heart.

Vau l'eau, Vonderjan thought. Which meant, going downstream, to wrack and ruin.

He could not sleep, and turned on his side to stare out through the window. The stars were so unnaturally clear. Bleumaneer was in the eye of the storm, the aperture at its centre. When this passed, weather would resume, the ever- threatening presence of tempest.

He thought of the white horse, galloping about the Island, down its long stairways of hills and rock and forest, to the shore.

Half asleep, despite his insomnia, there was now a split second when he saw the keys of a piano, descending like the levels of many black and white terraces.

Then he was fully awake again.

Vonderjan got up. He reached for the bottle of schnapps, and found it was empty.

Perhaps he should go to her bed. She might have changed her mind. No, he did not want her tonight. He did not want anything, except to be left in peace.

It seemed to him that after all he would be glad to be rid of every bit of it. His wealth, his manipulative powers. To live here alone, as the house fell gradually apart, without servants, or any authority or commitments. And without Anna.

Had he been glad when Uteka eventually died? Yes, she had suffered so. And he had never known her. She was like a book he had meant to read, had begun to read several times, only to put it aside, unable to remember those pages he had already laboriously gone through.

With Anna it was easy, but then, she was not a book at all. She was a demon he had himself invented (Vonderjan did not realize this, that even for a moment, he thought in this way), an oasis, after Uteka's sexual desert, and so, like any fantasy, she could be sloughed at once. He had masturbated over her long enough, this too-young girl, with her serpentine body (apple-tree and tempting snake together), and her idealized pleas always for more.

Now he wanted to leave the banquet table. To get up and go away and sleep and grow old, without such distractions.

He thought he could hear her, though. Hear her fast-starved feeding breathing, and for once, this did not arouse him. And in any case it might not be Anna, but only the gasping of the sea, hurling herself far away, on the rocks and beaches of the Island.

It – he – paints her lips with its long and slender tongue, which is black. Then it paints the inside of her mouth. The tongue is very narrow, sensitive, incites her gums, making her want to yawn, except that is not what she needs to do – but she stretches her body irresistibly.

The first set of hands settles on her breasts.

The second set of hands on her ribcage.

Something flicks, flicks, between her thighs . . . not the staff of the penis, but something more like a second tongue . . .

Antoinelle's legs open and her head falls back. She makes a sound, but it is a bestial grunting that almost offends her, yet there is no room in her body or mind for that.

"No –" she tries to say.

The *No* means yes, in the case of Antoinelle. It is addressed, not to her partner, but to normal life, anything that may intrude, and warns *Don't interrupt.*

The black tongue wends, waking nerves of taste and smell in the roof of her mouth. She scents lakoum, pepper, ambergris and myrrh.

The lower tongue, which may be some extra weapon of the tail, licks at a point of flame it has discovered, fixing a triangle with the fire-points of her breasts.

He – it – slips into her, forces into her, bulging and huge as thunder.

And the tail grasps her, muscular as any of its limbs, and, thick as the phallus, also penetrates her.

The thing holds Antoinelle as she detonates about it, faints and cascades into darkness.

Not until she begins to revive does it do more.

The terror is, she comes to already primed, more than eager, her body spangled with frantic need, as if the first cataclysm were only – foreplay.

And now the creature moves, riding her and making her ride, and they gallop down the night, and Antoinelle grins and shrieks, clinging to its obsidian form, her hands slipping, gripping. And as the second detonation begins, its face leaves her face, her mouth, and grows itself faceless and *only* mouth. And the mouth half rings her throat, a crescent moon, and the many side teeth pierce her, both the veins of her neck.

A necklace of emeralds was nothing to this.

Antoinelle drops from one precipice to another. She screams, and her screams crash through the house called Blue View, like sheets of blue glass breaking.

It holds her. As her consciousness again goes out, it holds her very tight.

And somewhere in the limbo where she swirls, fire on oil, guttering but not quenched, Antoinelle is raucously laughing with triumph at finding this other one, not her parasite, but her twin. Able to devour her as she devours, able to eat her alive as she has eaten or tried to eat others alive. But where Antoinelle has bled them out, this only drinks. It wastes nothing, not even Antoinelle.

More – more – She can never have enough.

Then it tickles her with flame so she thrashes and yelps. Its fangs fastened in her, it bears her on, fastened in turn to it.

She is arched like a bridge, carrying the travelling shadow on her body. Pinned together, in eclipse, these dancers.

More –

It gives her more. And indescribably yet more.

If she were any longer human, she would be split and eviscerated, and her spine snapped along its centre three times.

Her hands have fast hold of it. Which – it or she – is the most tenacious? Where it travels, so will she.

But for all the *more*, there is no more *thought*. If ever there was thought.

When she was fourteen, she saw all this, in her prophetic mirror, saw what she was made for and must have.

Perhaps many thousands of us are only that, victim or predator, interchangeable.

Seen from above: Antoinelle is scarcely visible. Just the edges of her flailing feet, her contorted forehead and glistening strands of hair. And her clutching claws. (Shockingly, she makes the sounds of a pig, grunting, snorting.)

The rest of her is covered by darkness, by something most like a manta ray out of the sea, or some black amoeba.

Then she is growling and grunting so loudly, on and on, that the looking-glass breaks on her toilette table as if unable to stand the sound, while out in the night forest birds shrill and fly away.

More – always more. *Don't stop* – Never stop.

There is no need to stop. It has killed her, she is dead, she is re-alive and death is lost on her, she is all she has ever wished to be – nothing.

"Dearest... are you awake?

He lifts his head from his arm. He has slept.

"What is it?" *Who are you?* Has she ever called him *dear* before?

"Here I am," she says, whoever she is. But she is his Anna.

He does not want her. Never wanted her.

He thinks she is wearing the emerald necklace, something burning about her throat. She is white as bone. And her dark eyes – have paled to Venus eyes, watching him.

"I'm sorry," he says. "Perhaps later."

"I know."

Vonderjan falls asleep again quickly, lying on his back. Then Antoinelle slides up on top of him. She is not heavy, but he is; it impedes his breathing, her little weight.

Finally she puts her face to his, her mouth over his.

She smothers him mostly with her face, closing off his nostrils with the pressure of her cheek, and one narrow hand, and her mouth sidelong to his, and her breasts on his heart.

He does not wake again. At last his body spasms sluggishly, like the last death-throe of orgasm. Nothing else.

After his breathing has ended, still she lies there, Venus-eyed, and the dawn begins to come. Antoinelle casts a black, black shadow. Like all shadows, it is attached to her. Attached very closely.

Is this her shadow, or is she the white shadow of *it?*

9

Having sat for ten minutes, no longer writing, holding her pen upright, Yse sighs, and drops it, like something unpleasant, dank or sticky.

The story's erotographic motif, at first stimulating, had become, as it must, repulsive. Disgusting her – also as it should.

And the murder of Vonderjan, presented deliberately almost as an afterthought (stifled under the slight white pillar of his succubus wife).

Aloud, Yse says almost angrily, "Now surely I've used him up. All up. All over. Per Laszd, I can't do another thing with you or to you. But then, you've used me up too, yes you did, you have, even though you've never been near me. Mutual annihilation. That Yse is over with."

Then Yse rises, leaving the manuscript, and goes to make tea. But her generator, since the party, (when the music machine had been hooked into it by that madman, Carr) is skittish. The stove won't work. She leaves it, and pours instead a warm soda from the now improperly-working fridge.

It is night time, or morning, about three-fifty a.m.

Yse switches on her small TV, which works on a solar battery and obliges.

And there, on the first of the fifteen mainland (upper city) channels, is he – is Per Laszd. Not in his persona of dead trampled Gregers Vonderjan, but that of his own dangerous self.

She stands on the floor, dumbfounded, yet not, not really. Of course, who else would come before her at this hour.

He looks well, healthy and tanned. He's even shed some weight.

It seems to be a talk show, something normally Yse would avoid – they bore her. And the revelation of those she sometimes admires as over-ordinary or distasteful, disillusions and frustrates her.

But him she has always watched, on a screen, across a room when able, or in her own head. Him, she knows. He could not disillusion her, or put her off.

And tonight, there is something new. The talk has veered round to the other three guests – to whom she pays no attention – and so to music. And now the TV show's host is asking Per Laszd to use the piano, that grand piano over there.

Per Laszd gets up and walks over to this studio piano, looking, Yse thinks, faintly irritated, because obviously this has been sprung on him and

269

is not what he is about, or at least not publicly, but he will do it from a good showman's common sense.

He plays well, some melody Yse knows, a popular song she can't place. He improvises, his large hands and strong fingers jumping sure and finely-trained about the keyboard. Just the one short piece, concluded with a sarcastic flourish, after which he stands up again. The audience, delighted by any novelty, applauds madly, while the host and other guests are all calling *encore!* (more! More! Again – don't stop –) But Laszd is not manipulable, not truly. Gracious yet immovable, he returns to his seat. And after that a pretty girl with an unimportant voice comes on to sing, and then the show is done.

Yse finds herself enraged. She switches off the set, and slams down the tepid soda. She paces this end of her loft. While by the doors, forty feet away, the piano dredged from the Sound still stands, balanced on its forefeet and its phallic tail, hung in shade and shadow. It has been here more than a month. It's nearly invisible.

So why this now? This TV stunt put on by Fate? Why show her this, now? As if to congratulate her, giving her a horrible mean little failed-runner's-up patronizing non-prize. Per Laszd can play the piano.

Damn Per Laszd.

She is sick of him. Perhaps in every sense. But of course, she still wants him. Always will.

And what now?

She will never sleep. It's too late or early to go out.

She circles back to her writing, looks at it, sits, touches the page. But why bother to write any more?

Vonderjan was like the enchanter Prospero, in Shakespeare's *Tempest*, shut up there on his sorcerous Island, infested with sprites and elementals. Prospero too kept close a strange young woman, who in the magician's case had been his own daughter. But then arrived a shipwrecked prince out of the sea, to take the responsibility off Prospero's hands.

(Per's hands on the piano keys. Playing them. A wonderful amateur, all so facile, no trouble at all. He is married, and has been for twelve years. Yse has always known this.)

Far out on the Sound, a boat moos eerily.

Though she has frequently heard such a thing, Yse starts.

Be not afeard: the isle is full of noises,
Sounds and sweet airs, that give delight, and hurt not.

She can no longer smell the perfume, like night- blooming vines. When did

that stop? (Don't stop.)
Melted into air, into thin air ...

10: *Passover*

They had roped the hut-house round, outside and in, with their amulets and charms. There were coloured feathers and dried grasses, cogs of wood rough-carved, bones and sprinkles of salt and rum, and of blood, as in the Communion. When they reached the door, she on her bare, navy-blue feet, Jeanjacques felt all the forest press at their backs. And inside the hut, the silver-ringed eyes, staring in affright like the staring stars. But presently her people let her in, and let him in as well, without argument. And he thought of the houses of the Chosen in Egypt, their lintels marked by blood, to show the Angel of Death he must pass by.

He, as she did, sat down on the earth floor. (He noted the earth floor, and the contrasting wooden bed, with its elaborate posts. And the two shrines, one to the Virgin, and one to another female deity.)

Nothing was said beyond a scurry of whispered words in the patois. There were thirty other people crammed in the house, with a crèche of chickens and two goats. Fear smelled thick and hot, but there was something else, some vital possibility of courage and cohesion. They clung together soul to soul, their bodies only barely brushing, and Jeanjacques was glad to be in their midst, and when the fat woman came and gave him a gourd of liquor, he shed tears, and she patted his head, calming him a little, like a dog hiding under its mistress's chair.

In the end he must have slept. He saw someone looking at him, the pale icy eyes blue as murder.

Waking with a start, he found everyone and thing in the hut tense and compressed, listening, as something circled round outside. Then it snorted and blew against the wall of the hut- house, and all the interior stars of eyes flashed with their terror. And Jeanjacques felt his heart clamp on to the side of his body, as if afraid to fall.

Even so, he knew what it was, and when all at once it retreated and galloped away on its shod hoofs, he said quietly, "His horse."

But no one answered him, or took any notice of what he had said, and Jeanjacques discovered himself thinking. *After all, it might take that form, a white horse. Or she might be riding on the white horse.*

He began to ponder the way he must go in the morning, descending towards the bay. He should reach the sea well in advance of nightfall. The ship would come back, today or tomorrow. Soon. And there were the old buildings, on the beach, where he could make a shelter. He could even jump into the sea and swim out. There was a little reef, and rocks.

It had come from the sea, and would avoid going back to the sea, surely, at least for some while.

He knew it was not interested in him, knew that almost certainly it would not approach him with any purpose. But he could not bear to *see* it. That was the thing. And it seemed to him the people of the Island, and in the hut, even the chickens, the goats, and elsewhere the birds and fauna, felt as he did. They did not want to *see* it, even glimpse it. If the fabric of this world were torn open in one place on a black gaping hole of infinite darkness, you hid your eyes, you went far away.

After that, he started to notice bundles of possessions stacked up in corners. He realized not he alone would be going down the Island to the sea.

Dreaming again, he beheld animals swimming in waves away from shore, and birds flying away, as if from a zone of earthquake, or the presage of some volcanic eruption.

Nanetta nudged him.

"Will you take me to St Paul's Island?"

"Yes."

"I have a sister there."

He had been here on a clerk's errand. He thought, ridiculously, *Now I won't be paid.* And he was glad at this wince of anxious annoyance. Its normalcy and reason.

11

Per Laszd played Bach very well, with just the right detached, solemn cheerfulness.

It was what she would have expected him to play. Something like this. Less so the snatch of a popular tune he had offered the talk show audience so flippantly. (But a piano does what you want, makes the sounds you make it give — even true, she thinks, should you make a mistake — for then that is what it gives you. Your mistake.)

As Yse raised her eyes, she saw across the dim sphere of her loft, still wrapped in the last flimsy paper of night, a lamp stood glowing by the piano, both of whose lids were raised. Her stomach jolted and the pain of shock rushed through her body.

"Lucius —?"

He was the only other who held a key to her loft. She trusted Lucius, who any way had never used the key, except once, when she was gone for a week, to enter and water her (dying) plants, and fill her (then operable) refrigerator with croissants, mangoes and white wine.

And Lucius didn't play the piano. He had told her, once. His *amouretta*, as he called it, was the drum.

Besides, the piano player had not reacted when she called, not ceased his performance. Not until he brought the twinkling phrases to their finish.

Then the large hands stepped back off the keys, he pushed away the chair he must have carried there, and stood up.

The raised carapace of the piano's hind lid still obscured him, all but that flame of light which veered across the shining pallor of his hair.

Yse had got to her feet. She felt incredibly young, light as thin air. The thick silk of her hair brushed round her face, her shoulders, and she pulled in her flat stomach and raised her head on its long throat. She was frightened by the excitement in herself, and excited by the fear. She wasn't dreaming. She had always known, when she *dreamed* of him.

And there was no warning voice, because long ago she had left all such redundant noises behind.

Per Laszd walked around the piano. "Hallo, Yse," he said.

She said nothing. Perhaps could not speak. There seemed no point. She had said so much.

But "Here I am," he said.

There he was.

There was no doubt at all. The low lamp flung up against him. He wore the loose dark suit he had put on for the TV program, as if he had come straight here from the studio. He dwarfed everything in the loft.

"Why?" she said, after all.

She too was entitled to be flippant, surely.

"Why? Don't you know? You brought me here." He smiled. "Don't you love me any more?"

He was wooing her.

She glanced around her, made herself see everything as she had left it, the washed plate and glass by the sink, the soda can on the table, her manuscript lying there, and the pen. Beyond an angle of a wall, a corridor to other rooms.

And below the floor, barracuda swimming through the girders of a flooded building.

But the thin air sparkled as if full of champagne.

"Well, Yse," he said again, "here I am."

"But you are not *you.* "

"You don't say. Can you be certain? How am I different?"

"You're what I've made, and conjured up."

"I thought it was," he said, in his dry amused voice she had never forgotten, "more personal than that."

"*He* is somewhere miles off. In another country."

"This is another country," he said, "to me."

She liked it, this breathless fencing with him. Liked his persuading her. *Don't stop.*

The piano had not been able to open – or be opened – until he – or she – was ready. (Foreplay.) And out of the piano, came her demon. What was he? *What?*

She didn't care. If it were not him, yet it was, him. So she said, archly, "And your wife?"

"As you see, she had another engagement."

"With you, *there*. Wherever you are."

"Let me tell you," he said, "why I've called here."

There was no break in the transmission of this scene, she saw him walk away from the piano, start across the floor, and she did the same. Then they were near the window-doors. He was standing over her. He was vast, overpowering, beautiful.

More beautiful, now she could see the strands of his hair, the pores of his skin, a hundred tiniest imperfections – and the whole exquisite manufacture of a human thing, so close. And she was rational enough to analyse all this, and his beauty, and his power over her; or pedantic enough. He smelled wonderful to her as well, more than his clean fitness and his masculinity, or any expensive cosmetic he had used (for her?) It was the scent discernable only by a lover, caused by her chemistry, not his. Unless she had made him want her, too.

But of course he wanted her. She could see it in his eyes, their blue view bent only on her.

If he might have seemed old to an Antoinelle of barely sixteen, to Yse this man was simply her peer. And yet too he was like his younger self, clad again in that searing charisma which had later lessened, or changed its course.

He took her hand, picked it up. Toyed with her hand as Vonderjan had done with the hand of the girl Yse had permitted to destroy him.

"I'm here for you," he said.

"But I don't know you."

"Backwards," he said. "You've made it your business. You've bid for me," he said, "and you've got me."

"No," she said, "no, no I haven't."

"Let me show you."

She had known of that almost occult quality. With what he wanted in the sexual way, he could communicate some telepathic echo of his desires. As his mouth covered and clasped hers, this delirium was what she felt, combining with her own.

She had always known his kisses would be like this, the ground flying off from her feet, swept up and held only by him in the midst of a spinning void, where she became part of him and wanted nothing else, where she became what she had always wanted... nothing.

To be nothing, borne by this flooding sea, no thought, no anchor, and no chains.

So Antoinelle, as her vampire penetrated, drank, emptied, reformed her.

So Yse, in her vampire's arms.

It's how they make us feel.

"No," she murmurs, sinking deeper and deeper into his body, drowning as the island will, one day (five years, twenty).

None of us escape, do we?

Dawn is often very short and ineffectual here, as if to recompense the dark for those long sunsets we have.

Lucius, bringing his boat in to West Ridge from a night's fishing and drinking out in the Sound, sees a light still burning up there, bright as the quick green dawn. All Yse's blinds are up, showing the glass loft, translucent, like a jewel. Over the terrace the snake tree hangs its hair in the water and ribbons of apple-green light tremble through its coils.

Yse is there, just inside the wall of glass above the terrace, standing with a tall heavy-set man, whose hair is almost white.

He's kissing her, on and on, and then they draw apart, and still she holds on to him, her head tilted back like a serpent's, bonelessly, staring up into his face.

From down in the channel between the lofts and towerettes, Lucius can't make out the features of her lover. But then neither can he make out Yse's facial features, only the tilt of her neck and the lush satin hair hanging down her back.

Lucius sits in the boat, not paddling now, watching. His eyes are still and opaque.

"What you doing, girl?"

He knows perfectly well.

And then they turn back, the two of them, further into the loft where the light still burns, although the light of dawn has gone, leaving only a salty stormy dusk.

They will hardly make themselves separate from each other. They are together again and again, as if growing into one another.

Lucius sees the piano, or that which had been a piano, has vanished from the loft. And after that he sees how the light of the guttering lamp hits suddenly up, like a striking cobra. And in the ray of the lamp, striking, the bulky figure of the man, with his black clothes and blond hair, becomes transparent as the glass sheets of the doors. It is possible to see directly, too, through him, clothes, hair, body, directly through to Yse, as she stands there, still holding on to what is now actually invisible, drawing it on, in, away, just before the lamp goes out and a shadow fills the room like night.

As he is paddling away along the channel, Lucius thinks he hears a remote crash, out of time, like glass smashing in many pieces, but yesterday, or tomorrow.

Things break.

Just about sunset, the police come to find Lucius. They understand he has a key to the loft of a woman called Yse, (which they pronounce Jizz.)

When they get to the loft, Lucius is aware they did not need the key, since the glass doors have both been blown outwards and down into the water-alley below. Huge shards and fragments decorate the terrace, and some are caught in the snake-willow like stars.

A bored detective stands about, drinking coffee someone has made him on Yse's reluctant stove. (The refrigerator has shut off, and is leaking a lake on the floor.)

Lucius appears dismayed but innocuous. He goes about looking for something, which the other searchers, having dismissed him, are too involved to mark.

There is no sign of Yse. The whole loft is vacant. There is no sign either of any disturbance, beyond the damaged doors which, they say to Lucius and each other, were smashed outwards but not by an explosive.

"What are you looking for?" the detective asks Lucius, suddenly grasping what Lucius is at.

"Huh?"

"She have something of yours?"

Lucius sees the detective is waking up. "No. Her book. She was writing."

"Oh, yeah? What kind of thing was that?"

Lucius explains, and the detective loses interest again. He says they have seen nothing like that.

And Lucius doesn't find her manuscript, which he would have anticipated, any way, seeing instantly on her work-table. He does find a note – they say it is a note, a letter of some sort, although addressed to no one. It's in her bed area, on the rug, which has been floated under the bed by escaped refrigerator fluid.

'Why go on writing?' asks the note, or letter, of the no one it has not addressed. 'All your life waiting, and having to invent another life, or other lives, to make up for not having a life. Is that what God's problem is?'

Hearing this read at him. Lucius' dead eyes reveal for a second they are not dead, only covered by a protective film. They all miss this.

The detective flatly reads the note out, like a kid bad at reading, embarrassed and standing up in class. Where his feet are planted is the stain from the party, which, to Lucius' for-a-moment-not-dead eyes, has the shape of a swimming, three-legged fish.

"And she says, 'I want more.'"

'I want the terror and the passion, the power and the glory — not this low-key crap played only with one *hand*. Let me point out to someone, Yse is an anagram of Yes. *I'll drown my book.* '

"I guess," says the detective, "she didn't sell."

They let Lucius go with some kind of veiled threat he knows is only offered to make themselves feel safe.

He takes the water-bus over to the Café Blonde, and as the sunset ends and night becomes, tells one or two what he saw, as he has not told the cops from the tide-less upper city.

Lucius has met them all. Angels, demons.

"As the light went through him, he wasn't there. He's like glass."

Carr says, slyly (inappropriately — or with deadly perception?), "No vampire gonna reflect in a glass."

12: *Carried Away*

When the ship came, they took the people out, rowing them in groups, in the two boats. The man Stronn had also appeared, looking dazed, and the old housekeeper, and others. No questions were asked of them. The ship took the livestock, too.

Jeanjacques was glad they were so amenable, the black haughty master wanting conscientiously to assist his own, and so helping the rest.

All the time they had sheltered in the rickety customs buildings of the old port, a storm banged round the coast. This kept other things away, it must have done. They saw nothing but the feathers of palm boughs blown through the air and crashing trunks that toppled in the high surf, which was grey as smashed glass.

In the metallic after-storm morning, Jeanjacques walked down the beach, the last to leave, waiting for the last boat, confident.

Activity went on at the sea's edge, sailors rolling a barrel, Nanetta standing straight under a yellow sunshade, a fine lady, barefoot but proud. (She had shown him the jewels she had after all brought with her, squeezed in her sash, not the ruby earrings, but a golden hairpin, and the emerald necklace that had belonged to Vonderjan's vrouw.)

He never thought, now, to see anything, Jeanjacques, so clever, so accomplished at survival.

But he saw it.

Where the forest came down on to the beach, and caves opened under the limestone, and then rocks reared up, white rocks and black, with the curiously quiescent waves glimmering in and out around them.

There had been nothing. He would have sworn to that. As if the reality of the coarse storm had scoured all such stuff away.

And then, there she was, sitting on the rock.

She shone in a way that, perhaps one and a quarter centuries after, could have been described as radioactively.

Jeanjacques did not know that word. He decided that she gleamed. Her hard pale skin and mass of pale hair, gleaming.

She looked old. Yet she looked too young. She was not human-looking, nor animal.

Her legs were spread wide in the skirt of her white dress. So loose was the gown at her bosom, that he could see much of her breasts. She was doing nothing at all, only sitting there, alone, and she grinned at him, all her white teeth, so even, and her black eyes like slits in the world.

But she cast a black shadow, and gradually the shadow was embracing her. And he saw her turning over into it like the moon into eclipse. If she had any blood left in her, if she had ever been Antoinelle – these things he ignored. But her grinning and her eyes and the shadow and her turning inside out within the shadow – from these things he ran away.

He ran to the line of breakers, where the barrels were being rolled into a boat. To Nanetta's sunflower sunshade. And he seemed to burst through a sort of curtain, and his muscles gave way. He fell nearby, and she glanced at him, the black woman, and shrank away.

"It's all right –" he cried. He thought she must not see what he had seen, and that they might leave him here. "I missed my footing," he whined, "that's all."

And when the boat went out, they let him go with it.

The great sails shouldered up into the sky. The master looked Jeanjacques over, before moving his gaze after Nanetta. (Stronn had avoided them. The other whites, and the housekeeper, had hidden themselves somewhere below, like stowaways.)

"How did you find him, that Dutchman?" the master asked idly.

"As you said. Vonderjan was falling."

"What was the other trouble here? They act like it was a plague, but that's not so." (Malignly Jeanjacques noted the master too was excluded from the empathy of the Island people.) "No," the master went on, bombastically, "if you sick, I'd never take you on, none of you."

Jeanjacques felt a little better. "The Island's gone bad," he muttered. He would look, though, only up into the sails. They were another sort of white to the white thing he had seen on the rock. As the master was another sort of black.

"Gone bad? They do. Land does go bad. Like men."

Are they setting sail? Every grain of sand on the beach behind is rising up. Every mote of light, buzzing –

Oh God – *Pater noster – libera me –*

The ship strode from the bay. She carved her path into the deep sea, and through his inner ear, Jeanjacques hears the small bells singing. Yet that is little enough, to carry away from such a place.

13

Seven months after, he heard the story, and some of the newspapers had it too. A piano had been washed up off the Sound, on the beach at the Abacus Tower. And inside the lid, when they hacked it open, a woman's body was curled up, tiny, and hard as iron. She was Caucasian, middle-aged, rather heavy when alive, now not heavy at all, since there was no blood, and not a single whole bone, left inside her.

Sharks, they said. Sharks are clever. They can get inside a closed piano and out again. And they bite.

As for the piano, it was missing – vandals had destroyed it, burned it, taken it off.

Sometimes strangers ask Lucius where Yse went to. He has nothing to tell them. ("She disappears?" they ask him again. And Lucius once more says nothing.)

And in that way, resembling her last book, Yse disappeared, disappears, is disappearing. Which can happen, in any tense you like.

Like those hallucinations which sometimes come at the edge *of* sleep, so that you wake, thinking two or three words have been spoken close to your ear, or that a tall figure stands in the corner... like this, the image now and then appears before him.

Then Jeanjacques sees her, the woman, sitting on the rock, her white dress and ivory-coloured hair, hard-gleaming in a post-storm sunlight. Impossible to tell her age. A desiccated young girl, or unlined old woman. And the transparent sea lapping in across the sand...

'But he has said, the Island is quite deserted now.'

The Isle is Full of Noises
Chosen by Sarah Singleton

In essence, "The Isle is Full of Noises" is a novella about a vampire piano. Around this unlikely kernel is wrapped a complex, erotic, surreal and lyrical meditation about desire, imagination, frustration and the power of creativity – specifically, about writing. It is also, in my reading, an intensely personal story and within its arcane twists, word-play and the many oceanic fathoms of its depths, I see Tanith, and I hear her voice, and her exploration of what it means to write and the boundaries, or lack of them, between the creations of the imagination and the experience of an objective reality.

This thoroughly postmodern novella introduces the main character, Yse, a writer living in an island-apartment in an inundated city of the near future, and the process of her creation of a story – about another island, an unspecific post-colonial Caribbean island, in the (probably) first half of the 19th century. Two texts are referenced: Wide Sargasso Sea is woven into the fabric of Yse's story, with Rhys's 'madwoman' Antoinette becoming Antoinelle, and, of course, The Tempest, from which the story takes not only its title, the island location, but also the explicit reference to Prospero, the ageing magician-creator. The framing story is told in the present tense and here we are aware of the voice of an omniscient narrator ('Best to describe Yse at this point...') so even as we engage with the fictional writer and read the story this fictional author is writing, there is another, exterior voice reminding us this is all a fabulous construct.

It is difficult for me not to picture the writer Yse as Lee herself, even down to the physical description, and this is compounded by the appearance of the man Per Laszd, an actor Yse has long been obsessed with. Yse uses him in her writing, recreates and controls him, giving him life in the character of Gregers Vonderjan. In interviews, Lee has mentioned her obsession with Dutch actor Rutger Hauer (Vonderjan – tall, powerful, his hair 'a mass of silvery blond') and explained how she has cast Hauer in her novels (Malach in 'Personal Darkness', Hassinger in 'When the Lights Go Out') in just the same way. So into the layers – Rutger Hauer becomes Per Laszd, who is cast as Vonderjan (who is also Rochester and Prospero 'shut up on his enchanted island').

Yse feels 'slight guilt' for using the fictional Per Laszd in her stories (and destroying him in this one) and it is hard not to wonder if Lee felt the same with the way she 'used' Hauer. And yet, at the end of the framing narrative, Yse has her wish come true. Her (fictional) reality breaks down and Per Laszd appears, fulfilling her fantasy and sweeping her into his arms. At this point she disappears from the story and the invented inundated world. Her final thoughts – 'None of us escape, do we?' – are deliberately ambiguous. Are they hers, or do they come from the omniscient narrator? From Lee?

Yse's friend Lucius picks up a note that was left behind, and again it is hard for me not to hear Lee's own voice, and her frustration (perhaps my projection, as I read this first when she was already struggling with ill-health, and it has a terrible poignancy for me): "Why go on writing?... All your life waiting, and having to invent another life, or other lives, to make up for not having a life. Is that what God's problem is?" And then: 'I want more. I want the terror and the passion, the power and the glory – not this low-key crap played only with one hand.'

I could write so much about this story – the complex imagery, the use of colour (particularly black and white) the intense eroticism, a feminist reading, a post-colonial reading – but more than anything, it is this sense I have of Lee's own voice, thoughts and passion that makes it so moving. Those reviews of it I have read have not been effusive; some reviewers have found it overly complex or even dull – but for me, it is a story of beauty, depth, inventiveness, passion and searing honesty.

– Sarah Singleton

Publisher s Acknowledgement

Thank you to all who have made this project possible; to Craig Gidney, Mavis Haut, Stephen Jones, Vera Nazarian, Sarah Singleton, Kari Sperring, Sam Stone, Cecilia Dart-Thornton, Freda Warrington, and Nadia Van Der Westerhuizen for their careful selections and fascinating story notes, to Storm Constantine for both her choice and her constant support, to Allison Rich for her selection and her keen editorial eye, and to John Kaiine, not only for his artwork and his story choice but also for his willingness to see this volume come into being.

Most of all, of course, thank you to Tanith Lee, who continues to populate the world with her words and her wonder.

— Ian Whates
NewCon Press

Colder Greyer Stones
Tanith Lee

Cover art by John Kaiine

A unique collection of twelve stories from Britain's foremost Mistress of the Fantastic; all are previously uncollected, two have never appeared in print before and six stories are wholly original to this collection., including the bonus novelette "The Frost Watcher". The first paperback edition of *Colder Greyer Stones* was released in November 2013 to commemorate the author being honoured at that year's World Fantasy Convention with a 'Lifetime Achievement Award'.

Available now from NewCon Press
A5 paperback: £9.99

www.newconpress.co.uk

Splinters of Truth
Storm Constantine

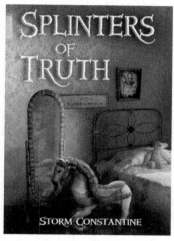

Cover art by Danielle Lainton

Storm Constantine is one of our finest writers of genre fiction. This new collection, **Splinters of Truth**, features fifteen stories, four of them original to this volume, that transport the reader to richly imagined realms one moment and shine a light on our own world's darkest corners the next. A writer of rare passion, Storm delivers here some of her most accomplished work to date.

"Constantine's talent for twisting the mundane and making it dark and delicious shines out on each page"
— *Starburst*

"Storm Constantine is a myth-making Gothic queen. Her stories are poetic, involving, delightful and depraved. I wouldn't swap her for a dozen Anne Rices." – *Neil Gaiman*

"Storm Constantine… is a daring romantic sensualist, as well as a fine storyteller." – *Poppy Z Brite*

"Storm Constantine is a literary fantasist of outstanding power and originality. Her work is rich, idiosyncratic and completely engaging. Her themes have much in common with Philip K Dick – the nature of identify, the nature of reality, the creative power of the human imagination – while her sensibility reminds me of Angela Carter at her most inventive." – *Michael Moorcock*

Available now from NewCon Press
www.newconpress.co.uk

IMMANION PRESS
Purveyors of Speculative Fiction

The Weird Tales of Tanith Lee

This anthology of twenty-eight tales comprises all the short stories by Tanith Lee that were published in the seminal magazine *Weird Tales* during her lifetime. Some of them are previously uncollected, and appeared in print only in the magazine, so will be new to many of Tanith's fans. Tanith Lee's highly-respected and influential work spanned every genre, and this sumptuous collection demonstrates the range of her versatility. From the dark high fantasy of 'The Sombrus Tower', through the Arthurian-influenced 'The Kingdoms of the Air', the achingly beautiful 'Stars Above, Stars Below' of a science-fantasy Mars, the sinister retelling of a fairy tale in 'When the Clock Strikes', the real-world mysteries of 'The Unrequited Glove' and 'Arthur's Lion', and the almost whimsical steampunk of 'The Persecution Machine', *The Weird Tales of Tanith Lee* showcases the myriad styles of the writer rightly known as the High Priestess of Fantasy. ISBN: 978-1-907737-79-4 £13.99 $18.99

Dark in the Day, Ed. by Storm Constantine & Paul Houghton

Weirdness lurks beyond the margins of the mundane, emerging to dismantle our assumptions of reality. *Dark in the Day* is an anthology of weird fiction, penned by established writers and also those new to the genre – the latter being authors who are, or were, students of Creative Writing at Staffordshire University, where editor Storm Constantine occasionally delivers guest lectures. Her co-editor, Paul Houghton, is the senior lecturer in Creative Writing at the university.

Contributors include: Martina Bellovičová, J. E. Bryant, Glynis Charlton, Storm Constantine, Louise Coquio, Elizabeth Counihan, Krishan Coupland, Elizabeth Davidson, Siân Davies, Paul Finch, Rosie Garland, Rhys Hughes, Kerry Fender, Andrew Hook, Paul Houghton, Tanith Lee, Tim Pratt, Nicholas Royle, Michael Marshall Smith, Paula Wakefield, Ian Whates and Liz Williams.
ISBN: 978-1-907737-74-9 £11.99, $18.99

A Raven Bound with Lilies by Storm Constantine

Wraeththu – a new species or the next step in the evolution of humankind? Androgynous, and stronger in mind and body than human, naturally magical, sometimes deadly, and often possessing unearthly beauty, the Wraeththu have captivated readers since Storm Constantine's first novel, *The Enchantments of Flesh and Spirit*, was published in 1988, regarded as ground-breaking in its treatment of gender and sexuality. This anthology of 15 tales collects all her published Wraeththu short stories into one volume, and also includes extra material, including the author's first explorations of the androgynous race. The tales range from the 'creation story' *Paragenesis*, through the bloody, brutal rise of the earliest tribes, and on into a future, where strange mutations are starting to emerge from hidden corners of the earth. With sumptuous illustrations by official Wraeththu artist Ruby, as well as pictures from Danielle Lainton and the author herself, *A Raven Bound with Lilies* is a must for any Wraeththu enthusiast, and is also a comprehensive introduction to the mythos for those who are new to it. ISBN: 978-1-907737-80-0 £11.99, $15.50

Animate Objects by Tanith Lee

"There is no such thing as an inanimate object… And how could that be? Because, simply, everything is formed from matter, and basically, at *root*, the matter that makes up everything in the physical world – the Universe – is of the same substance. Which means, on that basic level, we – you, me, and that power station over there – are all the exact riotous, chaotic, amorphous *same*. Here is an assortment of Lee takes on the nature, and perhaps intentions, of so-called non-sentient things. And you're quite safe. This is only a book. An inanimate object." – *Tanith Lee*

The original hardback of this collection, of which there were only 35 copies, was published by Immanion Press in 2013, to commemorate Tanith Lee receiving the Lifetime Achievement Award at World Fantasycon. It included 5 previously unpublished pieces. This new release includes a further 2 stories, co-written by Tanith Lee and John Kaiine, and new interior illustrations by Jarod Mills. ISBN: 978-1-907737-73-2, £11.99 $18.99

Immanion Press
http://www.immanion-press.com
info@immanion-press.com